The Bennett Family Saga

INTREPID JOURNEY

Book Two: Perils in Paradise

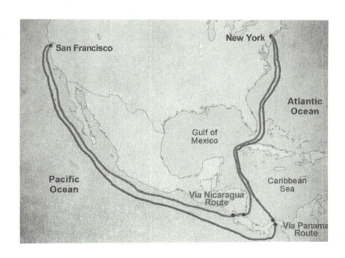

LILLY ROBBINS BROCK

Dedication

To my courageous pioneer ancestors

A Bennett Family Saga
INTREPID JOURNEY
Book Two: Perils in Paradise

River Cliff Publishing

Copyright © 2019 Lilly Brock

Official Website: http://www.lillyrobbinsbrock.com

Table of Contents

About the Story

Although this is a work of fiction, many of the events are based on fact. The theme of the *Intrepid Journey* series was inspired by a journal, which I came upon during my research. It was written by a pioneer woman in 1855 about her family's journey to Washington Territory. During that time, the route most people took to travel West was the well-known Oregon trail. This family, however, took a different course. They left New York City on a paddlewheel steamship to travel via the South American route toward their final destination--Washington Territory.

If you read *Intrepid Journey, Book One: An Untamed Frontier,* you followed Thomas Bennett and his brothers leave New York City on a paddlewheel steamship to travel the six-month-long journey to the southern tip of South America through the Strait of Magellan toward their destination, Washington Territory. You also know, that once they were properly settled, Thomas's wife, Jane, and their adult children would follow.

During my research, I learned about the Nicaragua route, which was much shorter--two months. The pioneer family in 1855 chose this route. It seemed fitting for my characters, Jane and the children, to travel on this route. Just as in Book One, through many hours and avenues of historical research, actual events and places are brought to life throughout this book.

The route through Nicaragua is true to life as well as the environment in nineteenth century San Francisco. I have touched on the rampant sex trade market in San Francisco, especially in the use of young Chinese women, along with the common danger of unsuspecting men becoming shanghai victims.

While Jane and the children are delayed in San Francisco,

Thomas and his brothers are called to serve in the 1855 Indian War in Washington Territory. Most of the battle scenes are based on firsthand accounts, which I uncovered during my research. I have inserted my fictional characters into these scenes and told the story from their perspective.

Later when the family was finally together in Puget Sound, my description of the area such as Olympia, the capital of Washington Territory, (now the state of Washington) is also based on research. Governor Stevens has been brought into the story, including the Governor's Ball. I have fictionalized the experience of the event using my imagination of what my characters experienced. The Bennetts settled in Teekalet, which is Port Gamble today. I have used the presence of a lumber mill in Teekalet as an integral part of the storyline. The name of the mill has been fictionalized. I mention the Point Julia Indian tribe, located on the other side of Hood Canal opposite the mill. It still exists today.

Further along in the book, my character, Robert Bennett, travels to England in 1857. By this time, the Panama Railroad had been completed, which cut travel time across the Isthmus of Panama from several days to less than one day, while linking the Atlantic Ocean to the Pacific Ocean. Robert takes this route. The history about the construction of this railroad is extraordinary. The project began in 1850 and wasn't completed until 1855. The cost of the forty-seven-mile railway was eight million dollars, which was eight times the original estimate. Approximately twelve thousand laborers died.

I have included a map showing both the Nicaragua and Panama routes. See references below for more information about the Panama Railroad.

I hope you enjoy the story. Stay tuned for Book Three as the Bennett family saga continues.

Lilly

http://www.rare-mileage.com/blog/2011/the-panama-canal-railroad-company/

http://www.panamarailroad.org/history1.html

http://www.bruceruiz.net/PanamaHistory/panama_railroad.htm

Cast of Characters

Cast of Main Characters (several were introduced in *Intrepid Journey, Book One: An Untamed Frontier*)

The Bennett brothers:
Captain Philip Bennett, captain of his ship, the *California II*
> Robert Bennett
> Thomas Bennett
> Edmund & Brenda McKenzie – Scottish couple who immigrated to Delhi, New York
> Jane McKenzie – Daughter of Edmund and Brenda
> Abigail McKenzie Barlow – Daughter of Edmund and Brenda
> Charles Barlow – Abigail's husband

Children of Thomas & Jane Bennett
> Jonathan Bennett (nickname: Jonny)
> Jeremy Bennett (nickname: Jemmie)
> Mary Bennett Spencer
> Elizabeth Bennett
> Emily Bennett (aka Désirée)

Benjamin Spencer – Mary's husband

Captain William Davis – Captain of the ship *Southern Light*

Victoria Davis – Captain Davis's wife

Sebastian Jones – passenger on *Southern Light*, owner of gambling house in San Francisco

Jack Miller – partner with Sebastian Jones

James Mitchell – passenger on the *Southern Light*, settled at Seabeck with his uncle

Oliver Scott – Private Investigator in San Francisco

Alberto De Leon – wealthy man in Mazatlán, Mexico

Francesco De Leon – Alberto's son

Rita – Love interest of Francesco in Mazatlán, Mexico

Peter Crandall – survivor of *Theodora* shipwreck, settler in the Bennett settlement, Teekalet, Washington Territory

Billy (Ying Chan) – survivor of *Theodora* shipwreck, settler in the Bennett settlement, Teekalet, Washington Territory

Margaret Dawson (Maggie) – Philip's love interest, owner of bakery at Bennett settlement

Rachel Bly – widow of Daniel Bly who perished in the *Theodora* shipwreck, Maggie's partner at the bakery.

Matthew Bly – Rachel's son

Annie Bly – Rachel's daughter

Pierre Mallet – French mountain man, lived near Teekalet

Red Feather – Pierre's wife.

Christopher Taylor – young stowaway on the *California II*, lived at the Bennett settlement.

Randolph Mitchell – James Mitchell's uncle, owned a general store in Seabeck, Washington Territory

Isabel Warner – worked at general store in Seabeck, love interest of Robert Bennett

Eleanor – Robert's first love in England

Chapter 1

*A*s the frosty November days passed, the cannon, *Le Achille*, stood vigil over the Bennett settlement. Each day when the settlers opened their eyes, they wondered if this was the day there would be an attack, but none came. Could it be there were rumors about the ominous presence of their cannon?

Then one day a man arrived by boat from Teekalet with the anticipated message for Captain Philip Bennett from Governor Stevens. It was time to sail the *California II* to San Francisco and retrieve the much-needed provisions and armaments.

* * *

Two Months Earlier

September 1855

Delhi, New York/New York Harbor

Jane Bennett and her children had finally finished packing for their upcoming journey. Soon, Jane's sister, Abigail, and her husband, Charles, would be driving them to the New York harbor to board Captain Davis's ship, the *Southern Light*. The soon-to-be travelers had longed for this day, but also dreaded it.

Jane was nervous, and fretted, "I hope I haven't forgotten anything." She avoided her parents' eyes for fear she would fall apart and cry nonstop. *Would she ever see them again?*

Jane's parents, Edmund and Brenda McKenzie, tried to stay cheerful, but the reality and agony of parting was upon them. At long last, Jane looked into their sad eyes and broke down in uncontrollable sobs, throwing herself into their arms. The three stood together in a silent embrace, while her sister stood a few feet away with tears welling in her eyes. Jane looked at Abigail and stretched out her arm inviting her sister to join the embrace. The possibility of never seeing one another again hovered like a black cloud, but they pretended otherwise.

"Ah expect ye to be writing us, Jane," implored Edmund.

"And our grandchildren, too," added Brenda.

"I promise I'll write often and I'll come back to visit," replied Jane. Her voice cracked, and her eyes were wet with tears.

Then Jane turned to Abigail and Charles. "It comforts me to know you'll be living near Mother and Father."

"We thank you again for turning your home over to us," replied Abigail. Her gaze swept from her youngest son, Thurston, to Jane's sons. "Thurston is going to miss his cousins." Then she called out to him, "Thurston, come and say goodbye to your aunt. It's time to go."

Thurston ambled over and kissed his aunt on her cheek. "I'm sure going to miss you all, Aunt Jane."

"I will miss you and your three brothers as well. I understand you plan to apply to West Point in two years when you turn seventeen?"

"Yes, they accepted my brothers; I hope they take me."

"I'm sure they will. You're a fine young man. How proud your parents will be to have four sons attending West Point. I'm very proud of my nephews. It's too bad your brothers couldn't have been here to say goodbye, but I understand, duty calls."

One by one, the Bennett children hugged their grandparents, aunt and uncle, and cousin for a final goodbye. The children, now grown, began their lives in Delhi and had never fathomed they would someday embark on a journey to the other side of the nation. The twin brothers, Jonathan and Jeremy, were nineteen, Mary was nearly eighteen, and her baby, Mollie, was nearly six months old. Elizabeth was sixteen and Emily, fourteen. They were sad to say goodbye, but excited about the new adventure ahead of them. So many mixed emotions lingered in the air.

Mary had been married just a little over three months when

her husband, Benjamin, joined her father and two uncles, Robert and Philip, on the journey. She still felt like a newlywed and looked forward to reuniting with her husband and introducing him to his new daughter.

Jane yearned for Thomas and worried about him relentlessly. They had been married twenty years in June, but he wasn't there to celebrate with her. Instead, they were separated for the first time. A year had passed since they had been together.

With the hour of departure at hand, Jonathan and Jeremy helped Charles load the baggage onto the wagon—the same wagon that carried their menfolk away several months prior. Once the baggage was loaded, the family climbed into the back of the wagon, sitting on the bench seats Charles had built for them. He sat in the front as the driver, and Abigail took her place beside him.

Brenda was holding a basket brimming with food she had put together for her loved ones and handed it up to Jane. "Ah'm sure ye will need this. Ye have many miles to travel."

Jane lifted the cloth. "This looks as good as what you handed to Thomas when he left. Thank you, dear Mother. We'll think of you while we enjoy every morsel." She bent over and hugged her mother one last time.

Charles turned in his seat and looked to the back at his passengers, shouting out, "Everyone ready?" Then he snapped the reins, and Jane, her children, and little Mollie were on their way to the New York harbor. Edmund and Brenda, clutching hands with heavy hearts, watched them leave.

* * *

"I see the harbor," shouted Jonathan as he balanced himself into a standing position for a better view. "I can see the ships!"

As the family approached the harbor, they felt the breeze from the bay drifting through the air and heard the blasts of ships' horns signaling the impending hour of departure.

"There's the *Southern Light*," exclaimed Charles. "We best hurry."

The roadway was jammed with carriages delivering passengers. Charles adeptly wove his way through the mass and maneuvered the wagon close to the ship's embarkation area. Then he and the twins unloaded the baggage as the family exited the wagon.

The wharf was crowded and hectic. People pushed against each other in their haste to board the ship. While the passengers boarded, their baggage was hoisted up to the ship and loaded.

"Well, I guess this is goodbye," said Abigail, her voice cracking. She was on the verge of tears and trying unsuccessfully to hold them back. They all hugged, and the travelers quickly boarded the ship, finding a space along the railing for a final goodbye. They looked down at the wharf and saw clouds of white handkerchiefs being waved for one last farewell to loved ones. Jane singled out Abigail's blue kerchief and leaned over the railing to blow a kiss to her sister. Charles had stayed behind to mind the wagon.

Promptly on the hour, the ship's horn sounded three short blasts and the majestic side-wheel steamer glided from her berth, leaving the harbor toward her destination—Nicaragua.

The throng of passengers milling about in confusion was almost overwhelming to Jane and her family. Before long, they found their bearings and followed the signage to the roped-off section for first-class passengers. A porter immediately greeted them. "You must be the Bennett family?"

"Yes, we are," replied Jane. "How did you know?"

The porter answered, "Welcome aboard. There are ten first-class cabins, and you are the only family unit listed." Then he signaled another porter to assist with their baggage. "Please, allow us to carry your bags while we take you to your cabins. You'll find your trunks already there."

The porters led the Bennett family toward the center of the ship to their cabins. After unlocking the doors and setting the bags inside each cabin, the lead porter turned to Jane, "I believe you'll be quite comfortable here, Mrs. Bennett. You'll feel very little of the ship's movement in this location. Is there anything else we can do for you?"

"We are fine, thank you. You've taken good care of us."

He tilted his hat. "Then we will leave you to your cabins, Mrs. Bennett."

The Bennett ladies were in a state of wonderment when they entered their cabin. They had never seen such luxury.

Their cabin was generous in size and included two washbasins, a sofa, and three berths. Each berth was large enough for two people. The berths were finished in satinwood and draped in elegant curtains providing privacy. Steam heat warmed the cabin, and a bell rope system installed on the wall provided the means to summon a steward.

Emily exclaimed, "It's like we're royalty!" She had to touch everything, examining every detail. She opened a door, thinking she had found a closet.

"Look Mother, we have our own privy." She dashed to a wall across the room. "And look at the bell pull. I can summon a servant any time I please." Then she plopped onto one of the beds. "I want this one."

"Yes, this is a beautiful cabin. I know you're excited, my dear Emily, but we're not going to be summoning a servant every minute. Your Uncle Philip has graciously arranged all of this for us. We must be grateful and humble. And you and Elizabeth will be sharing a berth. Mary will have her own to share with Mollie."

Emily frowned, "Yes, Mother. Now, let's explore the dining saloon. It's just a few steps away. Can we Mother?"

The family had glimpsed the lavishly decorated dining and grand saloons on the way to their cabins. The saloons were richly carpeted, the furniture was of the finest quality, and a sense of spaciousness had been created by the clever use of mirrors on the walls.

Jane answered in a patient tone, "In due time, Emily. Right now we need to settle in and unpack our belongings."

Elizabeth noticed the desk and chair in the room. She walked over and sat down.

"This is where I'll be writing in my journal for Father. There's even a porthole so I can look out. It's all so beautiful here." She promptly brought out her journal and writing supplies.

Mary made herself comfortable on the sofa and nursed Mollie. "Mother, I should take the berth furthest away from all of you. Mollie has been fussy. I hope she doesn't keep everyone awake."

"That's very thoughtful of you, Mary. She does seem unsettled. If you like, I'll unpack your belongings so you're free to give little Mollie all the attention she needs."

"Thank you, Mother. That would be most helpful."

Emily brought out her dresses, found the wall mirror, and held each one up to her.

"Oh, Mother, I'll be able to wear my prettiest dresses when we dine. There haven't been many opportunities to wear them. I can't wait. Don't you love how this green dress brings out my eyes?"

Jane smiled. "Yes, my dear."

Next door, Jonathan and Jeremy explored their shared quarters, which were as nicely appointed as the larger cabin, complete with two berths. They eagerly unpacked their bags and made themselves comfortable. Jonathan brought out his collection of maps and laid them out on the desk.

"Do you think the captain might let me spend time with him in the pilothouse?" asked Jeremy.

"It's possible, if Uncle Philip told him about your obsession to become a captain. And, if he lets you, I'm coming with you. I have a feeling there isn't going to be much to do. I'm glad I brought my books."

* * *

Once the family had gathered together in the larger cabin, Jane looked at her children and said, "My darlings, from this moment on, we're beginning a new chapter in our lives. We don't know what lies ahead of us, but as your father always says, we must meet every challenge square in the face."

Everyone was quiet for a moment as they listened to their mother's words. Then Emily broke the silence, exclaiming, "Brothers, I want to see your cabin!"

"There'll be plenty of time for that, little sister," replied Jonathan.

Jane looked at her watch. "Goodness, where has the time gone? It's nearly past the hour for our midday meal. Emily, you may now use the bell pull. We'll dine here in our cabin."

The Bennetts were famished and thoroughly enjoyed their first meal on the ship. Soon after finishing an exceptional repast, there was a knock on their cabin door.

"That's most unexpected," said Jane as she answered the door.

The visitor removed his hat. "Mrs. Bennett, I presume? I'm Captain William Davis."

Jane smiled, "Yes, I'm Jane Bennett. Please, do come in, Captain Davis."

The captain stepped in. "Thank you, Mrs. Bennett. I trust you and your family are comfortable?" He glanced around the room at the other occupants. "It would be my great pleasure if all of you would join me at my table for a light supper this evening."

Jane replied in her usual gracious manner, "We would be honored, Captain Davis. If I may, allow me to introduce my family." She turned toward her children. "These are my daughters, Elizabeth, Emily, and Mary. Mary is now Mary Spencer and is holding our first grandchild, Mollie. Her husband, Benjamin, joined my husband and his brothers on their voyage to Washington Territory. And these are my sons, Jonathan and Jeremy."

Each of them acknowledged the captain.

"I'm pleased to meet all of you. I had the pleasure of meeting your family while Captain Bennett's ship was in port in San Francisco. As planned, the captain visited me to finalize the details of the Nicaragua journey and also to introduce me to his brothers and Benjamin." Then the captain looked at each family member, "Captain Bennett has spoken fondly of you all and entrusted you to my care. Is there anything you need, or are there any questions I may answer?"

Mary inquired, "Did my husband, Benjamin, look well, Captain Davis? He's never been on a ship before."

"Yes, he looked fine." The captain had been asked not to say anything about Benjamin's near-death experience on the ship.

"And before you ask, Mrs. Bennett, Thomas looked fine too. They were all quite tired when they arrived, but they had a good night's sleep as guests in our home."

Jonathan asked his burning question, "Captain Davis, would you mind if I come to the pilothouse and observe you? Perhaps my uncle might have mentioned my desire to become a captain like him one day?"

"Yes, your uncle and I discussed that, Jonathan. Of course, you may." Jonathan beamed. The captain looked over at Jeremy. "Maybe your brother would like to come too?"

Jeremy answered, "Yes, I'd like that Captain Davis, thank you."

"It's been a pleasure to meet the rest of the Bennett family. I must excuse myself now, and get back to work. Young men, you may come with me to the pilothouse now if you'd like."

"Yes, sir!" exclaimed Jonathan.

The captain donned his hat as he exited the cabin and turned toward Jane and her daughters, "Ladies, until this evening, then? Supper is served at eight o'clock."

"Thank you, Captain Davis. We'll look forward to this evening," replied Jane.

The captain left with Jonathan and Jeremy in tow. On the way to the pilothouse, he gave the brothers a quick tour of the main deck. First, he showed them where his quarters were located along with a top-quality class kitchen, barbershop, and wood-paneled smoking room.

As they continued, the captain pointed at the helmsman's cabin. "When I need to communicate with my helmsman, I use a bell signal located near the wheel where I stand. I'll show you when we get to the pilothouse."

After the captain and the brothers left, Jane suggested they rest before supper. It had been a long day and she was ready for a nap.

Mary was exhausted and hoped Mollie would nap so everyone could get some sleep. She laid the baby beside her on the berth, and with the rocking motion of the ship, they soon fell into a peaceful slumber.

Elizabeth opened her journal and penned her first entry. She thought, *I wonder where Father is at this moment? He would be so happy to know I'm writing in my journal for the first time.* A few minutes later, she began to feel drowsy, so she set her quill in its stand and laid down for a nap.

As Jane rested her head on the pillow, she thought about her life. This wasn't her first time on a ship. She was only two, and Abigail four, when the family fled Scotland to come to America in 1820, leaving the turmoil of the Highland Clearances behind. She and Abigail were too young to retain any memories of the hard times. Jane had never realized the hardships her parents had gone through. It wasn't until she and Thomas had come to them needing shelter, that her father shared his Highland Clearances story. Then later, he recounted about their experience of staying in the steerage section of the ship for weeks at a time. A set of steep steps led them to the crowded, low-ceilinged quarters, which were situated between decks. The atmosphere was stuffy and stale, and the only relief for fresh air was when the hatches were open, but during bad weather, there was a standing order to batten them down.

When she and the children had boarded, she felt pity for the people she saw following the sign to steerage. She thought, *How grateful I am that we aren't among them, thanks to my brother-in-law, Philip. Here we are now—in a first-class cabin.* She fell asleep on that thought.

Emily was busy lining up her dresses on the sofa. She had an important decision to make. Which dress should she wear tonight? This was her first opportunity to dress as a fine lady. She decided on the green satin gown and held it up to herself again in front of the mirror. She was pleased with her reflection. *Oh, yes. This will do nicely. It brings out my green eyes, and I shall wear my hair up to show off my neck.* With her decision made, she laid the dress down. She sighed, *I'm just not ready for a nap yet.* Emily looked at the door, then her mother and sisters. *They're asleep. Before I rest, I'll just slip out and get some fresh air.*

Emily cautiously opened the door. She glanced back at her mother to be sure she was still sleeping. Emily knew her mother wouldn't approve of her going out on the deck unescorted, but she couldn't help herself. *I'll only be a few minutes. They'll never know I was gone.* She slowly and quietly closed the door as she backed into the hall.

She strolled the deck, enjoying every stolen moment of freedom. With so many passengers milling about the deck, it didn't take long for her to be noticed.

A well-dressed tall gentleman walked past her. He stopped and turned, then smiled and tipped his hat. She realized she had seen him when they boarded. He, too, was in the first-class section. Suddenly, she was startled from her reverie, when out of nowhere, a rough-looking man abruptly brushed against her as he passed, nearly knocking her down.

The gentleman reacted instantly to assist her. "Are you all right, miss?"

"I—I guess I'm fine. Thank you for your concern." She gazed at him. "I believe I saw you earlier when we were boarding."

Emily had indeed seen him. From the moment she noticed the handsome and debonair man, she was intrigued. He was well-dressed and looked quite dapper with his black silk top hat. His dark brown hair was cut short and his long sideburns met a trimmed beard. He wore a waxed mustache, which turned upward on each side into a curl. Emily had never seen such a mustache, or a top hat. The men in the quiet town of Delhi looked nothing like this man.

"That's possible," he answered. *Oh yes, I saw her,* he smirked to himself. "I'm quite sure if I had seen you, I wouldn't have forgotten. You're very beautiful. Please, allow me to introduce myself. I'm Sebastian Jones. And what's your name, pretty lady? Where are you heading?"

"I'm Emily Bennett from Delhi, New York. My mother, brothers, and sisters, and I are going to San Francisco and then on to Puget Sound to join my father and uncles." At that moment, she saw her brothers leaving the pilothouse. They saw she was alone and talking to a strange man. They were heading toward her and looked unhappy. "Oh dear, I see my brothers coming. I must leave."

"I hope I see you again, Miss Bennett."

"I'll be dining at the captain's table tonight. Perhaps you'll be dining this evening?"

He tilted his hat. "Yes, indeed."

Jonathan and Jeremy caught up to their sister and scolded her for being on the deck alone and talking to a stranger. They marched Emily back to her cabin. She entered without a sound, not wanting to wake anyone. *I've been scolded enough!* Then she lay down gently next to Elizabeth to nap and fell asleep thinking about the handsome stranger who told her she was beautiful.

Meanwhile, Sebastian Jones rendezvoused with the rough-looking man who had strategically bumped into Emily. He handed the man a couple of coins. "I'll let you know if I need you again."

* * *

By the time the supper hour had come, the sea was tranquil,

making perfect conditions for dining. The servers were always grateful when the sea was calm. They had their hands full when trying to serve a meal during rough weather. As the family entered the dining saloon, they immediately saw the captain's table with their host sitting at the head. The captain stood and greeted them warmly and seated Jane at the opposite end of the table.

The family felt at ease with the captain, and the conversation flowed effortlessly. They were a captive audience when he provided a vivid description of what to expect on their Nicaragua journey. He added, "Once we arrive at Greytown, I'm afraid we'll have to say goodbye and you will board the river steamer, *S.L. Tucker.*"

"We'll miss you, Captain Davis," Jane lamented. Everyone nodded in unison.

"And I you. Captain Bennett was correct. You're a fine family." He smiled broadly. "Now, shall I tell you more about Nicaragua?"

"Yes, Captain Davis. Please do," replied Elizabeth in an exhilarated voice, excited about the prospect of filling her journal pages.

"It's a beautiful and exotic country. One of my passengers on my last trip had been there and shared his experience. He said it was like a lost paradise. He described orange groves so loaded that the branches hung low to the ground. He saw towering coconut trees, banana and pineapple plantations, and beautiful forests. And the culture was nothing like a man from New York City had ever seen. Just be prepared for many hot, muggy days and nights."

"It sounds like I'll have plenty to write about in my journal," exclaimed Elizabeth.

Mary took a moment to turn the conversation to their current travels and asked the captain if there was a doctor on board. She was worried about her baby. She explained that Mollie had been extremely fussy, but now seemed listless. Even while Mary held her at the table, the baby had been abnormally quiet. Jane took turns holding Mollie while at the table and was concerned about her as well.

"Yes, Mrs. Spencer, there is a doctor on board. I'll ask him to check on your babe right away."

"I appreciate that so much, Captain Davis," said Mary. "Thank you."

Jane added, "You've set our minds at ease, Captain."

Jonathan and Jeremy asked the captain if they could continue to observe him navigate the ship.

"Yes, you're welcome to come to the pilothouse, but if the weather changes, which it frequently does, and the seas are rough, I want you secured in your cabin."

"Understood, Captain," saluted Jonathan.

Jeremy was interested in the business side of piloting a ship. During supper, he asked questions about delivering freight and materials to the different ports. Was it profitable? Or, was the business of transporting passengers more profitable?

"Let's talk about all that later, so we don't bore our ladies. I must say, conversing with you and your brother is quite refreshing. I've never experienced so much interest from young men such as yourselves. We'll get together soon for our discussion."

Elizabeth found herself distracted from the conversation. She couldn't stop looking at the beautiful room, and its beautiful occupants, dressed in their finery. She made a mental note to pen a description of the surroundings and the meal in her journal as soon as they returned to their cabin. *It's all so exciting!*

Emily flaunted her entrancing personality, which was by no means subdued, and as always, her beauty and kittenish charm didn't escape anyone's notice. Her bright green eyes scanned the room to see who might be looking her way. When she felt someone staring at her more intently than the other admirers, her eyes stopped at a man who had been attempting to make eye contact. It was Sebastian Jones. He nodded, stood up, and sauntered toward her table.

"Good evening, Miss Bennett. I trust you've recovered from your little mishap." He cast a glance at the assemblage of diners sitting at the table. "Is this your family?"

The family reacted with a look of surprise and alarm. Emily had said nothing about a *mishap*, and who was this man? Jonathan and Jeremy bristled. This strange man was much too forward and friendly toward their sister.

"Thank you for asking, Mr. Jones. I'm quite fine. It's very nice to see you again."

Then Emily introduced him to her family and Captain Davis, explaining what had happened. Sebastian remained standing. There was an awkward silence. It was obvious he was waiting to be invited to join them at the table, but neither the captain nor the family said a word. Emily thought it wasn't like her family to be so rude. *Where are their manners, for goodness' sake?* She took the matter into her own hands.

"Please, Mr. Jones," she said, looking toward the captain, "if Captain Davis doesn't mind, do sit down."

The captain felt uncomfortable, but didn't want to offend a passenger. "Of course, please join us, Mr. Jones."

During the remainder of the hour, Sebastian Jones coyly attempted to learn as much as he could about the family. The family members were polite, but purposely not forthcoming of many details. Emily noticed they weren't very friendly or talkative. Oblivious to their discretion, she promptly filled in any missing information.

The evening, however, was about to be cut short. The weather changed and the sea transformed from its tranquil state to rolling waves. The captain asked his passengers to return to their cabins and settle in for the night. They were in for a night of rough seas.

Captain Davis approached Mary, "Mrs. Spencer, I'll send Dr. Osborne to your cabin within the hour to check on your daughter."

"Oh, thank you, Captain Davis. I'm very worried."

Chapter 2

September 1855

The Atlantic Ocean

*T*he following morning, the passengers opened their eyes to a blue sky. The sea was calm, and rather than the rolling and pitching motion, which had continued throughout the night, they felt the steady, subtle movement of the ship plowing forward.

When Elizabeth woke, her first thought was to write in her journal. She looked out the porthole at the placid waters and knowing the sea could turn angry at any time, she seized the tranquil moment and penned her next journal entry. She wrote as though talking to her father. She described what it was like to board as first-class passengers and how beautiful their cabins were. She wrote about the luxurious dining saloon and the dinner with Captain Davis, as well as the unexpected appearance of the stranger who seemed much *too* interested in Emily and the family.

Elizabeth grew accustomed to the movements of the ship and continued to write in her journal almost daily.

1855

September 21.

It's cloudy today. Some of the passengers are suffering from seasickness. Little Mollie is very sick and isn't able to take her mother's milk. Mary is so worried and feels helpless. Dr. Osborne continues to look in on Mollie. He doesn't know what's wrong with her.

September 23.

We're heading south. The weather is pleasant and it's getting warmer. Everyone is feeling better now and spending time on deck. Jonathan and Jeremy aren't letting Emily out of their sight. Off and on, Mr. Jones walks by them and tips his hat. Emily loves the attention. Mother and Mary are busy caring for our Mollie.

September 24.

There are more passengers spending time on deck, especially those who are staying in steerage. They hang on to every moment they can to be on deck breathing in the salt air and enjoying the ocean breeze. Some of the people are playing cards to entertain themselves. They use their trunks as tables. There is little to entertain oneself. One nice man plays his violin. While the weather is pleasant, he plays it at night and some of the passengers dance in the moonlight. Mother enjoys standing at the railing watching the movement of the water, illuminated by the moon and the light of the railing lanterns.

September 25.

The further south we go, the warmer the weather. Jonathan referred to his map and announced when we started passing through the West Indies.

September 26.

This morning we passed the Isle of Cuba. At dusk, we watched the sun disappear behind the mountains of Jamaica. It was one of the most beautiful sunsets I've ever seen. Mollie seems better today. Mary and Mother are much relieved.

September 28.

Jonathan told me we're almost to our destination. It's been about ten days since we left New York harbor.

September 29.

Our ship entered the mouth of the San Juan River and will stop at the Caribbean coastal town of Greytown where we'll disembark and board a smaller steamer, the S.L. Tucker. We must say goodbye to dear Captain Davis. He has taken such good care of us. We will miss him, especially Jonathan and Jeremy who have become his shadow. I do believe the captain will miss my brothers' company.

Jonathan learned that Greytown is also called San Juan del Norte and it is considered to be the Atlantic port of Nicaragua in Central America.

Oh, how I beheld the scenery as our ship approached. I heard and saw the white surf crash onto the sandy beach. I marveled at the tall palms with their feathery crowns swaying in the wind lining the shoreline and the contrasting layer of dark foliage in the background.

As we came closer, I noticed the land surrounding the town to be perfectly level giving way to creeper vines festooned with pink and rose-colored flowers, covering every bare patch of ground.

Jonathan wondered why the buildings of Greytown looked so new. He inquired, and learned in the prior year, 1854, the town had been destroyed by the U.S. Navy sloop, USS Cyane, in retaliation for local actions against American citizens over tariffs and the control of transit routes. Since Greytown was considered to be such an important port on the Atlantic side, it was immediately rebuilt.

I watched the river steamer, S.L. Tucker, slide next to our ship. It's a smaller vessel with a flat bottom and as Jonathan describes, a shallow draw. I'm learning so much from my brother. After our baggage was transferred, we boarded. When we boarded, it became obvious to me we would no longer be enjoying the same luxury and comfort the Southern Light afforded.

As soon as our steamer was fully loaded, it paddled away parting the thick, humid air, leaving the cove and Greytown behind.

The S.L. Tucker chugged its way from the mouth of the Atlantic Ocean to the entrance of the San Juan River. Large sharks were swarming the entrance, alarming all of us at the sight of them. As we traveled further past *the mouth into the river along the shoreline, we saw cattle wading in the long grasses in the shoal water. There were marshes filled with aquatic birds, white cranes, and chocolate-brown jacanas with lemon-yellow markings under their wings. Alligators floated slightly submerged in the water with only their eyes showing above the surface. At first sight, they looked like a log. The land along the river was dotted with a variety of trees—palms, breadfruit, orange, and mango. The trees provided landings for the flocks of screaming bedazzling green parrots and toucans with brightly colored beaks.*

At first, I observed the riverbanks as low and marshy, intersected by numerous channels. Then the banks changed and became dense with thick jungles and vines intertwining the trees. We saw more palms, beds of wild cane and grass. As our steamer continued, the riverbanks changed again, becoming higher and dryer.

Then our vessel rounded a bend, and approached the Machuca Rapids followed by the Castillo Rapids. At this point the ride was extremely rough, and we all hung on tight, white-knuckled. After successfully maneuvering the rapids, the S.L. Tucker approached the small town of El Castillo.

We glanced upward at the bluff above the town and saw an old abandoned Spanish fort at the top of the hill, and cows and goats were grazing on the grassy land around it. Sitting at the bottom of the hill next to the rapids was the little town with several thatched-roof huts.

Jonathan was in awe of the sight and asked some of the crew about it. He said they were proud to share their knowledge and told him the history of the two-hundred-year-old fort. They told him that because the rapids were so formidable, the Spanish colonial authorities built the fort El Castillo de la Inmacuboya Concepcion high above the rapids in 1675 to guard the river communities. They knew the rapids were big enough to slow down the Caribbean pirates or enemy ships on their way to attack Granada.

September 30.

Captain Davis's passenger was correct, this is a beautiful, exotic paradise. When we stopped at El Castillo, the sun shone brilliantly upon a scene of dense foliage all along the riverbanks and created sparkling reflections in the water.

We left the steamer to find a place to get breakfast and discovered there was only one small street to follow, which was narrow, dirty, and rugged. We ate at a place called the American Hotel. The food was disappointing. Afterward, we left the hotel and walked about a half mile to board another small steamer. It was hot and muggy just as Captain Davis described. Mollie wasn't doing well in the heat.

We boarded the small steamer, San Marco, *and proceeded up the river for twelve miles heading to the small village of San Carlos. The river was more placid with tall palms, tree ferns, and banana and orange trees lining the riverbank. The abundant wildlife was a new and exciting spectacle for us. We saw Black Congo monkeys, tanagers, toucans, and screaming macaws dressed in vibrant colors of blue, yellow and scarlet.*

Once again, Jonathan educated me, so that I may continue to fill my journal with details of the spectacles we encounter. San Carlos sits at the foot of Lake Nicaragua where it empties its waters into the San Juan River, the only outlet to the Pacific Ocean. The lake spans one-hundred-ten miles from north to south, and thirty-one miles across, covering more than three-hundred square miles. According to legend, the locals named the lake after Nicarao, a chief of an Indian tribe who lived on the lake shores. The lake, in turn, inspired the name Nicaragua for the country.

Late in the day, September 30.

We came to San Carlos where we transferred to a lake steamer to cross Lake Nicaragua. The lake was a quiet expanse of water. We saw a great conical peak emerging from the lake, which I learned is called Ometepec. Jonathan told me it's almost five thousand feet above the lake's surface. On our left, we saw the cloud-capped mountains of Costa Rica. To our right, we saw low hills and ranges covered with dark forests. We saw flocks of Muscovy and whistling ducks flying above us.

Our next stop was Virgin Bay. We found the National Hotel where we ate and spent the night. We paid $12.50 for a single dirty room. We paid for two rooms. The rooms were full of insects and spiders. We killed several tarantulas. We all tried to clean the floors since that's *where we had to make up our beds. All night we fought mosquitoes. Oh, how I miss our cabin on Captain Davis's ship.*

October 1.

We are still at the hotel, and it looks like we'll be here for some time waiting for our ship to arrive from San Francisco. It's so hot and humid. Mollie isn't feeling well, her breathing is shallow. Meals are one dollar a day and the food is so poor and the conditions so filthy, we almost prefer to go hungry. Our cash is quickly depleting.

October 2.

We are still waiting for word of the ship. Everyone is tired and bored. Some of the other men found a way to amuse themselves outside by getting the natives to run races. Mr. Jones pursuaded the men to start betting on the runners. Emily is bored and insists on watching the races. Mother gave in, but told Jonathan and Jeremy to stay with her.

October 3.

The day started so very warm. Mollie was doing worse. Mother sent Jeremy and Jonathan to fetch Dr. Osborne. It's fortunate he stayed in the hotel. He came right away. After Dr. Osborne examined Mollie, he said she might have whooping cough. She has developed a wheeze in

her chest, and her breathing is very labored. Mary is
frantic.

October 4.

We received news by noon that the ship was arriving
soon at San Juan del Sur and we would need to cross
overland for thirteen miles to get there. We were
assigned a guide and interpreter who informed us there
weren't enough mules and wagons to take all of the
passengers at one time. One wagon arrived but was
only large enough to hold thirteen women and children.
Because of Mollie, Mary was chosen to be one of the
thirteen passengers. The rest of us walked. We knew we
might fall behind, but were told another wagon would
be sent back for us.

After several miles of traveling in the intense heat, the mules
became too exhausted to continue to pull the wagon with the weight
of the passengers. The guide instructed everyone to get out of the
wagon and walk except for Mary. It was agreed she should stay in the
wagon with her baby.

The road was in terrible condition making it difficult to walk
safely. During the first hour of walking, Elizabeth tripped on a
tenacious vine sprawled across the road, causing her to fall and
sprain her ankle. Her brothers rushed to her aid and lifted her. They
helped her walk, each of them supporting her by the arms. Her ankle
throbbed and was beginning to swell.

Periodically, the group experienced torrential rain showers. Jane
handed Mary her shawl to cover little Mollie. Nightfall was close
upon them, and with a distance yet to travel to the halfway house
ahead, the group wondered if they might be spending the night
outdoors without the benefit of any shelter. Earlier in the day, one
of the men in their group had run ahead and disappeared. No one

knew what his plans were except perhaps he didn't want to be slowed down by staying with the slow-paced group.

Later and unexpectedly before dusk, the young man returned with three mules. The group had already halted. The man explained he had recognized there were at least three women in the group who were in a bad way so he ran as fast as he could to the halfway house hoping there might be another wagon and more mules available. There wasn't another wagon, but he was able to bring back three mules.

The young man continued, "The halfway house is about four miles ahead. I spoke with an English couple who are the owners and convinced them to let me borrow their mules. At first, they only wanted me to take two, but I told them there are at least three women in this group who need help. We must hurry if we're going to get there before dark, which will be soon."

He walked up to Mary who was still in the wagon, extending his hands out to take Mollie from her. He turned to Jane, standing close by, "Will you take the babe while I help this lady from the wagon and onto a mule?"

The young man handed Mollie into Jane's arms. "You're a true gentleman, young man."

He led Mary to the mule and helped her up. "When we leave, I'll walk next to you and carry your babe, if you like."

"Thank you, kind sir, but she'll be more comfortable in my arms. I'm so grateful to you. She needs food and shelter soon."

The man took Mollie from Jane's protective arms. Mollie had been crying constantly. He handed her to Mary. He could see Mary would have a difficult time holding the baby and hanging onto the mule. He pondered for a moment and glanced over at his baggage on the wagon. "I believe I can make it easier for you to hold your babe." He walked over to the wagon and brought out a small blanket from one of his bags. Then he fashioned a sling for Mary and helped her position the baby. "This should do nicely."

"Oh, yes, this is much better, and she'll stay warmer as well. Thank you again. You are such a thoughtful man."

Next, he led the second mule to a woman in the group who was about seven or eight months along with child and had been walking the entire time. He helped her onto the mule. Unfortunately, her husband wouldn't be able to walk by her side since he needed to stay with their four children who would surely lag, whose ages ranged from five to fourteen years old.

Elizabeth stood next to her mother, still supported by her brothers. She was impressed with this gallant young man. Then she saw him walking toward her with the third mule.

"You're next, Miss. Please allow me to help you up."

She smiled, accepting his assistance. He had expected her to sit astride the mule, but not wanting to lift her skirts and spread her legs in front of this engaging man, she blushed and attempted to sit sideways. "Miss, you must ride astride. If not, you'll surely fall off and hurt yourself again."

Jeremy smiled and shook his head, "She has always insisted on riding sidesaddle." Then he swung her other leg around before she even had time to protest. The young man nodded to Jeremy and focused his attention on Elizabeth's ankle. He pulled a neck scarf from his pocket and wrapped it around her ankle.

Elizabeth enjoyed his attentiveness. "Thank you for your concern for all of us. We don't even know your name."

He tilted his hat. "I'm James Mitchell, at your service. And now I need to get you ladies to shelter before it gets so dark we won't be able to see the trail. With so many trees blocking the moonlight, it will be of little help to us. I brought a lantern with me just in case."

They proceeded forward. Elizabeth twisted around and waved goodbye to the rest of her family. The group continued walking as they watched James and the women slowly disappear. About an hour later, the guide called the group to a halt. The exhausted mules pulling the wagon wouldn't go another step. It was about nine-thirty, and it was so dark they could barely see the road in front of them. Because of the torrential rain showers, everyone was covered in mud.

Further ahead, James and the women had finally reached the shelter. They were soaked from the rain showers, cold, and exhausted. The innkeeper's wife rushed out to assist and introduced herself as Mrs. Taylor.

When Mrs. Taylor saw Mary with the baby, she approached her first, "Let me take your little one from you while this young man helps you ladies down from the mules. I'll have her warmed up in no time." She dashed back to the inn with Mollie in her arms.

Soon after, James escorted the exhausted women to the welcoming sanctuary. Swinging the door open, he ushered them in, at which point they were immediately comforted by the warmth of the crackling fire in the stove.

"Make yourselves comfortable," said Mrs. Taylor while handing Mollie, freshly bundled, back to Mary. "Your poor little girl, she doesn't seem well, does she? Would you like to sit over there in the corner by the fire to feed her?"

"Thank you, Mrs. Taylor. I'm sure she's hungry," replied Mary.

Elizabeth and the expectant mother also sat near the fire. Mrs. Taylor made tea for everyone.

"After you all finish your tea," said Mrs. Taylor, "I'll show you where you may sleep."

As Elizabeth sipped her steaming beverage, she looked up and saw James Mitchell walking toward her.

"May I check your ankle, Miss, and ask your name?"

As Elizabeth extended her foot, she answered, "Oh, yes, of course. My name is Elizabeth Bennett, and the lady with her babe is my sister, Mary Spencer." She continued the conversation by telling him their plans to join her father, uncles, and Mary's husband in Puget Sound to begin their new life.

"That's my plan as well. I'll be joining my uncle who has been there for some time. He owns a store, and his business has grown so much, he needs help and asked me to come."

James looked up and saw Mrs. Taylor leading Mary and the other lady to their sleeping quarters. Regrettably, his conversation with this intriguing young woman was coming to an end.

"Well, Miss Bennett, as much as I would like to continue this conversation, I think we should get some sleep. I plan to go back early tomorrow morning to see how the rest of the group fared. They probably had to stop traveling and spend the night by the road. They must be miserable. I'll take the mules back with me. Miss Bennett, before I take my leave, is there anything else I can do for you?"

"Thank you, Mr. Mitchell, I'm sure I'll be fine. I appreciate everything you've done. I feel guilty for being so comfortable with my poor mother out there. Thankfully, my brothers are there to look after her and my other sister, Emily."

"What are their names? I'll seek them out to see how they're doing."

Elizabeth gave him their names. "That's very thoughtful of you, Mr. Mitchell. It would be a great relief to me knowing you'll be checking on them."

James bid her good night, and as he walked away, Elizabeth studied him. She could see why he was able to run ahead of the group and return to them on the same day. He appeared strong and healthy. She admired his wavy dark brown hair, and it seemed as though his amber brown eyes looked deep into her own. *He's very handsome and gallant.* She thought about how lucky she was that this man entered her life. *He was on the ship the entire time, and I never noticed him.* She wondered if she would ever see him again when she and her family settled in Puget Sound. She pulled out her journal, which was always with her, and entered the latest experience including meeting Mr. James Mitchell. Soon, she put her quill down for the night, collapsed into her assigned bed, and fell fast asleep.

Before James turned in, he chatted with Mrs. Taylor and learned about her and her husband's history. The couple was originally from England and had migrated to California. Mr. and Mrs. Taylor had been running the inn since the California Gold Rush in 1848. While witnessing the population explosion in California, they realized people from the East traveling through Nicaragua to California would need a place to stay along the way. Mr. Taylor had said to his wife, "We won't have to dig gold to make our fortune!" The passage of time proved that the Taylors had made the right decision.

The next morning, Elizabeth took the time to pen another entry before the remainder of the group arrived.

October 5

This morning was most pleasant. The halfway house where we are staying is cleaner and more organized than the previous lodging. We've enjoyed a good breakfast, and it was served on clean dishes! Even though it's quite rustic here, it feels like a luxury. I'm so

happy Mr. Mitchell didn't have to go back alone. Mr.
Taylor went with him, and they took fresh mules. Poor
Mollie is still sick. Mary is beside herself with worry.

By noon, the Bennett family was thankful to be safe and together again. Conversations buzzed as the family exchanged stories about their experiences of the night before. The women and children had spent the night inside the wagon with blankets spread over the top forming a tent. Some of the men slept on the ground under the wagon. Jonathan and Jeremy propped themselves up next to each other against a heavily branched tree and draped themselves with a blanket. Jane told Elizabeth about the thoughtful Mr. Mitchell who, upon arriving, had asked if she needed any assistance. Elizabeth was impressed to learn he had kept his promise.

The rest of the passengers were still yet to come, but they had been delayed a day while waiting for transportation. Sebastian Jones was in this group. Emily wondered if he would continue to ignore her. It seemed he had lost interest. Even when she had made an appearance to watch the natives running races, where she knew he was actively placing bets, he hadn't acknowledged her presence.

That night, Mollie worsened and had developed a fever. The coughing was deeper in her chest and more frequent. Then the vomiting and spasms began. Mary and Jane were frantic and summoned the doctor. After examining her, he knew what was wrong. With a grim expression and a solemn tone in his voice, he said, "I'm afraid it's what I suspected—whooping cough." He brought out a bottle of powdered Ipecacuanha and mixed a portion with water and administered it to Mollie. "Time will tell," he said dolefully.

With such grave news, Mary broke down into uncontrollable sobs. She felt helpless. How could she put Mollie through more traveling?

Jane put her arms around Mary. "We're here together as a family, my sweet daughter, and we will help you keep Mollie as comfortable as possible. You've always had a strong will, and this is the time to bring it forth. We have no choice, Mary, we must move on. I've heard rumors of war, and we may be in danger."

By the end of the next day, the second group had arrived. The following morning they would begin their final trek to the port of San Juan del Sur. As Jane had feared, they found themselves in the middle of a revolutionary war. A battle was already in progress nearby.

October 6

We arrived at San Juan del Sur. We saw several armed men who had taken over the town quartered at the Columbia House. These soldiers were an arresting sight. They wore heavy felt hats accented with red ribbons, blue woolen shirts, course pants with a leather belt holding a revolver on the left side and a knife on the right, and heavy boots. They appeared well-mannered and disciplined. We asked one of the locals who spoke English about the soldiers and why they were there. The man told us the people in his town and towns nearby were caught in the middle of a civil war. A man called The Butcher and the Democrat General Castellon had started the war. The General had hired an American man by the name of William Walker and his army who came from San Francisco to fight for him. He said they were grateful for Walker's presence and considered him their civil and military governor. They said more of Walker's men had arrived just three days prior on the ship Cortez.

The passengers were relieved to see the steamer ship, *Maria*, waiting for them in the harbor. Soon they would be on their way to San Francisco. For some of these passengers, San Francisco was to be their final destination. Others would go on to Puget Sound. Everyone was excited and jubilant. Their joy, however, was short lived.

* * *

While the passengers chattered about their excitement of going to San Francisco, a man approached them wearing a somber expression. Then he gave them the worst news they could have ever contemplated. There was cholera on the *Maria*. Six people had died during the journey and two more passengers died that day. Others still on board were sick.

The ship remained in the harbor for several hours beyond the scheduled departure time. The only passengers leaving the ship were the recently deceased. There in San Juan del Sur, they would rest in eternal peace while those who survived would be forced to leave their loved ones behind.

The passengers waiting on the wharf of the San Juan harbor watched as the bodies were carried to shore. Now they had a difficult decision to make. Should they take their chances and board the ship, or stay and possibly become a victim of the civil war? They had heard rifle shots in the distance the entire day, and they heard stories about kidnappings and ransoms. There would be another steamer, but it could take several days before arriving. Several chose to stay in town for the next steamer, but most took their chances and waited to board the *Maria*.

Shortly after the corpses were brought ashore from the ship and new supplies loaded on, a blast was sounded from the *Maria*, signaling the passengers to board. Doctor Osborne decided to continue the trip, feeling obligated and duty-bound to be where people needed his help. After much discussion among themselves, the Bennett family chose to board the ship as well. They were concerned about Mollie not being near the doctor and were anxious to get to San Francisco. The trip would take about two weeks. Since they did not know how cholera was spread, they reasoned that if they stayed in their reserved first-class cabins as much as possible, and if they kept to themselves when venturing out, they might escape exposure to the outbreak.

October 7

We settled into our cabins on the ship and spent the night in the harbor. The cabins aren't as spacious and comfortable as the ones on Captain Davis's ship. The doctor has been checking on Mollie regularly. He told Mary to try to get Mollie to take her breast. The poor little babe is hungry but she is so uncomfortable, it's difficult for her to feed. My heart is breaking for my sweet niece.

October 8

The ship is finally heading out to sea. It's still warm, and the seas are rough. Many people are seasick including mother, Mary, and Emily. I haven't been affected yet. Two more passengers died from the cholera. One was a nine-year-old girl. They were sheeted and slipped into the sea. Many people prayed for them. It broke our heart to see a child meet the Lord so soon. It appears the cholera is mainly affecting the passengers in steerage. I thank my Uncle Philip daily for making sure we had the best accommodations available for this entire journey. We are fortunate indeed.

October 9

There's a bit of a breeze—a nice relief. Mollie was able to receive some nourishment today and seems a little better. We're all so hopeful.

*At midmorning, our ship stopped at Acapulco for
fuel, provisions, and water. The officials told us that
we wouldn't be going ashore because of the cholera. It
looked like it would have been a beautiful place to visit.*

October 10

*Our Mollie has taken a turn for the worst. The doctor
attends her every hour. Captain Lewis has been
extremely attentive and offered his cabin to Mary, which
he said would be more comfortable and private. Mary
didn't want to be separated from us, so she declined his
offer but expressed her gratitude for his generosity.*

Late afternoon.

*I cry as I write this. Near the end of the day, Mollie
suddenly left us. She seemed at peace when she
passed. We have never experienced such grief. Mary
is inconsolable. Mother, Emily, and I dressed Mollie in
her baptismal gown and wrapped her in her favorite
blanket with her little rag doll next to her. Mary didn't
want her to be alone. I cut a lock of Mollie's hair for
each of us to always have a part of her with us.*

*The captain and the pastor came to our cabin to prepare
Mollie for burial at sea. As Captain Lewis gazed at
Mary and her babe, he said he would give Mary a little
more time, and he and the pastor left the cabin.*

*When the captain returned, he brought one of the
passengers with him. The captain introduced the man*

and said he was a portrait artist. He thought Mollie's angelic beauty should be preserved, so at his own expense, he commissioned the artist to sketch Mollie's portrait before sending her to the Lord. After an hour, the artist finished the portrait. The captain told Mary it was time. She became hysterical and wouldn't let go of Mollie. She held her tight against her bosom. Mother asked the captain for a few more minutes. The captain nodded and stepped back. Mother was so gentle with Mary. She lovingly took Mollie from her arms and handed Mollie over to Captain Lewis.

We all proceeded to the deck with the heaviest of hearts. I've never felt so much heart pain. We were surprised to see so many people congregated to witness her burial. We tried to distance ourselves without appearing obvious or ungrateful. We bowed our heads while the pastor led us in prayer. Several people sang a hymn, and the violinist played "How Can I Leave Thee". I saw a familiar face come forward. It was James Mitchell. He orated a beautiful poem. I felt my heart fill with warmth. Then Captain Lewis held Mollie, wrapped tightly in a sheet, in his arms and spoke the kindest words, and he told us that never before on his ship had such a large group of people participated in a burial. We felt honored. When the captain finished speaking, he gently slipped our babe into the sea. Mary wailed and collapsed. Jonathan and Jeremy, who had been by her side, held her up and carried her to our cabin. Oh, how we all wept. I've never seen Emily so quiet.

October 12

We've been spending most of our time in our cabins. It's still very warm. Mary hasn't left her berth since Mollie's burial. Burial at sea is the worst fate, for there will be no gravesite for us to visit our dear Mollie. At least we each have a lock of her hair. My bereaved sister clings to the portrait gifted to her by Captain Lewis and her body is now aching to nurse her babe.

Mother has woven a lock of Mollie's hair into one of her brooches, which she plans to give to Mary at a later time.

Another man from steerage died today. Space is so confined there, it isn't a surprise.

October 14

The weather is more tolerable than before. We have remained in our cabins and only venture out on the deck for fresh air.

October 16

A woman died today. She was a steerage passenger. We learned it was the woman we met earlier who was with child. She didn't die of the cholera, but in birthing her babe. The babe lived. We heard the husband and his four children are devastated.

* * *

There was a knock on the Bennett family's cabin door. It was Captain Lewis. The man who had just lost his wife accompanied him. The man held his newly born baby swaddled in his arms and his four children were huddled behind him. The baby boy cried out in hunger. He needed a wet nurse as soon as possible. The captain knew Mary could fulfill such a need and hoped in the process the baby might ease her body's need and help her heal.

Jane invited them in. "Please, come in." She gestured toward the settee. "Feel free to sit."

Captain Lewis addressed Mary. "Mrs. Spencer, I know you're grieving, but I wondered if there is any possibility you would be willing to help this baby boy? His mother died shortly after giving birth to him. Mr. Johnson has nowhere to turn but you."

Mary was hesitant, but when she looked at the tear-stained and worried face of the father with his four children, she reached out her arms for the baby. With a sigh of relief, Mr. Johnson handed over his son to her. She caressed the baby's head and went over to a corner, draped one of Mollie's blankets over him, and began nursing him. The baby boy took to her breast immediately and sucked fervently. Jane gazed at the scene, and for the first time since they lost Mollie, felt a sense of calm. *This is a mixed blessing. The Lord works in mysterious ways.*

Mary felt physically relieved and an overwhelming feeling of nurturing returned to her. She felt a sense of purpose to be helping the motherless baby and the distraught family. She agreed to care for and feed the baby during the remainder of the voyage.

Mr. Johnson gazed at his son in Mary's arms for a moment. "I'm sorry for your loss, Mrs. Spencer, and I'm grateful to you. I must confess, I don't know what I'm going to do once we reach San Francisco."

Mary looked up and nodded.

"I won't impose on you any longer. Thank you." He gathered up his children and left the cabin.

Before the captain departed, he spoke softly, "Well done, Mary."

* * *

October 17

*The woman who died during childbirth was sheeted
and buried at sea today. We attended the burial. It was
difficult to watch the children witness their mother's
body being slipped into the sea. Mr. Johnson looked so
sad. Mary stayed in the cabin to nurture the babe.*

October 18

*None of us got much sleep last night. It seemed like the
babe was awake every two hours. We all tried to help
Mary care for him.*

*The weather has cooled down. We are about a week
away from San Francisco. Captain Lewis informed
everyone that the supplies are low. Food and water will
need to be rationed out.*

* * *

The following day the Bennett family gathered together to
discuss their plans. There was a knock on their cabin door. Jane
answered it to discover Mr. Johnson and his children standing in
the hall.

"Good morning, Mr. Johnson, please come in. I imagine you
want to check on your son?"

Mr. Johnson thanked Jane and stepped in. He instructed his
children to wait in the hall until he told them they could come in.

"Would you like to sit, Mr. Johnson?" Jonathan and Jeremy immediately stood to free up the settee.

Mr. Johnson looked over at Mary holding his son who was sleeping soundly in her arms. He noticed Mary's face was no longer tear-stained and the baby was peacefully content in her arms. He chose not to sit. He seemed anxious and was wringing his hands.

Then he spoke. "Mrs. Spencer, I paced the entire night pondering my situation. We're only a few days from San Francisco and I've learned from Captain Lewis of your plan to continue to Puget Sound to join your husband. My children and I are going to the north central valley in California to start a farm. I know if I take my son with us in our present state, he'll surely die. I'm sure you must see where I'm heading."

Mary nodded. The father continued. "Would you consider taking my son to raise as your child? I attended your babe's burial, and I know no other child could replace *your* babe, but I believe the Lord has led me to this decision, and that it is the right thing to do." His voice faltered for a moment. "This is an emotional and difficult decision for me, Mrs. Spencer. Most likely, we'll never see him again, but it comforts my heart to know he would be loved and be part of a good God-fearing family."

Mary had been guarding her emotions toward the baby knowing he would be torn away from her when they reached San Francisco. How much more pain must she endure? But regardless of checking her emotions, she had begun to form an attachment to the baby. They had bonded physically and emotionally. She gave Mr. Johnson the answer he prayed to hear.

"I'll take your son, Mr. Johnson, and you can be assured he'll be loved and enjoy a good life. I already love him. It seems he doesn't have a name yet. Would you like to name him? You and Mrs. Johnson must have been discussing names."

Mr. Johnson's eyes welled up with tears. "That would mean everything to me. We had decided if we had a boy, we would name him after her father, Parker Daniel."

"Then Parker Daniel it will be. It's a fine name."

Mr. Johnson asked, "May I ask one more thing from you? My children are standing outside the door. Could they come in to see Parker one last time and say goodbye to him?"

"Of course, Mr. Johnson, bring them in," said Mary.

Jane opened the door, and Mr. Johnson motioned his children to come in. The children were very quiet and solemn, and it was obvious they had been crying.

Jonathan and Jeremy were anxious to do something to help make the children feel better. They knew Mr. Johnson had very little money. Jonathan and Jeremy were running low on their small stash of money, but they decided to give each of the children a coin and reached into their pockets.

Jonathan said, "Hold out your hands." As Jeremy placed a coin in each palm, Jonathan continued, "Let this coin be the beginning of a savings account for each of you and be a symbol of the connection to Parker between our two families."

The children gazed at their coin, now in each of their hands. They had never held a coin in their palm, and now they each had their own. Jane was proud of her sons. They had created a thoughtful and generous distraction as the time came for the children to leave. They looked at Parker one last time and then looked at their coin. Somehow, the symbolic coin was a comfort to them.

* * *

October 23

Mary is beginning to heal now that she has little Parker. She no longer has time to stay depressed. It's surely God's will. I know we'll all love him. Benjamin has no idea they lost their daughter and now have a son. I know he and Mary will grieve together over Mollie. At least Mary has the portrait for Benjamin to see what his daughter looked like and they'll always have her lock of hair. Mother chose this day to give Mary the beautiful brooch embellished with Mollie's hair. Mary cried and held it against her heart. I wonder, will Benjamin resent Parker who is not of his blood and who so quickly has taken Mollie's place? Perhaps knowing they're saving Parker's life will make a difference. Benjamin is a gentle soul. I can't imagine him being resentful and he would never want to hurt Mary. She already loves Parker.

The weather has turned very cold now. We're only a couple of days away from San Francisco. I'm excited to see the Golden Gate city.

The cholera seems to have run its course. It's been several days since anyone else died. It has taken about thirty lives. I hope they let us leave the ship. I don't think I could tolerate Emily's restlessness much longer. Mother is an angel—she's so patient with her. Jonathan and Jeremy have been very nice to let me spend time in their cabin for some peace and quiet.

October 25

We're coming into sight of the Golden Gate Bay. It's shrouded in fog making it difficult to see very far ahead. Jonathan and Jeremy are out on the deck. They don't want to miss anything. I can hear foghorns. The sound must be coming from the lighthouse that I see through our porthole. We're moving past the lighthouse, but I still hear the sound, and it's getting louder. Now I hear the whistle from our ship, which seems to be in unison with the other sound. Both are getting louder. What—"

Suddenly, the sounds of the whistle and horn blasts collided.

Jonathan and Jeremy had been helping the captain keep a lookout through the fog. Without warning, they saw another ship breaking through the fog and coming directly toward them.

They shouted out, "Ship dead ahead, now!"

Then they heard a loud scraping noise at the port bow and at the same time felt an abrupt jerk of the ship. The captain had already seen the ship coming and had reacted instantly, turning his ship. This caused the ship to heel on the starboard side. The paddle wheel on the port side was nearly out of the water and whirred, throwing foamy water into the air. Meanwhile, the deck on the starboard side leaned downward nearly to the water line. In the same instant, as the ship pitched and rolled, the crew members and passengers on deck were thrown starboard against the railing. Fortunately, the railing prevented them from going overboard, but not from getting wet. There was shouting, screaming, and confusion. The crew quickly picked themselves up and instinctively ran to the port side of the ship to distribute the weight to reduce the degree of heeling. Jonathan and Jeremy followed suit to help stabilize the vessel. With the shift of weight, the ship sprang back and righted herself.

The two vessels had nearly collided in the thick fog. The damage on the port bow didn't disable the *Marie*. Repairs could be made once they dropped anchor in the bay. The other ship suffered some damage, and the captain turned his ship around back to the harbor to assess the repairs needed.

Most of the passengers got by with only bumps and bruises. One woman suffered a broken arm. Dr. Osborne was summoned to tend to her. Once the ship was steady, Jonathan and Jeremy dashed to the lower deck to check on their family.

Elizabeth had been writing in her journal and was knocked off her chair, landing on the floor. Her journal flew into the air along with her quill, which rolled across the cabin. Her inkwell spilled, leaving ink puddling on the floor. Her journal entries were over until she could get more ink.

Jane, Emily, and Mary had been thrown to the floor as well. Mary was holding Parker and protected him as she fell.

Jeremy and Jonathan burst into the cabin as everyone picked themselves up from the floor. "Are you all right?" they both asked breathlessly.

Jeremy exclaimed, "We saw it happen! The fog was so thick the captain didn't see the oncoming ship until it was almost too late."

Jonathan chimed in. "We yelled out a warning, but the captain had already seen it coming and veered away before the collision. There's some damage on the port bow, but we're okay. A few people got banged up and wet."

Jonathan noticed Elizabeth's ink sprawling across the floor with the movement of the ship. "Looks like we're going to have to find you some ink, sister, once we get to the city."

The ship crept into the harbor and took its place at the long wharf, which extended several hundred feet out into the bay. The wharf was crowded with people coming and going. Baggage and supplies were either being loaded or unloaded. On the street next to the wharf, cab drivers had lined up waiting for prospective customers.

Much to everyone's relief, the passengers were allowed to disembark. The Bennetts left the ship and located their baggage, then summoned one of the nearby cabs.

Jonathan and Jeremy helped the cab driver load their baggage, then joined their mother and sisters in the cab. Jane said, "Driver, please take us to the Elliot Hotel." The driver nodded, snapped the whip, and the horses trotted toward the hotel.

Sebastian Jones disembarked closely behind the Bennetts. He had stayed in earshot and heard where they were going. He grabbed his bags and hailed one of the cabs. "Driver, the Elliot Hotel please."

The family was excited to be in San Francisco. Mary exclaimed, "It feels so good to be on dry land."

"And not to be in the middle of a civil war," Elizabeth added.

As Jane gazed out the cab window at their new surroundings, she remarked, "This city looks much different from New York City. There are so many hills. I'm looking forward to our arrival at the hotel. Your Uncle Philip said he would leave any letters for us there from your father and Benjamin when he was here on business. It won't be long before we see them. I miss them so much."

Jane noticed the pensive look on Mary's face. "Are you thinking about Benjamin, Mary?"

"Yes. If there's a mail ship going to Puget Sound, I must post a letter to him. It breaks my heart to have to tell Benjamin about our Mollie. I pray he'll be able to accept Parker." She looked down at the baby sleeping contently in her arms and gently caressed his head. She wondered how Parker's family was faring. San Francisco was the crossroads for the two families.

"I must post a letter to your father as well," said Jane. "There is so much to tell him. I wonder if they heard about the war in Nicaragua? Your uncle may have possibly heard about it on one of his trips here. If he did, I'm sure they would have been frantic, wondering if we were in the middle of it."

Jonathan, in a take-charge manner, replied, "As soon as we settle into the hotel, Jeremy and I will check the schedule for the next passenger ship departing for Puget Sound along with the mail ship. If the mail ship is scheduled before our departure, we'll post your letters."

Jane smiled lovingly at the twins, "What would I do without my sons?"

Mary nodded in agreement, remembering the two of them by her side during Mollie's burial. "You're always looking out for us. Thank you, dear brothers."

Elizabeth clutched her journal. She was anxious to begin writing again. "Do you think the hotel will have an inkwell in the room?"

Emily had been leaning her head out the open window of the cab absorbing the city sights and sounds. Once they left the wharf area, the conditions improved, which she found most appealing. The buildings were much nicer, having been made of brick, and the roads were paved in cobblestone rather than planks like some of the streets in the lower section. Emily looked forward to staying at the Elliot Hotel. *It's bound to be high-class in this part of the city,* she told herself.

Emily announced, "When we get there, I want a nice bath and a proper meal. I wonder if they dress for dinner here?" She thought about which dress she should choose.

Chapter 3

October 25, 1855

San Francisco

*A*fter the brief excursion through the city, the family arrived at the hotel. As they exited the cab, the driver unloaded their baggage and set it in the hotel lobby. Jane dipped into her reticule and paid the driver. Then they checked in, knowing Philip had made reservations for them.

"Hello, I'm Mrs. Thomas Bennett. I believe you have reservations for us?"

The clerk checked his book. "Oh, yes, Mrs. Bennett, I see we do." He handed her a key for room seven and one for room eight. She asked, "Is there a letter here for us?"

"Yes, Mrs. Bennett, as a matter of fact, there is something here for you." He handed her the packet Philip had left. She peeked inside and saw a letter for her from Thomas and one for Mary from Benjamin. They were both eager to read their letters, but held off until they could settle into their room.

"Oh, let's hurry," said Mary. "I can barely wait to savor every one of Benjamin's words."

"I don't know if I could have stood it if there hadn't been a letter from your father," said Jane.

Jonathan queried the clerk, "Do you provide filled ink wells in the room? My sister lost hers during a mishap on the ship."

"No sir, I'm sorry we don't. Most of our guests bring their own."

At that moment, the family heard a stranger's voice enter into the conversation. They hadn't noticed the man standing behind them, Sebastian Jones. He had skulked in, unnoticed.

"Please, forgive me. I couldn't help but overhear your inquiry. I happen to have an extra inkwell you may have. After I'm settled into my room, I'd be happy to bring it to you, Miss Bennett. May I ask your room number?"

Before Elizabeth could answer Sebastian's question, Emily had maneuvered herself into a position for easy eye contact with the man and gave him their room numbers. He tilted his hat to her.

"Ah, Miss Emily Bennett. I trust you didn't suffer any discomfort during our recent misadventure on the ship?"

She smiled flirtatiously. "I was safely secured in our cabin. We had no idea what was happening. It was rather unsettling. Thank you for asking."

Jonathan and Jeremy were uneasy seeing Emily flirt with Mr. Jones, and they certainly held a strong dislike for him. Jeremy offered his arm to his sister, "Come, Emily, let me escort you to our rooms."

Emily turned to see if Mr. Jones was looking at her as she left. To her disappointment, he wasn't looking in her direction. He was busy talking to the clerk. She was undaunted, however. *The hotel isn't so big that it wouldn't be impossible to cross paths with Mr. Jones. I'll have to make sure I do.*

Sebastian asked the clerk if room five was available. It was an easy request to fill since the hotel didn't have many occupants at the time.

"Yes, sir, here is your key for room five." Sebastian looked at his key, checking the number, as he walked to his room. *Ah, yes, this will do nicely. Room five keeps me at a proper distance from their rooms, but close enough to keep an eye on Miss Emily Bennett.*

Sebastian trailed slowly behind the family as they followed the bellhop up a flight of stairs and down a long hall to their rooms. Jonathan and Jeremy each had a key and unlocked the doors while Jane directed the bellhop to place the baggage in their rooms.

"Will there be anything else, Madam?" asked the bellhop.

"No thank you, that will be all," replied Jane as she handed the young man a tip.

Jonathan noticed room eight was smaller, so he suggested he and Jeremy take that room and give the larger room to his mother and sisters.

Emily peeked at room seven confirming it was the larger of the two. "An excellent observation, Jonathan," said Emily.

Jane and her daughters made themselves comfortable in their

room. Finally, Jane and Mary were free to open their letters. Jane sat down on the edge of one of the beds, her hands trembling.

"I've been waiting so long for this letter. I feel a little lightheaded now that I have it in my hands," Jane confessed.

Mary laid Parker on the other bed and sat next to him while she opened her letter from Benjamin.

After Jane read her letter, she set it down on her lap. She couldn't hide the alarm on her face. "Elizabeth, would you tell your brothers to come to our room? I have some unsettling news from your father."

Elizabeth hurried to her brothers' room to summon them, wondering what was going on. Jeremy answered the door, surprised to hear a knock so soon. "What is it Elizabeth?"

"Mother needs you both to come to our room. She has news from Father and she wants all of us together when she tells us."

Jonathan was worried. "Do you have any idea what it's about?"

"No, I just know that mother looked very serious. I don't understand it. She was so excited about receiving a letter from Father."

Elizabeth and her brothers continued their discussion as they walked down the hall expressing their concern about what might be wrong.

Now together, the family sat in silence while they awaited the news. Mary appeared to be upset as well. Her letter contained the same news.

With a somber expression, Jane looked at her children and said, "It seems we won't be able to continue to our destination for some time until your father informs us it's safe to come. There's been an Indian uprising in the Territory, and Puget Sound is in imminent danger of attack. It's even possible they will all be called into service.

"Your father says we'll be safe here. Your Uncle Philip has left a letter at the residence of his close friend, Captain Davis, about our new situation. At least the captain isn't a stranger to us. Captain Davis and his wife will be our contact to help us settle somewhere. I'm afraid we're all going to have to find a way to earn some money, for we will surely deplete our remaining funds."

The family was stunned. They thought they would have been boarding a ship destined for Puget Sound soon. Most of the passengers from their ship, the *Maria*, were traveling on to settle in

Puget Sound except for those who had chosen California as their final destination. It was doubtful the other passengers who were continuing on would learn about the Indian war in time to change their plans.

Elizabeth thought about James Mitchell. *He would surely be on that ship. Will he be pressed into service to fight the Indians too?* She prayed that he, her father, uncle, and Benjamin would be safe.

* * *

A few hours later, there was a knock on the door. Emily was sure it would be Sebastian Jones with the inkwell. She rushed toward the door. "I'll answer it," she said.

Sebastian smiled broadly, the curled ends of his mustache nearly rising to his cheekbones. "Good evening, Miss Bennett. I have an inkwell filled with ink for your sister."

"Thank you, Mr. Jones. Elizabeth will be pleased."

He lingered in the doorway before producing the inkwell. Earlier, he had eavesdropped on Elizabeth and her brothers talking in the hallway. He prompted Emily. "So, you must be looking forward to continuing your journey in a couple of days. I'll be disappointed to see you leave our fair city."

"I'm afraid we won't be leaving, Mr. Jones. We've just learned from my father that we won't be able to go to Puget Sound for awhile. My father says there's an Indian uprising and he wants us to stay here until he believes it's safe for us to leave."

"Your father sounds like a sensible man and cares about your welfare."

Jane decided it was time to end the conversation. She stood up and approached Sebastian Jones, extending her hand to take the inkwell from him.

"I'll relieve you of the inkwell, Mr. Jones. Thank you. I'm sure Elizabeth will be grateful to return to her journal. I would invite you in, but we're getting ready to go down to dinner."

"Yes, of course, I understand."

Emily broke in, "Are you going down to dinner as well?" Jane frowned at her impetuous daughter.

"Yes, Miss Bennett, I have a meeting with some of my business associates for the dinner hour." He bowed. "Until another time, I bid you adieu."

Abruptly, Jane closed the door before either of them could speak another word. Sebastian left with a smirk on his face. *Aren't I the lucky one? It looks like I have more time to make my move if I need it.*

The family prepared for dinner. With the possibility of Sebastian Jones being present, Emily took great care of her appearance. She chose the same dress she had worn that first night when they dined with Captain Davis on his ship—the dark green satin, styled with a neckline that bared her shoulders. Surely, Mr. Jones wouldn't tire of seeing her in it again.

When the family entered the dining area, Emily turned heads. Women were still scarce in comparison to the number of men in that part of the country. Being young, single, and beautiful, attracted even more attention. The family chose a table and sat down. Emily looked around and saw Mr. Jones and two other men sitting at a table across the room. Sebastian had already seen her. He made eye contact and nodded. Then he looked away and continued to converse with his associates.

Emily noticed the men were involved in a vigorous conversation. They were energized and pleased with themselves. Every once in awhile, they glanced over at Emily. Sebastian lowered his head toward the two men and whispered, "Did I not tell you I had found an excellent commodity?"

One of the men answered in a lowered voice, "Ah, ya, she should bring in top dollar!"

The other man joined in, laughing loudly, "Guaranteed!"

Emily wondered if Mr. Jones would come over to her table to greet her and the family. He seemed inattentive toward her. *Surely, his friends must want to be introduced to me.* Then the three men pushed away from their table and stood. Emily watched them as they walked away. *They don't appear to be coming to our table.* When they left the room without coming by, she felt slighted. *He didn't even say goodnight.*

Jane and the brothers were aware of Sebastian Jones's presence across the room. They were relieved to see he seemed to have lost interest in Emily. They certainly didn't need any more problems.

* * *

The next morning, as per Thomas's instructions in his letter, the family prepared to contact Captain Davis's wife, Victoria. She knew the ship on which the family travelled had arrived, and was expecting a visit from them at any time.

Jane felt anxious, "We can't waste a day. It's urgent we get help. The cost of this hotel will deplete our funds quickly."

Emily announced she was too tired to go and would like to stay behind and rest. *Perhaps I will have a chance meeting with Mr. Jones.*

Jane said, "Emily, we're likely to be gone for several hours so I don't want you leaving the hotel. I noticed there are several books in the parlor available for hotel guests to read. Perhaps reading might entertain you. I'm sure they would allow you to take a book to our room."

"I always find ways to entertain myself, Mother. I'll be fine."

"That's what worries me."

"Don't fret. How far can I go if I stay in the hotel? Goodbye, Mother. I'll see you all later."

"I guess you can stay, but keep to yourself."

"Yes, Mother."

* * *

The hotel clerk told Jane they could catch a ride on the omnibus, a horse-drawn bus, to and from their destination. Thomas had provided the address for Captain Davis's residence in his letter. The captain would not have yet returned from the New York trip. After taking them to the Greytown port, he planned to continue south toward Cape Horn to take care of other business along the way.

As the family entered the neighborhood of Rincon Hill, they saw beautiful parks situated near luxurious homes. Before long, the omnibus stopped at the address of Captain Davis's residence.

The Bennetts followed the manicured walkway to the impressive entrance of the home. Jeremy grasped the bronze lion's head door knocker and tapped on the door. Within minutes, the Davis's servant, Bridget, answered. The Bennett family introduced themselves.

"Yes, Mrs. Davis has been expecting you. She wasn't sure when you would arrive."

Bridget led them to the parlor. "Please have a seat. I'll let Mrs. Davis know you've arrived." She scurried from the room.

Shortly, Victoria Davis appeared. "Hello, I'm Mrs. William Davis, but do call me Victoria, and make yourselves comfortable. I've ordered tea."

Jane introduced her family. "You'll meet my youngest daughter, Emily, later, I'm afraid. She was weary and asked to remain behind at the hotel to rest. Thank you, Victoria, for welcoming us *vagabonds* to your home."

A few minutes later, Bridget brought a tray laden with an inviting assortment of tea sandwiches and a pot of tea. As Victoria poured the tea, she said, "You must all need some refreshments by now. Please help yourselves." After Jane told her of their plight, Victoria explained how she could assist them.

"We own several rental houses, and at the moment, there are some vacancies. You're welcome to stay in one of them until you're able to go on to Puget Sound. If you'd like, I can take you to one of the houses after we finish our tea. I have a certain residence in mind I believe would be the most accommodating for you and your family." She offered the tray. "More refreshments?"

As the family partook of another helping from the tray, Victoria continued. "I can also refer you to a friend of ours who has many connections. I'm certain he could help you find employment."

Then Victoria noticed Mary holding Parker, and commented, "What a beautiful child."

Mary thanked her but couldn't bring herself to tell her story about Parker and Mollie. She was sure if she talked about what had happened, she would lose control of her emotions.

After they finished their tea and sandwiches, Victoria ordered her driver to bring the carriage around to the front of the house. Everyone boarded while Victoria gave the address of the prospective vacant house to the driver.

* * *

Back at the hotel, Emily left her room and wandered about hoping she might cross paths with Mr. Jones. She decided to go to the dining room for a cup of tea, hoping she might find him there. She wasn't disappointed. Sebastian was well aware of her presence and knew she was alone. He had heard her family leave the hotel earlier that morning. He also heard Emily leave her room after her family had gone, and proceeded to shadow her. As he skulked down the hall behind her, he stopped for an instant at room four, tapping the door twice. Continuing to distance himself, he followed her down the stairs, and finally, to the dining room. Sebastian waited until she found a table, then strolled toward her. She had barely sat down when he appeared.

"Good day, Miss Bennett. What an unexpected surprise to see you here! Is your family joining you?"

She sighed, "No, they've gone out on business to secure our living arrangements. I didn't want to rush around this morning, so I decided to stay behind."

"I see. May I be so bold as to join you?"

Emily wondered if this would be appropriate but rationalized since she was in public, it was probably acceptable. "Yes, of course. Do sit down."

"You're looking quite lovely this morning, Miss Bennett. What is your pleasure? Tea? Coffee?"

"I was planning to have tea. With cream, please."

"Then tea it is." He summoned the waiter and ordered a pot of tea, a small pitcher of cream, and two cups. While waiting for the tea, they carried on a polite conversation. Soon, the waiter arrived. Before Sebastian poured the first cup, one of his associates, appeared out of nowhere and approached the table. Emily recognized him as one of the men she saw with Sebastian the night before during the dinner hour. She assumed he wanted to be introduced.

"Well, Sebastian, my man, I see you've found pleasant company this morning. Are you going to introduce me?"

"Of course. This charming lady is Miss Emily Bennett. I found her all alone this morning. Miss Bennett, this is Jack Miller."

"Indeed, a pleasure, Miss Bennett," he said as he half-bowed. "I saw you last night during dinner."

Jack Miller remained standing, positioning himself so that

Emily was forced to turn her head away from the table to continue her conversation with him. While she chatted with Miller, Sebastian poured and served the tea. During this orchestrated distraction, Sebastian brought out a small pouch from his pocket and sprinkled a generous serving of potent powder into Emily's cup. The powder dissolved instantly once the hot tea hit the cup.

After watching Sebastian *enhance* Emily's tea, Jack Miller said, "I see your tea has been poured, Miss Bennett, please don't let it get cold on my account." He tilted his hat and said goodbye to Emily and Sebastian, and walked away, pleased with himself on how well he played his part.

He chuckled. *That Sebastian always has something special in his pocket for the opportune moment. Our plan is in play.*

Chapter 4

October 26, 1855

San Francisco

*E*mily and Sebastian drank their tea, engaged in a flowing conversation. Emily enjoyed Mr. Jones's charismatic personality immensely, but she was beginning to feel a little strange. *I didn't eat this morning. That must be why I feel so lightheaded.* Sebastian continued to talk. His voice sounded like he was talking under water, and everything she looked at, including him, was blurry.

Finally, she said, "Mr. Jones, I'm not feeling well. I need to go back to my room."

"I'm sorry to hear that, Miss Bennett. Come, I'll help you." Sebastian looked around the nearly empty room before assisting her. Then he helped Emily rise from her chair, grasping her arm. She could walk, but not without assistance. She felt herself wobbling and wondered if she would be able to climb the stairs. She squinted at the staircase. It appeared to be one big mass of steps melded together.

Jack Miller lurked nearby. Then he walked up to the hotel clerk, handing him some cash. He looked straight into the clerk's eyes, and spoke in a low threatening voice, "You didn't see us here, isn't that right? If you say otherwise, we'll pay you a personal visit, and you won't like it. Understand, George?!"

The clerk's eyes widened with fear. His voice faltered. "Ye—, ye—, yes, I mean no. I didn't see anything. It's none of my business."

The clerk was accustomed to the many forms of corruption such as kidnapping and shanghaiing in San Francisco. He knew his singular voice wouldn't make a difference. Even the police and politicians were crooked.

Sebastian continued to assist Emily up the staircase. She had to concentrate on maneuvering every step. When they were in the hall, she fumbled for her key and handed it to Sebastian to unlock her door. Jack had sprinted ahead up the back stairs and unlocked and entered Sebastian's room, then waited in a dark corner.

Instead of taking Emily to room seven, Sebastian took her to room five, his room, now unlocked. He pretended to be unlocking room seven with her key. She was so disoriented, and her vision was so blurred, she couldn't read the number on the door. She thought she was entering her room. The room was dim and seemed to be spinning. The surroundings looked different, and was that another person sitting in the room? Was that the shape of a man blended into the shadows? She was confused. Then everything went black and she passed out, crumbling onto the floor. Sebastian snickered, picked her up, and threw her on the bed.

Jack and Sebastian congratulated themselves at how well they had set the trap. They were experienced and knew how to pounce on their prey instantly once they perceived an opportunity. Sebastian still held Emily's room key in his hand.

"Jack, keep a lookout while I go down the hall to her room. I'm going to fetch some of her things."

When he entered the room, he looked for the baggage labeled with Emily's name and decided to take it all. *Her family might think she ran off on her own accord.*

When Sebastian returned, he looked hungrily at Emily lying helplessly on the bed. *What a shame. I'd like to have a taste of her, but I don't want to damage the merchandise. A virgin will get top dollar.*

Jack scowled at Sebastian. "I see how you're licking your chops at her. Forget it! I'll hurry and pull the wagon to the door at the back stairway. Wrap her in that rug."

Sebastian sneered at his partner, "Don't you think I know better. Just get the wagon ready and I'll bring her out." Sebastian laid Emily on the rug. He thought, *She looks so helpless. I could do whatever I wanted with her.* He stroked her body, savoring his control over her. Then he wrapped her in the rug and chuckled, "You're in for a nice surprise, Miss Emily Bennett."

Then Jones and Miller took Emily to their gambling house and locked her in one of the rooms at the back of the building.

The two partners ran a large operation. They were proud of it and possessed no fear of doing whatever they pleased. Gambling was one of the most prominent branches of business in the city, and the gambling saloons were the main entertainment in the evenings. Their building was always crowded with men willing to take a chance with their money to win the big pot in the middle of the table. At times, there could be as much as $10,000 in the pot.

Their building was designed to attract customers. Fine crystal chandeliers lit up the room and elegant pictures and mirrors adorned the walls. There was a large bar with an endless supply of liquor available to anyone who asked for it. Poker, Roulette and Faro tables took center stage in the room. Chairs ready for occupants surrounded the tables. An attractive elegantly dressed woman usually assisted the dealer.

Along with gambling, the customers were often entertained by a female singer dressed in her finery accompanied by musicians. If the men needed another kind of entertainment, they only needed to ask, then hand over the money.

Sebastian Jones and Jack Miller also owned a large building adjacent to the gambling house. Auctions were held in this building. There were two types of auctions.

Publicly, they held auctions for certain merchandise, but it was the private auctions that were the most popular, attracting a large following of men from all walks of life. Jones and Miller auctioned off women. Men outnumbered women twenty to one in the area, so the opposite sex was in high demand. The attendees wanted wives and they were willing to pay well. The followers checked periodically to see if an auction was scheduled any time soon. They were aware that the women were not participating in the auction of their own volition; therefore, the auctions weren't publicized. These men had no problem with how the women got there, and they knew that Sebastian Jones was their contact to learn about the schedule and details of the *merchandise.*

With his newly acquired prize under lock and key, Sebastian let it be known that they had an extra special private auction scheduled. They had brought in a group of young Chinese women to be sold, and they had a beautiful young, white female available. He made sure the men were informed they should be prepared to pay a high

price for such a rare virginal commodity.

Chapter 5

October 26, 1855

San Francisco

*B*y the end of the day, thanks to Victoria Davis, Jane not only possessed the name and address of the man who could help them with their needs such as employment, but she and her children knew where they would be living for their sojourn in San Francisco. The house was already furnished and perfect for the family. The next morning they would check out of the hotel and move into their temporary home.

Jane thanked Victoria for her help. "Victoria, you've been so kind to us. We're forever grateful."

"It's been my pleasure, Jane. Now, allow me to do one more thing for you. Let my driver take you back to the hotel."

"I'll take you up on your offer, Victoria. I wasn't looking forward to waiting for the omnibus and I'm anxious to share our news with my daughter, Emily. I hope you can meet her one day soon."

"I would like that. I'll visit you once you're settled into the house."

* * *

After the family enjoyed a pleasant ride down Rincon Hill, Victoria's driver arrived at the Elliot Hotel. They exited the carriage and thanked the driver. Upon entering the hotel lobby, the family waved at the hotel clerk, but instead of acknowledging them, he quickly turned away. Jane thought he must have been preoccupied, so she dismissed it. She was in too good of a mood to let the clerk's snub bother her. They walked past him and went upstairs to their room. They hadn't seen Emily downstairs, so they assumed she would be there.

Not surprised to find the door locked, they knocked expecting Emily to let them in. They waited. Nothing. They knocked again, louder. Not a sound of any movement in the room. Had she fallen into a deep sleep? She did say she was tired. Jeremy volunteered to get another key from the clerk. The clerk wasn't surprised to see one of the family members coming to ask for another key. He did his best to act normal. "May I help you, sir?"

"Yes, we need another key for room seven. We seem to be locked out. My sister must be asleep and hasn't heard us knocking."

The clerk reached for a duplicate. "Of course, here's another key for you."

Jeremy sprinted up the stairs with the key. The clerk knew they would find an empty room and decided to be conveniently absent before he was besieged with an onslaught of questions. He asked one of the other men who worked there for a favor.

"Albert, I've received word of a family emergency. I need to leave as soon as possible. Would you mind covering my shift? I can do the same for you in a day or two."

"Sure, George. Go ahead and take off."

"Thanks, Albert," he said as he rushed toward the back door.

* * *

When the family entered the room, Emily was nowhere to be seen. Her bed looked exactly the same as when they left that morning. They looked for a note. Nothing. Suddenly, Elizabeth noticed Emily's baggage was gone. Jane's face lost all color and a feeling of panic engulfed her.

Jeremy said, "Could she have run away? I noticed how much she enjoyed the attention of that Sebastian fellow. Do you think she might have runaway with him?"

"I can't imagine she would do such a thing!" exclaimed Jane.

"I think that's where we start anyway," said Jonathan. "Let's check to see if he's still here. I saw him check in to room five. If he's here, we can at least ask him if he saw her anywhere."

Jonathan and Jeremy soon learned that Sebastian was no longer in room five nor in the hotel, so they went out into the city to ask around about him.

Jane and Elizabeth rushed downstairs to question the clerk. As Jane and Elizabeth approached the front desk, they realized the clerk on duty was a different person.

"Good afternoon, sir. Is the man who was here earlier available? We need to ask him some questions," said Jane as she looked behind him hoping to catch a glimpse of the clerk who had waited on them.

"No ma'am, I'm sorry, he isn't here. There was some kind of family emergency, so he left awhile ago."

Jane didn't give up. She described what Emily looked like to the clerk. "Is there any chance you may have seen her today?"

"No, I haven't seen her. It's pretty quiet around here these days with the recession going on and all. From the sound of her description, if I saw her, I'd remember her."

Jane explained they would be checking out of the hotel the next morning. She asked for paper and quill. "I'm writing down the address of where we'll be living in case the other clerk has any information, or, if Emily happens to come back looking for us. I'll settle up this evening before I retire." *Maybe I'll see the other clerk when I come back down tonight.*

"I'll be sure to inform George when he comes back on duty, Mrs. Bennett," replied Albert. He laid the note under the counter in a tray where George would easily see it.

The brothers looked everywhere for Sebastian Jones. They knew he ran some sort of business in the city. They asked several people if they knew of him. Finally, someone was able to give them some information.

"Sure, I know Sebastian. You can find him at his gambling saloon called the Lucky Lady. It's on the other side of town."

They thanked the man and rushed to find the saloon before nightfall. Just as the day turned into night, the brothers found the Lucky Lady. They walked in. The room was large and illuminated with brightly lit chandeliers. At least a hundred men occupied the place. Some were gambling at the tables, and some were drinking at the bar while enjoying the attention of flirtatious women trying to lure them to a room. The rumble of loud voices and boisterous laughter dominated the saloon.

Jonathan and Jeremy had never experienced such an environment and were overwhelmed at first glance. Once they regained their composure, they approached the bar to ask the bartender if they could speak to the owner. The bar was noisy with drunken men yelling and laughing and clinking their glasses. The bartender was busy serving customers, so it took a few minutes for Jeremy and Jonathan to get his attention. While they waited, two aggressive women approached them and draped themselves all over the brothers.

They instantly pulled away from the women and said, "No thanks." The women, feeling chagrined, huffed away.

Finally, the bartender noticed Jonathan and Jeremy. "What's your pleasure, young fellas?"

Jeremy answered. "We're looking for Sebastian Jones. We have something to discuss with him."

"Oh sure, he's in the back." He turned his head toward a man at the end of the bar. "Hey Ned, go fetch Sebastian. He has company!"

After a few minutes, Sebastian Jones appeared. "Well, the Bennett brothers. Have you come for a taste of Frisco? How about a drink? On the house!"

The brothers thanked Sebastian, declining the drink.

Jonathan said, "We're here on serious business. We had to leave the hotel for several hours earlier today, but our sister, Emily, didn't go with us. When we returned, she wasn't there and there's no sign of her. We've looked everywhere, and we haven't a clue of where she might be. Did you see her at anytime today?"

"No, I'm afraid not. I've been working at my businesses all day. Let me know if there's anything I can do to help." Then he looked out into the room. "Now, if you'll excuse me, I see a matter that requires my attention."

Jonathan and Jeremy returned to the hotel hoping Emily might have returned. They were discouraged and exhausted. No one knew anything. Emily had vanished. Jane told her family they had no choice but to prepare to leave the next morning. Their funds were nearly gone.

Elizabeth walked over to the desk to pen an entry in her journal. When she was about to sit down, she discovered Emily's cameo locket lying on the desk. The locket held a picture of their father. Being the youngest and nearly dying during childbirth, Emily and her father shared a special bond. She would never have left the locket behind if she had left on her own accord.

Elizabeth picked up the locket. "Mother, look, Emily's locket. This is proof she didn't run away. She would never have left this behind!"

Jane took the locket from Elizabeth. She opened the locket and gazed at the picture of her husband. Then she closed it, clenching it in her hand.

"How am I going to tell your father that Emily is missing?" Jane had been holding back tears but could not any longer. Then she brushed the tears away and summoned her strength.

"Let's try to get some sleep if it's at all possible. I promise we *will* find her."

The children gathered around their mother and embraced her. Then they all went to bed, but no one slept that night, except little Parker.

Chapter 6

*T*he following morning, the family stopped at the front desk to check out. No one was there, so they left their keys on the counter since Jane had settled up their bill the night before. As they left the hotel, Jane glanced back imagining Emily rushing down the stairs shouting out to them to wait for her, but she knew Emily was gone. They caught a cab and headed to their temporary home. Their next step was to meet with the contact provided by Victoria Davis. Maybe he would have advice on what they should do next to find Emily.

Back at the hotel, the clerk returned to the front desk once he learned the Bennett family had left. He saw Jane's note with their address information lying under the counter. He picked it up and read it, then set it aside. He hadn't been there long when Sebastian Jones showed up. He asked George about his conversation with the Bennett family.

George told Sebastian, "I managed to avoid talking to them." He picked up Jane's note and handed it to Sebastian. "But they left this."

Sebastian snatched the note and read it. He stuffed it into his pocket and sneered, "Glad to see you're cooperating, George. If you're smart, you'll keep it that way."

Sebastian walked away. The clerk wasn't proud of himself. He wished he wasn't such a coward.

* * *

When Emily woke from what seemed liked a deep sleep, she looked around the room and realized she wasn't in her hotel room. She looked down at herself. *I'm still wearing the same clothes. Where am I? How long have I been asleep?* She stood up. She felt dizzy but walked over to the door to open it. It was locked. Suddenly, it was becoming horrifyingly obvious she had been drugged, and she was in a great deal of trouble. Her heart felt like it was pounding a thousand beats per minute.

A few minutes later, she heard someone unlocking the door. An overweight man with a sarcastic manner walked in with a breakfast tray.

"I see you're up," he said. "You'd better eat. You missed dinner last night." He chuckled to himself, *Of course she did, she was passed out.*

"Who are you, and where am I? Why am I here?"

"The boss will be in soon and he'll tell you what you need to know."

He left the room and locked the door behind him.

A few minutes later, Emily was alerted to the sound of a key turning the lock on the door. Sebastian Jones walked in. *What is he doing here?* She saw a different man. It seemed as though he towered over her and his sinister eyes pierced her. She felt sick to her stomach as she realized how gullible she had been.

Emily glared at him and summoned her courage. "What do you want from me?"

"Well, Miss Bennett," he smirked, "I see you have some spirit left. That pleases me. Tonight, you're going to be making a special appearance. Shortly, there'll be two women coming in to prepare you. You'll have a nice bath. You should like that, and you'll be perfumed and dressed."

"But why?"

Sebastian leered at her with a malicious grin, "Because you're going on the auction block, of course."

Emily gasped. "I won't cooperate."

"Oh, I think you will." He brought out the note written in her mother's handwriting and showed it to her.

"Is this not your mother's handwriting? You can see she's written down the address where your family will be living. Your family's lives are in your hands, Miss *Emily Bennett.*"

"What do you mean, their lives are in my hands?"

"That's what I said," he sniggered.

"You would hurt my family?"

Sebastian narrowed his eyes and leaned toward her. "Only if you give me trouble."

Emily's voice was barely audible. "What is to be my fate?"

"Well, princess, there are two options, both of which will be out of my hands. You could end up as a high-class prostitute in some other country, or you could become some man's wife. Since you're so young, you'll produce children for your husband-to-be for years to come. And because you're a virgin, you're even more valuable. A man likes being the first to break in a woman."

Emily glared at him with hate in her eyes. "You've stolen my life from me. I hate you," she replied vehemently.

"Huh! Do you think I care? That means nothing to me. I laughed at you when you thought you had charmed me. Now, eat your breakfast. I don't need you fainting. If you don't do as I say, I'll find ways to punish your family. There's a chamber pot behind that door if you need it." He left the room, locking the door behind him.

Later, the man who had come in earlier brought in a lunch tray. Emily had eaten very little of the breakfast he brought in earlier.

"You better eat this lunch, girlie. You don't wanna cross Sebastian."

Emily still felt sick but forced herself to eat. The man was right, she didn't want to make Sebastian angry. If he was capable of doing this to her, what would he be capable of doing to her family? She also knew she needed to keep up her strength and her wits. *I have no idea what I'll be facing tonight. If I can find a way to escape, I'll need to be strong.*

An hour later, two Mexican women came in. They led Emily to a smaller room where there was a tub filled with hot water. They pinned her hair into a bun on top of her head, then stripped her clothes off and pointed to the tub. She didn't like being naked in front of the women and wished she could cover herself. She stepped into the water, gradually getting used to the temperature and immersed herself, hoping to gain some modesty. When the women finished washing her, they motioned for Emily to step out of the tub. At this point, she was fully exposed. They powdered and perfumed her entire body. The strong fragrance took over the room.

Finally, Emily was given a robe to wear while the women

continued to prepare her. They released her hair from the pins and vigorously brushed her long wavy hair.

Next, they brought out her undergarments and motioned for her to put them on. Emily was surprised to see her other clothes there. When she put her corset on, they laced her in so tightly, she could only take shallow breaths, and wondered if she might pass out from lack of oxygen.

Unexpectedly, one of the women left and returned with Sebastian while she was still in her undergarments. She was embarrassed and looked for the robe to cover herself, but to no avail.

"Don't bother," he said. Sebastian was holding her emerald green dress and handed it to her. He sneered. "Put this on but do it slow-like, so I can enjoy the show." He salivated as she buttoned the front of her bodice.

Sebastian looked Emily up and down with lustful eyes and stepped toward her. "Almost perfect."

He took hold of the front of her dress and ripped it open nearly down to her waist. The buttons were no longer there. She gasped and her eyes widened as he brought his hands toward her bosom and opened the front of the bodice further, displaying a larger proportion of her breasts.

He smacked his lips. "Now, it's perfect."

He turned to one of the women and instructed her to stitch the front of the dress so that it stayed open. In a gruff voice, he spoke to both women as he headed for the door, "Finish her up and let me know when you're done."

The women nodded.

Next, the women brought out the matching shoes Emily's father had made for her. Tears filled her eyes. When the women noticed her tears, they shook their finger at her and shouted, "No, no!" The final touch was to apply rouge to her cheeks and lips.

One of the women said in broken English, "You finished now," and left.

Moments later, the woman returned with Sebastian. He looked her up and down and was pleased with what he saw, and thought, *Ah, I'll be making good money tonight.*

Sebastian was about to leave the room when he looked back at Emily. "Oh, one more thing, your name is no longer Emily. You're now Désirée. It's a French name meaning *desired*. Aren't I clever?" With a sadistic chuckle, he added, "We don't know what your last name is going to be yet."

Sebastian's sinister laugh reverberated around the room as he left. The two women followed him. Emily looked at herself in the mirror. She hardly recognized herself. This time she wasn't looking out of vanity.

* * *

Soon a man escorted Emily into a large room and led her to a raised platform. She looked around the room for any possible avenue of escape. She saw a door at the opposite end of the room. Then the man instructed her to stand behind the heavy velvet curtains that spanned the platform.

"Stay here," he said.

Emily heard women's voices, but they weren't speaking English. She peeked her head out where the curtains parted. A group of young Chinese women was herded to stand next to the platform. They wore nothing more than sheer gowns allowing full view of their nude bodies. Emily was grateful to be fully dressed except for her bosom being so exposed. She thought the young women must have been about the same age as her—fourteen or fifteen years old.

A man unlocked and opened the door at the other end of the room. Swarms of men who had been waiting to enter rushed in. Emily's heart raced. Then the man in charge of the Chinese women saw her peeking out the curtain. He pushed her away from the curtain and roared, "Get back!"

Emily could hear exhilarated voices filling the room. She heard whistles and laughter and the voices grew louder and louder. She wondered how many men were on the other side of the curtain.

A drumroll sounded, and Sebastian Jones walked out onto the platform. This was the moment Emily dreaded. He looked out at the sea of excited faces. The room was filled beyond the normal capacity. He was pleased.

"Welcome, gentlemen. Tonight's auction will top all other auctions we've held thus far. First, we have twenty young Chinese women for you and I can guarantee their maidenhead is still intact and ready for you to take. For those of you with unlimited funds, as I advertised, we have a special prize right behind this curtain." He stroked the curtain. The men cheered. Emily could hear everything and felt nauseous.

"Now, let's begin." He motioned to the man overseeing the Chinese women and instructed him to send the first woman out. The platform was well lit, and it was easy to see her body through the sheer gown. Sebastian brushed his hand down her body. He snickered. "As you can see, gentlemen, I've made it easy for you to view the merchandise." The young woman lowered her head in shame. Sebastian put his hand under her chin and abruptly raised her head. "Do I hear the first bid?"

The men who participated in these auctions came from all sectors of society and nationalities. They had money to burn and attended the auctions regularly. It was exciting to have enough money and power to buy whatever they wanted. It was a competitive sport for many of them. Some men had struck it rich during the 1848 gold rush. Some were lucky in speculations, and some made their money through unscrupulous means.

The bidding process was infectious and frenzied. Since about a hundred men showed up for the auction, and there were only twenty women available, the bids rose quickly. When the men won their bid, they paid the amount, marched up to the platform, picked up the petite woman, and slung her over their shoulders like a sack of flour while they shouted their victory chant.

There was a slight opening on the side end of the curtain. Emily could see the men carrying the women toward the back door exit. Outside, a carriage and driver was waiting, and the men disappeared into the night with their purchase.

When the last Chinese woman was auctioned off, there was another drumroll. Sebastian's sinister smile stretched across his face as he parted the curtain, slowly, teasing the men. When the curtain was fully open, Sebastian told Emily to walk to the center of the platform. He stood next to her. The men applauded and whistled. They liked what they saw. Her golden hair draped against her fair skin and the emerald green dress she wore enhanced her bright green eyes.

Emily peered out at the room. There were so many men. Her heart pounded so hard she feared it could be seen with her bosom so exposed. Sebastian told Emily to tell them her name so they could hear her voice. She started to say her name was Emily until he glared at her, and checked herself.

Emily murmured the name, "Désirée."

Sebastian sneered, "I don't think they could hear you. Say it again, louder."

She looked at him with defiance, but did as he ordered.

Sebastian addressed the men. "As you can see, we have a young filly with spirit, and as I promised, she is a virgin. Who wants to be the lucky man to take her maidenhead? She's healthy and comes from good stock. She can provide many childbearing years. The bidding will start at one thousand dollars."

The bidding escalated into a war. Sebastian was pleased with himself. He figured he could get as much as five thousand dollars or more for her. Emily saw behavior unbeknownst to her. She had lived a sheltered life. These men were crude and rowdy. The thought of any one of them touching her made her sick. *I'll kill myself before I bear a child for any of these men.*

A voice from the back of the room sounded out. "Ten thousand dollars!" Sebastian jerked and tried to see who made the bid. His eyes darted about the room to see if anyone was going to top the bid. The room fell silent. He waited for a moment. No other bids.

Sebastian picked up the gavel. "Going once! Going twice!" He hesitated for a moment and scanned the room. Then he slammed down the gavel. Emily flinched. "Sold to the lucky man at the back of the room!"

Emily squinted to try to see who it was. She saw two men standing together near the door. One man wore a black cloak and a hat that shadowed his face. The man who made the bid was the mysterious man's assistant. The mystery man handed his assistant the cash for the payment and left the building. The assistant handed the cash to the greedy Sebastian Jones and escorted Emily by the arm out the back door to the carriage parked next to the building. He wrapped a blanket around her as he assisted her into the carriage and stepped up to the driver's seat. Emily was frightened but grateful she wasn't carried out like a sack of flour. She wondered where she was going.

She could see the man in the cloak riding a black horse ahead of the carriage. He made sure to keep himself distanced from the carriage.

A short time later, Emily was escorted onto a ship anchored in the San Francisco Bay. A man was waiting for her on the ship and took her to a cabin. He told her the ship wouldn't be sailing until morning and she would be spending the night. She asked where the ship was going, but he told her she didn't need to know. He left and locked the door. The cabin was comfortable enough. She was surprised to find her baggage already in the cabin. She felt some solace having some of her belongings with her, but she didn't have her coveted locket that held her father's picture. *Will I ever see his face again? Will I ever see my mother, brothers, and sisters?* She had been through so much in the last twenty-four hours. She collapsed onto the bed and sobbed.

Hours later, Emily awoke to the ship's movement. She had cried herself to sleep and slept the entire night. She realized it was the next day. During the voyage, Emily was allowed to leave the cabin for fresh air, but was never allowed to be alone while outside. Her meals were brought to her cabin. She learned from the cook's boy who brought her the meals, they would be at sea for about a week, and they were heading south. He wouldn't tell her anything else. She had no idea where the ship was taking her, only that it was the opposite direction of her family's destination.

Chapter 7

October 28, 1855

San Francisco

*J*ane was anxious to meet with the contact referred by Victoria. The family hoped he could lead them to a private detective. They also had no choice but to focus on employment. Now they would need money to pay for a private investigator as well as living expenses. For all they knew, they could be there for months. Jonathan and Jeremy insisted on going with Jane to meet the contact, Mr. Avery. He was extremely helpful in all their areas of concern. He told them he would make immediate inquiries regarding employment and gave them the name and address of a private investigator.

"You're doing the right thing acting fast while the trail is still fresh," said Mr. Avery.

Jane and her sons hailed a cab to take them to the office of Oliver Scott. After a short ride through the busy business section of the city, the cab driver stopped in front of a two-story red brick building. Jane's heart pounded when she saw the sign hanging above the entrance, which read *PRIVATE INVESTIGATOR*. She drew a deep breath and said, "This is it."

They entered the office and were greeted warmly by the receptionist. "Welcome. How may we help you?"

After Jane explained their situation, the receptionist put their minds at ease. "You have come to the right person. Mr. Scott has a high success rate. If you'll have a seat, I'll let him know you're here."

A few moments later, Dorthea ushered Jane, Jeremy, and Jonathan into the investigator's office. A distinguished gray-haired man who appeared to be in his sixties stood and introduced himself.

"Good day, I'm Oliver Scott. How may I help you, and who do I have the pleasure of addressing?"

His gray beard and mustache were neatly trimmed, giving the

impression of attention to detail. He was a well-preserved looking man who exuded a calming effect. His slate blue eyes were kind, and his mannerisms were telling of a man seasoned with experience.

Jane felt comfortable with this man. She introduced herself and her sons.

Oliver pulled out a chair for Jane. "Please, sit down. I'm happy to meet you all, but I sense there is something terribly wrong."

"Yes, there is," said Jane. Then she told him about Emily's disappearance. She brought out a picture of her daughter. Oliver extended his hand to examine the picture more closely while looking directly at Jane for permission to take it. She nodded. When he looked at the picture, he saw a beautiful young woman, perfect prey for the white slave marketeers that infested San Francisco. He knew immediately where he would begin his investigation.

During the discussion, Jeremy gazed at Oliver's office. The room revealed clues about this man's character. The American flag hung on the wall behind his desk. A sword rested on a bookcase. When the meeting came to a pause, Jeremy asked Oliver about the sword.

"Young man, I served in the War of 1812. The sword was awarded to me for my involvement in the capture of a British spy. I was prepared to lay down my life for this young nation. Many brave men gave their lives to preserve the victory of our freedom and independence from Great Britain. But don't get me started, I could talk all day about this country."

While Oliver spoke, he looked up at the flag and tears filled his eyes. He looked back at Jeremy.

"Son, don't ever let anyone take away your freedom." Then he looked at Jane, "I'll take your case, Mrs. Bennett. May I hang on to your daughter's picture? It'll be useful. Don't worry; I'll take good care of it."

Jane began to cry. "Thank you, Mr. Scott. I sense we're in good hands."

Jonathan shook Oliver's hand. "Mr. Scott, Jeremy and I would like to assist you in any way possible. We can be very resourceful."

"Why don't we start by you calling me Oliver? I look forward to

your help, lads."

Chapter 8

November 5, 1855

Mazatlán, Mexico

*A*s the ship steamed into the hill-screened harbor, Emily looked out the porthole and saw palm trees swaying in the wind. Straight ahead, she saw a lively town filled with pastel-colored buildings. On some of the buildings, black wrought iron bars covered the windows. She wondered if she would be confined behind iron bars. She realized she was no longer in the United States. Would her family ever find her? Where was she?

Unbeknownst to Emily, the ship had dropped anchor in the port of Mazatlán. It was one of the most important ports for ships traveling the South American route to San Francisco. Mazatlán was the capital of the state of Sinaloa situated in the northern part of Mexico. People became wealthy mining the prolific silver mines and manufacturing products such as cigarillos, cigars, matches, footwear, beer, soap, and carriages. The port was the stopping place to give weary ship passengers and crew a respite from their long voyage. There were restaurants, open markets, and a variety of services. If a ship was without a doctor on board, there was one available in Mazatlán for anyone needing a doctor's attention.

Emily sat frozen waiting for what was going to happen next. She listened for any sound outside her cabin door. Finally, she heard footsteps approaching. A key turned the lock in the door. Then the door swung open and a Mexican man entered. "Come," he said, with a stone-faced expression. He grabbed her upper arm, his large hand covering the entire circumference, and pressed his fingers so deep into her flesh, she was sure she would end up with bruising. Without speaking, he escorted her from the ship to the small boat that awaited, and then once ashore, a carriage. Another man followed with her baggage.

The mystery man who bought her had already disembarked from the ship. He had stabled his horse in town to be available upon his return, and as he had done before, rode a distance ahead of the carriage. Emily peeked her head out the window to look at him and assumed he was the same man she saw riding ahead of the carriage that frightful night in San Francisco.

The destination was the man's home, located on the outskirts of town. The mysterious man's name was Alberto De Leon who had built his wealth in the silver mines and from manufacturing cigarillos, cigars, and matches. As the carriage progressed down the narrow road, Emily studied the surroundings in the hope that she might find a way to escape her captors. A while later, the carriage slowed down. She leaned her head out the window to see what was happening. Ahead was a large arch with a sign that read *La Casa Grande*. As the carriage passed under the arch, straight ahead sat a large two-story adobe house surrounded with palm groves. It was obvious the owner of this grand house and beautiful grounds was wealthy. The carriage stopped in front. Then the driver helped her step down from the carriage, unloaded her baggage, and led her to the front door. He set her belongings inside and gestured for her to go in. Since he spoke minimal English, she had given up asking him questions, so she complied, after which she heard the carriage leave.

She stood next in the entry wondering what would happen next. The interior of the house was as grand as the exterior. Soon, a servant appeared and guided her upstairs to a bedroom. Although the servant was Mexican, she spoke some English. She showed Emily where she could freshen up. The woman told Emily she would find clothing in the wardrobe, but there was already a dress laid out on the bed for her. "I will return in one hour. Please be dressed and ready," said the servant. Emily smirked to herself. *Ready? For what? Another humiliating auction? This place looks big enough to hold several men.*

After the servant left, Emily noticed she hadn't locked the door, but she recognized there was no use in trying to run away at the moment. Where would she run? And how? An image of the crude ruffians at the auction bidding for her flashed through her mind. *At least I haven't been mistreated, thus far.*

When the servant returned, she took Emily downstairs to a

library. She was told to sit and wait. As Emily entered the room, she could smell the essence of leather and lingering vapors of tobacco. She sat on one of the crimson mohair settees, stroking its velvety texture. She gazed around the room. The walls were covered in wood panels interjected with bookcases filled with leather-bound books. There was a glass decanter holding some sort of spirits and two glasses set on a narrow table near a bookcase.

A low flame flickered in the tall adobe fireplace. Two large dark leather chairs decorated with brass studs stood on each side.

Above the fireplace, her eyes were drawn to a pair of sabres mounted on the wall. While they were beautiful as decorative objects, they were indeed weapons. The tapered curved blades appeared to be very sharp, and the ornate silver handle was encircled with a guard to protect the user's hand.

Finally, her eyes landed on the mahogany grand piano located on the opposite side of the room. She thought back to the last time she had played piano. It was on her father's birthday and she played his favorite song for him. The family had gathered around and sang along. Oh, how she missed her family. She wondered if they were gone from her life forever. She was deep in thought while she waited. She had been such a fool. She had so easily fallen into Sebastian's trap. Now, she had to keep her wits about her and show strength in the man's presence, even as she trembled inside. *I'm going to be fifteen soon. It's time I grew up, if it's not too late.*

Suddenly, she was startled by someone opening the door. She held her breath to prevent her heart from pounding, but to no avail. A tall dignified older man entered. *Who is this man? Does he want me to bear his children? He looks old enough to be my father!* She studied him wondering what kind of man he was. He had a dark complexion and his blackish hair was peppered with grey. He wore a broad mustache and sideburns that met a short beard. His clothes were those of a gentleman.

"Miss Désirée, I trust you're comfortable? I'm Alberto De Leon. I see you're as beautiful up close as you were on the auction stage. You should know, you're very fortunate that you belong to me. Many ruffians in the room would have liked to own you. They had money, but I had more. You must accept the fact that you are my property.

Depending on how well you accept it, your life can be pleasant or unpleasant. Do you understand?"

That was the first time Emily heard someone refer to her as Désirée. *I hate that name. What am I to do? For now, I'm Désirée, but I'll never forget who I am.* With a defiant face, she looked straight into Alberto's eyes. "Yes, I understand. I have no choice, do I? Am I here to marry you?"

"First, I demand respect, and I will not tolerate your insolent tone. No, I'm not to be your husband."

He signaled his manservant standing near the library entrance. Without a word, the servant left. Emily wondered what was going to happen next. She decided it would be wise not to speak for the moment.

The servant returned and opened the library door. A young man entered the room. He was a handsome Spanish man, and it was obvious from his demeanor he, too, demanded respect. As much as she tried, Emily couldn't ignore how striking he was. His long dark brown hair was parted in the middle and tied back with a narrow strip of leather. He wore long sideburns, a pencil-thin mustache, and a goatee. His dark brown eyes seemed almost black.

Alberto introduced him. "This is my son, Francesco. Francesco, this is Désirée, your soon-to-be bride."

Emily's eyes met Francesco's, then she looked away. She didn't care how handsome he was. She didn't like being forced to marry him or anyone. For all she knew, this prideful Spanish man would beat her to break her spirit and force her to carry his child.

Alberto added, "I'll give you two a few minutes to get acquainted. I'll be back in a little while."

After Alberto left, Emily stood up with her hands on her hips, looked straight into Francesco's eyes, and said in the strongest voice she could manage, "Don't expect me to be your brood mare!"

Francesco's eyebrows raised. He was shocked at her arrogance. He couldn't believe those were the first words she spoke to him.

He looked at her with disdain. "You're not starting this relationship out very well. I had hoped we might at least eventually come to care about each other. Am I so repulsive to you? I'll settle for civility. There are plenty of women who would like to be in your place. I'll see you at supper. Can I at least expect some courtesy at the table?"

Without waiting for an answer, he marched out of the room. *She'll be difficult to love, but at least it won't be unpleasant to have her in my bed. All I care about is that she gives me a son. If she wants to be lonely, so be it. I can easily find attention elsewhere.*

Momentarily, Alberto returned, looking very displeased. He had watched his son leave the library looking hurt and angry. Spanish men were accustomed to women being subservient and respectful. Emily read the expression on Alberto's face. She was nervous. She knew she had pushed Alberto too far by offending his son.

"My son did not look happy when he left this room. He told me how you treated him. He wasn't even in here five minutes before you managed to insult him. I'm extremely upset with your behavior. I paid a great deal of money for you and I expect a return on my investment. My plan was for the two of you to go through a courting phase. I'm not going to let my son waste his time on the courtship of such an insolent woman. I warn you for the last time, change your attitude or I will sell you to someone else.

"Now, let's move on to the next step. We're of the Catholic religion. You'll need to be interviewed by the priest for preparation of the marriage. Once you're married to my son, consummation will be expected on the wedding night. You'll be taken to the priest tomorrow. Now you're dismissed. Go to your room. And I expect you to be dressed for supper and to act civil. We have friends attending."

Alberto added in a stern voice, "Do not embarrass me, and you *will* be discreet."

* * *

The next day, Emily was taken to the priest and left under his supervision for the marriage preparation. She was fully aware of how much she had antagonized Alberto and Francesco. She didn't dare insult the priest, so she cooperated. The priest was happy to learn that Emily was also Catholic. Her parents had emigrated from the *Old World* where they were Catholics. They had thought about converting to another religion, but when they discovered

Catholicism in America was a different more desirable version, they embraced it. They were now Catholics of the *New World*. Alberto was pleased when he learned Emily was of the same faith. It simplified the process and meant the marriage date could be scheduled.

Emily had hoped, somehow, she would find a way to escape before the marriage. At least she wouldn't be forced to lay with Francesco before the ceremony. As the days passed, Emily acted more complaisant but showed no emotion. At the dining table, she and Francesco would coyly look at the other intermittently, and then look away. Mealtime was the only time Emily saw him. Subconsciously, she looked forward to mealtime so she could be in Francesco's presence, but continued to fight her attraction to him. She found herself thinking about him more than she wanted to admit. There was something about his vulnerability that she unmasked the first day she met him in the library. It affected her. She had never deliberately hurt anyone before. He hadn't done anything to deserve her stinging words. *Emily, stop it. I cannot weaken just because I hurt his feelings. I'm quite sure, sooner or later, he'll deserve it.*

One night when Emily came down to dinner, Francesco's chair was empty. *Where was he?* Her pride wouldn't allow her to inquire. She continued with the meal alone with Alberto, pretending she hadn't noticed Francesco's absence. She reprimanded herself each time she stole a furtive glance at the door wondering if he was coming, but his chair remained empty. It bothered Emily, and she took it personally. *He doesn't want to be around me. But that was what I wanted, wasn't it?*

Francesco was physically attracted to Emily and was determined to fight the invisible force controlling his mind and body. He wasn't about to be rejected by this defiant woman, so he distanced himself. He wished his father hadn't pushed him into this arranged marriage. He was miserable.

For Alberto, it was mandatory for the De Leon line to continue. Many young women in town would marry Francesco without hesitation, but Alberto felt his son would be marrying below his station. He decided once this marriage ceremony was over, the couple would live in La Casa Grande. If Désirée chose to live in a separate wing from her husband, he would allow it, but she would have to lay with Francesco until she gave him a son.

Chapter 9

*W*ith the help of Victoria's contact, the Bennett family found employment. Jane and Mary took on sewing jobs, Elizabeth became a private tutor, and Jonathan and Jeremy were hired as helpers in a tannery business, due to their prior experience with their father and uncle.

Jane stayed in contact with Victoria who had agreed to be Philip's connection with the family once they had found a place to live. He knew they would soon deplete their funds, so their stay at the hotel would be short-lived. Jane hoped and prayed that Philip's next trip to San Francisco would be soon. She was desperate to tell him about Emily.

Oliver Scott was busy on the case. He went undercover and requested to be included on the white slave marketeers' private lists for announcements of the auctions. There were many marketeers in the city. He attended several auctions hoping to find someone who could give him information about any auctions held in the past few weeks. Oliver was new to this kind of thing and wasn't sure what to expect. He discovered Chinese women were brought in to each auction he attended. They were easy to acquire since their parents sold them off to Chinese gangs called tongs. These gangs controlled the human trafficking to San Francisco and provided the white slave marketeers a steady supply of Chinese women to auction off.

Oliver infiltrated his way into Sebastian Jones's operation and attended the auctions. Once again, the only women being sold were Chinese. Just as he had done at the other auctions, he initiated conversations with some of the customers, especially if they were regulars. He focused on a few men standing at the makeshift bar that had been set up for the auction. Sebastian knew the more the men drank, the looser their pocketbooks would be. Oliver joined the men and drank with them, but was careful to drink less than his drinking partners. *Perhaps they'll have loose tongues.* He pretended to be bored about seeing only Chinese women on the auction block.

"Is that all they offer, Chinese women? Do they ever offer variety? A little excitement for us bored fellas?"

One of the men freely offered a clue. "A few weeks ago, Jones had a young white virgin up on the auction block. She was a feisty one. Beautiful! Sebastian said it was going to be the auction to top all auctions. Man, was he right!"

"Well, now you're talkin." Oliver rubbed his hands together and smacked his lips. "Tell me more!"

They blurted out a full account of the auction and a description of the young woman. It sounded like Emily. One of the men said, "Too rich for my blood. She went for ten thousand greenbacks to some mystery man."

Oliver had the beginning of a trail. Now, somehow, he had to find out who the mystery man was.

He slapped the men on the back. "Well, see ya at the next auction. I've had too much to drink. I'd better git home." He pretended to stagger out the door.

Oliver thought back to his initial meeting and conversation with Jane when she had informed him about her brother-in-law, Captain Philip Bennett, who periodically sailed to San Francisco.

"As soon as I speak with Philip," she'd said, "I'll give him your address and ask him to call on you. I know he'll be a great help to you, Oliver. Philip never gives up."

"I'll look forward to meeting him," he had responded. "If I don't happen to be in my office when he arrives, Dorthea will schedule an appointment for him to meet with me."

Oliver felt it was too soon to tell the Bennett family what he had already discovered, but he did want to connect with Captain Bennett and fill him in.

The investigator did his homework. He checked to see if any ships had departed the day after the auction. As a result, he learned three ships had left the harbor on that day. He didn't know if he was on the right track, but it was a good place to start. He figured

Captain Bennet would know other captains from whom he could gather information.

* * *

Two weeks later, Captain Philip Bennett was on his way to San Francisco. The mill owners were thinking ahead and had instructed him to bring back wheat, weapons, and other supplies to have on hand in case of an Indian attack. The Bennett settlers were of the same frame of mind. Thus far, Teekalet and the surrounding area hadn't been affected by the Indian uprising. Philip reflected on the cannon, a lone sentinel watching over their settlement. *Perhaps word was out about the cannon? Enough worrying for the moment, I have much to do.*

After Philip finished business, he hailed a cab to visit Captain Davis's wife, Victoria. She had promised him on his last visit she would watch over Thomas's family once they had arrived. His mind had been set at ease when Thomas received Jane's letter announcing the family had arrived safely to San Francisco.

Sadly, Benjamin had received his own letter from Mary with the devastating news that their baby girl had perished during the voyage. For the first time in his life, Philip witnessed a grown man sob. It was heartbreaking.

Now Philip was keeping his promise to his brother and Benjamin that he would check on the family once he was in San Francisco. He was anxious to find them and Victoria was his liaison.

Upon his arrival, Philip asked the cab driver to return in an hour. He exited and followed the familiar manicured pathway to the porch. He grasped the iron door knocker and tapped on the heavy carved door.

The Davis's servant, Bridget, answered the door. "Please come in, Captain Bennett."

He handed Bridget his hat, "Good afternoon, Bridget. Do I have the good fortune to find Mrs. Davis at home?"

Before Bridget could answer, Victoria swooped into the foyer. "Captain Bennett! I thought I heard your voice. You must be here to see what news I have for you?" She turned to Bridget. "Please bring us a tray. We'll be in the library."

Bridget nodded, "Yes, ma'am."

Philip followed Victoria into the library, looking forward to her update.

"My apologies for the unannounced visit, but yes, you are correct, Victoria. Do you have news?"

"Jane told me she sent a letter to Thomas letting him know they had arrived safely, so you already know they're here. I'm sure you realize they are no longer staying at the hotel. After they received your brother's warning to remain here, Philip, they needed a place to live. You'll be happy to know William and I have put them up in one of our rental houses on a gratis basis for as long as needed."

She walked over to the desk and picked up a folded piece of paper. "I prepared this for you. Here's their address."

"This is wonderful news, Victoria! Thank you for your kindness and generosity toward them. As soon as my cab returns, I'll go there directly. I know they'll be excited to see me, and I'm sure they'll want to know everything."

At that moment Bridget tapped on the library door and brought in the tray.

"Thank you, Bridget. Please alert us when Captain Bennett's cab returns."

"Yes, ma'am."

As Victoria poured a cup of tea for Philip, she looked up at him and spoke in a serious tone, "Jane has her own news, Philip. She needs you."

"What? What do you mean, Victoria?"

"It's not my place to say. Just know, I have done what I can to help."

The hour couldn't pass fast enough. Finally, Philip brought out his pocket watch, hoping the cab would be arriving soon. His heart felt like it was thumping out of his chest. *What bad news am I going to have to report to Thomas now?*

Finally, Bridget tapped on the library door announcing the cab's arrival.

Victoria grasped Philip's hands. "Philip, please let us know if there is anything we can do for your family. Now, go with God's speed."

* * *

Philip rushed to the address. When he arrived, once again, he instructed the cab driver to return in an hour. He was relieved to see the modest house situated in a safe neighborhood. *At least that's positive.* He walked up the sidewalk to the covered porch and knocked on the door.

Jane shouted from inside, "Who's there?"

"Jane, it's Philip."

"Oh, my prayers are answered!" She flung the door open and threw her arms around him. "Philip! It's so good to see you! I wasn't sure when you would arrive."

It was obvious to Philip when he looked into Jane's troubled eyes there was something terribly wrong. He didn't see any of the other children in the house.

He asked, nervously, "Where is everyone, Jane?"

"Elizabeth is tutoring a young woman, and Jonathan and Jeremy are working in a tannery." She pointed toward the hall, "Mary is in the bedroom nursing Parker. But Philip," she cried, with tears she could no longer hold back, "our Emily is missing."

Philip was stunned and immediately thought about Thomas. *How am I going to tell him this news? He already has to worry about fighting in an Indian war. How much can my brother handle?*

Through her sobs, Jane told him what had happened and about the private investigator she hired. Philip listened attentively. When she finished telling him everything she knew, he embraced her. Even though his strong arms around her were comforting, she wished they were Thomas's arms. She worried about how Thomas was going to handle the news about his daughter.

"Oh Philip, I'm so worried about Thomas. He's going to need your strength when he learns Emily is missing."

"Yes, I've already been thinking about my brother. I must see this investigator at once. Be assured, we *will* find Emily."

"I have his name and address written down for you. This man

cares, Philip. I know you'll make a good team to bring our Emily back to us. He'll be expecting you."

To put her mind at ease, Philip told Jane that none of their men folk had been pressed into service yet during the Indian disturbances. Also, thus far, their settlement hadn't been threatened due to its secluded location. He didn't, however, tell her the situation could change soon. She had enough to worry about.

"Before I leave, I'd like to hug my niece."

"I wouldn't have let you leave without Mary seeing you." She called out to Mary to greet her uncle. Parker was in her arms. When Mary saw her protective uncle, tears brimmed her eyes.

"My dear niece, it was dreadful to hear about your little Mollie. I'm so sorry, sweetheart. Benjamin took it hard." He brushed the top of Parker's head with a gentle hand and smiled down at him. "So this is the little one you took under your care. He'll be a lucky boy to have you and Benjamin as parents."

"Uncle Philip, do you know how he took the news about Parker?"

"It was an additional shock at first, but after a while, he accepted the idea. He's ready to call him his son."

"Oh, that lifts such a burden. Thank you for telling me."

"It's the very least I can do, Mary. And now, I need to concentrate on finding your sister."

He turned to Jane, "I'll be back soon to let you know how the meeting with the investigator goes."

Embracing them one last time, he left.

* * *

Philip headed straight to Oliver Scott's office. He was fortunate to find Oliver in his office. The receptionist announced him.

"Well, Captain Bennett, I've been anxious to meet you. Jane speaks highly of you."

"I was happy to hear you are on the case, Mr. Scott. You have my full support, of course. I won't quit until we find her."

"Excellent! Please, call me Oliver."

After becoming acquainted with Captain Bennett, Oliver

was confident the captain would be instrumental in finding and rescuing Emily. The two men put their heads together and reasoned it could take weeks for Philip to make contact with the captains of the three ships Oliver had identified. They ended the meeting shaking hands and agreed to stay in constant touch.

Philip added, "I'll see Jane before I head back to Teekalet and assure her we're on the case together. It's comforting to know you'll be watching over them. I will see you on my next trip, Oliver, which I anticipate to be soon."

"You can be assured I'll be looking after them, Captain Bennett."

"Until our next meeting then. I'll take my leave now." The men shook hands and Philip left.

Before Philip returned to visit Jane and the family one last time before departing, he purchased a newspaper to check the daily sailing schedules to see if any of the three ships were listed. He didn't find the ships listed, but a story on the front page of the paper voicing outrage, titled *Massacre of Americans at Virgin Bay in Nicaragua,* caught his attention. With all the bad luck Jane and her children endured on their voyage, they had been fortunate to have just missed being caught in the middle of a massacre. Some people were killed and many others suffered wounds.

The massacre happened the week after Jane and her family boarded the cholera ship. Many of their fellow passengers had decided to wait for the next ship and had no choice but to join the hundreds of others who were also stranded in the La Virgen settlement waiting for a ship. Without warning, a detachment of Legitimista troops marched into the town and fired indiscriminately upon those who happened to be on the streets at the time.

Thomas had shared Jane's letter with Philip wherein she described the terrifying experience of being caught up in the Nicaraguan civil war. They were in dire straits, forcing them to make the life or death decision to either board the cholera-infected ship, *Maria*, or take their chances by staying in La Virgen and wait for another ship. They chose to board the ship. Jane had noted the departure date of when they left La Virgen.

Philip was sure Jane and the family had no idea what had

happened to their fellow passengers who chose to stay behind. He took the paper with him when he went back to see them.

"Jane, I have something you'll all want to see," said Philip as he handed her the newspaper, pointing to the front page.

Jane exclaimed, "Oh my heavens! This is shocking! Thank the Lord we boarded that ship. Surely, we would have been in the middle of the massacre."

"Those poor people. We met some of them," added Mary.

Philip also told her about his meeting with Oliver Scott. "Oliver Scott is a good man, Jane. With the two of us working together, I'm confident we'll bring Emily back safe and sound."

He chose not to tell Jane *everything* he had learned from Oliver. He didn't want to get the family's hopes up only to be dashed if he and Oliver were on a wild goose chase. He did, however, have some news he could share.

"Jane, Oliver found out some new information and asked me to pass it on to you. He learned that Emily was sold for ten thousand dollars."

Jane found the news shocking, but encouraging. "That must mean she's still all right! No one would spend that much money and harm her. Wouldn't that be true, Philip?"

"Yes. I'm certain of it. And now, dear ones, I'm afraid it's time for me to head back to Teekalet. I wish I could have stayed longer. Give my love to Elizabeth and the boys. I'm sure I'll be returning soon. I expect the Governor will be sending me back here for munitions and supplies presently."

Jane cringed, "Oh, Philip, is the situation that dire? I can't imagine Thomas with a weapon in his hands with the intent of shooting another human being."

Philip tried to make her feel more comfortable, "I'm sure it's just a precaution, Jane. It's better to be prepared than not." He hugged her and Mary one last time and left.

Within an hour, Philip was on his ship. The cargo was loaded and the *California II* sat ready for departure.

Captain Bennett shouted out to Samuel, his first mate, "Weigh anchor. We're ready to head back to Teekalet."

Philip left San Francisco with a heavy heart. He wasn't looking forward to telling Thomas about Emily.

* * *

In the meantime, Oliver continued to seek more clues by fraternizing at Jones's next auction. He left empty-handed, but at least he knew Sebastian's whereabouts and could keep an eye on him. Oliver vowed that after they found Emily, and she was safe with her family, he would take Sebastian Jones and his partner down. He also hoped he would be able to rescue the next group of Chinese women. It sickened him to watch those poor young women being carried off over the shoulder of a ruffian buyer and not be able to help them.

Chapter 10

November 1855
Puget Sound

The Indian war had been going on since October, but tensions had started even earlier.

Businesses had come to a halt, and many settlers were forced to abandon their crops and face starvation. To feel safe, they fled to the small villages near them where blockhouses had been built for protection. Several settlers fled to Olympia for safe refuge in a large blockhouse upon which a cannon had been placed. A large stockade had also been built. Food was scarce, and there was a shortage of firearms and ammunition. The government had not supplied anything, nor was any military assistance provided.

Volunteers, including Thomas, Robert, Benjamin, and Peter, had been called upon to cut in roads along with building blockhouses and stockades. As a result, a line of blockhouses was built the entire way to the foot of the western side of the pass across the mountains. The working conditions were miserable. It rained constantly. The men were drenched, covered in mud, cold, and had very little food. Lighting a fire to warm themselves was forbidden for fear of being easy targets for the Indians hiding in the dense brush and woods.

It was on that mission they experienced their first close encounter with death. Two of the volunteers had been stationed at the top of the hill above their camp to stand guard. A few hours later, shots were heard. A few volunteers rushed to the scene and found the men dead. Robert would have been one of the men killed if Thomas hadn't stopped his brother from volunteering. Death had put its claim on Robert, but Thomas intervened.

By November, a replacement company of men relieved the volunteers of their duties and they were able to go back to their homes.

The men's time at the settlement had turned out to be short-lived, however. Shortly after the acting Governor's proclamation for military enrollment had been issued, every able-bodied man was pressed into service, including Thomas, Robert, Benjamin, and Peter. They were assigned to the Olympia company named the Puget Sound Mounted Volunteers, and consisted of one hundred ten men. Matthew, Christopher and Billy were too young to go, and were left to guard the women at the settlement. Each of them possessed a rifle, as well as Maggie, Rachel, and Annie. The blockhouse on the Bennett land was fully stocked with supplies and weapons, including the cannon which had been hoisted to its rooftop. Settlers throughout Puget Sound were building blockhouses for protection.

Reluctantly, the four men left the Bennett settlement to join the Olympia company. When Philip returned from San Francisco, he found them gone. In faith that their family had arrived safely to San Francisco, Thomas and Benjamin left a packet behind for Philip to deliver to Jane and Mary on his next trip back to Frisco.

* * *

After settling into the camp with the other volunteers, Thomas said to Robert, "Philip should be arriving any day now, and he'll find us gone. My heart aches not knowing how Jane and the children are faring in San Francisco. I can only imagine how Benjamin feels. He's been very quiet since he heard about little Mollie."

"God seems to be testing our strength, Thomas, and I'm afraid he's not finished with us yet," replied Robert in a trepidatious voice.

Later that night, they heard a report about a young man riding with a small group of men who were on their way to join the volunteers. Without warning, the group was attacked by Indians. The young man was wounded and fell from his horse. The other men wanted to try to save him, but he told them to save themselves. He was newly married and yelled out to them to tell his bride he loved her.

The next day a group of volunteers found his body. He was given a military ceremony and a musician played *The Girl I Left Behind*. It was a solemn burial. His new bride was inconsolable. The Bennett brothers, Benjamin, and Peter attended. Benjamin's heart went out to the bride, and as he watched her sob, he thought about Mary. They had spent too little time together as husband and wife before he left. Would this war turn her into a widow too?

Not long after the funeral, the Bennett group heard another disturbing report. Some settlers who thought they lived in a safe area, were tragically wrong. On one occasion, a man, his wife, and his wife's sister had attended church. Each of the women held a baby and sat in the horse-drawn cart. The husband walked slightly behind and to the side of the cart with the lines in his hands driving the horses. Suddenly, Indians emerged from the timber. The husband saw the Indians in time to whip the horses to take off with the women and babies in the cart, saving their lives. The Indians attacked him. He fought hard for his life, but he was unarmed and outnumbered, and was killed. The wife knew her husband would be killed and there was nothing she could do to save him. She was devastated. The next day, some of the neighbors went back and found the husband's body stripped of his clothes and mutilated.

* * *

The tension escalated. A few days later two men rode their horses into a lather riding the entire night toward Olympia and Steilacoom to warn the settlers of Indian attacks.

The man riding to Olympia charged into the camp of the Puget Sound Mounted Volunteers shouting, "ALARM! ALARM!" The captain and some of the men rushed to him and asked what was happening. "Indian attacks," he said as he dismounted.

"Ring the alarm bell! Everyone needs to hear this.," cried out the captain. Then he said to his aide, "Take this man's horse and care for it."

The Bennett group and the rest of the volunteers quickly gathered around. When the captain ascertained that everyone was present, he told the exhausted man to proceed with his report.

In a frenzied voice, the rider continued, "Three families have been killed and mutilated in the White River area. The local sheriff is also dead. Some of the settlers who thought they knew the Indians well and wouldn't be harmed, ventured out to reason with them, but were immediately killed."

"At this moment a family is trapped in their house on the Puyallup bottom. You must hurry. They need your help!"

The Olympia volunteers didn't waste a minute and rushed to rescue the family and any other families who were in danger. They arrived in time to save an English family. Indians had surrounded their house and anyone inside who could handle a firearm was shooting at the attackers. The Indians were about to break down the door of the house when the volunteers arrived.

After the volunteers chased off the Indians, they rode to the location of the other families who had been killed. There were three homes.

The first cabin they approached had been set ablaze, and they found the charred body of the husband inside. They found the body of the wife lying outside the house, mutilated. Their two small boys were missing. Later, the boys were found alive thanks to an old squaw who had hidden them in the brush.

The second family lived about a mile away. The husband was in the house, cut to pieces. His wife and baby were found at the bottom of the well. She had been stabbed several times. Her dead baby was still in her arms.

At the third cabin, the husband's burned body was found inside the house. They found his wife outside, cut open. Their two small children were missing, so they were presumed to have been kidnapped.

After witnessing the death and destruction, the volunteers hastened their search to locate any remaining survivors throughout the area.

They rode to another house a few miles away and found no one there. The family had fled and warned another family on their path who also fled.

Robert, Thomas, Benjamin, and Peter were sickened at what they saw and heard, and worried about everyone at their settlement. Were they in danger? They hadn't heard anything. All of the volunteers yearned to go back to protect their own families, but could not.

With very little time to rest, the Olympia volunteers were sent to the eastern side of the mountains to assist the troops in the Yakima

Valley where the Cayuse, Walla Walla, and Umatilla Indian tribes were on the warpath. The plan was to approach the Indians from the western side of the Cascades.

Thomas and Robert's friend, Pierre Mallet, had volunteered to act as a guide for the group. They hadn't realized Pierre had joined their group, and when they saw him, felt a sense of calm with him in their midst.

This part of the country was new to the Bennett group. The whole experience was new. They had never shot at a human being, and they had never shot at a moving target while riding a galloping horse. There hadn't been much time to develop this skill. Peter was the most seasoned man among them.

The volunteers marched east up the White River, but their route over the Cascades was blocked with snow. The company had no choice but to abandon their plan and turn back. They cautiously followed a road through a swampy area with fallen timber and underbrush on each side of the road. Finally, they came upon a safe place to ford the White River.

Suddenly, Pierre called out, "Ambush!"

The company faced about one hundred fifty warriors from the Puyallup, Nisqually, and Squaxon tribes. Some of the Indians whooped war cries and held poles with scalps attached, which they waved in the air to intimidate the volunteers. A long battle ensued. When the Indians retreated, the company followed them to the Puyallup River. The battle raged on for two days.

During the battle on the second day, Thomas became separated from Robert and the others. He was alone when his horse was shot out from under him. The Indian who shot Thomas's horse, rode at full force toward him to finish the kill. Thomas was now on foot, and his rifle had flown out of his reach when he fell, and there was no time to draw his revolver and shoot.

Suddenly, one of the volunteers appeared. He was too close to shoot, so he swung the butt of his rifle at the Indian, hitting him on the head and knocking him off his horse. The young man leaped from his horse, ready to fight the Indian hand to hand. Thomas quickly snatched the reins of the volunteer's horse. The Indian was only dazed and grabbed his tomahawk. The volunteer pulled out his knife. Thomas knew the young man would be no match for the

Indian since very few of them were experienced in battle. While holding the reins in one hand, he pulled out his revolver and shot the Indian dead.

"Much obliged," said the young man as he grabbed the reins to his horse. Reacting quickly, Thomas seized the Indian's horse before it ran off. He found his rifle and was ready to mount when two more Indians galloped toward him. One Indian leaned sideways on his horse swinging a tomahawk and the other shot an arrow at him.

The young man, who was without a weapon at the moment, saw them coming and yelled out to Thomas, "Behind you!"

Thomas turned and felt the thump and sting of an arrow on his right outer thigh. The Indian was about to draw another arrow. Thomas still had his revolver in his hand and shot every bullet remaining in the chamber in rapid succession. The bullets hit their marks and both Indians were dead.

Thomas thought about his father-in-law's gift of the revolver. *Thank you, Edmund McKenzie. You just saved my life.* His upper thigh hurt like the devil, but at least he was alive. Thomas asked the young man to help him break the arrow off. Pierre, who witnessed the scene from afar, charged toward them on his horse, yelling, "No, don't touch it. Let me tend to it."

He dismounted and turned to the young volunteer. "Help me get Thomas on to that Indian pony so we can find some cover."

The three of them rode to a thicket away from the line of battle. Pierre helped Thomas slide off the horse while the volunteer tied the horses to a nearby sapling.

"Lay down *mon ami* while I look at your wound." Pierre looked up at the volunteer. "Young man, hold his leg still."

Pierre cut open Thomas's pant leg and twirled the arrow to determine if the arrowhead had hit any bone. He was able to twirl it easily.

"Thomas, you are lucky. The arrow missed your thigh bone and went into the flesh instead. I can see the tip of the arrowhead. It nearly went all the way through your thigh. I'm going to have to push it through. Thomas, there are many feathers on this arrow."

"Is that supposed to mean something to me, Pierre?" replied Thomas, wondering why he should give a damn about feathers!

"It means the warrior used a large arrowhead. More feathers are needed to make it fly. You killed a formidable warrior, *mon ami*. I'm going to break off the shaft so I can push it through enough for me to pull it out, but first I need to make an incision. I'm sorry, *mon ami*, this is going to hurt."

Thomas nervously surveyed their surrounding area. "Let's get it over with."

The young man took off his leather belt and handed it to Thomas to bite on. Pierre brought out his hunting knife to cut a larger opening in Thomas's trouser leg and then cut the incision around the protruding tip of the arrowhead.

"Hold his leg, *monsieur*."

Thomas clenched on the belt with his teeth. When Pierre finished, the volunteer whipped off his long neck scarf and tied it around the wound.

Thomas grimaced. "Thank you both. Now, we need to find our group and get the hell out of here." Flashing back to the bear incident with Pierre, he said "Pierre, I'd say we're even, my friend."

"*Oui, mon ami*. Now, let us help you mount that horse."

Thomas was about to thank the young volunteer for saving his life, when suddenly he galloped off. The young man had spotted some warriors coming in their direction and drew them away from Thomas and Pierre. His horse outran the Indians' horses, as he caught up to his company.

Pierre rode with Thomas until they found his company. Robert, Benjamin, and Peter spotted them coming.

Robert shouted, "Thank God, Thomas, we thought you might have been killed. I've been worried sick. We were together and then we weren't. What happened?"

"It's a long story, and as you can see, I took an arrow in my leg. Guess I'll be limping for awhile. Pierre patched me up. He probably saved my life. If I had tried pulling it out, which is what I had in mind, there would have been a great deal of damage to my leg and a lot of blood. And if it wasn't for a young volunteer," he scanned the present group of men, "who seems to have disappeared, my head would have been split open with a tomahawk."

Pierre said, "I leave Thomas in your hands, *mes amis*. Thomas, make sure to watch for any infection on that leg. Get to the *docteur* as soon as you can. Now, I must find my own company. *Au revoir, mes amis.*"

After the second day, the Indians retreated. There were casualties on both sides. The Indians lost thirty warriors, and twenty-two volunteers were killed with four wounded.

The tired and crippled volunteers made their way to Fort Steilacoom for medical help and rest. Robert found a doctor to tend to Thomas's leg.

"I didn't like us getting separated, Thomas. Thank the Lord someone was close by to help you."

"After I rest, I want to find the young man to thank him properly."

"I'd like to thank him too, Thomas."

The following morning, Thomas limped around the barracks to find the young man. He found him resting on one of the cots.

"Young man, I've been looking for you. I'm here to thank you for saving my life. Three times! That was a brave thing you did. My family will be eternally grateful to you. May I ask your name?"

The young man stood up from the cot. "My name is James Mitchell, and yours?"

Thomas reached out to clasp James's hand.

"I'm Thomas Bennett. I want to introduce you to the rest of my party."

Robert, Benjamin, and Peter stepped forward.

"This is my brother, Robert, my son-in-law, Benjamin Spencer, and my friend Peter Crandall."

They all shook hands.

Thomas said, "This is the brave young man I was telling you about who saved my life. Meet James Mitchell."

"I'd have been lost without my brother. Thank you," said Robert.

Peter and Benjamin thanked him also.

James said, "Don't forget, Thomas. You probably saved my life as well when I was about to fight hand to hand with that Indian. My knife against his tomahawk.

"By the way, I met some Bennetts on the Nicaragua route who said they were headed to this region to be with the men of their family. But I didn't see them on the ship continuing to Puget Sound. Are you related by any chance?"

"Why, yes. My wife, Jane, my three daughters, our granddaughter, and two sons were on that route. When I received a letter from Jane they had arrived in San Francisco, I was a happy man, until I read further and learned our baby granddaughter had died during the voyage."

Thomas glanced over at Benjamin whose eyes were welling with tears. He continued talking to James. "It was the worst news anyone could receive. Before they arrived, I had left instructions for them to stay in San Francisco because of the tensions developing here with the Indians. I suspected there would be a war. I knew they'd be safer there. I would never have thought they had already suffered a tragedy."

They all sat down and conversed. Thomas was anxious to hear anything James could share about his family on the trip.

James described their experience during the journey. He told them how he came to the aid of Mary and Elizabeth when they were walking to the halfway house. While he was talking, he became aware that Benjamin was the father of the baby girl who had died.

"Benjamin, please accept my deepest condolences."

James wasn't sure if he should describe the burial at sea, but Benjamin wanted to hear everything. He told Benjamin in the gentlest words he could muster about the burial—how everyone on the ship showed the most profound support and respect, and how beautiful the ceremony was. There were a few moments of silence while they absorbed what had happened to Benjamin's baby, as well as what they had recently witnessed at White River. They were all tired and drained, but extremely grateful to be alive.

They continued to share their stories.

Robert told James about their settlement at Teekalet and their journey to Puget Sound.

James told them his story about his uncle's business in Thurston County and his uncle's plea for his help.

"I certainly wasn't expecting to join the Puget Sound Mounted Volunteers the moment I stepped off the ship, but I figured every man was needed. Unfortunately, my uncle has had to try to get along without me. He understood. He said he knew helping to keep everyone safe was more important."

"Considering you saved *my* life, I'm grateful you did," said

Thomas. "James, when this war is over, and when my family is finally settled at Teekalet, I'd like you to come visit us."

"I'd be pleased to pay you and your family a visit." The thought of Elizabeth flashed through James's mind. *I would especially like to become more acquainted with Miss Elizabeth Bennett.*

While the volunteers were recuperating at Fort Steilacoom, the captain asked them to gather around so he could give them the latest report. It wasn't good news.

They learned that a company of troops had been attacked and defeated by the Yakimas in Yakima Valley, and Indians all over the Northwest from British Columbia to California were on the warpath, rampantly massacring and scalping settlers.

Most distressing was the news that the Governor's efforts to quell the Indian uprisings on the east side of the Cascades had failed, and he and his troops had been surrounded and attacked by hostiles. Fortunately, the Governor escaped and returned safely to Olympia.

The captain continued, "Men, the situation in the Territory has become desperate. The Governor has initiated an appeal to San Francisco, Portland and Victoria for arms, ammunition, and provisions. He has also appealed to the Governor of Oregon to lend all the aid he can spare. There is a shipment available soon in San Francisco and I understand the Governor has requested Captain Philip Bennett to sail there to retrieve it. Aren't there a couple of Bennett brothers here?"

"Yes, sir," answered Robert. "I'm Robert Bennett and standing next to me is my brother, Thomas."

"Are you possibly related to Captain Bennett?"

"Sir, he's our brother," replied Thomas.

Thomas murmured to Robert. "I guess we know what Philip is going to be doing soon."

Chapter 11

*T*he wedding ceremony was scheduled for early December, which meant Emily was running out of time to make her escape. She needed to act fast. She knew by now all the servants and rancheros were accustomed to her roaming around the estate. Since there were several horses in the stable, she planned to rise early one morning before daybreak and escape by horseback. First, she selected the particular horse she would use. She chose a gentle mare, then visited her for a few days to form a bond, bringing treats each time. By the fourth visit, the mare whinnied and tossed her head each time Emily came. "Shhh," she said, stroking the mare's face. "Soon you will help me leave this place."

Emily hoped she would remember the way to town. She recalled there had been a fork in the road on the way to the estate. Would she choose the correct one? She had tried to memorize the landscape, but much of it looked the same. She rehearsed the plan in her mind. *I must make my escape on a Sunday when Alberto and Francesco aren't in town. Once I reach the town, I'll tie the horse to a hitching post. Surely someone will recognize the De Leon brand and return the mare to Alberto. Then I will dash to the wharf and pretend to be a traveler. I'll listen for any sailors who speak English and ask them if their ship is heading north. If I'm lucky and find the right ship, I'll sneak onto it and hide.*

Finally, on a pre-dawn Sunday morning, Emily seized her moment. The day before, she had slipped into Francesco's room and took a pair of his trousers, a shirt, and a hat, and hid them in her wardrobe closet. She brought Francesco's clothes out from hiding and slipped them on. Then she put together a small bundle of a few of her belongings and quietly crept out to the horse barn. She saddled the horse, tying her bundle to the saddle horn, and mounted the mare. She rode out at a slow pace, and once she was out of earshot, kicked the mare into a gallop.

When Emily came upon the fork in the road, she halted the horse. *Which way do I go? I think I must go left.* As she continued, the road became more narrow and brushy, so she slowed the mare to a trot. *This doesn't seem right. This road is much too narrow for a carriage.* She was beginning to worry. What was ahead of her if she continued to follow this road? Suddenly, a pheasant, startled by the sound of the horse's hooves, flew out from the underbrush and into the horse's face. Spooked, the mare reared up and threw Emily to the ground, knocking her unconscious.

The horse ran directly back to the ranch. One of the rancheros saw the mare trot to the stable with an empty saddle. He rushed to the house and alerted Alberto and Francesco about the horse. They were confused at first until Francesco noticed the small bag tied onto the saddle horn.

He looked at the contents of the bag and recognized Emily's belongings. "This is Emily's bag. I hadn't seen her yet this morning, but I assumed she was in her bedroom sulking. I must look for her. She may be hurt."

Alberto shook his head in disgust. "Foolish woman!"

The ranchero quickly saddled Francesco's horse. Francesco mounted up and followed the fresh tracks. Finally, when he came to the fork, he shook his head. *She took the wrong fork. She'll end up deep into the woods.* He was furious with Emily. *She's so much trouble. I don't know if I can put up with her anymore.* A few minutes later, he saw Emily lying on the road. She wasn't moving. Francesco panicked. He raced toward her and leaped from his horse. He raised her halfway up by the shoulders, supporting her in his arms. She was limp. Her head slung back causing her long hair to drape to the ground. Her eyes were closed as though in a peaceful slumber. *She looks like an angel when she's not spitting venom.* He realized he did care for her.

Francesco grabbed his canteen and splashed a small amount of water on her face. She blinked, opened her eyes, then half-closed them. He lifted her into his arms. Emily was half awake and unconsciously wrapped her arms around his neck and laid her head on his chest.

Francesco was startled at this show of unguarded closeness. He savored it for a moment, then laid her across his saddle until he had her positioned in front of him and rode back to the ranch. Upon returning, Francesco carried Emily to her bedroom and laid her on the bed. She was still half conscious. He took off her boots. The shirt she was wearing was long on her and hung down to her knees much like a nightshirt, so he removed the men's trousers. He laughed out loud when he realized she was wearing his clothes. Francesco felt confused. She was the most frustrating woman he had ever met, but yet he was drawn to her. He couldn't deny his attraction to this young woman but resolved to remain on the defensive. She would have to take the first step.

The next morning, Emily awoke completely disoriented. She looked down at what she was wearing—Francesco's shirt but not the trousers. Shortly, one of the female servants came into the room to check on her. Emily asked what had happened.

The servant replied, "It's not my business." She was only there to help Emily freshen up and dress, and if she was up to it, to come downstairs. Emily thought the servant's answer was strange. While she dressed, she began to recall her misadventure. *Alberto and Francesco will be furious with me.* She thought she remembered being in Francesco's arms, and how protected she felt. *It must have been a dream.*

Emily conceded that the marriage was going to happen. She went downstairs as requested. She held her head high knowing she was about to be scolded. Alberto and Francesco awaited her. They looked serious.

"I'm sorry," she said, in a contrite manner, with her head hung low.

Alberto looked at her with disdain. "Well, that's the first sign of any manners I've seen."

Francisco looked frustrated. "Don't you know you could have been killed or injured our horse?"

Emily looked down again, and nodded her head. *I suppose he cares more about their horse than me.*

Then Alberto surprised her. She was expecting some sort of punishment like being locked in her room. Instead, he said, "The day is set for the marriage. We're moving forward with the ceremony.

The entire town is waiting to attend. I have a woman coming today to fit you with a wedding gown."

In his typical controlling manner, Alberto chose the gown Emily would wear. The gown had belonged to Francesco's mother, Georgiana. Francesco had never known his mother since she had died during his birth. He was the only boy and grew up with two older sisters.

Alberto had decided not to show the gown to his daughters and kept it hidden away in a trunk. He knew they would have expected to receive the gown and would have argued over it. He didn't want to decide which daughter would receive it. He simply avoided such a decision, and instead, reserved it for his son's *futura novia*.

Alberto had not married for love. He had been content living in California while it was still under control of the Mexican government. Unfortunately, as the population grew with Yankees and foreigners, it became necessary to marry an Anglo woman to escape segregation, which had become a threat to Spanish people residing there. The woman he married loved him, but he hadn't returned her love. For him, the marriage was simply a means to an end.

When Alberto's wife died, he fled with his three children to northern Mexico. He took advantage of the silver mining opportunities, becoming a wealthy man. Then Alberto moved to the coastal town of Mazatlán to set up a manufacturing business. He had learned Mazatlán was becoming one of the three busiest ports on the Pacific side of the Americas. As he continued to increase his wealth, he built his beloved La Casa Grande and established a horse ranch. Alberto counted on his daughters to help raise Francesco. They dutifully stayed until they felt Francesco was old enough to be left on his own with their father. Afterward, they married and moved to Acapulco where their grandparents lived.

With the date of the marriage having been set, Alberto immediately brought the gown out from his large trunk, allowing it to air. When the seamstress arrived, he handed the gown to her for the fitting. The wedding gown required minimal alterations. Emily was close to the size of Francesco's mother. When Emily stepped into the gown for the fitting, she frowned, knowing she would soon be in the marriage bed.

Chapter 12

Early December 1855
Mazatlán, Mexico

*L*a Casa Grande bustled with activity in preparation for the wedding reception, which was likely to last until dawn the next day. Food and drink were made ready, and musicians were scheduled to arrive an hour before the reception.

Upstairs, two women prepared and dressed Emily. When she was ready, she was assisted into the carriage that would take her to the cathedral in town. She wondered about Francesco. He was nowhere to be seen. She didn't realize he had gone ahead on horseback. Francesco's two sisters and grandparents were arriving by ship from Acapulco and he and Alberto planned to greet them when they arrived.

It appeared the entire populace of Mazatlán was walking to the church. Many of them were friends and neighbors of the De Leons. There was one person of note who was attending the wedding. A young attractive Mexican woman, by the name of Rita, was burning with curiosity to see who Francesco was marrying. Rita had assumed he would marry her one day. She and Francesco had enjoyed a flirtatious relationship for the past two years, and she had intended to turn it into something more serious. She was in love with him. Many young Mexican and Mulatto women desired Francesco, and they all thought him to be a prize catch. This marriage was a complete surprise to all of them.

The townspeople had prepared a celebration to be held in the town square after the ceremony. The people loved fiestas with lots of music, dancing, food, and drink. Everyone was invited. A large mariachi band was already set up. Tables were laden with food and drink. Alberto De Leon paid for it all.

When the carriage arrived and stopped in front of the cathedral, all eyes focused on the carriage to see the mysterious woman emerge. Before stepping out, Emily veiled her face with the black lace mantilla, which was attached to a large tall comb in her hair. A man who had been sitting next to the driver placed portable steps in front of the carriage door for Emily. As she descended the carriage, he offered his arm to assist her and to escort her inside where she would wait in an isolated room. Her vision pleased the onlookers. She wore a traditional Spanish black full-length lace gown, which was tapered longer at the back and trailed as she walked. The slightly sheer bodice hinted at her youthful décolletage, and was overlaid with a bolero style lace caplet edged in a black beaded fringe. Black was the preferred color for upper-class brides in the Spanish and Mexican culture, symbolizing *til death do us part*. Emily, of course, was given no choice of what she would wear.

A duet of guitar players strummed the *Wedding March*. That was Emily's cue to walk down the aisle with Alberto. He held her arm. As she proceeded, she thought about her dream of walking down the aisle with her father toward the love of her life. Alberto noticed her mind was wandering and gave her arm a discreet jerk. Her veil still covered her face, so no one could see the tears filling her eyes. She looked up at Francesco standing at the end of the aisle. She couldn't deny how handsome he looked. His clothes resembled a matador style. He wore a black bolero jacket trimmed in silver buttons and silver embroidery. Layered under the jacket was a white shirt with tiny pleated tucks and an attached white ascot. His tight-fitted pants showed off his trim, muscular body and were decorated with silver buttons leading down the outside pant leg. A red sash wrapped his waist. He wore leather-heeled boots and a wide-brimmed black hat embellished with silver.

Francesco watched Emily as his father walked her toward him. She looked beautiful dressed in black lace, which contrasted with her peaches and cream complexion and her golden hair draping her shoulders. He felt sorry about his father stealing her life, but she might as well accept her fate. Many women would give anything to be in her place. He was sure his father thought she would recognize her enviable position. This was no different than an arranged marriage, which was common in this culture. Maybe she would eventually come to care for him instead of fighting him.

When they reached the end of the aisle, Alberto turned Emily over to Francesco. At this point Alberto signaled a translator who spoke English to stand next to the priest for Emily's benefit. Emily thought, *Alberto is always in control.* Each time the priest spoke, the translator repeated the priest's words in English.

The ceremony began with the El Lazo tradition. Alberto brought out two rosaries, which were connected to form a lasso. Alberto lifted Emily's veil and placed one looped end around her neck and the other looped end around Francesco's neck. The looped lasso was configured into the shape of a figure eight. The lasso would remain on the couple during the vow exchange symbolizing the statement of union.

Alberto stood close to Francesco. He held thirteen coins in his hands, and gave them to the priest. The priest blessed the coins and directed Emily to cup her hands as he handed them to her. Then he directed her to place the coins into Francesco's cupped hands. Alberto now held a gold tray. Francesco turned toward Alberto and placed the thirteen coins on the tray. As the ceremony progressed, Alberto handed the tray of coins to the priest. The priest faced Francesco and stated the symbolism of the thirteen coins representing Francesco's responsibility as a provider and his pledge to support and care for his wife.

The priest continued and said to Francesco, "I will now count out these coins to you. Please cup your hands. I will place each coin in your hand. It will represent the thirteen values to be shared between you and your wife."

As each coin was placed into Francesco's hands, thirteen phrases were spoken.

"Let there be love,… harmony,… cooperation,… commitment,… peace,… happiness,… trust,… respect,… caring,… wisdom,… joy,… wholeness,… nurturing." The priest looked at both Francesco and Emily. "May these thirteen coins be a symbol of love, fidelity, and trust between you."

The priest turned back to Francesco. "Francesco, please repeat after me." He recited the words for Francesco to repeat.

Francesco turned toward Emily and looked into her eyes, "I Francesco, give you Désirée, these thirteen coins to be a symbol of my trust and confidence in you as my wife. As we unite our lives this day, I share my material responsibility with you."

Emily cupped her hands to receive the coins. It felt strange to be called Désirée. In her defiant mind, she would always be Emily.

The priest turned to Emily, "Désirée, please repeat after me." He spoke the words she was to repeat.

Emily faced Francesco. "Francesco, I accept these coins as my pledge to you of my love, loyalty and devotion." She thought to herself, *I don't mean one word of this.*

Then the priest bound both their hands together with a ribbon and looked at them. "In exchanging these coins, you Francesco, and you Désirée, are pledging and saying, 'What is mine is also yours, and what is yours is mine.' I now bless these thirteen coins with the knowledge they symbolize the unlimited goodness the universe offers to you as a loving couple. Let it be so. Amen."

The priest freed their hands of the ribbon. The coins were placed on the gold tray and handed to Alberto. Alberto then handed Francesco two gold wedding bands and the exchange of the rings was made. As was always done in the Spanish custom, the rings were placed on the right hand. The priest lifted and removed the lasso from around their necks.

He blessed them and congratulated them. "You are now husband and wife."

The audience of well-wishers cheered. Alberto was pleased and relieved Emily hadn't caused any problems. Francesco took Emily's arm and led her out of the church. Emily hadn't shown any emotion, and her face showed it. Francesco noticed.

"Could you try to smile a little, even if it's only for appearance?"

She did as he asked. She certainly didn't want another confrontation with him or Alberto. After leaving the church, it was customary for the married couple and everyone else to walk to the town square. Alongside them, one of the townspeople led a donkey decorated with flowers and loaded with casks of tequila. It was the tradition for the wedding group to never be without a drink as they walked to the reception in the town square.

As they approached the square, they could hear the mariachi music and the merriment of people singing along. The aroma of a variety of foods permeated the air. The party in the square was for the benefit of the populace and would continue for many hours. After the couple received the personal congratulations from the people in the square, they would return to La Casa Grande where more celebration activities were waiting to begin.

The people at this town square party were curious to meet the mystery bride and surrounded Emily, which separated her from Francesco. But even with the distraction, she kept a watchful eye on Francesco. It became obvious to her that her husband was quite popular with the young women in Mazatlán. Several of the women took advantage of the party atmosphere. With drinks in hand, they caressed his face and gave him lingering kisses. They weren't the least concerned about Emily. It was common for a married wealthy man to be friendly with other women. They also knew that Emily was kept busy with many men who wanted a closer look and were lined up to meet her. Very few of them spoke English, so she had no idea what some of them were saying to her. All she knew was *gracias*.

Francesco was enjoying the festivities, and Emily could see the women displaying their affections toward him. She felt something she didn't want to acknowledge. Was she experiencing a twinge of jealousy? Francesco seemed to be enjoying the female attention. He had decided he might as well enjoy it since he figured he wouldn't be getting any attention from his wife.

Finally, the hour had come to return to La Casa Grande. Francesco assisted Emily into the carriage. She started to slide over to make room for him on the seat when, without a word, he closed the carriage door. She felt slighted, and it fueled her antagonism. Francesco chose to ride his horse back and connect with her at the celebration party.

Many people had already arrived at La Casa Grande and were ready to celebrate until dawn. As the carriage approached, music and laughter resounded from the house. Violinists, guitarists, and trumpeters were already playing. Francesco waited outside for the carriage to arrive. Emily was pleased to see him waiting for her, but she was determined not to show her feelings. He assisted her from the carriage, taking her arm, and led her into the house.

As the couple entered, the music stopped, and everyone applauded. Francesco smiled and waved. Then the music resumed and people began to dance. Without warning, one of the men grabbed Emily to dance with him. She felt awkward since she didn't know their dance style. The man sensed it and slowed the pace so she could follow him more easily. She was grateful for not being made to look like a fool. She began to catch on to the step. Several men waited their turn to dance with the bride. Emily wondered if Francesco would claim her to dance with him, but she realized he wasn't even looking at her.

The Mexican woman, Rita, was also in attendance. She noticed right away that Emily had been swept away by several dancing partners. She saw her chance and swayed her curvaceous hips toward Francesco, smiling flirtatiously at him.

"Francesco, you look so handsome!" Then she embraced him and gave him a polite kiss. His lips were so warm and full, she wanted more. They chatted for a while. Then she grabbed his hand.

"Francesco, I've noticed your wife doesn't smile at you. It troubles me. You know how much I care about you. She didn't try to talk to anyone at the square. She acts like she's above us all."

Francesco made excuses for his wife. "She's just nervous about meeting so many strangers, Rita, and she doesn't even speak our language." He knew it wasn't the most convincing explanation, but he was caught off guard with this straightforward comment. Rita didn't believe him. She sensed something was off.

She clutched his hand in hers and leaned close to his face. He could feel the warmth of her breath. "Francesco, I want you to know you'll always have my support and I'll do anything for you. Anything."

At that moment, Francesco knew Rita was offering to be his mistress. Many wealthy men kept mistresses. Francesco kissed Rita on the cheek and thanked her for her loyalty. He didn't want to bring the subject to the surface. The thought of a mistress hadn't crossed his mind. He didn't know what the future would hold, but he also knew he didn't want to be lonely for the rest of his life.

While Emily was being whirled around, the little scene with Rita didn't escape her notice. Once again, she felt a pang of jealousy. *Doesn't she understand he's married now?*

After a couple of hours, when Francesco and Emily were sitting together at the celebratory table, one of Francesco's friends clanged a glass with a spoon. He was about to make a toast. His friend said the typical meaningful words about the couple's future happiness and how fortunate Francesco was to have such a beautiful bride. Alberto smiled smugly at the couple. He was proud of his accomplishment and beamed. *Finally, the marriage is made. There's only one more step to seal it—consummation in the marriage bed.*

The food and drink seemed endless. There was a variety of chicken and pork entrees, spicy rice beans, tortillas, and an ensemble of fresh fruit. For drinking, there was no shortage of tequila, rum, whiskey, beer, and *Agua de Fresa*, fruit water.

Several hours later, the cake was brought out. It was the traditional rum-soaked fruitcake, filled with bits of pineapple, pecans and coconut. The couple cut the first piece and gave each other a bite. Everyone cheered and continued with their merriment.

After a short time, Emily decided she was tired and bored. Hardly anyone spoke English. Her wedding attire was beginning to become uncomfortable. She couldn't wait to take that pinching corset off. The servant had cinched her in so tight she could barely breathe. She was accustomed to wearing a corset but never cinched so tightly. She decided to disappear to her bedroom. Then it struck her. *Is that still going to be my bedroom?*

She poured herself a glass of *Agua de Fresa* and slipped away. As soon as she was in her bedroom, she took the wedding attire off. *Oh, to breathe again.* She stripped down to her chemise, pantaloons, and stockings, and lay down to take a short nap. It had been a huge day and night. She was exhausted, and her short nap turned into a deep sleep, which could have lasted until the next morning—but it didn't.

Francesco saw Emily leave and it angered him. He had never felt such embarrassment. He finished the drink in his hand and consumed several more.

Rita was always by Francesco's side, drinking with him. She had also seen Emily go upstairs. Rita made her play and took Francesco's hand and led him into the library. She giggled and pushed him down onto the settee. Then she unpinned her hair, pulled her skirt up, and straddled him. He could see she wasn't wearing anything underneath, affecting him instantly. They kissed hard and passionately. He was so drunk he didn't resist. Rita unbuttoned her blouse to expose her ample breasts and opened Francesco's shirt. She pressed her body against his. Francesco was aroused and ready to take her. Rita was ready to let him.

Alberto, too, saw Emily go upstairs without his son. He was going to have to take control of the situation. In his mind, the marriage had to be consummated that night. He looked for Francesco. He saw the library door, carelessly left ajar. He went in. There he saw his drunk son being ravished by Rita on the settee. Nothing significant had happened yet. He saw Rita's fully-exposed breasts, her hair draped in Francesco's face, and her cheeks flushed. When Alberto entered, he startled Rita. Flustered, she held her blouse closed and charged out of the room.

Alberto bellowed at Francesco. "You're with the wrong woman! Take care of the woman upstairs! Your wife!"

Francesco, still in an aroused state, marched upstairs straight to Emily's bedroom. The door was locked. He pounded on the door. Without waiting for her to open it, he kicked the door open. Emily bolted up in bed with eyes wide open. Then she stood up to stand her ground. It was obvious that Francesco was drunk.

"You're drunk. Leave!"

Francesco advanced toward her. Some of the effects of the alcohol had worn off, but not all of it.

He answered. "I'm not going anywhere. You're my wife, and I have every right to be here."

"Not this night," she said.

He stepped closer. She tried to slap his face, but he caught her hand in mid-air.

"Take your clothes off!"

"No!"

He ripped her chemise and pantaloons off and pushed her down on the bed. As he started to mount her, she scratched his face. He felt his face and saw the blood on his hand.

"You wild cat! You drew blood! If you want it rough, I can oblige!"

He held her arms down above her head, pressed his body onto hers while spreading her legs apart with his knees, and thrust himself into her.

Emily stopped fighting. It was done. She turned away from him and started to cry. Francesco stood up and dressed. He didn't feel good about himself. He hadn't expected their first night together to be filled with so much rage.

As he walked toward the busted door, he turned to speak to her.

"I'll leave you alone for the rest of the night. I never expected our first night to be like this. I drank too much. I'm sorry."

Francesco went downstairs. By now, the party had wound down. People were slouched or sleeping everywhere, including the floor. Rita had fled the house immediately.

Alberto was waiting and saw Francesco's face. He surmised that Désirée put up a fight. He was displeased with her.

"Is it done, Francesco?"

Francesco nodded. "Yes, Father, it's done." Francesco was physically and mentally exhausted. He said goodnight to his father and retired to his wing of the mansion.

* * *

The next morning, a sober Francesco went to Emily's room. He knocked on the damaged door and waited for permission to enter. Emily knew it was useless to fight anymore.

"Come in."

Francesco apologized again for coming to her while he was drunk and for being so rough.

Emily looked at his face. Her four fingernails had left four scratches on his face. She felt like she had branded him leaving the telltale clue that he had been with a woman. Whether it was from passion or an altercation, was anyone's guess. "I'm sorry about your face. Does it hurt very much?"

The scratches had turned into swollen welts. She walked over to the washbasin and dipped a cloth into the water. As she raised her hand toward his face to sooth the scratches, he instinctively flinched, then let her continue.

"I guess I deserved that," she said.

His vulnerability touched her heart. He liked her tender touch on his face and wished their relationship could always be as it was at that moment. They gazed into each other's eyes. Emily looked away and stopped what she was doing. He yearned to kiss her.

Emily asked, "Is there anything else you want to tell me?"

Francesco didn't want to feel the sting of rejection again, so he stuck to business.

"Yes, I've come to tell you about our arrangements. You're already accustomed to this room and wing, so you may continue to stay here. I'll stay in the other wing. You'll have your privacy." She glanced at the door. "I'll send someone to fix the door for you."

"Thank you."

He continued. "We'll see each other at meal times. Periodically, I will come to lay with you until we know you are with child. That's all I ask of you is to give me a son. If you don't give me a son, we will continue until you do."

She thought it sounded like a business transaction. She was tired of fighting and was beginning to weaken. She sighed.

"I understand, Francesco." Then her defiant pride emerged. "Will there be anything else?" She walked over to the door and opened it. He knew he was dismissed.

* * *

As each week slipped by, Emily received Francesco for his nightly visit. She removed her clothes, climbed into the bed, and let him take her. When he finished, he left. There were times when she wanted to kiss him. He felt the same way. Both were too prideful to let it happen or even to allow themselves to admit it. Despite being in an intimate relationship, it was a lonely time for both of them.

Francesco kept himself and his mind busy working with his father. Every week Alberto asked Francesco, "Do you think she is with child yet? Are you visiting her enough?" Francesco's standard answer was that he hadn't been informed of any news yet, it was probably too soon, and yes, he visited her frequently.

Rita continued to spend time with Francesco whenever he was working at the factory in Mazatlán. He had his own office, so she knew there would be privacy. She was very seductive, but he resisted her. Emily was on his mind constantly. He couldn't get her out of his head. It was driving him crazy.

Alberto never missed anything. He was aware of Rita's frequent visits and knew she was in love with Francesco. Alberto informed his son he had no objection if he wanted to take advantage of the companionship of a willing sensuous woman. Alberto didn't want his son to be lonely.

* * *

Life had become calmer, and some trust had been established. Francesco told Emily if she was ready to give up trying to leave, she would be granted more liberties.

One day a beaming Francesco asked Emily to come outside with him. Emily was curious and followed him. Her eyes widened. She saw a beautiful white mare outfitted with a silver-embellished side saddle and bridle.

She caressed the horse's face and neck. She noticed the saddle was a side saddle, meant for a woman. Was this for her, perhaps? "Francesco, this is such a beautiful horse."

Francesco nervously responded, "This horse is a late wedding gift. I've been waiting for the right moment. I hope you'll accept it." Emily was overwhelmed with his thoughtful gesture and saw for the first time, a tender smile light up his face.

She wanted to run to him and wrap her arms around him, but instead, politely thanked him. "I'm so grateful, Francesco. I love this horse." She caressed her horse with love. Although Francesco wished it was him she was caressing, he was excited to see her genuinely happy. He was like a little boy inside. *I made her smile. When she smiles like that, she's even more beautiful.*

Chapter 13

$\mathcal{B}$y the time Philip had returned to the Bennett settlement from his San Francisco trip in late November, the men had left. Thomas had gone to fight in a war with no idea that his beloved Emily was missing. Philip was deeply distressed when he learned Thomas was gone before he could tell him about his daughter. Then he thought, *Perhaps it's better this way. Such news would be a distraction, and he'll need his wits about him.*

Philip's time at the settlement was short-lived. By the time he arrived, it was already time for him to return to San Francisco.

When the *California II* arrived once again at the Golden Gate harbor, Philip had several tasks to carry out when he stepped onto the wharf.

His first task was to procure the provisions and ammunition requested by the Governor. When he completed the transaction, he left Samuel in charge to load the cargo on to the ship. Because of the weaponry, he instructed Samuel to assign armed guards to watch over the shipment during the loading process and to continue guarding it once it was loaded.

The next task preying on Philip's mind was to continue his quest to find Emily. On his prior trips to San Francisco, he had interrogated every ship captain he saw in the harbor. This time he caught up with two of the three ship captains he had been seeking and questioned them. Their answer—they had not seen anyone of Emily's description on their ship at any time. He still needed to find the third ship captain. After querying several captains, Philip finally found the information he was seeking. He learned the particular ship in question had sailed toward South America.

Armed with new information, Philip checked with the shipping office to see if a ship was due in from South America. The office schedule showed the ship, *Triumphant,* was to arrive in two to three weeks. Finally, the ship he sought. He would need to work with the mill on the timing for the trip back to San Francisco. He knew there would still be a need to bring back more supplies for the settlers. There was no telling how long the Indian war would last.

Philip immediately went to Oliver's office to give him the latest information. Oliver had continued to follow any possible lead in case he had been wrong about Emily being taken away by ship. There was the possibility she could have been transported on an overland route. He had been counting on Philip to turn up a strong lead on the ship theory. Now with Philip's new information, he could concentrate on his original notion. Philip also updated Oliver that he would be sailing to the Hawaiian Islands more frequently. Business was increasing in the islands and diminishing in San Francisco. His time in Frisco would soon be limited.

* * *

With his tasks finished and the *California II* being loaded with cargo, Philip was free to visit Jane and the family. He had left the visit for last, not wanting to feel pressured with unfinished tasks. Jane would be anxious for any news. She wasn't going to like the news he carried, along with Thomas not being aware of Emily's disappearance.

Again, Jane and Mary were the only members of the family present at the time. Philip embraced them both. Then Jane said, "Philip, I was wondering when we'd see you next. It's so good to see you. I've also been wondering if it would be possible for Thomas and Benjamin to come with you on your next trip to San Francisco? It would be so wonderful to put our arms around them again. If your schedule allows, maybe for Christmas? It wouldn't have to be exactly on Christmas, after if necessary. I can't imagine a more wonderful Christmas gift."

Jane didn't like the look on Philip's face. He held two small packets in his hands, one for Jane and one for Mary. Before leaving to join the Volunteers, Thomas and Benjamin had left the packets

114

behind for Philip to deliver on his next trip to Frisco for Jane and Mary.

"Jane, I believe the answer to your question is in the letter you'll find in this." He handed over the packets, then added, "Jane, you need to know that Thomas doesn't know about Emily yet. You will understand after you read his letter."

Jane and Mary nervously opened their packet. Inside they found that Thomas and Benjamin had each included an envelope with some money along with their letters.

Jane read Thomas's letter.

November 1855, Teekalet

My darling wife,

You will be so proud to see the progress we have made on our land. Robert and I established our business and started making money. Unfortunately, because of the Indian uprising, everything has come to a halt. I'm sending you the money I can spare right now. I don't know what the future holds. I trust you are all finding some form of employment to tide you over until I can send for you.

Tensions are high right now with the Indians, so the Governor has called us into service. Robert and I have joined the Olympia company. We even have a title, Jane. We're called the Puget Sound Mounted Volunteers. Do you think our sons will be impressed with their father?

Darling, I was yearning to hear about Philip's visit with all of you. Unfortunately, we had to leave before he returned from San Francisco. I am writing this letter the day before we leave trusting Philip will be able to deliver it to you on his next trip to San Francisco.

Benjamin has written his own letter to Mary. He will be leaving with us. I do hope Mary is healing with the loss of Mollie. It has been a slow process for Benjamin. We have all grieved for her.

You're all I think about, my love. It comforts me to know you are safe and that Philip will be checking on you each time he comes to San Francisco. Please send my love to our children. I have found myself reminiscing about my special moments with each of them. Being separated makes me appreciate what a wonderful family I have.

I must close now my love. I need to try to get a good night's rest. We leave at dawn tomorrow.

Until next time.

Your loving husband, Thomas Bennett

Jane clenched the letter in her fist in anger. She cried out to Philip. "How much more are we to endure? We should never have left New York!"

She was ready to scream at Philip that everything was his fault but held her tongue. She realized Thomas and Robert had been unsatisfied with their life back home and were restless. If Philip hadn't encouraged them to go by sea and take advantage of his connections, Thomas would eventually have had them traveling overland on the

Oregon Trail. Jane had recently joined a sewing circle and many of the ladies had shared terrible stories of hardship and death of people who traveled the overland route. Even being scalped or tortured was a real possibility by Indians on the warpath.

Jane was on the verge of tears. Philip put his arms around her to comfort her.

"They're going to be fine, Jane. They're riding with a large company of men. There is safety in numbers. In fact, supplies are being loaded onto my ship as we speak, which I will be taking back to the settlers and the volunteers. And we'll get Emily back. I won't stop looking until I've found her."

Then Philip walked over to Mary and kissed her on the cheek. "Mary, again, I'm so sorry about little Mollie." He smiled down at Parker who was resting in Mary's arms. "This little baby boy will never replace Mollie, but I do believe he's been put in your arms to save him."

Mary responded with some relief in her voice, "Benjamin told me in his letter that Mollie's death affected him deeply and he wishes he could be here to comfort me. He says he has come to terms with Parker entering our lives."

"Benjamin is a kind and generous man, Mary."

Philip checked his pocket watch. "Well, my dear ladies, I see that I must take my leave. My crew awaits me. It's time to go back to Teekalet. I had hoped to have been here long enough to see Elizabeth and the boys this time. This has become a pattern, something I must change. Please give my niece and nephews my love and tell them I'm sorry I missed seeing them again." He embraced Jane and Mary one last time. "Until my next trip."

Chapter 14

January 1856
Teekalet

All aboard for Teekalet! Thomas, Robert, Benjamin, and Peter boarded the ship along with the mill workers and loggers. All were part of the Puget Sound Mounted Volunteers, Company One. The first company of men that had been pressed into service, including the Bennett settlement men and James Mitchell, had completed their term of service, which was three to six months, or less if the war ended earlier. In their case, the expiration date was January 1, 1856. To relieve the first company, the Governor had formed a second regiment of volunteers.

The men were finally going home, but they were no longer the same men. They had seen too much. Being in the throes of death and witnessing so much brutality, made them acutely aware of how fast the flame of life could be snuffed out. Every moment with a loved one was precious and not to be wasted.

As the ship steamed out of the Olympia harbor, the Bennett brothers, Benjamin, and Peter stood at the ship's railing and looked ahead, facing the direction of home. They were worried since they had no way of knowing if there had been an attack.

Peter couldn't stop thinking about Rachel and how he would feel if he lost her. He decided to tell his friends he had made a decision.

"I want you all to know when we get back, I'm planning to propose to Rachel. It's been on my mind for some time now. She and I and her children have come to know each other over the past few months. I'm sure she has no idea about my feelings toward her. I feel in my heart, though, that Daniel would be happy to know I'd be taking care of his family. Better me than a total stranger. Sooner or later, she'll either be snatched up by some newcomer or decide to stay single. With everything we've just gone through, I'm resolved not to waste any more time. What do I have to lose, right? She can only say no. Somehow, I don't think she will."

Robert grinned, "You sly fox, I had no idea. The Bly family will be lucky to have you in their life. It looks like we could have a double wedding. Philip and Maggie have yet to set a date."

Thomas and Benjamin joined in with well-wishes.

Then Thomas said, "Speaking of Philip, he should be close to coming home from his latest Frisco trip. I'm anxious to hear about my beloved wife and children. I miss them so."

As the ship entered the Teekalet harbor, the town showed no signs of having been attacked. The area had remained unscathed due to its unique isolated locale, which protected the settlers. It had been a question on everyone's mind. They breathed a sigh of relief. At last, the ship docked at the mill's wharf, and the Volunteers disembarked.

Robert said, "We're going to need a ride home. I'll ask one of the managers if someone will take us in one of their workboats." Robert walked over to the mill office.

The manager answered, "We're happy to oblige, Mr. Bennett. We owe all of you our gratitude. You have our deepest respect. Just head over to the workboats, and I'll arrange for someone to take you home."

The manager looked out the window and chuckled, "Well, would you look at all those men coming off the ship heading straight to the cafe. The cafe is about to become very busy. There'll probably be a run on Maggie's Lady Kay apple pie. It's been quiet around here and it will be a welcome change."

* * *

As soon as the four men stepped onto the Bennett wharf, Britta spotted them and ran toward the wharf barking with excitement. Thomas patted her on the head, "I see *you're* fine, Britta." The settlement looked safe and sound, and for that they were grateful. One thing was for certain, if the settlement had been attacked, the invaders would have been greeted by Captain Bennett's cannon.

With Britta's announcement, everyone rushed toward the wharf to see who had arrived. They were excited and relieved to see their men home again. Philip had not yet returned from San Francisco but was expected at any time.

One person was missing in the group of Volunteers returning— Pierre Mallet. He didn't live at the settlement, but once his term of service had expired, he had planned to go to the settlement first with Thomas and Robert before returning to his cabin in the woods. He had instructed his wife, Red Feather, to stay with Annie Bly and her family if war broke out and he had to leave. Pierre didn't want her left alone. He feared since she was an outsider, being from the Cree tribe in Montreal, she wouldn't be safe.

As everyone gathered around the returning Volunteers, Red Feather stood solo waiting for Pierre to appear. She looked out past the men but saw no sign of her husband. Where was he? The four men were back, and they indicated the loggers and mill workers were back as well. Surely, he would have returned with his friends, Thomas and Robert. She felt a sense of panic. *Is he dead?*

She turned to Thomas, "Where is my husband?"

Thomas realized he hadn't noticed Red Feather standing by herself, watching for her husband to appear. She was always so quiet. "I apologize, Red Feather, I didn't see you. I can see you're concerned about Pierre. Allow me to put your mind at ease. He's fine, but he won't be returning right away. He's such a valuable guide, and they are few and far between I might add, the Governor has asked him to lead the militia while they travel the eastern side of the mountain. He asked me to tell you this, and he wants you to stay here among your friends until he returns."

"It's more dangerous on the other side of the mountain, yes?"

"I have to admit, Red Feather, it is, but if anyone can survive, it's Pierre. I saw him in action." Thomas pointed to his leg, "I must tell you, he saved me from bleeding to death. I was ready to yank an arrow out until he charged in to stop me. He knew exactly what to do."

"Thank you, Thomas. I'm sorry about your leg. It's true, my husband would know what to do. I will obey him and stay here until he returns. Annie has been so kind to me."

Annie joined the gathering in time to hear about Pierre. She put her arm around Red Feather, and said, "Come back to the house with me. You're welcome to stay as long as you like. Let's have a cup of tea together."

Thomas and Robert were anxious to check on their business. Orders, of course, had slacked off. Matthew and Christopher were trained well enough to handle the small number of orders they had received. When the brothers walked into their building, they found the lads supervising the Chinese workers. They were pleased to see several fur hats and leather gloves lined up on the order table. Now, with the anxiety of danger over, the pace of orders had accelerated.

Robert complimented Matthew and Christopher. "You're doing a fine job, lads. Perhaps one day you'll follow in our footsteps."

The Hood Canal Bakery had also slowed down. Without the mill workers and loggers around, Maggie and Rachel received fewer orders for their bakery goods. However, they still provided products for the general store and the hotel cafe in Teekalet, with Billy continuing to deliver the orders. After working at such a pell-mell pace baking their pies and cakes before the Indian uprising, the ladies hardly knew what to do.

They didn't stay idle, however. The gardens the men left behind needed tending. The two women couldn't save all the crops, but they managed to work on Peter and Benjamin's gardens, which were the largest with a winter harvest to be gathered. Thomas and Robert had planted small gardens. Due to being so busy establishing and running Bennett Bros. Co., they had cultivated the bare minimum to satisfy the rules of the Homestead Act. Philip was in the same position. Inevitably, while the Bennett brothers answered the call to serve during the Indian war, their abandoned crops sat in a state of neglect.

Benjamin retreated to his empty house. He knew Mary would love the house since he designed it to be a close likeness of the home in which she grew up. *Maybe my bride will be here soon.* His heart ached for her. He walked over to the cradle he had lovingly made for Mollie, who now, would never lie in it. Instead, she lay at the bottom of the sea. A tear rolled down his cheek. If he didn't believe she had been lifted to the Lord, he wouldn't be able to bear it. He prayed he could accept the baby boy Mary had taken in.

Peter went straight to Rachel while he still had the courage. She and Maggie were in the bakery building.

Rachel exclaimed, "You're back! All of you I trust? We've been so worried."

"Yes, we're here and unharmed, except Thomas. You'll notice a definite limp in his gait. He took an arrow in his leg, but he's fine now thanks to Pierre Mallet's fast action. Speaking of Pierre Mallet, I heard Thomas tell Red Feather her husband won't be returning yet. He's guiding troops on the eastern side of the mountain until further notice."

"Our prayers have been answered," said Maggie. "We weren't attacked and now you're back, except Pierre, of course. Poor Red Feather. Philip should be returning soon from San Francisco." As she spoke, she sensed that Peter wished to talk to Rachel alone, so she excused herself. "I best check on the pies before they burn. Welcome back, Peter."

"Thank you, Maggie." Then Peter turned to Rachel and asked if they could sit down. They walked to the other side of the room. Rachel wondered what was wrong. She sat down at the table, resting her hands on the surface. Peter sat across from her, looking quite serious.

Peter reached across the table and grasped Rachel's hands. "Rachel, fighting in this war made me realize how short life can be. It can be snuffed out in an instant. I'll never be able to forget the scenes of death and destruction we witnessed. I couldn't stop worrying about you and your children and could only pray you were all safe. We had no way of knowing. It made me realize how much I care about you, Rachel, and I want to take care of you and your children forever."

Peter looked straight into Rachel's eyes, drew a deep breath, and asked, "Rachel, will you marry me? I'm sorry I don't have a ring to do this properly, but I didn't want to waste another moment. You have been on my mind constantly. I believe I would have Daniel's blessing. And I want you to know I'm not trying to replace him in your heart and memory. I cared about him too."

Rachel raised an eyebrow. "Peter, you've taken me by surprise. I've enjoyed our friendship, and I enjoy your company, and I must admit, I did miss you. I hadn't thought about loving another man. I don't know how I feel, Peter. How do you feel? Do you love me?"

Still gazing into Rachel's eyes, Peter answered, "Yes, Rachel, I love you. I finally admitted it to myself when I realized I might be killed. I believe I've loved you for quite some time. I understand you may not love me right now, but maybe you might come to love me someday?"

Rachel leaned forward and asked softly, "Are you willing to marry a woman on that basis?"

"Not just any woman, Rachel, but you, yes. I want to take care of you and your children."

Rachel squeezed Peter's hands and met his gaze, "Yes, Peter, I'll marry you. I already care for you deeply. You will not be a hard man to love."

"You've made me a very happy man," Peter beamed. "I can't wait to tell everyone. Do you mind?"

"Of course, I don't mind. And we'll talk about a date soon."

"May I kiss you, Rachel?"

Rachel nodded and leaning across the table, their lips met.

Chapter 15

January 1856

Teekalet

A few days later after leaving San Francisco, Philip guided his ship into the Teekalet harbor and dropped anchor next to the wharf. To his relief, everything still looked normal, just as it did when he returned two months earlier. The Indian neighbors across the bay seemed calm. The mill looked busy. It appeared the community had not been attacked. Could it be because of his cannon?

He checked in with the mill managers to inform them he had their shipment as well as the Governor's. The mill had agreed to house and guard the Governor's supplies until he could send someone to retrieve them for distribution throughout the Territory. The mill workers and Philip's crew worked together to unload the shipments. When they finished, all that remained was the supplies for the Bennett settlement.

The manager was pleased to see Philip return on schedule.

"Well, Captain Bennett, welcome back. I see the crew is unloading our supplies. From the amount of cargo, it looks like you brought back the Governor's as well. With any luck we may not have to rely on this shipment. You've probably noticed we're returning to some normalcy. Most of our men who served in the first company of volunteers have returned, including the men from your settlement, praise the Lord, so we're back to being a well-run mill. We've been at nearly a complete halt."

"My brothers are back? That *is* good news. I must say, I was relieved to see no evidence of an attack as I entered the bay."

"I believe we have two factors in our favor, Captain. Your cannon and our isolated location. The settlers in the White River and Puyallup valleys have been in the most danger on this side of the mountain. I've also heard that most of the battles are on the eastern side. And of course, the Federal troops have stepped in."

"That's encouraging news. If I may, Mr. Richards, I have another matter I would like to discuss with you."

Philip apprised him of his niece's kidnapping. "I would be most grateful if you could allow me some time and flexibility. Rescuing my niece is my top priority. Failure, is not an option."

"Of course, Captain Bennett. You'll have our full cooperation. That's shocking news. Go with Godspeed, Captain."

"I am in your debt, Mr. Richards. Thank you for your understanding, and with that, if you don't mind, I shall take my leave." Philip tilted his hat and reboarded his ship.

With the mill business completed, Philip navigated the *California II* down the canal to his settlement. He was happy to learn his brothers, Benjamin, and Peter were all back home. Questions besieged his mind. Were any of them hurt? How much more hardship could this family endure? He thought about Thomas the entire way. He wasn't looking forward to telling his brother the bad news about his youngest daughter.

The *California II* sounded her horn and eased next to the wharf. Samuel and the crew tied her off and unloaded the cargo. Philip grabbed his sea bag and jumped onto the wharf. As they finished unloading the freight under Philip's watchful eye, the crew untied the lines and Samuel blew the ship's horn, signaling departure. He was ready to take the ship back to the mill's wharf, where the vessel would rest until her master returned.

Philip waved Samuel off, and yelled out, "See you on the next trip."

Britta heard Philip's voice and charged toward him, yelping. She jumped up and down, her tail wagging vigorously. Philip bent down and loved her and said, "Ah, Britta, you always make me smile."

Philip walked toward the Bennett Bros. Co. building with Britta close by his side. He dreaded giving Thomas the bad news about Emily. He had kept the news to himself, except for Maggie, because he wanted to tell Thomas personally. Also, he had hoped to have more information to share about the situation after his forthcoming trip to San Francisco. Now the moment had come. *This seems to be becoming a habit,* he reflected. *I don't like it.* He found Thomas and

Robert in their business building getting reacquainted with their tools. He breathed a sigh of relief to see them.

Robert looked up. "Philip, you're back!" He gave him a big bear hug. "I see Britta spotted you right away. I thought I heard the ship's horn."

Thomas looked up and noticed the serious expression on Philip's face.

He embraced his brother. Then with a concerned tone, said, "Philip, as I look at the expression on your face, I fear you have something to tell me. It's the same look you had the last time you had bad news. Philip, what is it?"

Philip fidgeted, which wasn't normal for him. "Thomas, as you know, I planned to check on Jane and your children when I went back to San Francisco this past November. They are now staying in one of the Davis's rental houses on a gratis basis. Victoria gave me the address, and I went straight to the house. When Jane greeted me at the door, it was obvious something was wrong."

Thomas sat down to regain his composure for a moment, then leveled his eyes at Philip, "Tell me for God's sake. What is it?

Philip spewed it out. "Dear brother, Emily is missing. We're certain a white slaver kidnapped her." Philip gripped Thomas's arm. "Thomas, I'm already on the hunt. Jane and I are working with a private investigator, and we do have a lead."

Thomas's face turned white. He gasped, "My God. My precious little girl. Gone? Tell me everything you know."

Philip brought Thomas up to date. He told his brother that as soon as he could question the captain of the ship, *Triumph*, they should be able to locate Emily's whereabouts and plan a rescue.

"Philip, I intend to be involved in the rescue of my daughter. I know I can speak for Robert too."

Robert walked over to Thomas and put his hand on his shoulder, "I wouldn't have it any other way. I want my niece back!"

"The Bennett brothers united will be a force to be reckoned with," replied Philip.

Thomas thought about Benjamin. "Let's not forget about Benjamin going with us. Mary would never forgive us if we left him behind. I'll let him know right away.

"It's going to be difficult to be patient, Philip. I expect many sleepless nights ahead until my daughter is rescued, and when we find out who sold her, I'll show no mercy." Thomas wondered how Jane must be feeling right now. "Philip, tell me, how is my dear wife holding up? And the children? They must be devastated." His mind overflowed with guilt. *Oh, Jane, I'm so sorry. Do you blame me for this? I know you would rather have stayed in Delhi.*

"They're holding up as well as can be expected, Thomas. You can be proud of your wife. She didn't waste a minute before she found a private investigator to help find Emily. Your entire family is strong and resilient," replied Philip.

Philip noticed Thomas was limping. "Thomas, is it my imagination, or are you walking with a limp? What happened to your leg?"

"An arrow got me. A long story for another time. Right now I know you must be anxious to see Maggie. Go to her, Philip. Our time with our loved ones is precious."

Robert added, "Philip, on your way there, you'll notice the loggers are back. They were in the first company of volunteers along with us. They're continuing where they left off. My point is, we can feel better about leaving knowing there are several men nearby, and I'm sure they wouldn't hesitate to protect our womenfolk if something were to happen."

Philip nodded, "A point well taken, but it doesn't sound like we're in much danger any longer. I had a conversation with one of the managers at the mill, and he credits our good fortune to our cannon and Teekalet's isolated location." He looked back at Thomas. "With that good news, it should be safe for your family to come to their new home after we rescue Emily."

"If only you're right, Philip. I pray you are. Now, go see Maggie."

Philip went straight to the bakery building with Britta happily trailing behind. When he walked through the door, Maggie ran to him and smothered him with kisses. After they finished greeting each other, Philip updated her about his family and Emily.

"Maggie, when I arrived today, I told the mill manager about our family emergency and told him I'd be needing flexibility and extra time to rescue Emily. They understand and are fully cooperating. I'll be using my ship, of course.

"Darling, that means I'll need to leave again in less than two weeks. I've learned the ship I've been tracking should be anchored in the Frisco harbor in that time frame. Thomas, Robert, and Benjamin will be coming with me. I'm certain we'll be going toward South America to find Emily. We know it was the destination of the ship she was on. My niece is likely being held somewhere along the coast. I pray we'll be successful."

Maggie embraced him. "Philip, I know you won't fail them."

"I refuse to fail them."

Maggie wanted to cheer him up. "Philip, would you care for a piece of pie?"

Philip pulled her closer to him, "No, my love. I have something better in mind."

"You're turning down my pie?" She asked with a smile.

Philip grabbed Maggie's hand and led her to the door. Maggie grinned and shouted out to Rachel who was working at the other end of the building, "Rachel, can you manage on your own for awhile? Philip and I have some *catching up* to do."

Rachel smiled and waved them on.

Chapter 16

January 1856, Two Weeks Later

San Francisco

*T*he three brothers and Benjamin stood shoulder to shoulder in the pilothouse of the *California II* as it approached the foggy harbor.

"I see many masts in the bay," said Philip. "Start looking for the ship *Triumph*."

Philip brought his ship in at a snail's pace. It was early morning, and the harbor was quiet. The only sound they heard was the sloweddown *whooshing* of the ship's paddle wheels. They looked at every ship, but the *Triumph* was nowhere to be seen.

Philip said, "I know the ship is due in soon. We'll check tomorrow to see if it has arrived."

Then Philip told Samuel to take charge of unloading the mill's freight and contacting the buyer.

Thomas glanced toward the city with his family on his mind. There was a cab waiting for customers near the wharf. "Let's grab that cab. I can't wait to see Jane and the children."

Benjamin had thought about Mary and the baby boy the entire trip, "I can't get there fast enough," he said.

Philip gave the address to the driver. The driver nodded, and with a flick of the reins, the horses broke into a trot. The Bennett and Spencer families would soon be together.

* * *

There was a knock on the door. Jane and Mary were working on a sewing project together for a customer. Jane looked out the window near the front door to see who was there.

"Mary, it's your father and both your uncles! And there's Benjamin!" She rushed to the door and thrust it open.

"Thomas, I can't believe you're here!" She rushed into his arms. Her momentum threw him slightly off balance, and a pain shot through his leg as he regained his stance, but he chose not to bring it to her attention.

Then Mary came over to hug her father and uncles. She hadn't seen Benjamin yet until he stepped in from behind Robert and Philip. He extended open arms to her and she dashed into his embrace.

"Oh, Benjamin, you're really here. It's been so long. I'm so happy to see you!" Tears spilled onto her cheeks. Benjamin lovingly brushed them away. Then Mary took her husband's hand and led him over to the baby boy asleep on the bed. "This is Parker," she said.

Benjamin looked at the baby with a gentle smile. "I've thought about this moment, and wondered how I'd feel. Now, as I look at him, I know I'm ready to accept him as my son."

Mary walked over to her bag and brought out the sketch of Mollie and the swatch of her hair. She handed the precious mementos to Benjamin.

Tears welled up in Benjamin's eyes. "My precious Mollie. One day when the Lord decides to take me, I will meet her."

Mary's father and uncles gathered around.

"My granddaughter was beautiful," said Thomas with sadness in his eyes.

Jane went into the kitchen to put the kettle on as an excuse to control her emotions, then came back into the room. "You must be hungry. I'll have a meal ready soon. Elizabeth and the boys are running errands and should be here any time now." She couldn't help but think, *What a surprise for Elizabeth and her brothers when they discover their father and uncles standing in the room and Mary sitting on the settee next to Benjamin with his arms wrapped about her! What perfect timing that it's Sunday and the children aren't working today.*

A few moments later, Elizabeth, Jonathan, and Jeremy arrived home. They were astonished at the scene before them. "We're together in the same room," exclaimed Elizabeth. "Am I imagining this? Oh, how I wish Emily were here."

They sat around the dinner table trading stories. There was so much for all of them to tell and they talked for hours, especially about getting Emily back.

Jane glanced at her watch. "The hour is late, I think we should all get some sleep. Thomas, tomorrow you can meet Oliver Scott, our private investigator. I don't know what we would do without him."

Philip and Robert said goodnight to the family. They planned to spend the night on the ship, giving them the advantage to spot the *Triumph* the moment it came in.

As Thomas prepared for bed, Jane saw the wound on his leg. She exclaimed, "Thomas! What happened to your leg?! I thought I noticed you limping."

"I took an arrow, my love. It's a rather long story which I'd rather not tell you at bed time. All I want to do right now is to slip into those covers, put my head on that pillow, and lay next to you with my arms around you."

"Now that you're safe, I can wait for your story. It's been much too long since we've laid next to each other. You have no argument from me, my darling husband."

* * *

The following morning, Philip woke to see the *Triumph* steaming into the harbor. He and Robert rushed out to the wharf, ready to speak to the captain. After dropping anchor, the crew of the ship began unloading the freight brought in from South America. Then the passengers disembarked. The wharf was a hub of activity and cabs lined up, as usual, ready to attract the passengers for transportation around the city.

Philip and Robert watched for a man wearing a captain's hat. Finally, they saw him step onto the wharf.

Philip motioned to the captain. "Good morning, Captain. Would you indulge me for a moment of your time?"

"Good morning to you, Captain. You look familiar. Have we met?"

"No, we haven't. You've probably seen me coming and going around here though. I'm Captain Philip Bennett, and this is my brother, Robert Bennett."

"I'm Captain Stannard. What can I do for you?"

Philip replied, "I've learned that you left this harbor last October to sail to South America. Is that true?"

"Why yes, what is the nature of your question?"

"We believe our niece may have been one of your passengers, Captain." Then Robert narrated a detailed description of Emily to the captain. "Do you remember seeing her?"

"Yes, I do remember seeing a young woman of that description. Indeed, a beautiful young woman leaves a lasting impression. Especially when there are mainly men on board. She stayed in her cabin most of the time."

"Did you happen to speak to her?"

"No, Captain Bennett, I never had the pleasure. When she ventured out on the deck, there was always an escort with her. I never heard her speak. She kept to herself."

Philip was encouraged. "Captain, do you recall at what port she disembarked?"

"Sure do, it was our first stop—Mazatlán."

Philip continued to push to gain more information. "Do you have access to the names of anyone who was with her?"

"I'm sorry, Captain Bennett, they paid a premium to keep their names private. I can't oblige you."

"I understand, Captain." Philip could see he would be wasting his time to try to extract any additional information from him. He and Robert thanked the captain and left.

Philip and Robert were certain this new information would lead them to Emily. Philip grinned at his brother. "Robert, I believe we're about to rescue our niece."

Robert nodded in agreement. "I'm feeling most encouraged."

Philip sought out Samuel and briefed him of his plans. "Samuel, as you know we're here for more than one purpose. I just came upon the lead I've been seeking. My niece may be in Mazatlán. We'll be leaving at first light tomorrow. I need you and a couple of the crewmen to remain here to coordinate the freight shipment. Hopefully, the vendors will warehouse the cargo until we return. I don't know what will happen or how long we'll be gone. I have an account at the Elliot Hotel. You and the two crewmen may stay there under my name. I'll alert the hotel clerk. Please tell the rest of the crew to be prepared to leave at dawn tomorrow morning."

Samuel saluted Philip. "Yes, sir. I'll take care of everything, Captain. Good luck to you and your brothers."

While Philip was delivering his instructions to Samuel, Robert secured a cab and waited. Every minute counted to put their plan into action and they were eager to give Thomas and Jane the promising news. When Philip finished briefing Samuel, he left his ship and walked briskly to the cab. After hopping in, he gave the address to the driver. "We're ready. Please drive on."

Robert gazed at Philip with a look of admiration. "Philip, I had no idea how much you've been juggling. You've continued working for the mill, doing your part in the war effort and dealing with this kidnapping. Now, we're about to go to Mazatlán on your ship to rescue our niece."

"I do what I have to do. You and Thomas haven't exactly been on a picnic. There's no doubt we come from strong English stock. If our parents were still with us in this life, I'd like to think they'd be proud of us. Now, let's plan a rescue. Thomas and Jane will be relieved to hear our news."

Thomas paced the floor while he waited, hoping his brothers would bring good news. He wasn't used to good news anymore. He braced himself. Jane and Elizabeth sat next to the window watching for any sight of Philip and Robert's return. Jane jumped up to greet them at the door when they arrived.

The door opened to a smiling Philip and Robert. "The rescue is on!" declared Philip. "Let's sit around the table and put our heads together on how we're going to pull this off."

Thomas sighed, "Good news for a change."

Jane cried, "Our baby is coming home!"

During the discussion, Philip told them it would take about a week to get to Mazatlán. The participants in the rescue would be the three brothers.

Benjamin interjected. "I'm a member of this family now. I want to join in the rescue." He turned to Mary, "I realize we haven't had much time together, but I want to help bring your sister back. Can you accept that, Mary?"

"Yes," Mary answered reluctantly. "It's difficult to let you go again, but I'm proud of you for wanting to help."

Jonathan and Jeremy had been granted permission to leave work early and came home in time to take a place at the table and hear about the rescue plan. Jonathan looked across the table at Thomas, "What about us, Father? Shouldn't Jeremy and I go?"

Thomas replied, "No, I want you two to stay behind and look after your mother and sisters."

"Whatever you say, Father," replied Jeremy. Jonathan nodded.

Then Thomas left the room for a moment. He went to one of his bags sitting in the bedroom and brought out his revolver given to him by Jane's father. He came back with it in his hand and laid it on the table. "Jane, this is the revolver your father gave me. How sly you were to hide it in my bag. I must thank your father after we resume a normal life. Jane, this gun saved my life. I'm leaving it here for all of you, just in case."

With a look of shock, Jane exclaimed, "What?! You almost died? Do you know what that would have done to me? To all of us?"

Thomas pulled Jane into his arms. "I know, my darling, I can only imagine. As promised, I'll tell you everything later. Right now all I can think about is getting our Emily back."

"I'm torn as to whether I should know or not, Thomas. It's all I can do to handle what I do know, and yes, Emily is our most important concern right now."

* * *

Philip, Thomas, and Robert paid a visit to Oliver Scott.

"Oliver, I'm happy to introduce you to my brothers, Thomas and Robert.

The brothers shook hands with Oliver, each responding to the introduction.

"I'm pleased to know all the Bennett brothers finally. I'm sensing there's a plan in the works, Philip?"

"You're correct, Oliver. There will be four of us. Mary's husband, Benjamin, is also going."

Philip continued to describe their plan. It was simple. Once they disembarked at Mazatlán, they would ask around about a young white woman of Emily's description. They figured she would stand out in a Mexican town. Someone should have seen her and could give them crucial information that would lead them to her.

"Oliver, Jonathan and Jeremy are staying here to look after their mother and sisters, but would you mind keeping an eye on my family as well?" asked Thomas.

"You can count on it, Thomas, I'll check on them regularly." Oliver had already thought about the possibility of Elizabeth, Mary and the baby being prey for the kidnappers, but had chosen to keep it to himself for the moment. He didn't want to alarm the family if he was overreacting.

The next morning the family said their goodbyes and the men headed to the *California II* to begin their trip to Mazatlán. Before they had left Teekalet, Philip and his brothers loaded the ship with arms and ammunition in case they ended up in a confrontation. They didn't know what to expect, but they weren't coming back without Emily. Thomas, Robert, and Benjamin were tougher men now after fighting in the Indian war.

* * *

As usual, Oliver's instincts were on the mark. The fact was, since the auction of the young white woman, there was a great demand for another such auction. The customers constantly asked the auctioneers when there would be another white woman available. There were very few white women around for the white slavers, so the Bennett family was a perfect target. They got away with kidnapping Emily, so why not target one of her sisters? They would need to use a different strategy, however, since the sisters would most likely not be as easy to entrap as Emily.

With the address already in his possession, Sebastian Jones and his partner, Jack Miller, watched the Bennett house. They noticed the activity of the men who had arrived, but didn't know why they were there, possibly because of Emily. Sebastian was happy the men didn't stay long and followed them the day they left. He saw the men board a ship and leave the harbor. He was pleased, but in case the men might return, they needed to strike while the time was right.

Before long, they recognized a pattern for each family member. They saw Jonathan and Jeremy leave the house early in the day and not return until late afternoon. Mary and Jane didn't leave the house very often, but received frequent visitors bringing them sewing work. Elizabeth's pattern was the most promising to manipulate. They watched her go alone to residences of people wanting to be tutored. They stayed in earshot when she knocked on the residents' doors and listened to the conversations. She always introduced herself and said she was answering their newspaper ad for a tutor. The newspaper was a common method for requests. After spending some time interviewing the prospect, Elizabeth set up an appointment to return for the tutoring session. As they spied on her, they watched her faithfully return for the scheduled tutoring session.

Sebastian placed a newspaper ad describing a young Chinese woman wanting to be tutored. The ad read, *URGENT.* As anticipated, Elizabeth took the bait and answered the ad. The prospective tutor was to come to the address on a certain date and hour. Sebastian and Jack were so sure their plan would work, they began advertising to their private list of customers that there would be a special auction soon of another young white woman and more young Chinese women, all virgins.

Elizabeth went to the address on the day requested. She was excited at the possibility of another job. There hadn't been many requests. Jane wanted Elizabeth to wait to let one of her brothers go with her since the address wasn't in the best neighborhood. Victoria had coached Jane of what areas to avoid.

"Mother, I feel comfortable meeting this Chinese lady. She probably can't afford to live in a better part of town. I imagine she needs someone to teach her English, so that maybe someday she could afford to live somewhere else. If I wait for my brothers to return from work, I'll be late for the appointment and might not get the job. We need the money, Mother. Besides, I already scheduled the cab driver to pick me up today at this hour. If it makes you feel better, I'll write down the address and leave it here with you."

The cab driver arrived on time. "He's here," said Elizabeth. She hugged her mother goodbye. "Wish me luck, Mother."

Jane watched her leave in the cab. Something didn't feel right, but she brushed it off and decided she was overreacting. "Mary, I wish your sister could have waited for one of her brothers. I don't like the part of town she's going to."

"She left the address with you, didn't she? I know Elizabeth uses the same cab driver each time and she and Henry have developed a rapport. I'm sure he'll look out for her. She never stays for more than an hour, and Elizabeth told me he's always prompt to pick her up."

"I guess she isn't completely alone then."

* * *

Elizabeth arrived at the address and instructed Henry to return in one hour. The cab driver left. This first meeting was about learning the customer's needs, which usually took about an hour. She looked around at the other houses. They were shabby and looked unlivable. She wondered if anyone lived in them. *Mother was right. This is a terrible neighborhood.* She felt out of her element but continued to follow the narrow sidewalk to the front door. Weeds had sprouted up through the cracks. The house was surrounded with overgrown shrubs and trees and sat isolated from the other houses. The wooden steps leading to the front door creaked and wobbled. The door had been painted at one time, but now the paint had nearly peeled completely off.

She knocked on the door. A timid young Chinese woman opened it, motioned for Elizabeth to come in, and closed the door. The woman didn't speak. Elizabeth assumed it was because she didn't speak English. *I'm right. She needs me to teach her English.*

Then Elizabeth looked around. The house was empty. There wasn't any furniture. With a questioning expression, she looked at the Chinese woman. The woman's face telegraphed fear.

Elizabeth's protective instincts shot to the surface. *This doesn't feel right. I need to leave now.* Elizabeth reached for the door, but when she opened it, she came face to face with three men. They shoved her back from the door into the room. One man locked the door, and the other two grabbed her. She struggled. The notebook she was carrying fell to the floor. They put a cloth soaked in chloroform over her face covering her mouth and nose. Elizabeth went limp and passed out.

Outside, there was a covered carriage sitting in front of the house. The kidnappers looked to make sure no one was around and quickly carried Elizabeth out of the house to the carriage. One of the men went back for the Chinese woman who was an unwilling participant. He pushed her into the carriage, as she would be auctioned off as well. She had been handy to use in their scheme. The whole abduction took less than fifteen minutes.

The cab driver returned at the appointed hour to pick Elizabeth up. He waited for several minutes, but Elizabeth didn't appear. He put the brake on and stepped out of the carriage to knock on the door. The door was ajar, so he swung it open. His eyes scanned the room. *That's odd, the room is empty, and no one is here.* Then he saw Elizabeth's notebook splayed out on the floor. He picked it up. Something was very wrong. Elizabeth was always dependable and would never stand him up, and she would never leave her notebook behind.

The cab driver whipped his horses into a fast trot to the Bennett household. He jumped out of the carriage and banged on the door. The banging jolted Jane. She rushed to answer it. When the cab driver identified himself, she opened the door to find him holding Elizabeth's notebook in his hands. Feeling a sense of panic, Jane quickly looked past him hoping to see Elizabeth, but she wasn't there. She felt like she might faint but controlled herself. Henry told Jane and Mary what he knew. Elizabeth was gone.

Jane needed to see Oliver Scott immediately. She hired the cab driver to take her to Oliver's office. The driver said he would take her but couldn't possibly charge her. When they arrived at Oliver's office, Henry tied his horses to the hitching rail. Jane was trembling. As he assisted Jane from the carriage, he held her arm and escorted her into the office. He told Jane and Oliver he wanted to help.

After Jane and Henry told Oliver what happened, Oliver said, "Leave it to me. I'll get Elizabeth back. This time I know right where to go. When I went undercover, I was given access to the private auctions. Don't worry. They won't hurt her. They need her to look as good as possible. Send Jonathan and Jeremy to me as soon as they get home from their work shift. I'm going to need their help."

In the meantime, Oliver paid a quick visit to the Lucky Lady to find one of the men he knew would be going to the auction. He wanted to see what they knew. He learned there was to be a special private auction the next night. It only took a few minutes for him to learn about it. Armed with his new information, he went back to his office to wait for Jonathan and Jeremy to arrive. When the brothers arrived, they were furious when they learned what had happened to their sister. They were ready to do whatever was necessary. Jonathan and Jeremy held a bitter grudge against Jones and wanted to inflict the worst punishment possible on him and his partner, Jack Miller.

"Be patient, my lads. After both your sisters are rescued, we'll come up with a plan to take care of Jones and his partner. Right now, let's concentrate on Elizabeth's rescue. How many guns do you have?"

Jeremy replied, "We only have the one handgun Father left with us."

Oliver went over to his gun cabinet and brought out a shotgun and handed it to them.

"Unfortunately, Elizabeth is going to have to endure the auction experience. I know for certain the buyers have carriages waiting by the back door of the auction building to carry the women away. They'll leave Elizabeth for the last to build up the frenzy, so the other carriages will be gone. There should be only one carriage remaining. When someone buys her and brings her out, we'll grab her. We'll be under cover of darkness and the element of surprise will be in our favor."

"It sounds like it'll work," said Jonathan.

"Oh, and we have one other person helping us. The cab driver that Elizabeth hired is joining us. His name is Henry. We'll have the use of his cab as well."

"I don't see how we can fail," said Jeremy. "Mother and Mary will be so relieved to know we have a solid plan."

* * *

Elizabeth woke up in a stupor to see Sebastian Jones standing before her. He told her what was about to happen. And, like her sister, he threatened to harm her family if she didn't cooperate.

"We know where they live," he said.

She realized it was the next day and her family would know she was missing. *I know how hard my brothers will work to find me. And Oliver will help them.*

The auction was scheduled for that night and Elizabeth was groomed and dressed to be a seductive prize on the auction block. Sebastian came to inspect her.

"Your name is now Christine," Sebastian smirked. He laughed, "Guess you won't be needing that inkwell now, Christine."

Elizabeth glared at him. "You're an evil man and you'll pay dearly one day." She spat at him.

He grabbed her arm and twisted it behind her back hard enough to hurt. "If I weren't about to get paid for you, I'd take care of you personally."

Then he looked at her neckline, which only hinted at her bosom and ripped the dress open so hard the buttons flew through the air.

"That's better. Now the men can see what they're buying." Sebastian enjoyed unnerving her.

As the hour approached, Elizabeth worried she wouldn't be found in time. Would Oliver and her brothers conclude that the same people who took Emily had now taken her? Had Oliver learned the location of the auctions when he went undercover?

The auction started with a drumroll. Sebastian walked onto the platform and told his audience the auction would be orchestrated the same way as the last one.

First, the young Chinese women were paraded out one by one. They wore sheer gowns exposing their nude bodies to the hungry men in the audience. Like Emily, Elizabeth stood behind the curtain. She could hear the boisterous noise erupting from the men. Finally, when all the Chinese women were sold, Sebastian dramatically parted the curtain to reveal Elizabeth.

Seeing so many men gawking at her and hollering for her, took her breath away. In desperation, she scanned the room looking for her brothers to save her. *They're not here. Where are they?* Sebastian pranced around her. He even threw her head back and opened her mouth to show her teeth. She thought about biting him but worried about a repercussion to her family. Sebastian lifted some of her hair, "Did you ever see a head of red hair like this?" Elizabeth shook her head away from him.

"Well, gentlemen, we have here a young virgin who is as spirited as a wild filly. You'll have an entertaining night breaking her in. The minimum bid is one thousand dollars."

The bidding went fast until the final bid of three thousand dollars came in.

"Going once! Going twice!" He hesitated as he always did, giving time for someone to up the bid. His greedy eyes scanned the room. "No more takers?" He crashed the gavel down, startling Elizabeth. "Sold!" The buyer was a gold miner who had struck it rich and spent his money flamboyantly. He needed a wife and wanted several children.

The miner hadn't been with a woman for some time, and yelled out, "Can't wait to strip those clothes off and take her tonight. Yahoo!"

Now Elizabeth was really worried. Someone actually owned her. The heavy bearded man with missing front teeth paid his money and went up to the platform to claim his prize. He gripped Elizabeth's arm to lead her away. She balked. Feeling cocky in front of the men, he picked her up and threw her over his shoulder, lifted her skirt, and swatted her on the derriere. The men whistled and howled. The miner repulsed Elizabeth. And he smelled! Being alone with him would be a nightmare. *Where are my brothers?*

As the miner carried Elizabeth out the back door, she pounded on his back with her fists. "I'll be teaching you some restraint tonight, my little filly," he cackled and threw her into the carriage. Elizabeth burst into tears. Her life was over. *Where are they?*

Oliver, Jeremy, and Jonathan stood in the dark shadows near the carriage with guns ready. They wore dark capes and dark wide-brimmed hats and covered their faces with black scarves. The loyal cab driver, Henry, waited with his cab a short distance from the man's carriage, which sat ready to whisk Elizabeth away.

The brothers were in earshot of their sister and could hear her sobs. It broke their heart.

The miner was half drunk. He wasn't alert, and his gun draw would be considerably slowed down. He was so preoccupied with his prize, he hadn't noticed the missing driver. Oliver had yanked him off the driver's seat, knocked him out, tied him up and gagged him, and hid him in the bushes. Suddenly, the miner felt a gun pressed to his head and the unmistakable sound of it being cocked. Oliver held the gun on him while Jeremy and Jonathan sprinted to the carriage to get Elizabeth. She was about to yell out their names in happiness, but they motioned her to stay quiet. They didn't want the miner to hear their voices. Then Oliver hit the miner on the head with the butt of his gun, knocking him out. They helped Elizabeth walk to the waiting cab.

Elizabeth was so happy she couldn't stop hugging her brothers and Oliver. "I knew you would come. I never stopped believing." Her eyes overflowed with tears.

When they reached the cab, Elizabeth was surprised to see Henry. "Henry, you're here too? How?"

He stepped down from the cab and embraced her and told her how much he wanted to help rescue her.

"I'm finished tutoring!" she exclaimed.

Jeremy said, "You're not going to need to tutor. As soon as we get Emily back, we're all leaving together for Puget Sound! Father said the Indian uprising has simmered down. It turned out Teekalet was safe the entire time."

Oliver looked at them and thought, *I'm going to miss this wonderful family.*

Henry hopped back onto the cab. "Is everyone aboard? Let's get out of here before that miner comes to."

The hour was late. Jane and Mary waited up for the return of their family. Sleep was out of the question. Finally, around midnight, the door opened. Elizabeth ran in ahead of her brothers and Oliver. She ran to her mother's arms, then Mary's open arms. They cried with joy.

Jonathan and Jeremy smiled at their mother and sisters. Oliver was overjoyed. He and the brothers worked well together. Elizabeth was safe, and they were back together.

Oliver said, "I hope Emily's rescue goes as well."

Jeremy admired Oliver, and he was impressed with Oliver's profession. He was beginning to think about himself as a private investigator. Would Oliver consider being his mentor? He had a deep respect for this war veteran.

Chapter 17

*R*ita was obsessed with Francesco. As far as she was concerned, he was hers. She decided to become more aggressive to win his heart and visit him openly at his home, regardless of his wife. She had become increasingly emboldened ever since she had noticed the scratches on Francesco's face shortly after the marriage. She couldn't stop thinking about their brief moment of passion they shared in the library at the wedding festivities. The sexy vixen had escalated her relationship with Francesco and thought she might be making progress.

Rita arrived at La Casa Grande unannounced. Francesco and Alberto hadn't arrived home yet from their business day. Emily was home alone, except for the servants. Now Mrs. De Leon, she had taken on the role of lady of the house.

When Rita tapped on the entry door, the servant allowed her in since she wasn't a stranger to La Casa Grande. She told Rita to wait in the parlor, then found Emily to alert her there was a visitor. Emily wasn't expecting to find Rita sitting in the parlor and Rita wasn't expecting to be greeted by Emily. The servant hadn't told Rita which De Leon was home. Emily decided to be hospitable and asked the servant to bring some *Agua de Fresa.* She was curious why Rita was there. They conversed with the pretense of politeness, but there was no denying the underlying tension. Rita spoke enough English to carry on a conversation and both women sized the other up as they spoke.

It became a contest of whose questions and innuendos were the cleverest. Rita implied she had Francesco's full attention while he worked in Mazatlán. Emily boasted about the beautiful horse and silver embellished saddle and bridle Francesco had given her as a wedding gift.

At first, Rita's claims about Francesco's attentions angered Emily, but not wanting to show her anger, stayed calm. It was then she concluded that the more Rita exaggerated, the less she believed her. During this dance of female wits, Emily realized she trusted Francesco and felt possessive of him.

Emily asked Rita if she would like more to drink. When she stood up to pour the beverage, she suddenly felt dizzy and had to sit down. "Oh, pardon me, I guess I stood up too quickly."

Rita was devastated. She guessed why Désirée was dizzy. Francesco's wife was carrying his child. She was supposed to be the one to give him a son. *Does Francesco know?* Désirée didn't seem to be volunteering any news about a child. Rita moaned internally. *It's too late.* Any glimmer of hope to capture Francesco's heart was gone. She knew a son meant everything to him and his father.

Suddenly, Emily and Rita heard the front door open. Francesco had just arrived. When he entered the parlor, he was surprised to see the two women conversing in the parlor. Awkward was an understatement. He wondered, *Why is Rita here?*

"Rita, I wasn't expecting you," said Francesco, nervously. "Have you two ladies had a nice visit?" *Has Désirée divulged what his father had done?*

"Yes, Francesco, we've been getting to know each other," said Emily, coyly.

"I just came by for a short visit. I didn't have an opportunity to see you earlier today. I'm sorry I missed you, Francesco. I must leave now." Rita couldn't leave fast enough. The visit hadn't gone as she intended, and she was upset.

After Rita left, Francesco tiptoed around the burning question. Désirée wasn't volunteering any clues about the conversation. In a cautious voice, he asked, "So, what did you two ladies talk about?"

"Just girl talk." Emily paused. Then her green eyes narrowed and stared straight through him. "You want to know if I told her what your father did to me, don't you? Don't worry. Your secret is safe!"

What began as a somewhat friendly conversation, turned into anger. Emily abruptly flipped around and left the room. *He doesn't trust me. Haven't I proven he can?*

Francesco was speechless. He marched out the door, slamming it behind him. Then he mounted his horse and rode off. He needed time alone to think.

Later that night when Emily went to her bedroom to retire for the night, she discovered a small box tied with a ribbon sitting on the table next to her bed. There was also a note. It read, *Thank you. Francesco.* She opened the box. Inside the box lay the most beautiful piece of jewelry she had ever seen. It was a ruby and pearl encrusted brooch. Her only real piece of jewelry she owned was the cameo locket that held her father's picture inside. She missed her cameo. She missed her family. Her birthday was in a few days. Never would she have thought she would be celebrating her fifteenth birthday without them. Now it seemed she had a new family and she would have to accept it.

Emily admitted to herself she let her temper control her actions toward Francesco. She could understand him being concerned about Rita knowing too much. What might she have done with the information? Would Rita have used it as a tool to turn Francesco against her? For Francesco, betrayal of a pact of trust would be unforgivable.

Francesco had retired to his bedroom. Emily summoned up her courage and knocked on his door. Upon opening it, he was surprised to see her standing in the doorway. She was momentarily caught off guard at his magnificence and gazed at him. He was wearing a sapphire blue satin robe banded with black velvet. She thought how handsome he looked and how well the robe complimented his bronze skin, deep brown eyes, and dark chestnut brown hair. She held the brooch in her closed hand.

Perplexed, Francesco asked, "What are you doing here? Is there something wrong?"

Emily uncurled her fingers revealing the brooch. "This brooch is beautiful. What did you mean in your note?" She knew what he meant, but she wanted to make him say it.

"I'm grateful you didn't reveal anything to Rita. The whole town would have heard about it. It means a great deal to me to know I can trust you. I apologize for doubting you. This brooch is a symbol of my trust in you. It was my mother's, and now it is yours."

Francesco touched her heart. Little by little she saw the gentle side of him. In her heart she wanted to give in to her growing feelings for him, but her mind refused to give up her feelings of defiance. Francesco was beginning to break through her barrier.

Emily looked straight into Francesco's eyes and responded softly, "I'm honored to receive your mother's brooch. It's the most beautiful piece of jewelry I've ever seen. I shall treasure it. Thank you, and thank you for believing in me. Please, tell me about your mother. I've never heard you mention her."

Francesco led her over to a pair of chairs by the fireplace and invited her to sit. The wood in the fire crackled, and the dancing flames illuminated Francesco's handsome face. The warmth from the fire calmed her. She could have stayed there all night.

They talked over an hour. He told her his Anglo mother died giving birth to him, and that his older sisters took care of him while he was small. He talked about how and why the family left California and how they came to live at Mazatlán. He also talked about Alberto and his obsession to continue the family name. Since Francesco had Anglo blood in him, Alberto wanted to continue the Spanish-Anglo bloodline, which was why his father insisted he marry an Anglo woman, and one who was of a high station. Alberto believed it would be more advantageous for a Spanish person to be part Anglo. Francesco felt uncomfortable to ask Emily about her family, so he changed the subject, bringing the conversation to an end. He kissed her on the cheek, and in the gentlest manner, led her to the door. They said goodnight.

Francesco had gone to bed, but he couldn't sleep. It was now midnight. A candle still flickered in his room, and a small flame lingered in the fireplace. He wasn't able to stop reliving his moments with Désirée earlier that night. He couldn't get her off his mind. When he was about to extinguish the candle, he heard the creak of his door as it opened. There stood Désirée. She was in her nightgown and barefoot. She entered the room and crossed in front of the fireplace. The glow of the flames illuminated the fabric of her nightgown, silhouetting the beautiful curves of her body. Her long golden hair draped on her shoulders and glimmered in the firelight. She was an exquisite vision. He blinked. *Am I dreaming? I must be.*

Neither of them spoke. Francesco stood up. He was nude. Désirée faced him and dropped her nightgown. If he was dreaming, he didn't want to wake up. He embraced her, and she could feel the heat of his desire pressed against her. For the first time, they kissed. Their lips parted, and their tongues met, and for the first time, she surrendered all of herself over to him, and they mutually made love. Désirée stayed in his bed wrapped in his arms throughout the night.

Early the next morning, she left Francesco's bed without waking him and went back to her bedroom. She prepared herself for the day and went down to breakfast. Alberto was already at the table. He noticed a glow about Désirée.

Then Francesco came down to the breakfast table wearing a coy smile. During the meal, they exchanged stolen glances. Alberto noticed everything and he hoped what he suspected was true. He wanted his son to be happy. The day before, Francesco had asked Alberto for his blessing for him to give Désirée his mother's brooch. Alberto always thought like a businessman and suggested the gesture might be a good investment. That morning, Alberto surmised the investment paid off.

* * *

Emily loved riding her beautiful horse. She rode every morning until one day she stopped. Alberto and Francesco always worked in town in the early part of the day so she knew they wouldn't notice her lapse in riding. She suspected she was carrying Francesco's child. She had missed two monthly flows and had begun to feel nauseous when she woke each morning. Should she tell Francesco? She decided to wait a little longer.

Chapter 18

Mid-February 1856
Mazatlán, Mexico

a week had passed since the Bennett brothers and Benjamin left the San Francisco harbor. When they entered the Mazatlán port, they saw several ships and schooners anchored in the bay. Philip gave the order to drop anchor, and instructed the crew to remain on the ship. He informed them he was uncertain of how long he would be gone. Within minutes after the steamer had come to anchor, she was surrounded by a flotilla of awning-covered boats ready to transport passengers to shore. Philip signaled the service of one of the boatmen whose boat appeared large enough to hold the four of them.

As the boatman rowed them toward the shoreline, they observed a clean, well-organized town. There were two-story pastel-colored buildings with flat roofs along with houses constructed of brick surrounded with whitewashed plastered walls. The arched apertures in these walls allowed a glimpse at inner courtyards fringed with fruit trees, shrubs and flowers. The rescuers wondered if Emily might be in one of those houses.

The foursome followed the narrow-paved street to the center of town. They showed Emily's picture to several street vendors and townspeople asking them if they had seen her. Although Philip spoke some Spanish, they still experienced a language barrier, and no one appeared to be interested in helping these outsiders.

The four men moved on and came across several large business establishments engaged in manufacturing and exporting products. Surely, someone in those businesses would speak English. They were correct. In the first building they entered, they found people who spoke English. Philip fabricated a story about a family emergency and their niece hadn't yet contacted them of her specific address.

When they showed Emily's picture, they purposely didn't say her name to prevent any possible confusion.

The lady at the front desk answered, "Oh, yes, the beautiful Désirée. She and Francesco were such a handsome couple at the wedding. There was a banquet in the Plaza Machado for the entire town to enjoy. I was there."

Philip said, "My goodness, we hadn't received word yet about the wedding."

Thomas was anxious for more information. "What's her last name now?"

"De Leon. A fine family. Their business is down the street. They manufacture cigarillos and cigars."

"One more thing if I may," said Thomas, "Where might we rent a carriage?"

"You'll find the local blacksmith who owns a livery stable with carriages at the end of the street. Carriages are made here you know."

"*Gracias*," said Thomas.

They left the building and followed the next step of their plan. While Philip and Thomas investigated the De Leon business, Robert and Benjamin walked to the livery to rent a carriage.

Philip and Thomas walked down the street to take a closer look at the De Leon business. They saw a large sign at the front, which read, *DE LEON*. They had learned a father and son operated the business. Once they identified the De Leons, they would wait for their workday to end and follow them to their residence. When Philip and Thomas walked into the business, an attractive woman at the front desk greeted them. She spoke English. Her eyes locked on Philip.

Philip picked up on her attraction toward him and spoke first. "Are the owners in?"

She smiled at Philip and answered. "Yes, but they're in the factory right now. They should be back in a little while."

Philip smiled with his boyish grin and spoke in a flirtatious manner to distract her from becoming suspicious. "We don't have much time at the moment. Could you possibly take us to the factory and point them out for us, just in case you're not here when we return? I'm sure you must take a lunch break?"

With a coquettish smile, she answered, "Follow me." The slow, easy sway of her hips telegraphed a direct message to Philip as she led them toward the factory. When they arrived, she pointed the father and son out to them.

Philip smiled again, *"Gracias, Senorita."*

She replied, "When I take my lunchtime at noon, one can find me at Buena Vida which is just across the street."

Philip tilted his cap and grinned. "I'll keep that in mind, *Senorita.*"

Thomas and Philip left the building and spotted Robert and Benjamin across the street with the carriage. They had halted the carriage at a cluster of orange trees to give themselves and the two horses some shade while they watched the De Leon building. Benjamin had obtained a keg filled with water to refresh their canteens along with a bucket to water the horses. They had no idea how long they would be waiting.

"Now we wait," said Philip.

"While we wait, we might as well help ourselves to some of these oranges hanging above us," said Robert as he picked a few and passed them around.

"Maybe by the end of this day, my daughter will be in my arms," Thomas lamented.

Late in the afternoon, Alberto and Francesco exited the building.

Thomas whispered, "There they are. We'll have to stay far enough behind so they don't see us." His heart pounded. He was another step closer to getting his daughter back.

One of the factory workers brought two horses to the De Leons. The father and son mounted up and trotted down the road leading out of town.

* * *

An hour later, Alberto and Francesco arrived at La Casa Grande. They dismounted, and one of the rancheros took their horses to the barn. When they entered the house, they heard piano music drifting from the library. Désirée was playing the piano. Francesco didn't realize she could play. He stood outside the library watching her. She looked beautiful and she played beautifully. The piano had sat for years in the library absent of anyone's fingers gracing the keys. She didn't hear them come in. They didn't announce themselves, they didn't want the music to end.

When the rescuers entered the property, they saw a large arch with a sign that read *La Casa Grande* straight ahead of them. As they passed under the arch, a large white plaster two-story hacienda with a terra cotta tile roof sat before them. Large windows paired with shutters punctuated the exterior of the house, and on the upper story, were glass window doors leading to balconies outlined by ornate black wrought iron railings. In the distance, they saw a barn, bunkhouse, and fenced land with horses grazing. They pondered how many rancheros lived in the bunkhouse. They kept their guns close.

Francesco heard the iron door knocker on the front door. Strange, they weren't expecting anyone. The servant answered the door and asked who they were and what they wanted. Francesco was within earshot.

Thomas said, "We need to speak to the De Leons."

Francesco marched to the door. "I'm Francesco De Leon. What do you want?"

Thomas stepped in without permission. "I believe you have my daughter. I'm here to take her back!" he declared in a commanding tone.

Thomas spoke so loudly, Emily thought she heard her father's voice. She stopped playing. She listened again. It had to be her imagination. By now, Robert, Philip, and Benjamin had also stepped inside. Thomas spoke again, louder, "Where is she?"

It *was* her father's voice. Emily dashed into the front parlor where they were all standing. "Father?"

"Emily!" He extended his arms out to her, and she rushed to his embrace.

"You're all here! I thought I'd never see you again!"

Francesco stood his ground. "Her name is Désirée, and she's my wife. You're not taking her."

At that moment, the three brothers and Benjamin pulled out their guns. Alberto had slipped into the library during the confrontation and grabbed the two fencing sabers off the wall. He returned and yelled out, "Francesco," while tossing one of the sabers into the air toward him.

Francesco caught it with his right hand, then pressed the tip of the sabre onto Thomas's chest.

Thomas glanced over at his daughter. "Emily, step away."

By now, Alberto was standing by Francesco's side holding his own sabre.

"All of you, drop your guns, or I'll run him through," threatened Francesco.

Emily screamed, "Don't hurt my father!"

Francesco turned his head away toward Emily when she screamed, just long enough for Robert to shoot Francesco in the right shoulder.

Emily screamed again. "Francesco!"

The metal saber crashed to the floor as Francesco fell to his knees and collapsed. Alberto turned and saw his son fall. Philip seized the moment. He charged at Alberto, knocking him off balance while disarming him.

Emily rushed to Francesco and knelt next to him. She cried out, "Father, help him!"

Francesco's wound bled profusely. Thomas shot his daughter a befuddled look, but quickly went into action whipping off his neck scarf to compress the wound. He told Alberto to get something to use for bandages. Alberto took off his shirt and ripped it into strips, which he handed to Thomas. A servant who witnessed the scene brought Alberto another shirt.

Thomas took the cloth strips and wrapped Francesco's shoulder area tight enough to keep pressure on the wound to slow down the bleeding. Thomas feared with so much bleeding, the bullet must have severed a large vein.

Thomas looked at Alberto, "You need to get him to a doctor immediately. We're leaving and my daughter's coming with us."

Francesco looked up at Emily with tears filling his eyes. "Please don't leave me."

Emily suddenly realized she didn't want to leave Francesco, especially seeing him wounded and in pain.

"Father, I can't leave." She turned, bent down to Francesco, looked at him, and back at her father, "I...I love him, and I'm carrying his child!"

Francesco heard her words just before he passed out. Alberto had gone to get blankets to cover Francesco. His son was going into shock and had started to shiver. As Alberto rushed back into the room, he heard Emily's proclamation.

Thomas was confused at what he had just heard. He knew one thing—they had a carriage sitting outside the door, and the young man needed to be taken to a doctor fast. He looked at his brothers and Benjamin, and said, "Quick, let's carry this young man to the carriage and get him to a doctor."

They reacted quickly and lifted Francesco into the carriage, laying him on the seat. Emily climbed in with him. Robert and Thomas climbed up to the driver's seat.

Two rancheros had heard the gunshot and rushed to the house to see if Alberto and Francesco needed help.

Alberto responded to the rancheros, "We're fine. Saddle my horse and two other horses, pronto!"

Thomas yelled out to Alberto. "We're going on ahead toward town. You can catch up with us and lead the way." Robert flicked the whip and the horses jolted forward, breaking into a fast canter.

Benjamin and Philip took the reins from the rancheros and mounted the two horses. Alberto was already in the saddle and told them he would ride ahead to alert the doctor. He galloped down the road, passing the carriage with Benjamin and Philip following closely behind. Once they learned where the doctor was located, they would ride back to lead the way for Thomas and Robert. Inside the carriage, Emily held Francesco's head on her lap. He opened his eyes for a moment, "You're going to have my child?" Then he passed out again.

While Thomas and Robert drove the carriage toward town, they discussed their current situation.

"Robert, I have no idea what to do about Emily. The family won't want to leave San Francisco without seeing her, and yet, we can't force her to go with us. She's legally married to this Francesco fellow and is carrying his child. If she stays, somehow, we need assurances we'll see her again. I can't bear the thought of never seeing my daughter again, and Jane would be frantic."

"We have something else to worry about, Thomas. The shooting. Our good deed at this moment could be our undoing. After all, we're outsiders in a foreign country."

"Yes, for all we know, Alberto may have a sheriff waiting for us. It'll be more than Jane can handle if we don't come back."

"It was self-defense. I was protecting you from being run through with a saber for God's sake."

"This is all so complicated, Robert. I'm at my wit's end."

In a little over an hour, they arrived at the doctor's clinic. It was situated in a two-story brick building with his residence on the second floor and the medical facility on the street level. The doctor was ready to treat Francesco while Alberto stood outside waiting for the carriage. With Philip and Benjamin in the lead, Robert and Thomas saw Alberto. They stopped the carriage, hopped down, and carried Francesco into the building. Emily followed closely behind.

The doctor swung the door open and pointed toward a long table. "Lay him there."

The doctor didn't waste a minute tending to Francesco's wound. Emily and Alberto hovered.

"Whoever dressed Francesco's wound probably saved his life," reported the doctor. "He could have bled to death. Now everyone, step back. Give me some room, and I need two of you to help me while I remove the bullet."

Francesco was conscious. The doctor said, "I need help holding Francesco down while I dig the bullet out."

Robert and Thomas stepped forward. "Tell us what you need, doctor," said Robert.

"I need one of you to hand me what I ask for from the tray and one of you to prevent Francesco from moving."

The doctor placed a leather strap in Francesco's mouth, and said, "I'm afraid this is going to hurt, son."

Emily squeezed Francesco's hand.

During the surgery, Robert and Thomas continued to glance outside to see if a sheriff was anywhere in sight. They made eye contact with each other from time to time, knowing what the other was thinking. Philip and Benjamin had remained outside with the carriage to keep a lookout for any undesired visitors.

Emily glanced at Alberto. She had never seen him look so

vulnerable. His facial expression of concern and fear said it all—he really did love his son.

During the surgery, Francesco passed out. As the doctor worked on his wound, he said, "I see the bullet missed the bone and entered the fleshy part of his shoulder but hit a vein. He's lucky." The doctor extracted the bullet and placed it on the tray, then stitched the wound closed. While the doctor was distracted, Robert took the bullet and slipped it into his pocket. Then in the guise of being helpful, he indicated he would carry the tray over to the nearby table. Purposely, he *accidentally* dropped the tray spilling everything on the floor.

"Excuse my clumsiness, doctor."

"I'm thankful you weren't clumsy during the surgery. Don't bother picking everything up. I have to clean it anyway."

Francesco began to regain consciousness. The doctor said there wasn't any reason why Francesco couldn't go home to recover. Francesco felt weak, but with assistance, managed to walk to the carriage. Emily hung on to his good arm to help him. Alberto stayed close by in case his son needed extra help. Emily's protective instinct had completely taken over. Perhaps maternal instinct? She helped Francesco as he stepped into the carriage, then followed him and sat next to him.

Thomas and Robert climbed back up to the driver's seat of the carriage and spurred the horses into a canter back to La Casa Grande. Philip, Benjamin, and Alberto followed on horseback.

Now that Francesco was conscious, he was happy to be awake and alone inside the carriage with Emily. He looked into her emerald green eyes.

"It was worth the bullet," he said.

"What was worth the bullet?"

"You said you love me. I heard you say it. Did you mean it?"

"I guess I did say that. Yes, Francesco, it's true. I tried hard not to love you, but I *do* love you."

"I have loved you from the moment I saw you despite the trouble you caused. I questioned myself how I could love you when we started so bitterly, but you bewitched me."

Emily beamed to hear his confession. She nearly wrapped her arms around him but remembered his injured shoulder.

He continued, "When you asked me the other night about my

mother and family, I felt terrible not asking about yours. I knew it would be too painful for you. That's why I ended our conversation so abruptly. We were too close to the subject." He chuckled, "Little did I know I would soon be meeting your father with his gun aimed at me. I want you to know I respect your family for fighting for you and they've proven to be compassionate people. I'll make sure my father doesn't press charges. I believe he's thinking the same way, or he would have already had the sheriff waiting for your family. Besides, knowing my father, he won't want anyone to learn how we came together. He'll want it to be our family secret."

"Thank you, Francesco. I *am* proud of my family. They're selfless. Now that I'm carrying your child, I feel selfless. Francesco, my mother must have been frantic when I disappeared. I need to see her and the rest of my family. Father told me they're still in San Francisco waiting for my return."

"Of course, I understand. I never had a mother. I don't want to be responsible for depriving you of yours. I believe I'm able to travel. How would you feel if I accompanied you to San Francisco to see your family?

"Oh, that would be wonderful!" Then she began to hug him forgetting about his shoulder.

"Be careful *mi amor*, it hurts," he grimaced.

Emily caressed Francesco's face and kissed him. "Francesco, there's something else." He looked at her with a quizzical expression.

"Could you please call me by my real name—Emily?"

He smiled. "I didn't realize your name had been changed. I think I could get used to calling you Emily though, but the paperwork may have to remain the same with the name of Désirée."

"I can accept that. My last name was Bennett. Now the Bennett family will be part of your family."

They all arrived at La Casa Grande and entered the house together. There was some awkwardness to overcome, but they made peace. Francesco was correct about his father. Alberto had already made up his mind not to have Emily's family arrested.

Instead of snatching Emily and making a fast getaway, they stayed and helped save his son's life. He forgave them. He knew if he were in their place, he would have done anything to save his child. Honor was of the utmost importance to Alberto. He admired Emily's family. They were courageous and honorable. Alberto asked his servant to bring in wine and glasses. He poured drinks for everyone, and made a toast in honor of the Bennett family.

Francesco echoed his father's words. Then he announced the plan he and Emily had worked out during the carriage ride. They would be going back to San Francisco on Captain Bennett's ship to see the rest of the family. This was news to all. Thomas breathed a sigh of relief. He was relieved with this initial step. Alberto interjected that he would like to join them.

Emily informed Alberto about Francesco agreeing to call her by her real name, Emily. Would he do the same? He nodded in acceptance.

Alberto addressed Emily's family. "It's late, and you have no place to stay tonight. Please accept our hospitality and stay here. We have plenty of room. I've alerted my cook to prepare supper for us. I hope you'll enjoy a meal with a local influence!"

* * *

"*La cena es servida,*" announced the servant.

"Ah, supper is served," declared Alberto, as he motioned to the dining area. "Please, come."

Alberto looked at his table with chairs no longer empty. It had been a long time since those chairs had been filled. Never would he have believed Emily's family would be sitting at his table sharing a toast in friendship. Especially this day.

The conversation flowed effortlessly. Thomas and Robert talked about their journey from New York City to the tip of South America to San Francisco and on to Puget Sound with Philip as their captain on his ship, the *California II*. They talked about their settlement in Puget Sound and about having to fight in the Indian war.

Thomas said, "Francesco, you got a bullet in your shoulder, but I got an arrow in my leg."

Emily gasped. She didn't know they had fought in the war or that her father had been wounded. As she listened to him, she saw him in a new light.

Benjamin talked about his experience of coming face to face

with the monster wave on the ship, which nearly took his life. Emily was wide-eyed as she listened. She wondered if Mary knew. Then with sad eyes, Benjamin shared about finding out about his baby girl perishing on the Nicaragua journey and how he learned about it through a letter from his wife when the family had arrived in San Francisco. He talked about how Mary saved the life of a baby boy whose mother had died giving birth to him during the voyage. She took him in and cared for him, and now he was theirs to raise. Francesco listened intently and reflected about his own mother's death when he was born.

Philip talked about their rescue of two survivors from a ship that sunk at the Strait of Juan de Fuca, and about the message in a bottle they found from a victim. Because of the message, Philip went to San Francisco and rescued the victim's family who was in imminent danger. He explained about the desperate situation of the settlers during the Indian war, and while still hauling shipments from the Hawaiian Islands for the mill, he used his ship to bring back food and weapons from San Francisco to the settlers of Puget Sound. They were facing starvation and were nearly defenseless.

Alberto and Francesco were in awe at how much this family had endured and now what they had gone through with Emily. Much of this information was news to Emily. She was so proud of her family.

Alberto lifted his glass, "I made a toast about the honor of this family, now allow me to toast to their courage and strength!"

Thomas lifted his glass, "And let me toast to two families coming together in friendship!"

They all clinked glasses, "Here, here!

The evening soon came to an end. The servant led the guests to their bedrooms. They looked forward to returning to San Francisco and joining the rest of the family. It would be a joyous occasion to be coming back with their Emily.

Chapter 19

February 1856, One Week Later
San Francisco

*T*he *California II* steamed into the San Francisco harbor. Philip dropped anchor and everyone disembarked. Samuel had been watching for Philip's arrival and greeted him on the wharf. He reassured Philip that everything was under control. Philip brought Samuel up to date and told him they would be delayed a day or two.

Thomas hailed two cabs for their group and directed the drivers to take them straight to the address of the house where the rest of the family was staying. Thomas was anxious to see his wife's reaction when Emily walked through the door.

Jane had been watching out the window every day for Emily's return.

Finally, Jane saw them coming, but there were two cabs and she wondered why. She cried out, "They're here, and I see Emily!" She ran to the door and threw it open.

Thomas instructed Emily to walk in first without Francesco and Alberto with her. They needed time to explain.

Emily ran to her mother and hugged her.

"Emily, you're really here. I thought I would lose my mind with worry."

"Mother, I missed you so. I missed everyone."

Elizabeth and Mary rushed to hug her.

Emily kissed each of her sisters. She didn't see her brothers. "And where are my dear brothers?"

"They're working, but they'll be home soon," said Jane.

Mary embraced Benjamin, and Jane flew into Thomas's open arms.

"We have so much to tell you, Thomas. It hasn't been easy." She could see Thomas looked alarmed. "I'll tell you later. I don't want to dampen our wonderful reunion with Emily."

"We have much to share as well," replied Thomas. Then he walked toward the porch and motioned for Francesco and Alberto to come in. Emily went to Francesco's side and held out her right hand to show her mother the wedding band.

"This is my husband, Francesco," she announced.

Jane looked confused. "I don't understand. I thought you were taken against your will, Emily?"

Thomas said, "Let's all sit down. We have so much to tell you. First, let me introduce you to Alberto De Leon, Francesco's father. They live in Mazatlán."

Jane needed a moment to absorb this news. "I'll bring us some tea." She scurried to the kitchen and prepared the tea. She wondered what was going on.

Elizabeth went in to help her and whispered, "When shall we tell them what happened to me?"

Jane spoke quietly, "Let's stay calm and let them tell us what happened. Then, we'll tell them. Something is amiss here. I want to know more about these men first." Jane handed one of the two tea trays to Elizabeth. "For the moment, let's serve the tea while we listen and learn."

Thomas sighed, "Where do I start?"

Thomas was about to begin telling their story when Jonathan and Jeremy walked in. With eyes wide open, they exclaimed in unison, "Emily!" They hugged her so tightly, she thought she might break. The brothers hadn't noticed the two strangers yet. Then Emily told them she was married and introduced them to her husband and father-in-law.

Jeremy and Jonathan looked puzzled.

"I'm confused," said Jonathan.

"Totally confused," said Jeremy.

Alberto and Francesco had been gracious the entire time, but they sensed they should give the family some privacy.

Alberto said, "If you'll excuse Francesco and me, we'll leave you to yourselves for awhile. We need to secure a hotel room for the night, and I'd like all of you to be our guests for supper this evening.

I know of a good restaurant, so I'll make reservations while we're out. We'll be back in a little while."

They both bowed and walked toward the door. Francesco and Emily exchanged longing glances as he and his father left.

Jane said, "Well, I must say they're gentlemen. Were you rescued by them, Emily?"

"That's not quite what happened." She proceeded to tell her story. As Emily described the auction experience, Elizabeth relived her own. Emily finished with the events that led up to their father's arrival.

Thomas interrupted. "This is where we come in."

Then, Robert, Philip, and Benjamin chimed in to describe the events.

Emily interjected, "They were all so heroic. I've never seen Father so tough or point a gun at anyone."

Jane asked, "I wondered why the young man was bandaged. Thank you, Robert, for protecting my husband."

Thomas looked at Emily. "Emily, don't you have something else to share?"

She nodded and looked at her family. "I'm with child."

Jane had to sit down. Mary gasped.

Elizabeth looked at her and said, "I can't believe it."

"Me either, but there's no turning back," replied Emily.

Jonathan said, "Little sister, you're the last person I could imagine as a mother."

Jeremy added, "I think we're going to see a side of you we thought we'd never see."

Jane took Emily's hand and held it in hers. "Emily, you've been forced to grow up. I like the person I see. I believe you'll make a fine mother."

"Thank you, Mother. Your words mean everything to me."

Jane went over to her small bag and brought out Emily's locket. "I imagine you've missed this? I had faith I'd be giving this back to you one day. My prayers have been answered. Shall I put it on you?"

"I thought about my locket and that I'd never see it again. Yes, please." Emily lifted her hair while Jane placed it around her neck.

"Thomas, while we are all here together and have some privacy, there's something you need to know. Something terrible happened while you were in Mazatlán," said Jane.

Thomas, his brothers, and Benjamin braced themselves.

Nervously, Thomas spoke first, "What happened?" *Will the bad news ever cease?*

"I'll tell," said Elizabeth. She told them she had been answering tutoring ads in the newspaper and was lured into a trap set by Sebastian Jones and Jack Miller. They kidnapped her and put her up on the auction block.

"Emily, when you described your experience at the auction, I was reliving my own. I know what you went through there. It was horrid."

Then Jonathan and Jeremy continued the story about their part. They were thankful they had the gun. They talked about Oliver Scott coming up with the plan and how they helped him. Even Elizabeth's cab driver, Henry, was involved in the rescue of Elizabeth.

Thomas was angry. "You mean we almost lost another daughter to those scoundrels?! I'm proud of you boys for helping to rescue your sister. When I left the gun, I didn't really think you'd need it." He clenched his fist and raised it in the air. "If it's the last thing I do, I'll get even with those scoundrels!" Philip, Robert, and Benjamin pledged to help make it happen.

Jeremy had a thought. "Mother, Father, Oliver doesn't know yet that Emily has been rescued. We need to tell him, and I think it would be good if Oliver could meet Emily. I thought maybe I could catch a cab and bring him back here for a few minutes."

"We do owe him that," said Jane. "Yes, go ahead, and hurry. We don't know how long Francesco and Alberto will be gone."

Emily interjected, "I have a better idea. Why don't you and Jonathan take me there to meet him?"

"Then let's go, little sister," said Jonathan.

Emily went out the door with a brother on each side of her, their arms linked. Before long, a cab came their way, and they were off to Oliver Scott's office. After a pleasant, but short visit with Oliver, they returned an hour later.

"Oliver is a very special man. I'm so glad I met him," said Emily.

"He's almost like family. I'm going to miss him," said Jane. "Now, let's not waste a minute of our time together."

The family conversed nonstop in Alberto and Francesco's absence. For the first time in many months, the family was together again.

Jane realized the hour was late and suggested they take some time to freshen up before going out to supper.

Soon Alberto and Francisco arrived. Alberto informed the family that he had carriages waiting to take everyone to the posh Palace Hotel restaurant. Alberto, Francesco, and Emily rode in one cab and the Bennett family rode in the second cab. A few minutes later, the cabs stopped in front of the luxurious hotel. Jane said to Thomas, "I could get used to this kind of treatment."

Thomas chuckled, "From what I have seen, Emily has become quite accustomed to such treatment."

For the first time, the entire Bennett family and the De Leons would dine together. Initially, Jane was nervous, but when she saw how much Emily and Francesco loved each other, she accepted the joining of these two families. The conversation flowed freely and by the end of the evening, the families had formed a friendship. Alberto suggested they spend the next day together as well. The family agreed.

Philip and Alberto developed an instant rapport. They were astute businessmen and recognized the advantage of doing business together. Philip had the ship and the ability to sell goods, and the De Leons had the products to sell. The family immediately saw the value of the relationship to mix business with pleasure, enabling them to visit Emily and their future grandchild. Travel time from Puget Sound to Mazatlán would be only two to three weeks depending on weather conditions.

After supper, it was time to say goodnight. Alberto informed the family they would have only a few hours together the next day. There was a ship scheduled to leave for Mazatlán that afternoon.

* * *

Francesco and Emily settled into their room. While she was happy to be with her husband, she felt a sense of melancholy. The reality of separating from her family was beginning to set in. Francesco understood how she felt and wanted to make her feel better.

"Emily, did you know my father and your Uncle Philip have already made a gentlemen's agreement to conduct business with each other? Do you know what that means? It means any member of your family, such as your charming mother, will be able to visit you often. Your family will always be welcome to stay with us."

"Oh Francesco, you've made me feel so much better. I noticed your father and my uncle had their heads together during supper. It made me smile. They seem like a perfect fit to be business partners. Thank you for telling me."

Then Emily shared Elizabeth's kidnapping experience by the same perpetrators and how badly she had been treated.

He replied. "I had no idea. Your family has had more than its share of adversity. One would never know when talking to them. I want you to understand I don't condone the slave market. After hearing how Elizabeth was treated, I'm happy my father was there to take you away from those crude men, and, we would never have met. I am so grateful you are in my life. Do you mind me saying this to you?"

"It's all right, Francesco. When Elizabeth told me the details of her experience, I did think about how much better I was treated, and I was thankful for that. Those poor Chinese women. They were practically nude, and the buyers slung them over their shoulders like a sack of flour while they laughed all the way out the back door to take them to who knows where."

Francesco put his good arm around her. "Enough sad talk. Let us retire Mrs. De Leon." He turned off the light. "*Te amo.*"

"What did you just say?"

"I love you."

Emily cuddled up to him, "I love you too."

Meanwhile, Emily's family took the carriage Alberto had arranged for them back to the house. While there, Philip wanted to talk to his brothers. He pulled Thomas and Robert aside and spoke in a muffled voice. "There's something we need to do before we leave Frisco. I have a plan. I'll tell you after everyone else goes to bed."

After everyone else had retired, Philip told Thomas and Robert what he had in mind. "We need to repay a debt to Sebastian Jones and his partner Jack Miller, but I don't want the De Leons or Emily to know about the plan. And, we're going to have to act fast."

Philip told them he knew of the arrival of a crusty unethical captain whose ship was one of the abandoned ships left to rot in the harbor from the days of the gold rush. The captain's idea of restoring the old rotting ship was to apply a few patches here and there and cover them in paint. The ship was the *Zephyr* presently anchored in the harbor.

"I have an idea how we can make use of the captain. He has a reputation for spending his time in shady circles. This captain has no problem taking shanghaied men on board and sailing off to sea with them." Philip smirked. "I think we can oblige our captain with two such men. Don't you agree?"

"I like your plan, Philip. Then, I'll get my revenge," Thomas rejoiced.

They decided they would put the plan into action after they said goodbye to Emily and the De Leons.

The next morning the family and the De Leons gathered at the house. After they visited for a little while, they went to a cafe for dinner. Alberto insisted on paying. When they finished, the dreaded moment of the farewells was upon them. They walked together to the wharf. Emily cried while she embraced her family. Thomas told Francesco he had something for him. He put his hand in his pocket and brought out the bullet that had been removed from Francesco's shoulder. Robert had hung on to the bullet he stole and thought Thomas might like to give it to Francesco. "I thought you'd like a reminder of us and that we can be tough if we need to be. Don't ever hurt my daughter."

Now that Francesco was going to be a father, he understood Thomas's implied warning. He would probably do the same if it were his child leaving his protective arms. "I don't doubt it for a moment, but I promise you, you'll never have cause. I love her with everything that is in me."

Suddenly, the ship's horn blasted the signal for boarding. Alberto and Francesco kissed each of the women on the cheek and shook hands with all the men. Then the three De Leons boarded.

Emily yelled out, "See you soon! I love you!"

The family stood transfixed with tear-filled eyes as they waved goodbye. They watched the ship leave the harbor until it disappeared over the horizon.

Thomas frowned, "There goes my little girl."

They walked away from the wharf to return to the house. Thomas asked his sons to escort their mothers and sisters. He and his brothers had some unfinished business to handle. Benjamin suspected they were up to something.

"Do you need any help, sir?"

"I appreciate your offer, Benjamin, but I think we'll be fine. Spend your time with Mary and Parker."

"Then, I'll see you later," replied Benjamin.

After the rest of the family was on their way to the house, Philip commented, "I recall hearing Oliver Scott express a desire to take Jones's business down and would like to be involved if there was ever a way."

"I'd say we should grant him his wish," said Thomas with a sheepish grin.

Chapter 20

Late February 1856

San Francisco

*T*he Bennett brothers walked into Oliver Scott's office. "Greetings," said Philip.

"Well, if it isn't the gallant Bennett brothers. This is an unexpected pleasure. What can I do for you, gentlemen?"

"Oliver, are you still interested in taking Sebastian Jones's operation down?" queried Philip.

"You had better believe it, Captain Bennett. After Elizabeth was taken too, I made a promise to myself to take Jones and his operation down. And, if there are any women locked up, I want to free them. What's the plan and when do we start?"

"Tonight," replied Philip. He told Oliver about the captain who had recently arrived in the harbor and welcomed *free* labor.

"Superb plan, Captain Bennett." The four men sat down and finalized the details of the plan.

Since Robert and Thomas were the least known in the city, they would be the first key to the plan. That night they approached the *Zephyr* and boarded it to find the captain. Robert and Thomas noticed the ship was a total contrast to Philip's ship. This ship was in complete disarray and filth.

"This seems like a fitting place for our soon-to-be sailors," snickered Thomas.

They walked toward the pilothouse. As they approached, they heard loud singing. The off-tune singing led them to the half-drunk captain holding a bottle of whiskey belting out a sailor's song. The two brothers startled him when they greeted him.

"Laddies, what can I do fer ya?"

Robert asked, "Could you use a couple of men for free labor on your ship?"

"Oh ya, I can always use some able bodies. I lose quite a few men down below shoveling coal into the furnace." He pointed downward. "I could use 'em there."

The first part of their plan was now in place. Oliver had access to chloroform that they would be using on Jones and Miller. They knew they would find the scoundrels at the Lucky Lady. It was about ten o'clock, and it happened to be a dark night.

They wrote a note to Sebastian with an offer he couldn't resist. The offer gave him the first opportunity to see the fresh cargo just brought into the harbor. It was a group of young virgin Chinese women. He should leave immediately and come to the wharf where the women were being held on a certain ship. If he delayed, they would make the offer to someone else. A man in a black cape and hat would be waiting for him in front of the ship *Zephyr*.

Robert handed the note to the bartender to give to Sebastian immediately. Then Robert stepped away, blending into the crowd of drinkers and gamblers.

The bartender called out, "Hey Sebastian! Someone delivered an urgent note to ya."

Sebastian was curious and responded. He grabbed the note from the bartender and opened it. Robert watched Sebastian as he read. Then Sebastian rushed out the door with Robert trailing well behind him. Robert smiled. *He took the bait.*

Philip and Oliver hid near the ship. Thomas was the man in the black cape and hat. The trap was set.

Sebastian showed up, and Thomas motioned him to board the ship. "The captain's waiting for you in the cabin."

The ship was dark except for the faint lantern light in the captain's cabin. Sebastian walked toward the dim light but never made it that far. Philip and Oliver jumped out of the darkness and grabbed Sebastian from behind. It wasn't difficult to restrain him. Sebastian was far too vain a man to have ever allowed himself to be involved in physical fighting. He always had others do his dirty work for him, such as Jack Miller. By this time, Robert caught up to lend any physical strength needed. Thomas quickly brought the chloroform-doused handkerchief out of his pocket.

"Does this look familiar, you scoundrel? You're going to get a dose of your own medicine. Your days of kidnapping and selling innocent women are over, you son of a bitch!"

Sebastian's vision blurred. He struggled to free himself but to no avail. Thomas reapplied the handkerchief over Sebastian's face as he exerted one last struggle. He moaned, then he was unconscious. They took him down to the hold of the ship, stripped him down to his underwear, and put him in irons.

Now they were ready for the next phase of their plan. Robert went back to the Lucky Lady with a note written in the guise of a man doing business with Sebastian addressed to Jack Miller, which appeared to have been delivered by a messenger. Robert gave a coin to one of the waiters in the room to hand the note to Miller who was leaning on the bar with a drink in his hand. Robert watched. Miller opened the note, which read:

Your partner Sebastian and I have struck a deal on a cargo of young Chinese women still on my ship. He wants you to come to the wharf with plenty of money and a wagon. There will be a man dressed in black waiting to direct you.

Miller shook his head. *Doesn't Sebastian ever do anything for himself? Can't he even write his own note?* He quickly went to the safe and brought out the typical amount of money for such *cargo*. Next, he went to their private stable to get their transport wagon.

Thomas waited in his disguise on the wharf for Jack Miller. Once again, Robert followed his prey.

When Miller arrived at the wharf and saw Thomas, he asked in a demanding tone, "Where's Sebastian?"

Thomas replied in a gruff voice, "He's inside with the captain looking at the women. Follow me."

Thomas led him up the plank onto the ship. He grimaced at Miller's size, a much larger man than Sebastian. Fortunately, Oliver was a husky man, and Robert had caught up. As Thomas led Miller onto the ship, Miller began to feel uneasy, but before he had a chance to react and pull his gun, Oliver and Philip jumped out of the shadows from behind to restrain him. He put up such a fight, it was necessary for Thomas to become involved in the struggle, although his strength was compromised due to the recent wound in his leg. Robert added his strength. During the struggle, Miller managed to free his right arm and punched Thomas in the face. Thomas retaliated and hit Miller in the face cutting his lip.

Then Thomas brought out the chloroform-doused handkerchief from his pocket. The white handkerchief was ominously visible in the dark shadows. Miller saw it and knew exactly what it was. He struggled harder. Thomas could see the look of terror on Miller's battered face and enjoyed it immensely. He covered Miller's face with the cloth and left it on for an extra minute or two. Miller's head wobbled, and he collapsed into unconsciousness.

Oliver took the money off of Miller's unconscious body. There were several thousand dollars. Miller had come prepared since he didn't know how many women they would be buying. Then Oliver found Miller's gun and tossed it into the water. It took all of them to drag Miller's dead weight down to the hold. Just as they had done with Sebastian, they stripped him of his clothes and put him in irons.

With the scoundrels now captive, Philip left the scene to talk to the drunk captain who was half asleep in his cabin. He figured the captain was drunk enough not to have a memory of who he spoke to once he sobered up. An empty whiskey bottle rested on the table next to him.

"Captain, you'll find your two coal shovelers chained up in the hold. We did as you instructed and stripped them of their clothes and shoes. They're all yours now." Philip tipped his hat and walked away with a large smile spreading across his face. He hadn't felt that good since he had proposed to Maggie. It was a good night's work.

Now they were ready to initiate the final phase of their plan. They took the wagon, which had so conveniently been brought to them by Jack Miller, and drove it to the back of the auction house. While Oliver had been investigating undercover, he sought out the location of where the women were kept while they waited for their turn on the auction block. He had also gleaned some information from Elizabeth. She told him she had been in a locked room for a short period of time and then taken to another room to be groomed for the auction.

It was now midnight, and because of the late hour, there weren't any guards. Jones and Miller had been complacent and felt confident their secret enterprise of trafficking the women would remain a secret. They figured no one would dare cross them, so they didn't need guards around the clock. Oliver brought out his handy lock pick tools from his pouch to use on the locked back door. Philip lit a match for light. In less than a minute, Oliver had the door unlocked.

When they entered the building, it appeared to be a maze of hallways and doors. It was dark. They lit their small lantern to light the way. Which way to go? They systematically checked each room. Each door thus far wasn't locked and opened to a small single room. They continued to check each room but found nothing. Then they came to a door that was locked. Oliver brought out his trusty tools, and within moments, successfully picked the lock.

They opened the door into a large room where they heard the sounds of women moaning, whimpering, and crying. There was also an overwhelming stench of human waste. They followed the sounds and lifted the lantern to illuminate the back of the room.

The men weren't prepared for what they discovered. Ten Chinese women stood before them locked in a cell behind cold steel bars. There were no windows. The floor was brick, and there was no heat. Bunks over bunks lined the walls with only a single blanket on each. In the corners of the space, they saw the source of the smell— open buckets to serve the function of chamber pots. It was obvious the space was intended for a short tenancy since Jones and Miller turned the women as fast as possible. However, even one night in that environment was unbearable.

When the women saw the men, they cried out and extended their arms through the bars toward them. Robert put his forefinger in front of pursed lips signaling them to be quiet. They understood. With a kind soft voice, Oliver convinced the women they would be freed soon.

Oliver fumbled with his lock pick to unlock the cell until one of the women pointed to the opposite wall where there was a hook holding the key. Philip quickly retrieved the key and handed it to Oliver. When Oliver unlocked the cell door, the women rushed out and jabbered incoherently. The brothers took the blankets from the bunks and wrapped one around each woman. The blankets comforted them, but Oliver's mature kind voice eased them the most.

The rescuers hustled the women out to the wagon while still motioning them to stay quiet and helped them climb in. The four men breathed in the fresh night air, a welcome contrast to the stench they left behind. They boarded the wagon and drove it to the wharf. The final phase of the plan was to take the women to Teekalet where they could be free and join the other Chinese people in the mill community.

The men stopped in front of the wharf and motioned for the women to exit the wagon and walk toward the *California II* to board, but the women wouldn't budge. They were too frightened to board the ship. For them, a ship meant enslavement. Philip understood their fear, so he rushed to his ship to fetch his Chinese cook, Meng, who by now was fast asleep in his cabin. Philip woke him, quickly explained the situation, and asked him to come out to the wharf to translate. The women needed to understand they weren't in any harm and would be taken to a place of refuge.

Philip had already warned Samuel to expect some activity that night. Knowing Captain Bennett as well as he did, Samuel was prepared to expect anything. He responded instantly and made preparations for the women. Meng's gentle manner with the Chinese women calmed them, enabling him to assure them it was safe to come aboard. Before the women boarded the ship, Oliver brought out the bundle of money he had taken from Miller. He divided the entire amount evenly among the women. Then Philip instructed Meng to tell the women the money was theirs to help them start a new life. Finally relaxed and happy, the women climbed down from the wagon still clutching their blankets. As they walked toward the ship, they bowed continuously in gratitude to their rescuers, finally boarding the ship. Samuel and Meng settled them into their cabins and made sure they were comfortable.

It had been a long day and a long night. The brothers thanked Oliver for his help.

"Thank you, fellas. I haven't felt so alive since the War. I was determined to take Jones and Miller down. I realize I couldn't have done it alone. You all helped make that happen. I'll stop by in the morning to say goodbye to everybody. You're a fine family. I'm very happy I was able to meet Emily and to learn she's happy. She's a beautiful young woman.

"Thomas, your son, Jeremy, has shown an interest in my line of work. If he ever wants to learn the business, I'd take him under my wing in an instant. He and his brother were both pretty good in action too. Guess it runs in the family."

"Why thank you, Oliver. I had no idea Jeremy had such an interest. Of course, we haven't had much time to talk since our arrival."

Philip and Robert stayed behind to spend the night on the ship to keep an eye on the women. Oliver and Thomas took the wagon and horses to the nearest stable, unharnessed them, and led them into the stable. The owner would find himself richer in the morning with one additional wagon and two horses.

With their mission complete, Thomas and Oliver found a cab that was still running late, taking each of them to their destination.

Jane waited up. When Thomas walked in the door, the first thing she saw was Thomas's now swollen black eye. "Thomas, what happened?!"

"It's been a long day and night. Can I tell you about it in the morning? I'm dead tired. Let's go to bed."

Jane smiled, "Is this something I should get used to? Your stories for *later* are beginning to stack up."

"I'll catch up my darling, I promise. Right now, I just want to sleep."

* * *

The next morning, Robert and Philip joined the family at the house. Jane and Elizabeth prepared the final meal in their sanctuary. Thomas kept his promise to Jane, explaining about his black eye as he described the events of the night before.

Elizabeth was elated about the fate of Sebastian Jones. "I told him he would pay!"

Before breakfast was served, Jeremy announced he wanted to discuss something with his parents that had been weighing on his mind. "I'm hoping Oliver Scott will agree to become my mentor so I can follow in his footsteps as a private investigator. I saw firsthand how people could be helped, and it inspired me, and I've become quite fond of Oliver."

Oliver had shared his life story with Jeremy. He learned Oliver was a widower and had no children of his own. He did have a niece, however. Oliver had married shortly after the war. He and his wife had been expecting their first child. Tragically, during the birth, both his wife and child died. He was devastated and never remarried. Instead, he plunged himself into starting his private investigation business.

Jeremy's decision was news for Thomas and Jane.

"Jeremy, you haven't seen your father for months. You aren't suggesting you want to stay in San Francisco, are you? We're already leaving without Emily. I thought we were all going to be together as a family again," moaned his mother.

Thomas interjected, "Jeremy, Oliver told me last night how fond he is of you, and it pleases him of your interest. I have a suggestion. Come with us and see what life will be like at Teekalet. I was looking forward to you coming into my business with me, but of course, your life is your own. Neither my brothers nor I followed in our father's footsteps, so how could I ask you to do what I wasn't willing to do? If, after some time you still feel strongly about coming back here to work with Oliver, then you have my blessing."

Thomas turned to Jane. "Jane, he would only be a week or two away from us and Emily three weeks at the most. Compared to the months of separation we've endured, the distance doesn't seem insurmountable. At least Jeremy will be a week closer to Emily than us."

Jeremy thought what his father said was fair. "Thank you, Father. I'm glad I was able to discuss it with you and Mother before Oliver arrives. Do you mind if I tell him what we've talked about?"

"That'll be fine, Jeremy. It's good timing."

A half hour later, Oliver arrived. Jeremy took him aside to tell him what he wanted to do and the agreement he had made with his father. Oliver was pleasantly surprised at Jeremy's sudden announcement.

"Your father is a wise man, Jeremy. If you decide to come, you'll be most welcome."

Oliver shook hands with the men and kissed each lady's hand as he said goodbye. The family thanked him for his help and ceaseless loyalty.

After Oliver left, they hailed a cab and dropped their baggage off at the ship.

Their last stop was the address of Captain William Davis and his wife, Victoria. Upon the family's arrival, they received a warm welcome with Victoria insisting on serving tea.

Jane handed Victoria the key to the house. "Victoria, you saved us. We were in such a bad situation. I don't know what we would have done without your help. The man you referred to us was so helpful and led us to dear Oliver Scott. You now have heard the rest of the story."

"Jane, it was my pleasure and I enjoyed our visits together. I was honored that you felt comfortable to confide in me about everything. You were always in my prayers."

"It helped, Victoria, to be able to talk to a friend. I'll miss you. We must stay in touch."

Philip gave William a bear hug. "William, you and Victoria have been true friends. You took good care of my family, and I thank you. You know you'll always have a friend in me."

William added, "Let me do one more thing for you all, Philip. My driver and carriage are sitting out front to take you to the wharf. No need to stand around waiting for the next cab to come by."

The rest of the family also thanked the Davis's. The family said farewell and stepped into the carriage awaiting them. They were finally on their way to board the *California II* and begin their new life together in Teekalet in Washington Territory.

Chapter 21

$\mathcal{S}$ebastian Jones and Jack Miller woke up thinking they were in the middle of a nightmare, but they were wide awake, and it was all too real. They looked at each other in the dim light. What happened to their clothes? Sebastian gawked at Jack. Didn't he leave him back at the Lucky Lady? And what happened to his face? They both attempted to stand to leave but learned they were restricted by the irons they were wearing.

Jack looked at Sebastian. "Who in Sam Hill did you make so mad they would do this to us? Where in the devil are we, anyway? This has to be your fault, Sebastian."

"My fault?! You have a long list of enemies. Look, it's not doing us any good to argue, we need to figure a way out of this! I want to track down who did this to us and put some irons on them, then throw them into the sea!"

Suddenly, they heard the hatch open and saw a ladder slide down. A man came down carrying some hard biscuits and water and set them down within their reach.

Jack yelled out, "Hey, who's in charge of this tub? I demand to speak to him. And where are our clothes? It's freezing down here."

The man didn't say a word but walked over to a chest and pulled out a blanket. He threw it at them and said, "Here, share this. The captain will be here shortly to assign you your duties."

"Duties? Nobody tells me what to do," sneered Sebastian.

The man laughed and replied, "I guess we'll see about that."

He climbed back up the ladder leaving it in place, and the hatch open. A shaft of light illuminated the dark hold just enough for the prisoners to view their surroundings. The rotten timbers and side walls were in full view, and they saw they weren't alone. Rats shared their quarters. Before long, a scar-faced captain and two sailors came down the ladder. The captain carried a small box.

"Good morning, gentlemen. I'm Captain Hanley, and you're on the good ship *Zephyr*. Did you enjoy your breakfast?"

Sebastian felt a moment of terror. *Hanley. I know that name. He's part of the Shanghai ring. No one's ever been known to make it back to San Francisco once they're in his hands. And I don't like what I see down here. This is one of those ships that was rotting in the harbor. We're done for.*

Jack yelled out to the captain. "What's this all about? We're men you don't want to cross. There'll be people looking for us. Where in hell are our clothes and shoes?"

The captain replied confidently and calmly, "I don't care who you are. As for someone finding you, well, I don't think that'll happen. We're on the high seas heading toward China."

Sebastian interrupted in an insidious tone. "Maybe I can appeal to your pocketbook. We're wealthy men. If you take us back, I'll pay you whatever you want. What do you say?"

"Sure, I take you back, you double cross me, and have me murdered. Your partner here already said you're not men to be crossed. Do you think I'm stupid? Besides, you two must be pretty bad apples for someone to go to the trouble to put you here. They didn't even ask for money. Oh, by the way, your *friends* left this note for you," chuckled the captain as he handed it to Sebastian.

Sebastian glowered at the note suspiciously, then read the words out loud, "*Payback is sweet. We always collect our debts.*"

"What the hell have you done to us Sebastian?" shouted Miller.

"Whatever I've done, you've done too," retorted Sebastian.

The captain interrupted them. "Okay, that's enough. We're wasting time. What's done is done. Now, let's get down to business."

Jones and Miller continued to scowl at each other and then turned the scowl onto the captain.

The captain opened the box he brought down with him. "I have a credit slip for each of you to sign. What this means is everything I provide you, including food and shelter, you'll owe me for. I'll owe you a minimal wage for your labor."

The captain burst out laughing thinking how clever he was. "But of course, you won't see wages, because you'll owe me more! This makes it nice and tidy and legal."

"I'm not signing your lousy paper," sneered Jack.

The captain replied, once again in a calm controlled voice, "It's up to you. You can cooperate, or I can let you stay down here half naked with nothing more than that blanket and starve to death. Then I'll feed you to the sharks unless the rats eat you first."

Jack answered with the fire within him suddenly snuffed out, "Give me your damned lousy piece of paper. I'll sign it."

Without a word, the captain brought out his quill and ink pot from his box and handed the agreement to Jack.

Then the captain turned to Sebastian, "And you, sir?"

Sebastian nodded in resignation and took the agreement to sign. They both noticed their names were already on the paper. Who told him their names?

Sebastian and Jack realized they were at this man's mercy and nothing seemed to bother him. It was true about the captain. In his past career, he had been a pirate.

Pleased with his signed credit slips, Captain Hanley said, "Thanks gentlemen, oh let me correct that. You'll be addressed as sailor." He laughed. "You'll be sea dogs before you know it!"

The captain climbed back up the ladder. The two men stayed behind. One of them went over to the chest and brought out some clothes and shoes and threw them at Sebastian and Jack. The other man unlocked their leg irons.

"Get dressed and come up to the deck. You'll be assigned to your duties," he said.

Sebastian and Jack put on the musty clothes and shoes and went up to the deck. The captain was waiting for them. Sebastian complained that the clothes were damp, and he was cold.

The captain laughed loudly, "When you see where you'll be working, you won't be cold for long!"

Then he led them down to the boiler area where men were shoveling coal into the belly of the fiery furnace. It was backbreaking work, and the blast of heat coming from the blazing furnace seemed unbearable. Sebastian looked at the sweaty soot-covered men shoveling the coal. *This can't be happening to me. I'm not cut out for this.*

As the weeks passed, Sebastian and Jack knew they had entered hell. It was a long way to China. Who knew whether the ship would make it in one piece for that distance? Would the captain stay sober? One fierce storm throwing the ship into rocks could finish her off. Maybe for Sebastian Jones and Jack Miller, a watery grave would be their refuge.

Chapter 22

March 1856

Puget Sound

*T*he first mate shouted out, "Anchors aweigh!" The throaty whistle of the *California II* signaled her departure from the Golden Gate harbor. The Bennett family was finally together, minus Emily, and for Jane and the rest of the children, their new home was just a week away.

Philip wanted to talk with the Chinese women, so he asked Meng to gather them together in the meeting room adjacent to the dining saloon. He wanted to tell them where they were going and what would be offered to them. Jeremy was interested and observed. Meng led the women to the room, and when Captain Bennett entered, the women squealed in delight, clapping their hands together. The room was suddenly filled with giggling Chinese chatter. Through Meng's translation, Philip told them about the mill town Teekalet and the Bennett settlement along the Hood Canal. He assured them there would be employment opportunity in the mill town and possibly at their settlement. He told them that the mill offered to house anyone they employed. His own crew lived in the mill's cabins. Most of all, Philip emphasized they were going to a safe place, and they would never have to fear being victimized again. Then he added, "You will be happy to know there is already a Chinese community in the mill town," Philip grinned as he continued his *communique*, "and I'm sure there are plenty of eligible men looking for a wife." The women were ecstatic and screamed in joy.

Jeremy couldn't imagine what the fate of these innocent young women might have been had they not been rescued. They appeared to be between sixteen and twenty years of age. He and Philip didn't like thinking about the women who hadn't been saved. At least Sebastian Jones and Jack Miller wouldn't be enslaving women any longer. Philip chuckled to himself as he thought about Jones and Miller waking up to find themselves stripped of their clothes and learning what lay ahead of them.

During the trip, one of the Chinese women approached Meng and asked if she could help him in the kitchen. He was pleased to accept her offer. The two had already made eye contact every time Meng was called in for translations.

* * *

The coastline between San Francisco and Puget Sound was a beautiful scenic experience for those on board who had never journeyed north of San Francisco. The further north they traveled, the more the vegetation and coastline changed.

Elizabeth opened her journal again to describe the final leg of their journey.

March 1856

March 3.

I marvel at the large dunes and expansive sandy beaches which give way to the surf pounding upon forested rocky shorelines dotted with reefs, tide pools, and sea caves. There are expansive grass and brushlands, rolling hills and rugged bluffs, fields of wildflowers, and stands of spruce and fir on the coastal mountain ranges.

The passengers are staying top deck whenever possible to enjoy the coastline.

March 4.

The Chinese women cheer in delight as they point at several groups of seals and sea lions lazily sunning themselves on the rocks sitting within the tide pools. They laughed out loud when they saw sea otters lying on their backs eating abalone, which they broke open with a rock. The sound of these women laughing warms my heart.

Meng enjoys acting as a tour guide for the Chinese women. They are a willing audience. I've noticed his new assistant always stands next to him.

It's such a pleasure to watch the Chinese women enjoying the sights. I'm so very happy for these women. Thanks to my father, uncles, and Oliver Scott, they've been given a second chance. I've noticed that Jeremy has taken an interest in them. He seems very curious about how they were kidnapped from China.

March 6.

Jonathan and Jeremy have stationed themselves at the railing. Today they spotted whales and shouted at us to look on the port side.

Everyone turned to see a group of whales breaching the ocean surface, propelling completely out of the water, twirling their bodies while still in the air, then flopping back down to the surface with a huge splash. We heard a loud smack as it happened and large masses of foamy sea water exploded into the air. It was an unforgettable sight for everyone.

March 8.

We have seen and heard many sea birds along the way. As we come closer to Puget Sound, large bald eagles are soaring above our heads.

March 10.

We are nearly there. Mother and Father look so happy to be finally together. They seem inseparable.

During the voyage, Thomas and Jane stood together at the railing as often as possible.

Jane was exuberant. "Thomas, this is the most beautiful country I've ever seen. I'm glad we came."

Thomas smiled at her, still sporting his black eye. He put his arm around her and pulled her close to him.

A week after departing the San Francisco harbor, the *California II* arrived at Teekalet. Philip guided his ship to the usual berth at the wharf, then Samuel dropped anchor and secured the lines. The crew went into action and began unloading the freight while the passengers disembarked. Everyone clustered on the wharf.

Philip jogged over to the mill office to check in and inform the managers that they not only had rescued his niece but also rescued ten Chinese women who had been victims of the white slavers. He hoped the mill would provide shelter and employment for them.

The mill managers assured Philip the women were welcome and agreed to provide for them. They congratulated him on the rescue of his niece and praised him and his brothers for rescuing the Chinese women. Now they would do their part.

It was agreed that Meng would be in charge of taking the women to the available housing. He determined that two cabins could accommodate them—five occupants in each cabin. After the women were settled, the mill managers would arrange employment for them.

Samuel and the crew finished unloading the ship and went to their cabins for a respite until the next trip.

Philip borrowed one of the mill's smaller boats to transport his family group to their new home. It took less than an hour to reach the Bennett wharf. Britta was the first to see everyone step onto the wharf. She barked and bounded toward Philip and nearly jumped up into his arms. Her barking alerted everyone else of the arrivals. Excitement filled the air.

Thomas introduced his family and then pridefully took them to their house he had built. Jane noticed it looked similar to the houses on the East coast.

"Oh Thomas, I had no idea our house would look like this. To be honest, I thought we might be living in a log cabin. This is a wonderful surprise."

Thomas had hoped Jane wouldn't be disappointed that the house was somewhat empty.

"Jane, I'm sorry there isn't much furniture in here. At least there are beds. Needless to say, I've been a little busy. Besides, you'll probably want to be in charge of furnishing our home."

"I love it, Thomas. I love it all. The land is beautiful, and I've never seen so many giant trees, and so many stumps!" She chuckled.

"We had a crew of lumberjacks clearing the land, but there was only enough time to remove stumps that were in the way of building the house. We managed to put in some crops around them. Unfortunately, because of the war, not much from the crops survived for harvest time. We have some work ahead of us." Then Thomas grinned. "Jane, follow me outside. I want to show you something."

Jane followed her husband to a small yard area next to the side of the house. She immediately noticed several small lilac bushes.

"Thomas! Lilacs! My favorite flowers! Where ever did you get them?"

"I know how much you love them. You had the room filled with lilacs when we married. A kind woman in Teekalet offered to give me some starts. I had visited her for a shoe fitting. Her husband had come into our building and wanted a pair of shoes made for his wife.

He expressed that she couldn't get around very well and wondered if I would come to her. I agreed to do so. While I was there, I noticed their yard was filled with lilacs in full bloom. When I mentioned how much you love lilacs, the wife insisted I take some starts home with me. Her husband went right out and dug up several good-sized bushes. It was their way of thanking me."

"What color are they, Thomas?"

"There's more than one color, but I want it to be a surprise. You'll have to wait until spring, my darling. The bushes are big enough, hopefully, to have many blooms."

"I can't wait! Thank you, Thomas. I'm going to love our new home."

Meanwhile, while her parents were looking at lilac bushes, Elizabeth and her brothers explored their new home. Elizabeth anxiously chose her bedroom and moved her bags into her new abode. She could hardly believe she was standing in her bedroom in a placed called Teekalet in Washington Territory, so many miles away from her bedroom in Delhi, New York. She brought out her journal and opened it. She was glad she had started writing in it again as they traveled to their new home. Before that, her last entry had ended abruptly when their ship and another ship nearly collided in the foggy San Francisco harbor. So much had happened while they were in San Francisco. She hadn't had any desire to write anything during that time.

Now, settled in, she sat down and prepared to write. When she brought out the inkwell, it reminded her of Sebastian Jones. She was angry for a moment. *I'm really going to have to replace this inkwell.* Then she daydreamed about something more pleasant for a moment and wondered what had become of James Mitchell. She knew he was going to Puget Sound to be with his uncle. Did he get pulled into the Indian war? Was he all right? *I must stop daydreaming. I need to finish this journal. Father will be anxious to read it.*

Thomas left Jane on her own to get acquainted with their new house and to start unpacking. He was excited to show his sons the business building.

"Lads, come with me. I want to show you what Robert and I have accomplished thus far."

Thomas had hoped his sons would become involved. Jonathan

and Jeremy were politely interested, but their father sensed they wouldn't be involved for long.

Jonathan hesitantly broached the subject, "Actually, Father, I've been wanting to talk to you."

Thomas recognized the signs, *I've heard this before from his brother. Him too?*

"You know I've always been interested in hearing all about Uncle Philip's voyages. I love the sea. This journey confirmed it. I was hoping Uncle might let me go along with him to learn. I want to be a captain someday, like him."

"I have to admit, Jonathan, I'm not all that surprised. I still remember when I used to find my missing ropes in your bedroom tied in nautical knots. Have you spoken to your uncle?"

"No, I haven't. I wanted to talk to you first."

"Like I told your brother, your life is your own. It's not up to me to tell you what you should do with it. At least we would still see you once in awhile. Has your brother shared with you what he wants to do?

"Yes, he has. That's what convinced me to talk to you right away. Do I have your blessing to talk to Uncle Philip? I could probably start immediately."

"I told your brother, and I will tell you the same. You will both always have my support."

"Thank you, Father. I'm going to go find Uncle Philip right now."

"Just make sure you don't have bad timing. He and Maggie haven't had any time alone for quite some time. If you follow me?"

"Understood."

With this new revelation, Thomas was already thinking ahead. If he and Robert weren't going to be able to depend on Jonathan and Jeremy's involvement, maybe they should discuss the idea of hiring and training some of the Chinese women. They would fit in well with the Chinese workers they had already hired.

Benjamin had taken Mary and Parker to their new home. She loved it at first sight. When they walked in, Mary saw the wooden baby cradle Benjamin had built. Inside, was a beautiful blanket, which Rachel Bly had knitted for their baby girl.

Benjamin spoke softly as he looked at baby Parker in Mary's arms. "I made this for our Mollie." Then he took Parker from Mary's arms and placed him in the cradle. "At least it won't be empty. I don't know how I would bear it."

"Benjamin, it's beautiful. Oh look, Parker is smiling at us."

Maggie had gone to the wharf along with everyone else. After Philip had finished introducing everyone, she hugged Philip so hard and long, he didn't think she would ever let go.

He kissed her and said, "Let's go to the house, soon to be *our* house, I should say, and talk there."

After Philip and Maggie entered the house, Maggie talked nonstop. She told him about the steady demand for their bakery goods from the mill. Her Lady Kay apple pie was so popular, a sign was displayed in the general store giving information of what day of the week the pies would be available. Philip smiled. He was pleased with himself as he thought back to that day in San Francisco when he suggested she should sell pies in Puget Sound.

Because of the Indian war, she lost the business from the lumberjacks. Now that the war had come to a close, they were back.

Everyone had worried that their Indian friends across the bay at Point Julia would go on the war path. Fortunately, they didn't take part in the war. Many of the Indians, in fact, had jobs at the mill and bought supplies at the general store. They even bought the bread Maggie and Rachel supplied to the store.

Philip said, "While we talk, let's get comfortable and lay on the bed so I can keep you close to me." There was something he wanted to talk about.

He swept her up and carried her to the bedroom. He gently placed her on the bed and lay down beside her.

"Maggie, I have so much to tell you, it'll take at least a couple of hours. But Maggie, first there's something else I want to discuss. Our marriage. We've held off while waiting for Thomas's family to come. Well, they are here! Let's set a wedding date. Now that we have a house to live in together, and I'm able to stay put for a little while, there's no reason why we shouldn't marry soon." He kissed her. "And we can look respectable sharing this bed."

"Yes, Philip, yes! And, there'll be two weddings. You probably haven't heard. Rachel accepted Peter's marriage proposal."

"We'll go congratulate them later tonight. Right now, I want to make up for lost time." Then Philip kissed Maggie passionately.

"Make love to me, Philip. I've missed you."

Unbeknownst to the lovers, Jonathan was on his way over to visit his uncle. He couldn't wait to talk to him. The front door was ajar, so he stepped in. He didn't see any sign of his uncle. Then he heard Philip and Maggie together in the bedroom. He quickly tiptoed back out. *Darn, bad timing. Father was right.*

Chapter 23

*N*early two weeks had passed since the family's arrival at the Hood Canal settlement. It was nearly spring, and with the help of Thomas's sons, Thomas and Robert juggled their time with the business to put in some crops. Developing the land was important not only for producing food, but it was a requirement under the Donation Land Claim Act. Fortunately, before the Indian war had begun, the orchard they had planted survived and stood ready to bloom.

Peter and Benjamin's land was further along. Their crops were well established and plentiful. By harvest time, there was enough for their supply of food along with enough to sell to the mill's general store. With the absence of the men during the war, Matthew and Christopher had helped Maggie and Rachel keep the crops alive and nurtured the orchard in the men's absence during the war. They also caught and smoked fish. Another skill they learned from their Indian friends.

While Maggie and Rachel had split their time from the bakery business working to keep crops alive, someone had to care for the horses and cows. Billy and Annie helped. Annie milked the cows, made buttermilk, and churned the cream into butter. She fed the chickens and gathered the eggs. Billy was in charge of delivering the baked goods to the mill town. It was a relief the war was mostly over, and the homesteaders were able to return to some normalcy in their lives.

* * *

When Billy learned about the rescued Chinese women living

in the mill's cabins, he was anxious to meet them. Perhaps one of those women might become his future wife. He still mourned the loss of his entire family when the *Theodora* sank. Now, he had no family and was ready to start his own. Peter wanted to help Billy and offered him some acreage from his own parcel at a reduced price of one dollar an acre. Under the rules of the Donation Land Act, Chinese people didn't qualify to claim land.

After Thomas learned of Jonathan's plans to follow in his uncle's footsteps, he followed through and spoke to Robert about the idea to hire and train some of the Chinese women.

Robert was in full agreement. "Thomas, maybe we should hire four of the women. What do you think?"

"Yes, I agree. I'm also thinking about hiring one of them for Jane. Our children are getting close to moving out, so Jane might like some extra help."

Robert added, "I spoke to Maggie and Rachel the other day and they mentioned they could use some extra help at the bakery. The girls they had previously hired part-time from Teekalet could no longer work at the bakery due to the slow commute back and forth. They said they would like to hire one of the women full time."

Thomas added, "Once we hire these women, we'll need to provide a place for them to live. They can't very well live in the bunkhouse with men still in there."

Jonathan and Jeremy overheard the discussion and approached their father with a solution.

Jonathan spoke first, "Father, Jemmie and I feel a little guilty about not joining the Bennett Bros. Co. But you know our hearts wouldn't be in it. We have an idea to help you."

"Yes," added Jeremy. "We believe part of the bunkhouse could be converted into living quarters for the women, even if an addition needed to be added on. Jonny and I are volunteering to work on the conversion."

"At least by working on the bunkhouse project, we're helping to make up for our absence," said Jonathan.

"I like the way you two think. You're truly Bennett men. I am pleased with the idea, and I accept it. I'll discuss it with Robert. I'm sure he'll approve."

Thomas was heartened by the idea and went straight to Robert.

"That's brilliant," said Robert. "Let's have a chat with Billy and get him involved in our little project."

Billy jumped at the idea and suggested he could be the women's representative and translate for them. He would even teach them English. Upon his next delivery of bakery goods, he contacted Meng and asked to be introduced to the women to discuss employment at the settlement. Meng was happy to assist and informed Billy that one of the women was already committed to work with him in the ship's kitchen. Her name was Jiao.

After spending some time with the women, Billy chose six of them to take back to the settlement to interview for the jobs. They were excited. He told the selected women when he would be coming back for another delivery, and at that time, he would take them back to the settlement with him.

Billy counted the days until the next delivery day. He was attracted to one of the six women. Finally, the day arrived. He loaded up the workboat with the goods, which included several of Maggie's special pies and Rachel's coffee cake. He sailed up the canal to the mill town and delivered the first order to the general store and the second order to the mill cookhouse. Then Billy found Meng and asked him to go with him to tell the six women he was ready to take them to the settlement.

As Billy and Meng walked to the women's cabins, Meng shared with Billy that he had developed a relationship with Jiao and he planned to marry her. Then Billy confessed that marriage was on his mind as well. One of the women had caught his attention.

Meng chuckled, "You'd better work fast. Many men at the mill have the same idea."

"Thanks for the warning. I will."

The women were excited to see Billy and Meng, and were even more excited when the two men explained why they were there. Billy thanked Meng and led the six women to the boat and helped them board. When they arrived at the settlement, he introduced the women to Robert and Thomas at their place of business, and then to Maggie and Rachel at the bakery. Thomas and Robert hired four of the women, two for each of them, and Maggie and Rachel hired one. Thomas also decided to hire one of the women to help Jane with the house. Emily's bedroom was vacant, so the woman would be able to live with them.

After Thomas had finished the hiring process, Jonathan cornered him.

"Father, I spoke with Uncle Philip about working with him and my desire to become a captain. He's excited about the idea. He thinks I'm a natural. We've agreed I'll start working with him on his next trip, which is in just a few weeks."

Thomas wasn't surprised. "Yes, I've been expecting this announcement. I appreciate your help with the bunkhouse. I believe the Chinese women are going to work out and I like the idea of helping them."

"Oh, and, Father, you were right about Uncle Philip."

"Right about what?"

"Right about timing. I had to go back the next day."

Thomas laughed. "That's my brother. He doesn't ever waste time."

Chapter 24

Late March 1856
Teekalet

*A*fter the hiring process, Billy took the Chinese women back to their cabins in Teekalet. Jeremy wanted to come along. He informed Billy he was interested in asking the women some questions. When they arrived, Billy gathered the women together in one of the cabins and introduced them to Jeremy. Jeremy proceeded, and Billy translated.

"Billy, please ask them how they ended up on the ship to San Francisco and then into Sebastian Jones's operation."

Jeremy continued his questions and Billy translated back and forth. He told Jeremy he would give more detailed information on their way back to the settlement.

Billy and Jeremy said goodbye to the women and went back to the workboat tied to the wharf. There was a nice wind, so they made use of the sails and skimmed down the canal. During their trip back to the settlement, Billy educated Jeremy about the background of the Chinese culture.

He explained, "Chinese women hold an inferior status. When a woman marries, it becomes her duty to maintain her husband's family and not her own. This makes her less valuable to her parents. Female infanticide is common, Jeremy. I want you to know I don't believe in this and neither did my mother and father."

Jeremy was shocked. "They kill their own child?!"

"I'm afraid so. Also, women are considered property and can be sold or traded. That's what happened to many of these young women. Their families were poor, and they sold them to tongs for a pittance. And they were aware they were selling them into the sex trade. Some of the women were even snatched off the streets. When they were taken to the ship, they were put in padded crates and handled as freight."

Jeremy was astonished over what Billy told him.

"Billy, what were the women saying to you when we were leaving the house?"

"They said they were glad you knew what happened to them and they'll be grateful to your family and the private investigator for the rest of their lives."

When Jeremy returned home, he told Thomas and Jane he had made a decision.

"You're not going to believe what I learned about the Chinese women. Billy helped me ask them some questions, but it was Billy who told me the most."

Jeremy continued to tell them everything he learned that day about the women and the Chinese culture.

"I know for certain now what I must do, Mother and Father. I'm returning to San Francisco to work with Oliver. There are and will be more Chinese women who need help. There are other white slavers in San Francisco. I believe, that together, Oliver and I can make a difference. If I have your blessing, I'd like to go back on Uncle Philip's next scheduled trip to San Francisco. Jonathan and I will have the bunkhouse project completed by then. Some of the mill workers heard about what we are doing, and have volunteered to come and help.

Thomas was concerned about Jeremy's safety. He had seen firsthand how evil those kind of people could be.

"Jeremy, do you realize you'll be inserting yourself into very dangerous territory? From what I learned, these tongs are organized Chinese crime groups that bring these women over. I'm frightened for you, Jeremy," his father said.

"I know it can be dangerous. I'm sure if Oliver ever thought we were in over our heads, he would back off. He has many contacts in all walks of life, even bounty hunters. I've been putting a lot of thought into this. Perhaps we can involve Christian groups or missionaries to purchase them out of bondage. I've been too close to this white slave market, Father, with two of my sisters being kidnapped."

"I'm proud of you son, but please be careful."

Jane nearly cried. "Jemmie, if something happens to you, I wouldn't be able to handle it. Please don't gamble with your life." She hugged him tightly.

"I promise to come back to visit as Uncle Philip sails back and forth. I'll even be able to check on Emily when he does business in Mazatlán. As you said, she'll be only a week away from me."

Thomas wanted to end the conversation on a positive note. "Jeremy, I want you to know your mother and I hope to take advantage of your uncle's business trips to Mazatlán whenever we can. Hopefully, we can all be together while we visit."

Jeremy exclaimed, "As Uncle would say. Brilliant!"

Chapter 25

*I*t was a beautiful spring day. Elizabeth Bennett was on her hands and knees working in the flower garden. The clothes she wore to work in the garden consisted of a pair of her father's trousers, which required a belt to prevent them from sliding off her, and one of his shirts which hung well below her hips. She wore her favorite straw hat equipped with a ribbon to tie under her chin, and her hair was tied in braids. She worked vigorously, breaking up the soil to plant her new flower seeds. Before long she was covered in dirt.

Suddenly, she thought she heard the sound of a horse whinnying. She looked toward the road that skirted the canal. It wasn't often they received visitors overland. Most people came up or down the canal by vessel.

A man riding a beautiful black stallion was riding in their direction. As he rode closer, she recognized him. It was James Mitchell! He wore a double-breasted frock coat, buckskin breeches with riding boots, and a plaid wool flat cap, which sat at a slight angle. His face was cleanly shaven except for a mustache. His dark brown hair was longer than it had been on the voyage. She liked it that way. She liked everything she saw. He was a magnificent sight sitting upon his horse. Then she remembered what she was wearing, and much of the dirt from the garden was on her, including dirt smudges on her face. She panicked. *He's seeing me at my worst!*

James held back a laugh but couldn't help grinning. He thought she was adorable messed up in her non-stylish ill-fitting attire. Their eyes met, and her heart fluttered. She could feel herself blushing, which greatly embarrassed her. James liked seeing her blush. It meant he affected her. *I'm going to marry this woman.*

Thomas spotted James and walked over to greet him, shaking

his hand. "Well, I see you took me up on my invitation to pay us a visit. Welcome."

Elizabeth was confused. *How does father know James?*

"Elizabeth, this is James Mitchell, the man I told you about who saved my life during the Indian battle. If it weren't for him, I'd be dead right now, and my scalp would be hanging from a pole at some lodge house."

Elizabeth looked at her father and then James. "It was you?" Her father hadn't mentioned the hero's name. He wanted to wait until James came to visit and make the introduction.

"Please, James, come up to the house to see Jane and the rest of the family. We'll have some tea, or something stronger if you like," Thomas winked.

Elizabeth was mortified to be caught looking so disheveled. She needed an excuse to break away to make herself more presentable. "Mr. Mitchell, I'll take care of your horse and give him some water, too. Such a beautiful horse."

"Thank you, Miss Bennett. You *are* coming up to the house, aren't you?"

"Yes, I'll be there, but I shan't join you for tea until I've made myself more presentable. You may not even recognize me."

James grinned at her. She blushed again.

Thomas was happy to see James again. His visit was a surprise. James felt at ease with the family, and the conversation flowed. Thomas retold his story about how James saved his life. Then Elizabeth entered the room. Her eyes sought James's eyes. He stood as she walked in and quietly gasped. He thought to himself, *What a beautiful vision is set before my eyes.* Jane noticed Elizabeth was wearing her best dress and wore her hair tied back with a large yellow satin ribbon to match the yellow flowers on her dress.

"Miss Bennett, you are looking quite beautiful, but I thought you looked just as beautiful out there in your flower garden." James wasn't making it a secret he was interested in Elizabeth.

Elizabeth smiled and blushed again. She couldn't seem to control the blushing. Not being in control of her emotions was new to her and she found it quite annoying. James, of course, enjoyed every moment of it. During the visit, Jane and Thomas noticed the little exchanged smiles between the two of them. Jonathan and

Jeremy enjoyed watching the flirtations and saw sure signs of a marriage coming up.

During the conversation, the Bennetts learned that James lived in Seabeck with his uncle. He and his uncle had both claimed land there. His uncle used to run a store in Olympia near the Government Custom House where ships paid duties and customs. It had been a perfect source of business.

"My uncle's business went downhill when the Custom House moved to Port Townsend about two years ago. Then the Indian war pretty much finished him off. A large lumber mill was recently established in Seabeck, and a store was badly needed to support the mill workers living there. So, my uncle set up his store in that location. Now the ship traffic coming and going for the lumber mill uses his store. It has become the ideal place for them to rest and spend their money. We're considering opening a small dining space."

Thomas saw this as an opportunity for Maggie and Rachel. "James, we need to talk." Before long, the concept of a dining space looked like it was about to become a reality. "We'll all come to Seabeck to meet your uncle and he can meet Maggie and Rachel to talk about a business plan."

"That sounds good." Then James stole a quick glance at Elizabeth. "Now, may I ask you a question, Mr. Bennett?"

"Of course."

"May I call on your daughter, Elizabeth?" Elizabeth looked startled and wide-eyed, and of course, blushed.

"I wondered when you were going to ask. Of course, young man, you have my blessing."

Since it was getting late, James announced it was time to leave. Elizabeth jumped up, "I'll walk him out."

While the couple walked toward James's horse, he said, "If you approve, Miss Bennett, I'll be back soon to pay you a visit."

She answered, "I'll look forward to your visit. In fact, why don't you come on my birthday? It's next week. Maggie is going to make a special cake for me."

"Do I dare ask the lady how old she'll be?"

Elizabeth blushed again. "The lady will be seventeen."

"I'll be there," he said.

* * *

It was Elizabeth's birthday. Maggie brought over the birthday cake, and the family was busy in the kitchen preparing the birthday dinner. Elizabeth continually watched the road for any sign of James. She was dressed in her best. She knew she was falling in love with him and thought it might have even begun on the Nicaragua journey. He had been such a gallant gentleman, and now she found out he had saved her father's life. He was truly a hero. Learning this, intensified her feelings. She paced across the lawn. *Where is he? Will he come?*

Soon her question was answered. She saw James on his horse trotting down the road. Elizabeth ran toward him and noticed him leading another horse behind him. It was a beautiful bay mare with a reddish-brown coat, a black mane, black tail, and black lower legs.

James dismounted his horse and took the reins of the mare and handed them to Elizabeth, and said, "Happy birthday, Miss Bennett."

"For me? She's so beautiful."

"Notice the saddle?"

Elizabeth looked at the saddle. "It's a side saddle!" She giggled.

James smiled. "You see, I didn't forget how you prefer to ride."

Her mind flashed back to the day in Nicaragua when she had been so contrary about riding astride on the donkey. She asked, "How did you find a side saddle in this part of the country?"

"I ordered it a while ago along with our regular order of saddles for the store with the off-chance I might see you again one day."

He reflected to that time when he couldn't get her off his mind. The more he thought about her, the more determined he was to find her, even if he had to search all of Puget Sound. Once he found her, he would marry her.

Elizabeth threw her arms around his neck. "Thank you, thank you. I love you so much!"

When she realized what she had just done and said, she stepped back, and embarrassed, said, "I didn't know I was going to say that. I hope I haven't made you uncomfortable."

"Uncomfortable?! I couldn't be happier. I fell in love with you back in Nicaragua. I never thought it could happen so fast. After fighting in the Indian war, I've come to realize how short life can be. I knew I would look for you. I didn't expect to find your father first.

"This isn't how I planned a proposal, but you did pave the way. I can't pass up an opportunity, and I don't want to waste another minute of not being with you, Elizabeth."

James bent down on one knee and took both her hands in his. "Elizabeth Bennett, will you marry me? I'm sorry I don't have a ring, but if you say yes, there will be one on your hand very soon."

Elizabeth threw her arms around James again. "Yes, Yes, I'll marry you. What a wonderful birthday present. A marriage proposal and this beautiful horse and saddle." She caressed her horse's face. "Now I'll say it intentionally, I love you, James Mitchell. Let's go tell everyone our news!"

"Yes, I want to tell the world!"

They tied their horses to the porch railing and joined the gathering inside the house.

Thomas smiled at Elizabeth and James, and said, "Well there's our birthday girl, and look who's here. How are you, James?"

James beamed. "I'm more than fine, sir."

Thomas noticed the way James and Elizabeth gazed at each other. "Ohhh?"

Elizabeth interjected, "I can tell you why. I just accepted James's proposal of marriage! And look outside at my birthday gift!"

Everyone went out to the porch and saw two horses tied to the fence post. It was obvious the beautiful chestnut mare equipped with a side saddle was meant for Elizabeth.

Elizabeth stroked her horse. "James," she said, "I've decided to call her Duchess."

Before dinner was served, Thomas poured everyone a glass of wine. He raised his glass. "I welcome you, James Mitchell, into our family. You have our consent and blessing to marry our daughter." He looked at Jane, and she nodded. He was certain she would agree with him. "I couldn't ask for a better son-in-law, not to mention one who risked his life to save mine. I'd say you've started out on the right foot. Let us toast."

They all raised their glasses. "Cheers!"

Jane whispered to Thomas, "This reminds me of the toast on our wedding day in New York City. We've had quite a life together, haven't we, my love?" Jane looked at her wedding ring with affection and proclaimed. "Now three weddings are coming up!"

Chapter 26

April 1856

Seabeck, Washington Territory

Shortly after Elizabeth's birthday, James returned to spend time with Elizabeth as often as he could. They spent much of their time riding horseback together.

One day while they were riding, James said, "You know, you haven't met my uncle yet, and your family has yet to schedule a visit to talk about the dining space. Shall we set a day when you can all come? Maybe, we can even discuss some wedding plans."

When James mentioned *wedding plans,* Elizabeth didn't want to waste a moment. "Let's go talk with everyone right now," she exclaimed. They nudged their horses into a trot back to the Bennett house. After a few minutes of discussion, a date was set for the following week to go to Seabeck

After James left, Elizabeth thought to herself, *If he's mentioning wedding plans, he must be close to getting a ring. It seems we're doing this a little backward. Of course, it's my fault. I was the one who blurted out I loved him without any warning. He's not had much time to get a ring.*

* * *

It was a pleasant day to be boating on the canal. Elizabeth, her parents, Maggie, and Rachel boarded the workboat and sailed to Seabeck. When they arrived, they were impressed with how well the harbor was set up for incoming ships. They tied the boat at the wharf and walked toward the uncle's store.

James had been watching for their arrival and saw them coming.

"They're here," he exclaimed to his uncle as he swung the door open to greet their visitors.

"I'm so pleased you all came," said James. "Please meet my uncle, Randolph Mitchell."

After the introductions, Randolph invited them to gather around a table to chat. There was much to discuss. Besides business, there was a wedding to talk about.

"I have a kettle on the stove if anyone would like tea."

Jane spoke for everyone, "That would be very nice. Thank you, Randolph."

While the group sipped tea and talked, James pulled Elizabeth away. "I want to show you where we'll live once we're married. It's walking distance."

James grabbed Elizabeth's hand and led her to a charming cottage complete with a white picket fence. It was perfectly situated to overlook the canal. Shortly after he had completed his term of service with the Puget Sound Mounted Volunteers, James forged ahead to build the cottage for the woman he intended to marry.

"I had barely filed my land claim before I was called to serve. Fortunately, my uncle had found this nice parcel for me knowing I would have less than two months to file once I arrived.

"Elizabeth, you were my inspiration for this white picket fence."

"James, it's so charming. I can't wait to plant flowers."

"Darling, I think there's just enough time to give you a tour of the house before we join everyone back at the store. Shall we?"

"Oh yes, I certainly don't want to miss out on that."

"It's not very large, so it won't take long," James chuckled. He added, "But if we are blessed with children, there is room to add on."

When James and Elizabeth returned to the store, they were pleased to see everyone gathered around the table participating in energized conversation.

While still holding hands as they entered, James squeezed Elizabeth's hand and commented, "I predict a prosperous future for us all."

Elizabeth smiled and nodded, then released his hand. She whispered, "It's probably too soon for them to see us holding hands, although in my father's eyes, you can do no wrong. And may I add, I feel the same way."

"Welcome back," said Randolph, amused as he caught a glimpse of the couple quickly separating their hands. "We're having a very productive meeting."

"I'm glad we came, Randolph," said Thomas. Then he addressed his daughter and her fiancé, "Now that you two have decided to join us, shall we discuss some wedding plans?"

The couple smiled and nodded.

"My favorite subject," said Elizabeth. "James and I haven't made any final decisions yet."

Jane interjected. "If everyone is in agreement, Thomas and I would like to host the wedding at our home."

"I would love that, Mother," exclaimed Elizabeth. She turned toward James, "If James agrees?"

"I would like nothing better," replied James with a wide smile.

Maggie said, "Of course Rachel and I will make the cake."

"And a beautiful cake it shall be!" exclaimed Rachel.

"Then it's settled," replied Thomas. "All that remains is a date!"

"We'll decide on a date soon, Father," said Elizabeth as she glanced at James.

Later that afternoon, Thomas peered outside and noticed grey clouds rolling in. "Well, I'm sorry to end this pleasant visit, but it looks like rain, so we'd better head back home."

James whispered to Elizabeth, "I'm looking forward to not having to say goodbye."

She smiled, hugged him, and joined her family as they walked to their boat.

James stood on the wharf and reluctantly watched them sail away until they disappeared around the bend.

Chapter 27

Late April 1856
Teekalet

A double wedding. Philip and Maggie and Peter and Rachel were about to wed. Everyone gathered at Philip's house. Mary, Elizabeth, and Annie filled the house with every flower that was available to pick. All of the Chinese women attended and happily helped with the decorations and food preparation. They added their own touch to the menu.

The minister who was to lead the ceremony arrived by boat along with a few of the Chinese women who lived at Teekalet. Meng, Jiao, and Samuel also arrived by boat. Meng walked in with Jiao by his side.

Billy had developed a relationship with one of the women living at the Bennett settlement whose name was Meifeng. They sat together. The room gradually filled up with family and friends. Meifeng stood and sang a song in Chinese. The family couldn't understand any of the words, but she sounded like a songbird.

The minister began the double ceremony. Finally, he said, "And now I pronounce both couples man and wife!" Everyone cheered.

Mary and Annie brought out the wedding cake they had made, which was beautifully decorated with flowers. They had used the bakery kitchen to bake the cake. Maggie and Rachel were moved by their kind gesture..

As Elizabeth and James watched the ceremony, they were thinking about their ceremony. They decided to marry the following month. "Let's announce right after the reception," said Elizabeth.

James had already thought about setting a date and announcing it at the wedding. Following the reception, James brought out a small box and handed it to Elizabeth.

"Open it," he said.

Elizabeth opened the box. She gasped. James took out an emerald and diamond engagement ring and slipped it on her finger. "Now, we can make the announcement."

"It's so beautiful," she said.

They joined the reception festivities. There were many toasts. James waited for the last toast, then he clanged his glass and stood. "I'm happy to announce our news. Elizabeth and I are getting married next month. We'll set an exact date once we check everyone's schedule."

James's uncle stood up with his glass, and toasted, "Here! Here!" Everyone raised their glasses and cheered.

Philip informed them he was scheduled to sail to San Francisco in the first week of June and Jonathan and Jeremy would be going with him, so James and Elizabeth decided the date for the wedding would be the last week of May.

Everyone else was fine with the schedule. Thomas and Jane said that of course the wedding would be held at their house. As previously promised, Maggie and Rachel would make the wedding cake. Another wedding was set.

Chapter 28

*E*lizabeth woke to the first rays of the morning sun streaming through her window ushering in a bright promise for this wedding day. She gazed about the room. It glowed in the soft, warm light. A single shaft of light spotlighted her wedding dress, her something old, which she had carefully draped over a chair. The ivory silk dress shimmered magically. It was her mother's wedding dress, who passed it on to her sister, Mary, to wear on her wedding day, and now it was Elizabeth's turn. Next to the chair on a small table was a string of pearls borrowed from her mother, and on the floor next to the chair was a beautiful pair of shoes adorned with blue ribbons. Her father made her the shoes to complete her wedding ensemble, just as he had done for his bride, and then daughter Mary. So Elizabeth had something old, something new, something borrowed and something blue. All that remained was a six-pence to put in her left shoe.

Although Elizabeth didn't feel hungry, her mother insisted she should eat a light breakfast. There were five place settings at the table set for her mother and father, her twin brothers, and herself. She thought, *This is my last breakfast with them as a single woman. There were once seven place settings and now, before long, there will be only two—each of us following our own path. Jemmie in San Francisco living with Oliver Scott, Jonny on the high seas with Uncle Philip, Mary running her household with her husband and Parker, and Emily in* Mazatlán, *soon to be a mother, but so far away.*

As Elizabeth sat down at the table, she said, "This is such a happy day for me, but I miss our whole family sitting together for a meal. At least I'll be able to see my brothers and Mary once in a while. But Emily is so far away. I miss my baby sister, terribly."

Thomas said, "Yes, I miss her too."

Jane added, "Thank goodness we know she is safe and where to find her. We'll be sure to visit her, especially when the babe is coming. I plan to be there with her when it's time."

Jonathan interjected, "I'll be checking on little sister every time Uncle Philip sails to Mazatlán."

"And don't forget about me," said Jeremy, "I expect to be picked up every time Uncle stops off at San Francisco on his way there."

Jane squeezed Elizabeth's hand, "Enough of this talk for now. Elizabeth, this is your day. Be happy."

"Thank you, Mother. I know I will. I'm marrying a wonderful, heroic man."

Thomas smiled at Elizabeth and reached into his pocket. "I have something for you, Lizzie." He handed her a silver sixpence. "This is for good luck. It's tradition for a father to give this to his daughter and wish her prosperity in her marriage. That's my wish for you and James."

Elizabeth raised from her chair and hugged her father. "What a special tradition. Thank you, Father."

Jane cleared the table and carried in a tray holding a pot of tea and six cups. "Mary will be here soon," she said.

Shortly thereafter, Mary arrived with a cheery smile, "Good morning, Mother, Father, Brothers. And you, dear Lizzy," she giggled, "Soon to be a married woman. I see I'm in time for tea."

After an enjoyable time conversing with her parents and siblings over tea, Elizabeth excused herself and returned to her bedroom to prepare for the wedding. Before her mother and Mary came in to help her, she brought out her journal and wrote:

Today, I become Mrs. James Mitchell.

* * *

James and his uncle arrived by boat along with the minister and many of the guests.

Although the house had been decorated, Elizabeth told her parents if it didn't rain, she wanted the ceremony to be held outside amongst the beautiful flowers and foliage. The lilacs were in full bloom, permeating the air with perfume, and she wanted them to be the backdrop for the ceremony. Like her mother, lilacs were her favorite flowers. She also had plans to surprise James with an unusual entrance.

The sun continued to shine for Elizabeth and James. Benjamin, Jeremy, and Jonathan escorted the guests to the garden where wooden benches, borrowed from the bunkhouse, provided seating.

On the stroke of the hour, the minister stood ready to marry the happy couple. Jane was the first to come down the aisle, escorted by her two sons, one on each side of her. Mary was the maid of honor and came down the aisle with Benjamin. Next came Maggie escorted by Philip, and then Rachel with Peter by her side.

Randolph had brought his violin and serenaded the audience with wedding music, and Rachel sang.

Then at the given signal, Randolph played the wedding march. James stood to one side near the minister awaiting his bride. To everyone's astonishment, Elizabeth entered on her horse, led by her father. James wasn't surprised over anything Elizabeth might do. He chuckled to himself to see she had even adorned her horse with flowers. He beamed and his eyes twinkled. His bride was a vision he would never forget. Her thin lace veil moved gently with the slight breeze as she moved toward him. She sat side saddle with her gown flowing to the side and held a bouquet of lilacs tied with a satin ribbon. Thomas led the horse in a slow walk to the end of the aisle. He lifted Elizabeth down and put her hand in James's hand. Jonathan stood ready to lead the horse away.

The ceremony began. As the couple looked into each other's eyes, Elizabeth and James exchanged their vows. Next came the ring ceremony with more vows pledging their love and devotion for one another. Then the minister smiled and announced, "May I present Mr. and Mrs. James Mitchell!"

As everyone clapped and cheered, the happy bride and groom embraced and kissed. It was their first real kiss.

The reception was held indoors. In May, there was always the possibility of a rain cloud passing through. The sound of merriment and toasts filled the air. For a final grand moment, Maggie and Rachel brought in a beautifully decorated wedding cake.

While everyone was conversing, Mary whispered to Benjamin, "I have something to tell you."

"What is it, Mary?"

Her eyes lit up. "We're going to have a child." She knew the reception would be a good time to tell Benjamin, so he could stand up and proudly share their news.

Benjamin could hardly contain himself. He kissed and hugged her.

Then he was worried about hugging her. "I'm not being too rough, am I?" He wasn't taking any chances with this child.

"No, Benjamin, you're not hurting me at all. I love seeing you so happy."

Benjamin took his first opportunity to announce their news. He stood up and clanged his glass, "I don't want to take anything away from James and Elizabeth, but I can't hold it in any longer." He grabbed Mary's hand and raised her to stand next to him. He put his hand around her trim waist. "Mary just told me we're going to have a child!"

James stood up, "Benjamin and Mary, we couldn't be happier for such a wonderful announcement with all of us here together. Congratulations. When might we expect this happy event?"

Mary replied as she smiled at Benjamin. "Possibly December. My birthday month! And Father's too!"

"Looks like another Christmas babe!" exclaimed Thomas.

James raised his glass, "Cheers!" Everyone joined in.

After the festivities, the bride and groom planned to go back to Seabeck. Rather than going elsewhere for a honeymoon, Elizabeth wanted to spend her first night with James in their cottage. Being with the love of her life was honeymoon enough for her.

Philip and Robert had volunteered to take them back to Seabeck in their workboat. To the couple's pleasant surprise, Jonathan and Jeremy had decorated it with garlands of cedar boughs and flowers.

* * *

Elizabeth and James looked forward to their life together in Seabeck, a young mill town situated along the Hood Canal. Elizabeth loved their little cottage with the white picket fence, and loved knowing she was the inspiration for the fence. She envisioned her favorite flowers in an English garden design.

Shortly after Elizabeth and James settled into the cottage, James surprised his bride with a lilac start from one of her mother's bushes. She would always think of her parents when she gazed at the lilac and the story of her father planting it as a surprise for her mother. Somehow, between creating a homestead and fighting in an Indian war, her father had managed to plant the lilac bushes. He knew his wife loved lilacs and wanted them to be waiting for her when she finally arrived at their new home after the long journey.

James and his uncle operated the general store together. There was no shortage of customers between the vast amount of lumber mill employees and the ship traffic coming into the port for the lumber.

With the involvement of the Bennett brothers, Randolph's business grew exponentially. Thomas and Robert continually provided their wares for the store, giving Randolph a much larger selection of items to offer his customers.

Soon, Randolph accumulated enough funds to make the diner a reality. He named his business *Mitchell's General Store & Diner* and made James an official partner.

"If it weren't for you, dear nephew, I would never have met the Bennetts. You've earned the partnership, and when I'm gone, this business will be all yours," said Randolph.

As ships came into port, the sailors anxiously disembarked and sprinted straight to the diner. The Mitchells served soup, sandwiches, pie, cake, and coffee. They kept Maggie and Rachel busy. Maggie's Lady Kay Apple pie was now famous and always sold out.

Before long, the Mitchells served breakfast. Elizabeth helped out and worked in the diner until extra help could be hired. She had noticed a very pleasant young woman who had become a regular in the diner. She always came in alone and routinely ordered a cup of the coveted Darjeeling tea, brought in from China. Elizabeth thought the woman would be a perfect candidate to interview for a job, so she approached her. The young lady was delighted for the opportunity.

During the interview, Elizabeth liked Isabel Warner so much, she offered her the job on the spot. Elizabeth felt confident that James and his uncle would trust her judgment.

Isabel was a single twenty-two-year-old attractive brunette who had come to Washington Territory with her family on the Oregon Trail in 1843. Her parents and six siblings were among the one thousand people who drove their wagons west from the small town of Elm Grove, Missouri. She was nine years old at the time.

Word spread about the hearty food and irresistible desserts at the diner. People stood in line for Maggie's apple pie and Rachel's coffee cake. Elizabeth didn't have the heart to quit, so she stayed on. Besides, she was very fond of Isabel and felt she had found a friend. As Elizabeth came to know Isabel, she began to think about her Uncle Robert. He was so alone, and Isabel was alone. Perhaps she should arrange a chance meeting for Isabel and her uncle. But how, with Isabel in Seabeck and Uncle Robert in Teekalet? *This was going to take some thought.*

Chapter 29

June 1856

San Francisco

*I*t was time for Philip to sail to San Francisco and then on to Mazatlán. Jonathan and Jeremy boarded the *California II*. The brothers had been looking forward to this trip.. Jonathan stayed by Philip's side in the pilothouse, and Philip let him take the wheel when the sea was calm. Soon the San Francisco Bay was straight ahead. As usual there was a fog bank, but the ship slid in without a problem.

Jonathan watched the crew unload the freight and then observed Philip as he negotiated with the buyers. He paid attention to every transaction, realizing one day he might be the one making the deals.

Jeremy followed through with his plans. He hailed one of the cabs lined up by the wharf and paid a visit to Oliver Scott.

"I'm back, Mr. Scott. If your offer still holds, I'm stopping by to tell you I want to join your business."

Oliver was excited to see Jeremy. He had wondered if he would ever see him again after he left to go to Puget Sound. He did need help in his business.

"I'm really happy to see you, Jeremy. I was selfish to hope you'd come back. I'm surprised to see you so soon. I insist you stay with me for your living quarters. I have plenty of space. I live one floor up above this office. No cabs necessary. By the way, please call me Oliver."

"Thank you, Mr. Scott, I mean, Oliver."

"If you have time, let's have a quick lunch before you return to the ship. We can discuss the business."

After Oliver and Jeremy talked business for an hour, Jeremy told Oliver about his passion for helping the Chinese women who were forced into the white slave market. He told him what he learned firsthand from the women they had rescued and also what he learned from his Chinese friend, Billy.

"I'd like to think we could help them somehow. We'll have to put some careful thought into it. It's dangerous, but I have people who can help us," said Oliver. "What are your plans at the moment, Jeremy?"

"I'm going on to Mazatlán with my uncle and Jonathan. Uncle has business with Alberto De Leon, and we'll be able to check on Emily at the same time. After we leave Mazatlán, we'll make a quick stop here to finish business before going home to Teekalet.

"Then in August, Uncle Philip will take Mother to Mazatlán, so that she can be with Emily during the birth of her babe. Jonathan and I will be going, too. After we leave Mazatlán, Uncle Philip will stop here to drop me off, and I'll be all yours."

"Sounds like you'll be busy for awhile. That'll give me time to prepare your room. It's filled with a lot of mementos from over the years. Lots of stuff. It's about time I did some sorting."

"I'm looking forward to working with you, Mr. Scott, er, Oliver. I'll see you in a couple of months." Jeremy shook hands with Oliver and caught a cab back to the ship.

Chapter 30

June 1856

Mazatlán

*P*hilip finished his business in San Francisco and navigated the *California II* to Mazatlán. Jonathan and Jeremy had never been to Mazatlán. They were excited and couldn't wait to see their sister. After a week of traveling, the *California II* entered the harbor. Samuel dropped anchor and Philip told Jonathan to sound the whistle. A boatman rowed out to transport them to shore. Philip's crew would be staying on board with the privilege of rotating shore leave while Philip, Jonathan, and Jeremy were gone.

Philip hailed a carriage and directed the driver to take them to the address of La Casa Grande. The brothers gazed out the carriage windows at the surrounding scenery and were enthralled with everything they saw. Puget Sound was beautiful country, but Mazatlán had its own special beauty. When the carriage driver entered the property, they passed under a large arch with a sign above, which read La Casa Grande. Then they saw the large two-story house surrounded with lush tropical vegetation, and just beyond, several Andalusian horses grazing in the fenced pasture.

The driver stopped in front of the house and the passengers climbed out, clutching their bags. Philip paid the driver. They walked up to the large carved door and tapped with the iron knocker. A servant answered, and Philip announced themselves. Alberto and Francesco weren't home yet, but Emily heard their voices and charged from the library to greet her family, embracing each of them.

"I'm so excited you're all here. Your first visit, dear brothers. Let's go into the living room where we can be comfortable." She used the bell pull for the servant to come to the living room and requested a refreshing drink for them.

"You seem to be doing okay, little sister. I always knew you'd be using a bell pull one day," chuckled Jonathan.

"Jonathan, you're just as silly as ever. Now tell me everything that's happened since I last saw all of you."

There was so much to talk about. The family had all agreed that the subject of what they did to Jones and his partner and the rescue of the Chinese women would be off limits. They knew it would make Emily happy to hear about it, but there was no guarantee she wouldn't share the story with Francesco and Alberto. Alberto was too close to the subject. How could they know who Alberto's connections might be? By happenstance, someone might learn about what they had done and take revenge. It was best to play it safe.

There was plenty of other news to share. Jeremy told her about his plans to work with Oliver Scott.

"Oliver said I have a natural talent to become an excellent private investigator, especially with his guidance. He's offered to allow me to live with him. That also means, sis, I'll only be a week away from you for visits."

Philip told her he was taking Jonathan under his wing to teach him everything about piloting a ship. "One day, your brother may be captain of his own ship."

"I'll be able to visit you too, Emily," Jonathan interjected. "Every time Uncle and I come to Mazatlán for business, we'll come to see you, and hopefully, pick up Jemmie along the way."

"That all sounds absolutely perfect," said Emily in an energized voice.

Philip interjected, "There's more good news, Emily. We had a double marriage ceremony—Maggie and me, and Rachel Bly married Peter Crandall."

"I'm so happy for you, Uncle. I hope I get to meet Maggie someday. Maybe you could bring her with you some time. Of course, I haven't met Peter and Rachel either."

"We're not finished yet on the subject of weddings," said Jonathan. "Elizabeth is married. Do you remember the man who brought back the mules and helped Mary and Elizabeth while we were in Nicaragua? His name is James Mitchell."

"I do remember him and what a handsome gentleman he was. I'm thrilled for her. But how did they end up together?"

"Well, there's more to the story." Then Jonathan told her about him being the man who saved their father's life, and how their father had invited him to come and visit the family after the Indian war was over. "The rest is history."

Jeremy added, "There's one last piece of good news. Mary and Benjamin are expecting a child. Possibly December. Wouldn't it be something if their babe was born on Mary's birthday?"

"You've brought so much good news." Then she stood up and gave them a profile image of herself. "I guess you can tell there's a babe in here." She patted her tummy. "It should be born sometime in September, I think. Would you ask mother if she could come and stay with me when the time is close?"

The brothers answered in unison, "Of course."

"Will you bring her, Uncle Philip?"

"You can count on it, Emily. I'll make sure Alberto and I schedule a business trip around that timeline. It'll be a nice change of scenery for her," said Philip.

Alberto and Francesco walked in. They were happy to see Philip and Emily's brothers had arrived. They all shook hands.

Alberto smiled warmly. "Welcome. I assumed you'd be here soon for the shipment, Philip. I see you brought along some help. Are you all enjoying your visit with our Emily?"

"Yes, we are. She looks a little different now," replied Jonathan.

Francesco put his arm around his wife. "She's carrying a precious package."

Emily chimed in. "They've brought so much news. And it's all good!"

Alberto invited them to stay as his guests, and they accepted. Philip said he would like to conduct business and load the products onto his ship the next day. "I already have buyers in San Francisco who advanced funds for the goods. The mill did as well. I must admit, the cigarillos and cigars seem to be in high demand, Alberto."

The next morning, they shared a hearty breakfast. Emily asked her uncle and brothers if they could stay an additional night. "I'm afraid we can't stay any longer this time, my sweet niece," replied Philip. "We have a schedule to keep."

The time went by much too fast. Emily dreaded seeing them leave.

As Philip and the brothers said goodbye, they hugged Emily and promised to see her again soon. Alberto's carriage and driver waited outside to take them back to town. Alberto and Francesco were going along to complete the business transaction.

When the transaction was finished, Philip shook hands with Alberto and Francesco, and said, "It's a pleasure doing with business with you. I foresee a long and profitable relationship. Until the next time."

After the cargo was loaded, Jonathan shouted to Samuel, "Release the lines and weigh anchor. We're ready to head back to San Francisco."

Chapter 31

Summer 1856

Teekalet

Spring had been a memorable and busy time with three marriages, Mary and Benjamin's announcement, and Jonathan and Jeremy announcing their plans. Now it was summer, and life was calmer. The Indian uprising on the western side of the Cascades had subsided, and the settlers heard rumors the militia on the eastern side had taken control of any Indians still on the warpath.

The Bennett family and their friends embraced their new life in Puget Sound. They worked hard, and with hard work came prosperity. The crops were plentiful once again and the orchards promised a good harvest.

* * *

The Hood Canal Bakery was thriving. With the help of the Chinese woman they had hired, Maggie and Rachel managed to keep up with the onslaught of orders.

Annie had been waiting for the right moment to ask her mother if she could leave the bakery. She had confided with Red Feather about her aspiration of becoming a nurse, and Red Feather encouraged her. Annie finally approached Rachel.

"Mother, do you think you and Maggie could manage without my help now?"

"I, I suppose so. Yu Yan is an excellent worker and has been a godsend. She could probably pick up the slack. What's on your mind, daughter?"

"I want to pursue nursing. I've known for quite some time it's what I must do. Dr. Ames said I'm a natural. He's even offered to teach me."

"Dr. Ames lives in Teekalet. Does this mean you want to move away? Where would you stay?"

"Yes, I would be moving. Dr. Ames and his wife have offered to take me in. Their children no longer live with them. He says they've all left the nest. They won't charge me anything either. Mrs. Ames had to step in to help her husband when his nurse married and moved away. She's anxious to be replaced. Ever since Red Feather came to stay with us, I've become even more determined. She's taught me many of her healing methods."

"I can see you're determined. It's an admirable profession. You've been looking rather preoccupied. Now I know the reason why."

"I mentioned it to Matthew a while ago. I needed someone to talk to before coming to you."

"He certainly kept your confidence. He didn't say a word to me. Now that you've mentioned Red Feather, how is she? I haven't spoken to her in quite some time. How is she faring with her husband being gone so long? She's so quiet, Peter and I hardly know she's around."

"She misses him terribly. She thought about going back to their cabin now that we seem to be out of danger, but Mr. Mallet told her to stay here until he comes to get her."

"Red Feather is welcome to stay as long as she likes. I'm sure Peter feels the same way. Now, my dear, I must get back to work. Maggie will wonder what has happened to me."

"One last thing, Mother. Do you think Peter would let me go with him the next time he goes to Teekalet so I can let Dr. Ames know?"

"I'm sure you can. I'll talk to him tonight."

* * *

Later that night, as Peter and Rachel prepared for bed, Rachel told Peter about Annie's plans to become a nurse.

"I'm not at all surprised. Since I was destined to become involved in Annie's plan, Matthew told me about it. Forgive me for not telling you, but I didn't think it was my place. And of course, I'll take her to Teekalet."

"You're a man of integrity, Peter." She smiled and laughed. "So, Mr. Crandall, are you holding on to any other secrets?"

He smiled back but didn't answer. Then as he removed his shirt, he said, "It's getting late, shall we turn in dearest?"

She gazed at the scar under his left shoulder blade, which had become a familiar sight to her since their wedding night. She reached out and lightly touched it, catching Peter by surprise. Her touch was warm and gentle, and he felt a comforting flow of energy between them.

Rachel asked, "Peter, how did you get that terrible looking scar on your back? It must have been painful."

Peter hadn't planned on telling her about his past, but he didn't want to start his marriage out with a lie.

"All right, Rachel, make yourself comfortable. This won't be a quick story, and it's not one I'm proud to tell."

"You have me very curious, Peter."

Peter stared at the floor for a moment and looked up with a solemn expression.

"Rachel, please understand the man you know right now, Peter Crandall, is who I want to be."

Rachel looked confused. "What do you mean? Aren't you Peter?"

"In my past life, I was Michael Harris and lived and worked in Montreal. I worked on ships, which transported furs to England, and so, I was in constant contact with the fur traders. They were a rough, surly bunch. Many of them married Indian women from the nearby Cree tribe, giving them an advantage over others to trade for fur pelts.

"One day I walked into the local trading post to secure some supplies and heard one of the trappers shouting obscenities at his Indian wife. I looked over in disgust. I noticed her face was terribly bruised. Then suddenly, he started hitting her in the face. He hit her so hard, he knocked her off the bench she was sitting on.

"Next, he grabbed her hair, yanking her up. I couldn't take it. I marched over and struck him in the face so hard my knuckles bled. Then I threw him across the room. I had never felt so strong, but I was so angry. While he was sprawled out on the floor, I went over to his wife and helped her to a chair.

"The trapper had several friends with him, and they promised they'd get even with me, so I decided I'd better make a fast exit. I turned to leave when suddenly, I felt a *thump* on the back of my left shoulder as though I had been punched, hard. It took my breath away and my knees buckled. Then I felt flashes of hot burning pain.

"I reached back using my right arm and felt a knife and warm blood on my hand. I reacted and turned around to see the coward rushing toward me. While we scuffled, he yanked his knife out from my back. I didn't realize it at the moment, but a gush of blood spurted out. I started to feel lightheaded, but when he shouted he was going to skin me alive, my adrenalin took over. I was sure he meant it quite literally. He swiped at me with his knife, back and forth, and cut my arm as I brought it up to defend myself. Next, when he lunged toward me, I managed to pull my gun from my waistband and shot him.

"At that point, I knew I needed to get out of there before someone tried to finish me off. While the trapper's friends hovered over him, I staggered out the door and got out of sight as quickly as possible. When I left, the trapper was still alive and moaning.

"My shoulder burned with pain and by then I had lost a lot of blood. Fortunately, my arm wasn't as bad since my jacket sleeve took the brunt of the cut. Instead of going to the sole doctor in town, I rushed to a certain ship where I knew there was a doctor on board. The last thing I wanted was to be found being treated by the same doctor who would soon be treating the trapper.

"Two days later, I saw wanted posters with my face on them plastered around town. I was wanted for murder, and there was a reward. Someone had sketched a pretty close likeness of me, including the scar over my left eye. Evidently, the trapper had died. I knew no one would testify on my behalf of it being self-defense, so I ran, and ran fast. My choice was to go to England or to go West.

"I ended up in San Francisco and planned to do what I knew best, work as a crewman on a ship. That's when I met your husband, Daniel. We struck up a friendship and decided to stay together and work on the same ships. Daniel was the one who convinced me to go to Washington Territory and claim land. The next ship was going to take us there, but it ended up in dry dock for repairs. And as you know, we ended up on the ill-fated *Theodora*."

"Oh, Peter, you've been through so much. Did Daniel know your story?"

"No, you're the only one I've told. From now on, I'm Peter Crandall."

"I like the man I see before me, and nothing you have said will go beyond these walls. You've touched my heart deeply to know you were willing to risk your well-being to help that poor Indian woman."

"It was just instinct, Rachel."

"No, Peter, it was much more than that, and I'm honored that you trust me with your secret."

* * *

Maggie and Rachel rushed to finish the pie and cake orders for the addicted dessert lovers of Teekalet. It was Tuesday, delivery day, and a cheerful, bubbly Annie assisted, humming to herself.

Rachel looked up at her daughter and commented, "Annie, I don't think I've ever seen you so excited." With tears welling in her eyes, she said with a voice full of sadness, "I'm happy for you, but the thought of you not being in my life daily saddens me. How am I to cope not seeing your sweet face at the breakfast table each morning? And when you are here with us, working by our side, you bring a ray of sunshine into the building."

"Mother, stop it now, you're going to make me cry. I promise to come and visit. I'm sure there will be times when Dr. Ames will be needed here, and I will be with him."

As mother and daughter embraced, they heard the bell chimes on the front door.

"Peter," said Rachel quickly composing herself, "you're right on time, and you have a most eager passenger."

Peter glanced at Annie, whose eyes were shining brightly. "Are you ready to go, young lady? If you like, you can give me a hand loading these delicious confections on to the boat."

"Oh yes, Peter. I'm ready." She looked at Rachel and Maggie, and gleefully announced, "I'll see you when we get back and fill you in on all the details."

* * *

After Peter finished loading the bakery order into the workboat, he helped Annie board.

"Looks like we're going to have a nice breeze to push us along, Annie."

"Does that mean we'll get there faster?"

"It certainly does."

While the boat sailed along, the two chatted.

Peter commented, "I understand Red Feather has had quite an influence on you. How did you meet her?"

"Do you remember when Thomas Bennett's shoulder was injured on the way back from Teekalet?"

"I do recall the story about a bear and a French mountain man."

"Yes. Afterward, the man and his wife, Red Feather, visited Mr. Bennett. She felt her husband was at fault, so she wanted to make up for it by healing Mr. Bennett's shoulder. She came regularly, so that's how I met her. We became good friends, and she taught me all about healing."

"Red Feather seems to have a different appearance than the local Indians. What tribe is she from?"

"She's from the Cree tribe in Montreal, Canada. That's where she met her husband Pierre Mallet. French is her second language, and Pierre began teaching her English soon after they married."

Although it was a warm summer day, Peter suddenly felt a chill. "Did you say Montreal?" *How could that be? What were the odds of someone from Montreal ending up here in the wilderness of the Pacific Northwest?* Wanting to know more, he probed, "That's a long distance away. How did they end up here?"

"Mr. Mallet worked in the fur trade with the Hudson Bay Company. According to Red Feather, he got tired of them trying to cheat him, so he worked his way to Fort Nisqually. He didn't find much improvement, so he quit working with them."

The more Peter learned, the less he liked it. *This is beginning to feel a little too close for comfort.*

As the boat skimmed up the canal, Annie looked over at the cluster of houses and buildings they passed. *I wonder if Dr. Ames lives in one of those houses.* The wharf was straight ahead.

"Here we are, Annie." Peter tied the boat off and helped Annie disembark. "Why don't you stay here and watch over our delivery while I get some help to unload it? Normally Billy comes along, but there wouldn't have been enough room for three of us. The order is so large, it's taken up most of the space!"

Peter walked over to the mill office and asked the manager if a couple of men could give him a hand dispersing the delivery.

"Part of the delivery goes to your cookhouse."

"Of course, Mr. Crandall," answered the manager who was suddenly in a merry mood. "Everyone's been waiting for the Tuesday delivery."

"Thank you. If I may inquire, sir, could you tell me where the doctor lives?"

"I'll have one of my men lead you to his house. It's not far away. I trust no one is ill or injured?"

"No, all is well. Just a visit."

The two men followed Peter to the boat. They nodded at Annie and helped Peter unload the orders.

"Annie, one of these men is going to lead you to Dr. Ames's house. It's only a couple of blocks away. Shall we agree to meet here at the boat in two hours?"

"That will be most satisfactory," quipped Annie. She picked up a parcel she had brought with her and followed the man to a two-story building with a sign above the front door, which read, *Medical Clinic.* Her heart beat a little faster as she read the words.

* * *

Annie thanked the mill hand and walked up a gravel path to the front door. She saw a sign in the window which read, *Open, Come in,* so she did. Dr. Ames was reading a chart, and a woman, most likely Mrs. Ames, was folding bandages.

They both looked up when the door chimes jingled.

"Annie! This is a pleasant surprise. Are you here with what I hope is good news?" Before she could answer, he turned toward his wife. "Annie, this is Mrs. Ames. She's been looking forward to meeting you."

"Pleased to meet you, Mrs. Ames. And, yes, Dr. Ames, I've come to let you know I'm now available." Then she held out her parcel to Mrs. Ames. "My mother insisted on sending her apple coffee cake along. She hopes you'll enjoy it."

"Marvelous, marvelous, on both counts," said the doctor in an exuberant voice.

"It's a pleasure indeed, Miss Annie," said Mrs. Ames. "Please thank your mother for us. We'll enjoy this cake immensely. Mr. Ames and I occasionally walk over to the hotel diner and treat ourselves to your mother's coffee cake."

"And sometimes the Lady Kay apple pie," interjected Dr. Ames. "Now, let us show you around. The clinic is on the ground floor."

The doctor gave Annie a tour of the entire clinic, taking up the first hour. Then he pointed to a staircase. "If you would like to follow us upstairs, we'll show you where we live, and soon, you. Speaking of soon, when can you start?"

"I thought I could come back next Tuesday with my belongings when Mr. Crandall delivers more orders. Maybe I could even bring a pie with me."

"Ah, Miss Annie, you're already learning to charm the doctor," chuckled Mrs. Ames. "Are you able to stay for a light supper, darling?"

"Thank you, Mrs. Ames, but I promised Mr. Crandall I would meet him back at the boat in two hours. I can't believe my time is nearly up. There was so much to see. As soon as I finish my tour up here, it will be time to say goodbye for now."

"Until next Tuesday, then," answered Dr. Ames.

* * *

While Annie was visiting the doctor, Peter finished the deliveries. His last delivery was at the hotel diner, so he decided to order a cup of coffee, and take a few private moments to ponder

---

over the unexpected and alarming piece of information he gained through Annie. He was still stunned to learn of Red Feather and Pierre Mallet originating from Montreal. It was obvious to him Red Feather hadn't shown any signs of recognizing him, which calmed him. *I can only pray it is the same with her husband. I'll be keeping my distance. I wonder how much longer he'll be gone?*

Peter was just finishing his coffee when he overheard a conversation at the next table.

One man said to the other. "I heard there's a ship coming in soon. The handful of volunteers and the guide who continued to the eastern side of the mountain are coming home. The Indian uprisings have slowed down, thanks to the militia."

Suddenly they heard the clatter of a coffee cup hitting the saucer. They turned to see that a man had just spilled his coffee.

* * *

After the two hours had passed, Peter and Annie rendezvoused at the workboat. Annie was bursting with excitement and chatted tirelessly the entire way back to the settlement. Peter was fine with that. He was in a despondent mood. Fortunately, Annie didn't seem to notice. When they returned to the Bennett wharf, Peter helped Annie from the boat.

"Thank you so much, Peter, for taking me with you. I'm so happy I could burst!"

"It was my pleasure, Annie. I know you'll make a fine nurse. We're going to miss not having you around here though."

Suddenly, Annie bounced over to Peter and surprised him with a hug, then dashed off to the bakery building to tell her mother and Maggie about her visit with the doctor and his wife.

* * *

A few days later when Peter and his new family and their guest, Red Feather, had sat down to supper, there was a knock on the door. They weren't expecting anyone, so Peter said, "I'll answer it."

When Peter opened the door, the unexpected visitor was Pierre Mallet. He and Pierre had never met face to face. Pierre couldn't believe who was standing before him. *This is the man on the poster!*

Pierre regained his composure and asked, "Good day, I've come for Red Feather. I was expecting to find Annie and her family here. Who are you?"

"I'm Peter Crandall. Welcome to our home." Peter shuddered when he realized who was standing in front of him. Trying to remain calm, he said, "You must be Pierre Mallet, Red Feather's husband? Please come in. Red Feather has been most anxious for your return. I heard about your excellent tracking skills as a guide. I'm surprised we never crossed paths while we dodged bullets and arrows during the uprising. The fact that you're back must be a good sign."

Although confused about the house belonging to Peter, Pierre replied, "Yes, the Governor finally released me. The militia has completely taken over. I believe we can all rest easy now." His eyes darted past Peter wondering where the family was. He didn't like the idea of Red Feather being alone with this man.

Peter sensed Pierre's uneasiness. "We have all just sat down for supper. Would you care to join us?" He motioned Pierre toward the dining area.

"*Merci, monsieur, j'accepte.* I haven't had a good meal in months."

The family could hear voices, and by the sound of Pierre's French accent, Red Feather knew her husband was back. She beamed when he walked in with Peter.

Peter looked at his wife, "Rachel, would you set another plate? Mr. Mallet is joining us for supper."

Matthew quickly stood up and said, "I'll get another chair."

Pierre kissed Red Feather on the cheek and sat down. "I've missed you, Red Feather."

"And you, my husband. Mr. And Mrs. Crandall have been so kind and generous to me."

Pierre raised a quizzical eyebrow.

"Oh Pierre, of course, you wouldn't know," said Annie. "My mother and Peter married a few months ago."

Pierre looked at Peter and Rachel, "My congratulations." Then he decided it was good timing to delve into Peter's background. "Where are you from, Peter?"

Peter and Rachel exchanged glances. "Well, Pierre, I like to say I've come from the brink of death." He continued to tell him about the *Theodora* disaster. "Rachel's husband and I had become very close. I'm sure he'd be happy if he knew I was watching over his family."

Rachel nodded.

Pierre continued his questioning of Peter. "If you don't mind my asking, where did you hail from before San Francisco?"

Rachel sensed Peter was beginning to feel cornered. She didn't understand why Pierre was so inquisitive about her husband. She glanced at Peter, smiling, and craftily changed the subject.

"Pierre, I must tell you. Red Feather has had quite an influence on my Annie." She looked over at Annie. "Annie, why don't you tell Mr. Mallet about your special plans."

Annie was only too happy to talk about her upcoming nursing career. After that, the conversation continued to flow away from Peter. He was impressed with Rachel's agility to protect him. Other than Daniel Bly and the Bennetts, he wasn't used to anyone being on his side.

The meal ended on a cordial note. Pierre had caught on that perhaps he was coming across too intense in questioning Peter and backed off. He created a diversion by talking about his experience on the eastern side of the mountain.

* * *

Red Feather was happy to be back in their little cabin in the woods with her husband. Although it was summer, there was a slight chill in the air as dusk crept upon them. Pierre lit the stove, already filled with wood. Red Feather put on the kettle to brew one of her relaxing teas. Pierre was exhausted and told her he was retiring early. He pulled the curtain across their sleeping quarters. He intended to be alone while he retrieved the wanted poster from under his mattress. He set the poster on the bedside table next to the lamp and studied it. *Yes, it is the same man right down to the scar over his left eye, and I now have a name to go along with the face.* He needed to come up with a plan.

As he lay in bed, scheming of what he should do next, he fell asleep, neglecting to put the poster back into its hiding place.

The next morning, Red Feather woke to shafts of early light washing over her face. She looked over at Pierre, who was deep asleep. She would let him sleep and have a hearty breakfast waiting for him. Before she left their room, she glanced back at him. Next to the lamp, she noticed some sort of poster lying on the table. She was alarmed to see it was a wanted poster for murder. And more importantly, the face staring back at her, was none other than that of Peter Crandall. She picked it up to examine it more closely. The assailant's name was unknown, but the victim's name was listed. She was shocked when she recognized the man's name who had been killed. It nearly took her breath away. She clutched the poster and gasped.

Red Feather knew of this incident.

Pierre woke to see Red Feather holding the poster in her hand with a look of horror on her face. He snatched it from her.

"My husband, now I understand why you asked Peter Crandall so many questions. Are you planning to turn him in to collect the reward? You mustn't do it!"

"Yes, Red Feather, I'm going to turn him in, and you can't stop me. All I have to do is bring the Hudson Bay authorities from Fort Nisqually here to arrest him. I have it all planned. We can use the money."

"But husband, I know who the dead man was, and I know what happened. Please, let me tell you what I know."

Pierre sat down on the edge of the bed, staring at the poster. He frowned. "I guess it can't hurt to listen."

"Like you, my husband, the man killed was a trapper who traded with our tribe. He did the same as you and asked to marry a woman from our tribe. He chose my cousin, Spring Rain. Soon, our chief granted him permission. They lived not far from the trading post, and some times I visited my cousin. There were times she wouldn't let me in even though I begged her and pounded on the door.

"Finally, one day she opened the door. She was crying. She told me after her husband had beaten her, she made the mistake of turning away from him in their bed. He was furious and raped her. She said her husband was always cruel to her, especially when he drank. It was around this time you began trading with my people, and you seemed interested in marrying me. I feared I would have the same fate as Spring Rain. I also knew the chief would grant your wish.

"One day Spring Rain came back to our tribe. She arrived badly beaten. Even some of her hair had been ripped from her scalp. Some of the other women and I rushed to comfort her. It was then that she told us her husband had been killed. I for one was not disappointed the evil man was dead.

"Spring Rain spoke about a kind white man who came to her aid. She watched the white man give her husband a sound beating. Immediately afterward, the man hoisted her up from the floor and helped her to a chair. Spring Rain said when the white man turned to leave, her husband picked himself up from the floor and threw his knife into the man's back. Spring Rain was horrified and feared her husband had killed the man.

"The white man started to fall but grabbed the back of a chair to hold himself up. Then she said her husband rushed to the man and pulled the knife from his back and blood started spurting everywhere.

"She watched her husband attack the man again with his knife shouting he was going to skin him alive. When her husband lunged at the man, Spring Rain saw the man turn, pull out his gun, and shoot her husband. She said it was self-defense. The white man stumbled out the door, and Spring Rain never saw him again. She would have liked to thank him. He had set her free.

"Not long after the killing, you asked to marry me. I could not disobey. The chief said it was for the good of the tribe. Our marriage didn't begin with love, but you were kind to me and treated me with respect. I thank you for that, my husband."

Pierre was quiet for a moment. He contemplated what he should do next. He decided to give Peter Crandall a chance to tell his side of the story. If his story matched Red Feather's story, he wouldn't turn Crandall in.

"Very well, Red Feather. I'm not an unreasonable man. I'll confront Crandall and allow him the to tell his side of the story. If it doesn't match what you've told me, I'm turning him in."

Red Feather sighed with relief, "Thank you, my husband."

Pierre never realized Red Feather had been afraid to marry him.

It was true, the marriage had started as a business deal, but gradually he had come to love her. *Does she know? Should I tell her now?*

That night when they went to bed, Pierre said, "Red Feather?"

"Yes, my husband?"

"Do you ever fear me?"

"No, you have always been kind."

"Red Feather, do you know that I love you?"

"You have never said so, but when you were worried about my safety, I felt your love. I am happy you have finally told me."

"Do you love me, Red Feather?"

"Yes, my husband, I've loved you for many moons."

* * *

"May I come with you, my husband? I want to be there for Rachel." She was nervous for her friend.

"Only if you promise to say nothing to Peter Crandall, Red Feather."

"I promise, my husband."

The couple arrived at the Bennett settlement by canoe. After securing the canoe to the wharf, Pierre and Red Feather walked up the path toward Peter Crandall's house. They found Peter working in his garden.

Pierre stopped, and said, "Red Feather, I prefer to be alone with Peter Crandall. Why don't you go to the house and visit with Rachel. If you don't find her there, you'll probably find her at the bakery."

"Yes, my husband."

The couple went their separate ways.

Pierre waved to Peter as he approached him. Peter put his shovel down, to Pierre's relief, and walked toward him.

"Well, Pierre. What can I do for you?" He noticed Pierre looked quite serious and wondered why. *This doesn't feel right. I don't think it's a social visit.*

"*Bon jour,*" he said in a serious tone. "I have something to show you."

Pierre brought out the poster from inside his shirt and held it up. "This looks like you, does it not? What do you have to say about this?

I've been waiting for this moment since before the Indian uprising. I didn't turn you in because we needed every man with a gun. What is to stop me now? All I need to do is go to Fort Nisqually and send the Hudson Bay authorities here to arrest you. And, I'll collect the reward."

Peter couldn't believe the wanted poster had made its way to Washington Territory. He swallowed hard. His face felt like stone. *My worst fear is happening.* He asked, "How did you get this?"

Pierre told him he and Red Feather were originally from Montreal. He traded with the Cree Indian tribe, which is where he met Red Feather, and not long after, chose her to be his wife. One day as he was entering the trading post, he noticed the poster with a reward on the front of the building and took it.

Peter implored Pierre to listen to his story.

Pierre listened without saying a word. Peter couldn't read him. He could only pray Pierre believed him. Peter didn't want to run any more. If he ran, he would have to desert Rachel. It was an impossible situation, and the outcome appeared to be in this Frenchman's hands.

Pierre prided himself as a fair and honest man. He had to admit to himself that Peter's story matched Red Feather's story, right down to the trapper saying he would *skin Peter alive.* A trapper who was accustomed to skinning pelts and hides could easily do such a thing if he could forcefully restrain a man and the trapper had friends to assist him. Pierre decided he believed Peter, and not only did he believe him, but he judged him to be a courageous and honorable man.

Pierre extended his hand out to Peter. "I believe you, Peter, and I will tell you why."

Then Pierre told him about Red Feather's story and the two stories matching.

Peter could breathe again. He sighed. His wonderful new life was no longer in jeopardy. He responded, "Pierre, I could use a swig of whiskey. How about you?"

Pierre put his arm on Peter's shoulder, and the two men walked to the house together.

Red Feather and Rachel walked up just in time to witness this unexpected act of friendship. Red Feather had shared her story with Rachel, and Rachel realized it matched Peter's story. The ladies happily walked arm in arm to the house to join their husbands.

When the two women entered the house, they noticed Peter had grabbed the jug of whiskey, and the two men were passing it back and forth, smiling and laughing.

As Pierre took another swig, he slurred to Peter, "*Mon frère*, did you know we have the same name? My name Pierre means Peter in English. A very good sign, *non*?"

Rachel breathed easier to see the joviality filling the room and walked toward the stove. "Shall we have tea, Red Feather? I still have some of the tea you brought us."

"I would like that, Rachel."

Rachel put the kettle on and opened the stove to stoke the wood.

Pierre noticed and walked over to her. "Let me do that, *ma chère*."

Then he pulled out the poster from his shirt and threw it into the flames. Rachel caught a glimpse of Peter's face on the sheet of paper as the flames devoured it. Pierre shut the stove door. A final act of closure.

That night Peter asked Rachel, "My dear, since there's no need to hide my face anymore, would you like me to trim some of this bushy beard off?"

"I would indeed, Peter. I have wondered what the man whom I love looked like behind that beard."

Peter's eyes widened in a state of wonderment. Had he heard her correctly or was it just wishful thinking and his imagination? "Did I hear you say love, Rachel?"

"Yes, Peter, I *do* love you."

Peter was ecstatic and wrapped his arms around her.

Chapter 32

Early August 1856
Seabeck

*I*t was Wednesday, the Seabeck delivery day for Thomas and Robert. On this trip, Jane decided to come along for a visit with her daughter and son-in-law. She was scheduled to leave the following week on the *California II* to sail to Mazatlán to be with their youngest daughter, Emily, whose due date for the Bennetts' grandchild was sometime in September.

In the pale light of dawn, Robert and Thomas loaded the workboat with the Seabeck orders. Jane had been waiting patiently on the wharf.

"You're next, my lady," said Thomas as he extended his hand out to her, "Let me help you board."

Robert hoisted the sails. "There's a good breeze. We should make good time."

* * *

As the Bennetts entered the Seabeck harbor, they noticed an increased flurry of activity since their initial visit in the spring. The recently built lumber mill had rapidly flourished and along with it, the once sleepy little town of Seabeck. Thomas and Robert were impressed by what they saw.

Finally, they eased the workboat next to the store's wharf. Robert hopped out and tied the lines, and said, "I'll let Randolph and James know we're here. It'll take all of us to transfer this order to their warehouse."

Thomas helped Jane disembark. Then Robert extended his arm to her. "Allow me to escort you in, Jane."

"Thank you, Robert. I'm so excited to see Elizabeth. She didn't know I was coming along. She'll be surprised."

"See you in a few minutes," said Thomas, who was already starting to unload the order onto the wharf.

Robert opened the door, and the brass bells jingled indicating the arrival of a visitor. He ushered Jane in first. A young woman whom they had not met greeted them.

"Good day," she said. "How may I help you?"

Jane replied, "Good day to you. I'm Jane Bennett, Elizabeth's mother." Then she turned toward Robert, "And this gentleman is her uncle, Robert Bennett."

Robert removed his beaver fur felt hat, and responded in a deep voice, "I'm pleased to meet you, and what is your name if I may ask?"

Isabel was so mesmerized with Robert's penetrating hazel eyes and his rugged good looks, she was stunned. She wondered if she might fall into a swoon.

Then the awestruck young woman broke from her trance and replied, "You certainly may ask. My name is Isabel Warner."

Robert, in turn, was transfixed by the spark he felt between them. For the first time since England, he found himself drawn to a woman. Isabel was like a younger version of his beloved Eleanor, not only because of her large brown doe eyes and warm brown hair but her demeanor. He suddenly realized he had been staring too long, and he needed to get back to business. *Poor Thomas is out there waiting.*

Jane noticed the chemistry between Robert and Isabel. She thought, *It's about time Robert finds a love interest.*

Momentarily, James and Randolph walked in. After hugging Jane, James said, "Mother Jane, this is a surprise. You'll find Elizabeth in the diner. She'll be excited to see you, and now that you are here, she has some news to share."

"You have piqued my interest, James. I'll dash right over while you men tend to business." *I wonder if we're going to be blessed with another grand baby?*

After the men shook hands, Randolph said, "Have you met Isabel, our new employee?"

Robert glanced at Isabel, and with a slow smile, locked eyes with her. He held his gaze with Isabel as he answered Randolph. "Yes, it has been my pleasure." Then he opened the door and gestured toward the wharf. "Thomas and I have your order. He's unloading it from the boat as we speak. We'll need help to transfer it to your warehouse."

"We're right behind you, Robert," said James.

As soon as the men exited, Isabel hurried to the window to watch Robert lead the way to the workboat. Her face was still pink from the rush of heat she felt when Robert gazed at her while he answered Randolph's question. *My goodness, that man makes my heart flutter.*

* * *

Elizabeth was surprised and excited when her mother walked into the diner. She had just finished waiting on a few sailors who had disembarked from the latest ship in port. Each appeared to be in ecstasy eating a slice of Lady Kay apple pie.

"Mother! I'm so happy to see you." Elizabeth threw herself into her mother's open arms. "Come, we can sit in the corner by the window. Would you like a cup of tea?"

"Yes, Lizzy, that sounds most appealing." *Hearing good news over a cup of tea couldn't be more perfect,* she thought.

Shortly, Elizabeth brought a tray with a teapot, cups and saucers, and a plate of shortbread. "I brought out my best china," she said, "This is a special occasion." Then she poured the tea, grinning.

Jane took a sip of tea and smiled. "I understand from James you have something to tell me?"

Elizabeth shook her head back and forth, "Oh that James. I'm surprised he didn't tell you himself. He's so excited." She broke into a gleeful smile. "Mother, you and Father are going to be grandparents again!"

Jane quietly clapped her hands. "I was hoping that was the news. I'm absolutely thrilled, sweetheart. And when will this happy event occur?"

"If I have calculated correctly, it will be in the spring. May, I think."

"How wonderful. The season of new beginnings, and I might

add the month of your wedding anniversary. Your father will be ecstatic. It will be such a blessing to have a grandchild near us."

"You must be thinking about Emily. How soon are you going to Mazatlán?"

"Soon, darling. That's why I came for a visit. I'll be gone at least a month. I want to be with her during and after the birth of our grandbaby."

"You'll be busy, Mother, especially with Mary and Benjamin's babe expected in December."

"We are truly blessed, Lizzy. Our family is growing."

Elizabeth pondered for a moment. "Mother, I worry about Uncle Robert. He's been alone for such a long time. There's always a faraway look in his eyes. He needs someone in his life, and I've been think—"

"Sorry to interrupt, but I know exactly what you are thinking. Perhaps the delightful lady I met when we came into the store? Isabel, by any chance?"

"Yes, Mother, exactly. She's alone too. I really like her, and I don't want her to end up as a spinster. From the moment I met her, I thought about her being a perfect match for Uncle Robert. I just have to figure out how to make it happen!"

"From what I witnessed this morning upon our arrival, you may not have to try very hard to get them together. They couldn't keep their eyes off each other. It was rather entertaining to watch them."

Elizabeth had the same habit as her mother when she was excited. She quietly clapped her hands. "That is the best news. It couldn't be more perfect! I thought I was going to have to come up with some elaborate plan to have them *accidentally* meet." She pondered, "But now I have to figure out how to keep the pendulum swinging. There's a bit of distance between here and Teekalet."

"I have no doubt you'll come up with something, dear daughter. You've always been very resourceful."

At that moment they heard the men come in. They had finished transferring the order to the warehouse.

James grinned at Elizabeth, "I'm afraid I couldn't keep from blurting out our news to your father. "Do you mind, darling?"

Before Elizabeth could answer, Thomas hugged her. "Lizzy, I couldn't be happier with the news. Don't be too hard on James," he chuckled. "He looked like he was about to burst about *something,* so I pried it out of him."

The family continued to chat while Randolph served coffee to Thomas and James.

Elizabeth looked for Robert. "Where's Uncle Robert?"

"He said he wanted to check the fur displays in the store," replied Randolph.

Elizabeth and her mother grinned at each other.

Thomas noticed and asked, "What are you two up to?"

Jane snickered, "Don't you realize why he's *really* there? Is there not a charming young lady there as well?"

"You mean Isabel?"

"Honestly, Thomas, sometimes men are so oblivious to what is right in front of them."

Thomas's mind flashed back to the early days of their marriage. *Jane thought I hadn't noticed the red-headed Anita eyeing me. Little did she know.*

* * *

Robert walked over to one of the display tables holding several fur accessories. He straightened an item, which didn't need straightening. Acting preoccupied, he periodically stole a glance at Isabel when he thought she wasn't looking. The intriguing young woman was on the opposite side of the room also tending to fur displays, which didn't need tending.

Robert couldn't help noticing how Isabel slowly stroked the fur accessories, which seemed extremely sensual to him. He loosened his shirt collar. He was beginning to feel warm. He reprimanded himself, *What am I thinking?!*

Isabel was well aware of Robert's attention, and she knew exactly how she was affecting him as she stroked the fur. Although she shocked herself, she smiled. *How else am I going to get his attention?*

Much to the couple's disappointment, their subtle *mating* dance was cut short. Thomas and James entered the room.

Grinning, Thomas said, "Well, Robert, you missed out on coffee, but somehow I don't think you mind. I'm afraid it's time for us to leave, if we're going to get back before dark."

Everyone said their goodbyes. Isabel extended her hand to Robert, smiling demurely. Robert half-bowed, then lightly kissed the delicate hand, and lingered, while meeting her eyes.

After the Bennetts arrived back to the settlement, Robert pulled Thomas aside and offered a suggestion. "Thomas, I should be able to handle the next Seabeck delivery alone. That will free you up to continue our work here."

"If you insist, Robert." Thomas could hardly contain his laughter.

Chapter 33

August 1856

Mazatlán

*J*ane began making preparations for her trip to Mazatlán. She wanted to arrive well before the babe was born, and September wasn't far off. Thomas's foresight to hire one of the Chinese women made it easier for Jane to leave, and also easier for her to stay awhile with Emily after the babe was born. By now, enough time had passed for Lien hua to become familiarized and comfortable with the household.

It was mid-August when the *California II* entered the Mazatlán harbor. Jane saw Mazatlán and its majesty for the first time. She had been told about the grandeur of the house and gardens of La Casa Grande, but upon entering the estate, it was beyond anything she had visualized. She followed Philip, Jeremy, and Jonathan to the carved front door while the driver unloaded Jane's baggage and set it on the porch. Philip tapped the iron knocker, and the servant promptly answered the door. Knowing they were family, she invited them in. Emily had been expecting her mother to arrive any day. When the servant informed Emily she had company, she charged into the room with excitement.

Jane embraced her tightly and laughed. "Emily, there's more of you to hug it seems. You look beautiful. I see you've kept your weight down. Good girl."

"*Bienvenidos a nuestra casa!*" exclaimed Emily, grinning at her mother and brothers.

Jane laughed. "I see you're learning the local language. So tell me, what did you just say?"

"I said, welcome to our home!" Emily replied proudly. "I've been learning from the servants. They're having fun teaching me. Oh,

Mother, I'm so happy you're here to stay awhile. We'll have the rest of the summer together. You'll like it here."

As Jane's eyes darted around the room, she answered, "From what I've already seen, I'm quite sure I will. Emily, you'll be happy to know I didn't forget to bring your wardrobe trunk. All those pretty dresses will give you the incentive to get your figure back. Also, I have gifts from your father and me. We have each made something for your babe. My gift to you will carry on a family tradition, which started two generations ago."

"Thank you, Mother. I can't wait to open it, but I'll force myself to wait for some quiet time for us together."

"That sounds perfect, Emily."

Jonathan teased Emily. "Little sister, you've certainly changed since we saw you last."

"I think that's an understatement," replied Jeremy, chuckling.

Emily hugged her brothers and uncle. "I'm so glad you're all here. Thank you, Uncle, for bringing Mother to me."

"You're very welcome," replied Philip.

Alberto and Francesco were in the library and recognized the voices. They hastened to greet their visitors.

"It's wonderful to see you again," said Francesco. He and his father kissed Jane on each cheek and shook hands with Philip, Jeremy, and Jonathan.

"Welcome," said Alberto. He turned to Philip. "How long are you staying? Naturally, you're welcome to stay as long as you like."

"That's very gracious of you, Alberto," said Philip. "We would love to stay longer. However, I'm afraid it will be a short visit for us. We'll need to get an early start in the morning to take care of business at your factory and head back to Frisco. We'll plan to visit longer on the next trip when we return to take Jane back home."

"I was quite sure that would be the case, but for now, relax. And now Francesco and I will leave you all to enjoy your visit with Emily. We'll look forward to dining with you tonight."

Francesco leaned down to kiss Emily on the cheek, who was sitting in the only chair in which she felt comfortable. "I will see everyone this evening," he said, nodding at the family.

That night the De Leons and the Bennetts shared good food, good wine, and good conversation.

The following morning, Philip, Jonathan, and Jeremy said goodbye to Jane and Emily, and left with Alberto and Francesco to go back to Mazatlán. This time Philip needed a larger quantity of De Leon products. Alberto and Francesco were more than happy to oblige and instructed their workers to help Philip's crew load the large shipment.

"Business is good at the moment, Alberto. I'm sure I'll be back for another order in a few weeks. I'm expecting an order from the Hawaiian Islands next."

The men shook hands, and Philip and his nephews boarded the ship. Samuel weighed anchor as Jonathan sounded the whistle, and the *California II* steamed her way back to San Francisco.

Chapter 34

August 1856

San Francisco

*O*ne week after leaving Mazatlán, Philip guided his ship into the Golden Gate harbor.

After turning the ship over to Samuel, Philip and his nephews disembarked. Philip took a deep breath. "Smell that moist marine air. Mazatlán is a little too warm and humid for my liking.

"Jonathan, say goodbye to your brother. While I take Jeremy to Oliver's office, I'm leaving you in charge to oversee the unloading of the De Leon merchandise. I won't be gone long. On my way back, I'll be bringing the buyers here to finalize the sale. Make sure everything is orderly and appealing."

"Wow, do you trust me to do all that, Uncle Philip?" responded Jonathan while looking wide-eyed at the intimidating size of the shipment.

"I have confidence in you. I'm sure you won't disappoint me."

I sure hope he's right, thought Jonathan. Then he gave his twin brother a big bear hug. "I'm going to miss you, Jemmie. This is our first time to be separated. I'm more than a little sad."

"And I as well, Jonny. Tell you what, let's promise to look up at the stars at the same time. I know how you love all that. How about every Sunday night at nine o'clock? Maybe we'll even feel each other's energy."

"Agreed," said Jonathan, "and every time Uncle Philip and I come to Frisco, I'll be seeing you. Maybe you'll be joining us to visit Emily when we go to Mazatlán. That is if you're not in the middle of some *big* case Mr. Private Investigator."

Philip had hailed a cab while the twins said goodbye. "Okay, boys. Time's up. Grab your bags, Jeremy."

With a final wave to Jonathan, Jeremy followed Philip to the cab.

Jonathan lingered for a moment as he watched the cab pull away. *Now, I have work to do. I'm going to make Uncle proud of me.*

A few minutes later the cab rolled to a stop in front of Oliver Scott's building. "Welcome to your new home, Jeremy," said Philip. They both stepped from the cab. "I'm glad I had the opportunity to become better acquainted with Oliver. He's compassionate and a man of integrity. If I didn't feel confident about him, I would have a difficult time leaving you here alone."

"I'm very fond of him, Uncle. He almost seems like a grandfather to me. Something I was going to miss."

"I understand, Jeremy. For now, I'll say goodbye. I emphasize, *for now.* I'll be back. The cab is waiting, so I won't go in. I'm short on time to meet the buyers. Please give my regards to Oliver, and tell him we'll all get together for a visit on my next trip."

"I will Uncle, and thank you for taking me to Mazatlán and for bringing me here."

"You're very welcome, Jeremy." Philip handed Jeremy his duffel bags, then watched him walk up the steps and enter the building. *What does the future hold for him?* He hopped back into the cab. "To the next address, driver."

* * *

Jeremy entered Oliver's office and greeted the receptionist. "Good morning, Dorthea, I don't know if you remember me. I'm Jeremy Bennett, and I'm here to see Mr. Scott."

"Yes, Jeremy, of course I remember you. I don't think it would be possible to forget you. Mr. Scott talks about you all the time. Let me tell him you're here. He'll be very pleased."

Dorthea returned with Oliver following close behind her.

"Jeremy, my man! You're here. To stay, am I correct?"

"Yes, sir."

Oliver was barely able to control his excitement. He pointed at the stairs. "Follow me, young man. Your room awaits you. Are you hungry? We can go out for a nice mid-day meal if you like. I usually eat here. Do you like to cook?"

"Eating here will be just fine. I cook a little, but I can learn to do more."

"Excellent, it will be nice to taste someone else's cooking for a change. Once a week my niece comes and cooks a nice meal for me. I've told her all about you. She's looking forward to meeting you."

"I'm looking forward to everything, Oliver. This is the most exciting thing I've ever done, and the first time to be away from my family. At least I'll see my uncle and brother when they come to Frisco, and every once in a while I'll be able to visit Emily if our schedule allows. Oh, and Uncle Philip passes on his regards, he was short on time this trip. He said we'd all get together on his next trip here."

"I'll look forward to that. Day after tomorrow, my niece will be coming, so you two can get acquainted. Now, let me show you around."

* * *

Back at the wharf, Philip arrived with his buyer. The sale closed quickly. Philip was pleased with Jonathan's presentation of the merchandise. "Jonathan, you did an excellent job. You orchestrated a good first impression for my buyers. Did you see how fast our shipment sold? I had to use self control to save some merchandise for the mill owners in Teekalet. You did such a good job I'm going to pay you a small commission." *My nephew passed his first test. He's going to work out just fine.*

"Thanks, Uncle. At first, I felt intimidated, but I wasn't about to disappoint you. I'm determined to handle any task you give me. Did Jeremy get settled?"

"I'm sure he did. I didn't go in. I waited a couple of minutes to make sure he found someone there. I told him to tell Oliver we will all get together on our next trip here."

"I'll look forward to that for sure. I already miss my brother."

"Are you ready to go back to Teekalet? Why don't you let Samuel know we're ready to weigh anchor."

"Yes, sir, Captain Bennett," said Jonathan with a wide smile.

Chapter 35

September 1856

Mazatlán

The time passed too quickly for Emily and her mother. Now it was September, and the time for the baby to enter the world was close at hand.

Emily complained, "Mother, my back hurts and the pains are starting. I think I'm in labor." The labor continued for several hours. "I never imagined so much pain," Emily said as she stood, gripping onto the back of a chair.

"It won't be much longer, Emily." Jane thought about her own experience of giving birth to Emily. The two of them could have died. She prayed her daughter would have an easier time.

Jane called out, "Francesco, tell the midwife it's time. Please hurry."

Francesco sprinted up the stairs to fetch her. Since the midwife lived so many miles away, Alberto had insisted she stay at the house when the due date was close. He wasn't taking any chances with his grandson. At first, the midwife protested, but Alberto was a very persuasive man, especially when he handed the midwife more money than she could have earned in several months. Many of the people she helped had little or no money, and for payment, gave her baked goods or produce from their garden.

"You'll be very comfortable here, Mrs. Santiago," Alberto had told her.

She had countered with her own terms. "I'll stay on two conditions, Mr. De Leon. People must know where to find and contact me, and if I receive an urgent request while I'm waiting for Emily's time, you must allow me to respond, and you'll provide transportation."

"I'll agree to that, Mrs. Santiago, as long as you don't try to leave when my grandson decides he's ready to come."

Now the baby was ready. Mrs. Santiago and Francesco rushed down the stairs. Emily and Jane were in the library.

"Francesco, carry your wife up to your bedroom where she'll be more comfortable and private. You and your father will have to stay out of the room until we call you in," ordered the midwife.

More hours passed. Finally, with the help of the midwife and Jane, Emily gave birth to a baby girl. Francesco and Alberto had been pacing the hall outside the door the entire time.

Mrs. Santiago handed the infant to Jane while she tended to Emily. Emily craned her head to see her baby while Jane cleansed her.

As Jane handed the baby to Emily, she said, "Here is your beautiful baby girl. She reminds me of you when you were born."

"Oh, Mother, I hope Francesco won't be disappointed. I wonder how Alberto is going to react. He was sure we were having a boy."

Jane answered in a protective voice. "They'll have to accept it and be grateful you're both fine. You couldn't control if it were a boy or girl, and I'll tell them so."

The midwife was finished taking care of Emily and called the men in.

Francesco rushed to Emily's bedside. Alberto stood a polite distance away.

"Francesco, we have a daughter," exclaimed Emily as she studied Francesco's face to read his reaction.

He bent down and kissed Emily and his daughter. "I can't help it," he said, "She already has my heart. I've been thinking about names. I already knew if we had a son my father would want us to name him Alberto. Would you mind if we name her after my mother, Georgiana?"

Emily smiled and nodded. "It's a beautiful name, Francesco."

Emily looked over at Alberto. She couldn't read his face, but said, "I promise we'll keep trying until we have a son."

Alberto came to her bedside, bent down, and kissed her on the cheek. He caressed the baby's head. "You have no idea how much that means to me. Thank you."

Emily nodded, and thought about how she came to this point in her life. *Oh, yes, I do know how much it means to you, Alberto.*

* * *

October 1856

Mazatlán

As promised, Jane stayed another month with Emily and enjoyed every moment with her granddaughter, Georgiana. By mid-October both Emily and Jane knew their visit was coming to an end. Even though Jane missed Thomas immensely, she dreaded having to say goodbye.

Thomas had been impatiently waiting for the month of October. *Soon Philip will be sailing to Mazatlán to bring my wife back to me.* Thomas didn't like being separated from Jane. They had already experienced too many months of separation. *On the next trip to Mazatlán, I'm going with her. I miss my Emily, and I want to see my grandchild. I wonder, do I have a grandson or a granddaughter?*

It was the middle of October when Philip navigated his ship into the San Francisco harbor. Jonathan, of course, was always by his uncle's side. Philip had told Jeremy he would stop at Frisco on his way to Mazatlán to see if he'd be available to go with them. He also wanted to say hello to Oliver. The timing worked out well. Jeremy was available to go with them to Mazatlán. The brothers were excited to see each other and chattered nonstop. After about an hour of visiting with Oliver, Philip announced it was time to leave.

During the voyage, Jeremy told Jonathan about the case he and Oliver had been working on. He had also met Oliver's niece. "She's awfully cute, and a little shy. I'm suspicious that Oliver is trying to matchmake us. I think she likes me. To be honest, Jonathan, I'm just not interested in getting involved with a woman right now. There's so much to learn from Oliver. I don't want to be distracted."

"Have you started *investigating* her yet?" snickered Jonathan.

"Very funny," replied Jeremy as he punched his brother's arm.

The *California II* glided into the now familiar Mazatlán harbor. As soon as they anchored, a boatman paddled his small boat close to the ship offering his services. Captain Bennett left Samuel in charge, and he and his nephews hopped into the vessel to go to shore. Once ashore, he thanked the man and paid his fee.

Philip pointed toward the town and said, "Lads, we're in walking distance of the De Leon factory. I expect we'll find Alberto there."

After Philip and Alberto finished business, Alberto summoned a carriage to take them all to his home.

During the ride, Philip asked Alberto, "Tell me, Alberto, am I about to meet a grand niece or nephew?"

"Francesco and Emily have a daughter," replied Alberto. "but they've promised to keep trying until they have a son."

Alberto was quiet the rest of the way. It was obvious he was disappointed he didn't have a grandson.

Francesco met them at the door. "Welcome! Are you staying more than one night this time, Philip?"

"I think we can squeeze in a couple of nights this time."

Jane said, "I'm so happy to see you all!"

"Hello, Mother," said Jonathan and Jeremy in unison, as they each hugged and kissed her.

Emily stood up with her baby in her arms and walked over to her brothers. "Do either of you want to hold her?"

"She looks awfully fragile, I wouldn't want to break her," said Jonathan in jest. "I think she's just beautiful, little sister."

"You've made me a proud uncle, Emily, with this beautiful little girl," said Jeremy.

Philip joined in. "I'd like to hold her," he said as he carefully took the baby into his arms. He wondered what holding a newborn would feel like. *This is a first for me,* he thought. Philip smiled and looked down at her. "She's beautiful, Emily. A new generation for the Bennett and De Leon families. And what have you named her?"

"We have named her Georgiana, after Francesco's mother," replied Emily.

Philip handed Georgiana back to Emily. "That's a beautiful name."

Francesco and Alberto stood back and watched the happy scene. Then a servant entered the room and spoke quietly to Alberto. He thanked the servant and turned to his guests. "I've just learned supper will be served soon. Please, come to the dining room where we will create another lasting memory."

* * *

The two days passed much too quickly for the family.

"I wish I didn't have to leave you my dear daughter, but it's time to go home to your father," said Jane. She bent down and kissed Georgiana on the forehead and Emily on the cheek.

"I'm going to miss you so much. Be sure to thank Father for the little leather shoes. They're adorable. And thank you, Mother, for the beautiful quilt. I guess I'll have to learn how to make one to pass on to Georgiana when she has a babe. At least I have a few years."

"I'll teach you, Emily. That means I'll be back from time to time."

"I'll bring your mother back as often as we can, and hopefully one of these days, your father," said Philip. He shook hands with Francesco and Alberto, thanking them for sharing their home, and kissed Emily and Georgiana on the forehead.

Jeremy and Jonathan shook hands with Alberto and Francesco as well. They saved their goodbye to their sister until last. They hugged and kissed her, then they each softly kissed their little niece.

"Goodbyes are so sad," said Emily. "Don't forget your promise. You're all coming back."

Jane thanked Francesco and Alberto for their hospitality. "You've been most gracious for having me underfoot for so long."

"It has been our pleasure," said Francesco. Then he and Alberto kissed Jane goodbye.

"My carriage awaits you," said Alberto. "Until next time."

* * *

Once the *California II* returned to the foggy Golden Gate harbor, Philip kept her anchored just long enough to unload the Mazatlán products for the buyers. This was the stopping point for Jeremy.

While the cargo was unloaded, Jeremy spent the remaining time with his mother. Looking at her son with sad eyes, Jane said, "Jemmie, it's so hard to believe we're leaving you here in San Francisco. I know you'll be in good hands with Oliver, but please be *extra* careful and don't take *any* chances."

"Don't worry, Mother," replied Jeremy. Then they heard the ship's horn, signaling the ship was ready for departure. He embraced his mother one last time and brushed a tear away from her cheek. "I love you, Mother. Give my love to Father, and I promise to write."

Jeremy turned to his uncle and brother. "Well, this is it. I look forward to seeing you both whenever possible. In the meantime, I'm going to miss you." As he jumped off the ship, he yelled out to them, "See you on the next trip. And Jonny, don't forget about nine o'clock on Sunday night!"

"I won't," responded Jonathan.

Jeremy stood on the wharf waving goodbye as the *California II* steamed out of the harbor. Then he hailed a cab and headed to his new address.

Chapter 36

December 15, 1856
Teekalet

*D*r. Ames exclaimed, "Mary, you have a beautiful daughter," as he handed the babe to Annie to cleanse and swaddle before presenting the baby girl to her mother.

"She's beautiful, Mary," said Jane. "She has rosy pink cheeks and wide bright eyes. And listen to that exuberant cry!"

"I'll tell Benjamin and Thomas they can come in now," said Dr. Ames. "I swear I could hear them pacing the floor out there the entire time."

Benjamin rushed to Mary's bedside who was now clutching their baby girl to her breast. "What a beautiful sight," he said. "I understand we have a daughter." Then he bent down to kiss them both on the forehead. "We'll have to decide on a name very soon."

"Are you disappointed it's not a boy?" said Mary peering up at him.

"It is impossible to be disappointed, dearest," said Benjamin smiling down at their baby girl. "She has already bewitched me."

Thomas stood on the other side of Mary. While beaming, he said, "Hello, little granddaughter. Welcome to our family." Then Thomas turned to Jane. "I've just realized our granddaughter is the first babe to be born in our settlement. Jane, I think this calls for a celebration."

"Yes, what a wonderful idea, and of course we'll celebrate Mary's birthday as well. Now we have their birthdays and yours to celebrate every December. We'll host the party at our house." Jane smiled at Mary and Benjamin. "What do the proud parents think of our idea?"

"Oh yes, Mother, I would love that." Glancing at her husband, Mary said, "I'm sure Benjamin would too!"

"An excellent idea!" replied Benjamin.

Dr. Ames interrupted. "Mary should get some rest now, and it's time for Annie and me to be returning to Teekalet. Thanks for putting me up for the night, Mr. and Mrs. Bennett. Benjamin, you were smart to fetch us early at the first hint of contractions. It was a bonus for Annie to have the opportunity to stay with her mother."

"Mother was so happy to see me, and Matthew of course. We had a wonderful visit. Yes, Benjamin, your timing was perfect," replied Annie.

Then Dr. Ames and Annie said goodbye and left.

Jane whispered to Thomas, "Did you bring the gifts?"

"Yes, they're in the other room. I'll bring them in." Thomas returned with two gifts in hand. "We have something for our grand baby. We each made something just as we did for Emily's babe. Benjamin, since Mary has her hands occupied, would you like to open the gifts?" Thomas handed the two packages to Benjamin.

Mary eagerly watched Benjamin unwrap the gifts. The larger package revealed a beautiful colorful quilt with a note from Jane, *"When my arms can't be there to wrap around your babe, this quilt will."*

"Oh Mother, this is beautiful. Something made by you."

Benjamin held it up, "Just beautiful, thank you."

"You're very welcome. I want you to know that this quilt continues the family tradition of giving a quilt when a babe is born. The tradition goes back two generations."

Thomas said to Jane, "I remember a certain quilt years ago."

Jane smiled, "As do I. What a surprise for us when we were blessed with two children."

Next, Benjamin opened the smaller package. Inside a small box was a pair of tiny soft leather shoes with a note from Thomas. *"Your child shall never be without shoes as long as I am here."*

"Thank you, sir. When she has outgrown them, we will save them as a special keepsake for her," said Benjamin, while handing the shoes to Mary.

Mary caressed the shoes. "I love them, Father. Our daughter's first pair of shoes."

Jane leaned toward Thomas. This is how it was when I handed Emily and Francesco our gifts. They were as happy as Mary and Benjamin are now."

"I appreciate hearing that." replied Thomas.

"It's time to give the parents some privacy now," said Jane. The grandparents hugged Mary and the baby girl, then Benjamin.

As Jane and Thomas were leaving, Jane said, "Thomas, we need to plan a trip to Seabeck to share the good news with Elizabeth and James, and while we're there, we'll set a date for the party."

Now that everyone was gone, Benjamin went over to the crib and picked up one-year-old Parker. "It's time for you to meet your sister, sweet boy."

Mary smiled. They were now a family of four. Tears came to her eyes as she thought of their little Mollie, forever gone.

Benjamin saw her tears and knew what they meant. He said a silent prayer for Mollie. *I didn't get to meet you, my precious baby girl, but you will always have a place in my heart.*

Benjamin was about to ask what they should name their new arrival, when Mary said, "I have an idea for a name, Benjamin."

"Please, do tell me. I was just wondering about that."

"We should name her Katherine, after your mother. And her middle name Jane, after my mother."

"Katherine Jane Spencer. I like it," said Benjamin. "I like it very much. My mother will be honored. I'll post a letter right away to my parents with our good news."

"Her nickname can be Katie."

"Yes, our little Katie."

* * *

December 18, 1856
Seabeck

"Thomas, Elizabeth will be so excited to see us. The last time she saw me was just before I left for Mazatlán. Now I have two babes to tell her about."

"I'm looking forward to seeing her too, as well as James and Randolph."

They tied the boat at the wharf, then entered the store, ringing the bell chimes on the door.

Isabel, who was standing behind the counter, smiled and greeted them. "Hello, Mr. and Mrs. Bennett." She glanced behind them and out the window wondering if Robert was with them. *Maybe he's tending the boat?*

"Good day, to you, Isabel," said Jane. "We're here on a social visit. Is Elizabeth nearby?"

Realizing that Robert wasn't going to walk through the door, Isabel answered in a quiet voice, "Yes, she's in the office. I'll fetch her."

Jane murmured to Thomas, "I think Isabel was hoping Robert was with us. Did you see how she glanced out at the wharf? Poor girl, she has it bad."

"I believe Robert does have some interest. It's been a long time coming, that's for sure. He happened to mention that he should handle the deliveries here by himself, giving me time to keep working on our products." Thomas laughed, "As if I couldn't see right through him."

Jane giggled, "Perhaps this party can serve more than one purpose?"

"Oh, you are a sly one, my lady."

At that moment Elizabeth burst into the room, embracing her parents. "Mother! Father! What a wonderful surprise. Mother, I want to hear all about Emily and the babe. And what did you think of Mazatlán?"

"We have much to share with you, Lizzy. Perhaps over a cup of tea?"

"Follow me. We'll sit in our favorite corner, and I'll bring out my best china. I have three kinds of Darjeeling tea now, thanks to Isabel's persuasion. James and my father-in-law will join us in a few minutes. But of course, you must tell me everything without a moment's hesitation. They'll just have to catch up."

While the three of them sipped their tea, Jane told Elizabeth all about Emily and the baby, and how overwhelmed she was by the beauty of Mazatlán.

"Mazatlán possesses a different kind of beauty, certainly very little rain. I must admit, though, I prefer the beauty here in the Sound, despite the rain. Everything here is so green and fresh."

Thomas beamed as he listened to Jane. *She's actually happy here.*

Elizabeth nodded, then thought about her other sister, Mary. "How is Mary doing? She must be ready to burst."

"That's the other news we have for you. Mary gave birth to a little girl three days ago. They named her Katherine Jane. Of course, our granddaughter is as beautiful as I remember her mother," said Thomas reflecting back to why they named her Mary. She was their Christmas baby.

"I have another niece?" Maybe it will have to be up to me to provide you with a grandson," chuckled Elizabeth as she patted her belly.

At that moment James and his uncle joined the circle.

"I'll be happy with either," said James, smiling, having overheard his wife's comment.

Jane added, "Now that we're all here together, Thomas and I want to tell you that we're hosting a party to celebrate Katherine Jane being the first babe born in our settlement.

"And since it's so close to Christmas, not to mention your father's and Mary's birthdays, we're going to have one big celebration."

"You all must come and spend the night, of course," said Thomas.

"The answer is yes!" exclaimed Elizabeth. James nodded.

"I would be honored to come," said Randolph. "Surely, the townspeople won't be upset with us for closing the store and diner during Christmas."

"We'll give them plenty of warning," said James.

Elizabeth thought about Isabel. Her parents had recently moved to Victoria. They wanted Isabel to move with them, but because she had met Robert, she declined. *Isabel will be alone on Christmas.*

"Mother, Father, would you mind terribly if I invited Isabel? Her parents moved to Victoria a month ago, and they're unhappy with her for not going with them. I just hate the thought of her being alone on Christmas."

Jane grinned to herself. *This party idea is working out extremely well.* "I was already thinking about inviting Isabel, and I think we all know by now who will be most pleased to see her in attendance."

Everyone chuckled. "I'm sure she could stay the night with Philip and Maggie. They have an extra room," said Thomas.

Finally, after a lively conversation about the party, Thomas scraped his chair back and stood. "Well then, it's settled. And now my lady and I need to head back to Teekalet before dark. We shall be pleased to see all of you on Christmas Eve day. I hope Philip gets back in time from his business trip. He doesn't know about our party, but he said he wouldn't miss our first Christmas together in Teekalet for the world."

Chapter 37

Christmas Eve 1856

Bennett Settlement

*I*mmediately after returning from Seabeck, Thomas and Jane worked swiftly to prepare their home for the celebration of the first baby born in their settlement, Thomas's birthday, Mary's birthday, and Christmas. They had a little over a week to transform their house into a festive haven.

Everyone in the settlement participated. Benjamin helped Thomas construct extra tables and benches. Christopher, Matthew, and Billy foraged the woods and brought back armfuls of fir and cedar boughs, then hung the greenery around the house. For the Christmas tree, Peter cut a small Douglas fir and set it up on a table in a tub of sand. Thomas brought in the log he had cut and debarked during the summer to be used as their Yule log for Christmas Eve. It was tradition to burn the log in the hearth the night before Christmas to bring in good fortune to family and friends. Maggie and Rachel brought sugar cookies and dried fruit to hang on the tree and helped Jane string popcorn garland. In honor of her Scottish heritage and her parents, Jane added red and green plaid fabric at the base of the tree, covering the sand and tub. Finally, candles in holders were strategically placed on the tree, ready to be lit at the set time.

The women planned the menu and prepared the food for Christmas Eve supper, Christmas morning breakfast, and the main meal on Christmas Day. Jane was grateful for the extra help since she had given Lien hua the time off to be with her own family who lived near the mill.

Robert continued his family's Christmas tradition by making Old English Wassail, a sweet, spicy beverage of hot mulled cider.

It was the first Christmas for the Bennetts to celebrate as a family in their frontier settlement with the exception of two of their children, Emily and Jeremy, who lived so far away. It was a fact they had accepted, but they were thankful everyone was safe. As Jane and Thomas prepared their home for family and friends, they pushed the absence of their two children to the back of their mind.

On Christmas Eve day, Jane took a moment and marveled at their home. She breathed in the scent of the evergreens and the wonderful fragrance emanating from Robert's pot of hot wassail brewing on the wood stove. Even the Christmas tree gave out its own mix of aromas from the dried fruit, cookies, popcorn garland, candle wax, and its own essence.

Soon their guests started arriving. Those who had been involved in helping Thomas and Jane with the party were already present, still lending a hand where needed.

Peter had gone to Teekalet to Dr. Ames's home early in the morning to bring Annie back. Rachel was excited to see her daughter. "Peter, I can't wait to put my arms around Annie," she said gleefully.

Pierre and Red Feather arrived by canoe. Jane welcomed them, "It's wonderful to see you. Peter went to Teekalet to fetch Annie. They should be here soon."

"*Merci*, we have been looking forward to the festivities," replied Pierre. Then he handed Jane a bundle of mistletoe tied with a cord. "I have brought you, a *Porte Bonheur,* a gift for luck."

Red Feather smiled and embraced Jane, "I am honored to be here." She handed Jane a small pouch. "I've brought you some dried herbs to use for seasoning."

"Thank you for coming and thank you for the herbs and the mistletoe," said Jane. Grinning, she thought, *I know of another purpose for this mistletoe, and I know exactly where to have Thomas hang it,* as her mind drifted to the door leading to the kitchen porch.

Next, Elizabeth, James, Randolph, and their guest, Isabel, arrived by boat.

Jane greeted them and hugged Elizabeth. "Oh, I think there's something growing in your belly, Lizzy," teased Jane. Jane turned to their guest, "Isabel, we're very happy you could join us."

"Thank you, Mrs. Bennett. I was excited to receive your invitation from Elizabeth." While answering, her eyes scanned the room to locate Robert.

Isabel may have thought she was subtle, but she didn't fool Jane.

"Isabel, would you like a nice hot drink? You must be chilled. There is some delicious mulled cider simmering on the stove in the kitchen. It's Robert's specialty. Feel free to help yourself. We're very casual around here." *With any luck, Robert might happen to be there serving our guests.*

"That sounds delightful, Mrs. Bennett. Can I bring anyone a cup?"

"We'll have some in a few minutes, Isabel, but thank you," replied Elizabeth winking at James and Randolph.

Isabel followed the aroma of mulled spices into the kitchen. As she hoped, she found Robert there. He was lining up cups to fill and serve to the guests.

"Hello, Mr. Bennett," said Isabel softly.

Robert looked up and felt his heart beat a little faster. "Miss Warner, it's very nice to see you." Not wanting to appear too anxious, he said, "May I serve you a cup of wassail?"

"Only if you will join me. Perhaps after I help you serve the guests?"

"I would like that very much." Then he ladled the wassail into two cups and handed them to her. He followed with two more filled cups. While they continued this process, Robert periodically glanced over at Isabel interacting so easily with the guests. He smiled. She seemed to always know when he looked at her, and when she returned the gaze, her eyes locked on him, embracing him. He sensed what she wanted. She wanted him. He felt the tension and energy, like a storm breaking loose, building to a crescendo. For him, it was like the first rain after many months without rainfall.

After every guest had been served, they returned to the kitchen. Robert filled a cup for Isabel and himself. He motioned toward the kitchen table, and said while pulling out a chair for her, "Shall we sit?"

"I would be delighted, kind sir," replied Isabel flirtatiously as she smoothed her skirt and took a seat. They sat at the table and chatted for an hour, slowly sipping their drinks, and although people came in and out of the kitchen, they didn't notice.

While deep in conversation, Isabel happened to see the mistletoe hanging above the door leading to the kitchen porch. "Oh my," she said, "this hot drink has made me rather warm."

"Would you like to step out onto the porch for a moment for some fresh air?" asked Robert.

"What a good idea."

They didn't linger long on the porch since it was quite chilly outside. Robert said, "Miss Warner, you're shivering. Let us go in."

"Yes, it didn't take long to cool off."

Robert opened the door, and before he could step into the room, Isabel stopped him at the threshold. Chuckling, she said, "Mr. Bennett, do you not see what we're standing under? You know, according to tradition, it's bad luck not to kiss beneath the mistletoe."

"Well," he said, "we can't have that." Then he leaned down to her and kissed her lightly on her inviting lips. *I've wanted to do that since Seabeck.*

Isabel wanted more and pulled him closer, her lips slightly parted, "I think we need to make sure, don't you?"

Robert, unable to contain his imprisoned passion any longer, pulled her into a fiery, intense kiss. Isabel could feel his pounding heart against her own fluttering heart. She broke away for a breath, then looked deep into his eyes and caressed his face. Their lips crushed together, and they kissed again, harder and longer.

Jane started to enter the room, but when she saw them in the embrace, she hesitated, then made a sound so they would know someone was entering. She grinned to herself. *I see the mistletoe worked.*

Robert and Isabel quickly broke apart, both their neck and faces flushed. Jane said, "I'm about to bring the sandwiches out and put them on the sideboard in the dining room. Robert, would you like to give me a hand?"

"Of course, Jane," answered Robert.

Isabel said, "I'll help." *Any excuse to be near Robert.*

When they finished bringing the food out, Jane announced, "Everyone, our Christmas Eve celebratory supper is ready. Even though some of our guests haven't arrived yet, we'll go ahead and start. Please come and help yourselves." Then she called out to Thomas, "Would you say a prayer?"

Everyone bowed their heads while Thomas gave a prayer of thanks for the presence of so many loved ones and for the events they were fortunate to be celebrating.

After the prayer, the guests served themselves buffet style. They filled their plates with ham sandwiches, hard boiled egg slices, stewed carrots, and applesauce. For dessert there was mincemeat pie and sugar cookies.

Jane wondered why Philip and Jonathan hadn't arrived yet. She at least wanted Jonathan to be there, even if his brother couldn't be. "Maggie, did Philip make it back? I thought I heard activity at the wharf last night."

"Yes, he did. He and Jonathan should be here soon. Jonathan didn't want to disturb any of you, so he slept in the bunkhouse last night."

"Odd, he should know he wouldn't have been a bother."

"Jane, why don't I go check on them. I'll be back in a few minutes." Maggie scurried out the door before Jane could ask her another question.

A few minutes later, Maggie returned. Philip followed behind her with a case of champagne in his arms, along with Jonathan, carrying a crate of oranges.

"There you are," exclaimed Jane. Then, from behind Philip and Jonathan, a grinning Jeremy stepped out.

"Jemmy!" Jane yelled out to Thomas. "Thomas, come, Jemmy is here." She wrapped her arms around her son.

"Oh, my Lord," said Thomas. He looked over at Philip. Are you responsible for this wonderful gift?" He embraced Jeremy, and then Philip. "You're a wonderful brother, Philip."

Philip smiled. Then Thomas and Jane thought they heard the sound of a baby crying outside the door, but Parker and Katie were inside the house. Philip, beaming, said, "Well, I guess that's my cue." He walked to the door, glanced back at them with a mischievous grin, and said, "I'm not finished yet!" He opened the door and motioned for someone to come in. Emily with baby Georgiana in her arms, Francesco, and Alberto walked in.

Jane's mouth dropped open, and Thomas put his hand on his heart.

"I didn't dare to dream of such a thing. All of our children here together," cried Jane. She embraced Emily and kissed Georgiana on the cheek. Then she acknowledged Francesco and Alberto. "Welcome to *our* home."

"Yes, welcome, we'll shake hands right after I properly meet my granddaughter," said Thomas. "Emily, may I hold this little bundle of joy?" Emily transferred Georgiana over to her father. "I'm enjoying this, my Emily. It brings back so many memories. How long can you stay?"

"Only a few days, Father, and that includes Jeremy." She grinned at Francesco and Alberto. "These two *conspirators* and Uncle Philip planned this surprise when Mother was with us in Mazatlán. She had no idea. Naturally, they worked it around business. I'm so excited to be here, and we have birthday and Christmas presents! Where's Mary and Benjamin and their babe? The little *cousins* need to meet," she chuckled.

By now, everyone in the house realized what was happening and gathered around. The buzz of voices grew louder as they were all introduced. Philip stood in the background, smiling contentedly. Maggie put her arm through his. "You did good," she said. "It was hard keeping the secret. Jane started questioning me, which was why I fled to our house. I had to get away from her before she caught on that I was hiding something."

"Then you did good too, my love. I think it's time we have some champagne and make a few toasts, don't you? I'm sure glad I brought a case of champagne. I had no idea there was a party going on." A few moments later, everyone heard the sound of corks popping and champagne being poured.

* * *

December 25, 1856
Teekalet

Jane was up at the crack of dawn to prepare Christmas breakfast. As she dressed, she thought about her family in Delhi. She missed them terribly, and it didn't seem natural to be enjoying the holidays without them. Had they received the Christmas card she sent? She was overjoyed when she received their card and letter. She almost felt guilty for being happy this Christmas, living in this untamed frontier. She prayed that one day they would all be together again.

The house was quiet, unlike the night before. The party had continued into the late hours with laughter, music, singing, and conviviality. There was even a little romance. Now, on the dawn of this Christmas day, their beloved guests slept peacefully.

Emily, Francesco, and Georgiana slept in Jeremy's former bedroom. Jeremy bunked with Jonathan in his bedroom. Elizabeth and James slept in her short-lived former bedroom.

Jane smiled contentedly thinking about their loved ones here together for Christmas. She thought, *A Christmas wish can come true,* and she would savor this moment of ecstasy, knowing it would soon come to an end.

While Jane began the preparations for breakfast, she heard a tap on the kitchen door. She opened it to the smiling, chipper faces of Maggie and Rachel.

"Good morning, dear ladies," said Jane. "Please come in."

"Good morning to you," said Maggie and Rachel in unison. Maggie handed off a basket brimming with steaming muffins to Jane.

"These smell so good and they're still warm. I'll keep them covered and put them on the sideboard in the dining room. I see you two were up as early as me. How did your overnight guests fare? Who ended up where?"

Rachel said, "Randolph and Alberto stayed with Robert. Annie, of course, stayed in her former bedroom, and Pierre and Red Feather stayed with us. We all had a wonderful visit. Annie and Red Feather chatted all night. I'm sure by now they are enjoying a cup of coffee with Peter."

Then Maggie added. "Isabel stayed with Philip and me. It gave me the opportunity to get to know her. We had a nice chat. When I happened to mention how busy we are at the bakery, she immediately indicated an interest in moving here and working for us. That is, of course, if Elizabeth can find a replacement for her. She is very fond of Elizabeth and doesn't want to abandon her. Now that part of the bunkhouse has been converted into women's quarters, she could probably stay there." Maggie chuckled, "We have an extra bedroom, but I'm selfishly not ready to give up alone time with my husband."

Jane laughed out loud. "Oh, my goodness. Isabel is a woman on a mission."

"Am I missing something, Jane?" asked Maggie.

"I guess I'm in the dark as well," said Rachel.

"I realize you were both so busy helping me as hostesses last night, you missed the romance blossoming between Isabel and Robert right under *our* roof."

"Our Robert?!" exclaimed Maggie. "I can't wait to tell Philip!"

Jane added, "They don't know it, but I saw them kissing. Oh my, there was so much heat, I had to fan myself. Before they saw me, I made a noise to warn them someone was coming into the room. You should have seen how fast they separated. I could barely stop grinning watching them act as though nothing had happened. Their flushed faces were a dead giveaway."

"So, I suppose for Robert's sake, we could hire Isabel if it works out for Elizabeth. After all, I've never been one to come between two lovers," said Maggie, giggling.

"I'm in," said Rachel.

Jane said, "I do believe I hear people stirring. Shall we get the breakfast started, ladies?"

* * *

"Breakfast is served," announced Jane. The cheerful guests had melded together and were even more relaxed than the night before. This time Jane chose to have everyone seated at the custom-sized table, as well as who sat next to whom, while she, Maggie, and Rachel served them. Each guest was served grilled rashers of bacon, a poached egg on toast, and baked mushrooms on a warmed plate. Stewed fruit and sweet muffins were set on the table as accompaniments. Finally, the three women seated themselves.

Thomas stood, and smiled, "I would like to say a prayer of thanks, once again, for all who are here and this fine meal." He continued the prayer.

Everyone bowed their head. "Amen," they said in unison.

It was no accident that Robert and Isabel were sitting next to each other, thanks to a little help from Jane. Isabel was beaming.

Robert tried to remain expressionless. He had not slept the entire night. In fact, he tossed and turned. While he ate, he mulled over the thoughts ravaging his mind. Was he allowing this *thing* with Isabel to be moving too fast? Was he even interested in a relationship with a woman? He still loved Eleanor. Was he unfair to Isabel because she resembled his beloved Eleanor? *On the other hand,* he thought, *Eleanor is lost to me. Do I want to remain alone for the rest of my life? Isabel is right here, and I know she wants me.*

Isabel could barely keep her emotions under control sitting next to the man with whom she was falling in love. She hadn't slept either, but not over questions. She relived *that* kiss over and over. Robert was everything she wanted in a man. He was ruggedly handsome and quietly suave. And the piece de resistance, he was a brilliant businessman, and because of that, on his way to becoming a wealthy man. He already had a house of his own, in which she would be quite content to reside. She imagined herself as the lady of the Bennett house. Marrying him would secure her financial future. In return, she would give him children. The act of making a child with Robert would be eagerly welcomed.

* * *

After breakfast, the family and friends milled about the house enjoying each other's company. Benjamin played his violin and Matthew joined in with his harmonica. Everyone sang along with the music.

Thomas and Jane spent a good portion of their time with Emily, Georgiana, and Jeremy, knowing they wouldn't see them again for several months.

Thomas also spent some time getting to know Francesco and Alberto a little better. He asked them if they would like to see his and Robert's operation.

Alberto replied, "Yes, please do show us. Business is my favorite subject."

"The walk isn't terribly long. You would have walked past our building when you left the wharf. The fresh marine air will do us good."

Pierre was in earshot. "If you don't mind *mon amis*, I would like to join you. If you have any questions about trapping, Alberto and Francesco, I'm your man."

Emily was happy to see her father conversing with her husband and father-in-law. After she saw the men leave the house, she felt free to spend some private time with her sisters, Mary and Elizabeth. They had fun reliving old memories as children and looked forward to making new memories with their children. Elizabeth's child was due in May.

Jonathan and Jeremy, as usual, were inseparable, sharing stories about their new lives. Periodically, they mingled among the guests.

Maggie had anxiously shared with Philip about Robert's romantic interlude. He went straight to Robert.

Philip sat down next to Robert, who happened to be sitting alone at the moment. He leaned over to him, whispering, "Robert, you son of a gun. I hear you have a little romance going in your life with a certain young woman by the name of Isabel?"

"Don't spread this around," said Robert, in a very quiet low voice. "I'm still undecided about letting it progress. I'm not rushing into it, that's for sure. To be honest, this infatuation, or whatever it is, scares me to death. Slow and easy is my way. I don't think she wants to go slow though. I was shocked when I felt her hand under the table on my leg at breakfast."

Philip laughed. "That must have been the moment when I saw your eyes get large. I would be very happy for you, Robert, if she's the one for you. She's lovely, despite being a little aggressive. I guess you're just so irresistible, she can't help herself. I hope you know you can always come to me to talk, and of course, I won't say anything. Does Thomas know?"

"Probably, because of Jane. I sense a little matchmaking going on with her. Do you think it was an accident that Isabel and I happened to be sitting next to each other at breakfast? And what do you think the odds are of the same seating arrangement at supper tonight?"

Philip laughed, "Knowing how women are, the odds are pretty good."

* * *

The final Christmas meal was about to be served. The Bennetts had outdone themselves. The guests were about to fill their plates with roasted turkey and cornbread stuffing, cranberry sauce, potatoes and gravy, stewed carrots, and squash. Dessert was plum pudding, and a spice cake baked by Maggie and Rachel.

After the prayer, each of the men stood and made a toast thanking their hosts for their unsurpassed hospitality and unforgettable meals. There were even three people's birthdays to toast—Thomas, Mary, and little Katie.

Thomas stood up with his glass in hand. "I hadn't planned on my birthday being included in this celebration since we celebrated it earlier this month. But I'm not about to turn down a toast from all of you dear people." He raised his glass, "Cheers to you all."

"Cheers," exclaimed everyone.

Thomas and Jane beamed. This would be an unforgettable Christmas and celebration.

Later that night, Thomas embraced his wife, "Jane, because of you, our party was a grand success. Thank you. You did a wonderful job."

"I did have help, Thomas."

"Yes, I know, and I thanked every single person. At dinner, as I stood to pray, I marveled at our gathered group of family and friends gracing our table. As I gazed at each of our children's faces, now young adults, I thought how blessed we are, despite constant adversity, that they are safe and sound, and now here with us sharing this celebration. We have had a difficult year, Jane. A frightening year for much of the time, but we came through it. We Bennetts are a strong family."

"I just couldn't imagine a better ending to this year, except for having to say goodbye to our family and friends on the morrow, especially Emily and Jeremy who are separated from us by a vast ocean." A tear trickled down her cheek.

Thomas smiled, brought out his handkerchief, touched her face, and gently wiped the tear away.

Chapter 38

*I*t was Wednesday, delivery day for the Bennett brothers. Elizabeth, still in matchmaking mode, made sure Isabel would be alone in the general store. "Isabel, I'll leave you here to greet Thomas and Robert when they arrive. I'll be next door in the diner if you need me. James and his father are working in the warehouse. You can alert them when it's time to receive the delivery."

Knowing Robert would be coming, Isabel took special care of her appearance. She was nervous. Since she didn't get to say goodbye to Robert privately after the Christmas celebration, she wasn't sure where she stood with him. Did he still think about her, or had she just been *good* company for him while everyone was in a party mood? She hadn't approached Elizabeth yet about leaving to work at the Hood Canal Bakery. She would wait and see how Robert acted toward her.

It was the usual mid-morning hour when the Bennett workboat arrived. Isabel kept a watchful eye waiting for the Bennett brothers' arrival. Finally, she saw the workboat. Robert had come alone. She scurried away from the window, and instead of standing behind the counter, stood in front. She didn't want any barriers between her and Robert.

The door chimes jingled, announcing Robert's arrival. As he walked in, he smiled at Isabel.

"Mr. Bennett!" She rushed to hug him, and looking deep into his hazel eyes, said in a hushed tone, "I've missed you."

With her body still pressed against him, Robert felt a warmth envelope his entire being. He realized how much he had missed her, and kissed her, gently. "I've missed you too," he said in a low, almost whispered, voice.

At that moment, they heard James and Randolph coming into the store through the back door. They quickly separated.

"Robert, you're right on time as usual." The three men shook hands. "Is Thomas waiting out there with the workboat?"

"No, I'm alone this time. Thomas had a lot of work to catch up on."

Walking toward the front door, Randolph said, "James and I will help you unload the boat." Robert followed, glancing back at Isabel as he closed the door.

Isabel frowned. *That just wasn't enough time. I'm talking to Elizabeth as soon as possible.*

* * *

A few days later, while waiting for the right moment, Isabel mustered up the courage to tell Elizabeth about her desire to leave Seabeck.

"Elizabeth, with your babe due in May, I imagine you'll be looking for someone to replace you?"

"Yes, you're correct. Now that people know I'm with child, there have been a few applicants." Elizabeth noticed that Isabel seemed anxious. "What's on your mind?"

Wringing her hands in anticipation, Isabel answered. "Would you consider hiring a replacement for me as well?"

"I've been wondering when you were going to ask. Mother told me about your interest in working at the Hood Canal Bakery." Elizabeth grabbed Isabel's hands. "You want to be closer to Robert. Am I correct?"

Isabel answered, with pleading eyes, "Yes, he's all I think about, but with the distance separating us, I fear he'll forget about me. I'm desperate to find a way to spend more time with him. Our attraction toward each other at the Christmas party was undeniable. Bless your mother's heart, I do believe she was nudging us along. Elizabeth, I'm falling helplessly in love with your uncle."

"Mother loves giving people a little push when she thinks they need it. I'll just have to join forces and help you two as well. Uncle Robert has been alone far too long. He needs someone in his life, and

I hope it'll be you! Yes, I will release you, but first I'll need your help to hire and train two people now instead of one. I'll stay until April, but as soon as we have our new employees trained, you'll be free to leave."

"I'll post a help wanted sign on the window today," said Isabel. Then she hugged Elizabeth tightly and said, "I'm so excited. I don't even know if I'll be able to sleep tonight."

Elizabeth smiled and replied, "The sign should be quite helpful, Isabel." *My, she sure doesn't waste any time.*

* * *

By the end of the month, Elizabeth and Isabel were training two new employees. One was a young man by the name of Frank, who was experienced in handling fur and leather goods. Randolph and James were pleased with Elizabeth's choice. They could use another man around to help haul inventory in and out of the warehouse. The second employee was Betsy, a middle-aged widow, who needed work, desperately. She was a perfect fit for the diner.

* * *

March 1857

Seabeck/Bennett Settlement

"Pack your bags, Isabel. Tomorrow, James and I are taking you to Teekalet," exclaimed Elizabeth.

"How wonderful," said Isabel gleefully. "It won't take very long. I have very little to pack. I'll be ready first thing in the morning. This is so exciting!"

"This trip will allow James and me to have a nice visit with my parents. My father-in-law suggested that James and I spend a few nights with them since he'll have Betsy and Frank to help him mind the store and diner. Of course, for you, my dear Isabel, it will be a one-way trip. Does Robert know what you're planning?"

"No, he has no idea. I hope he'll be happy about it. I am doing the right thing, aren't I, Elizabeth?"

"Well, at least this way you'll find out. You are right. If you stay here, your chances of anything happening are meager."

* * *

Early the next morning Isabel arrived at the wharf carrying two bags, the sum total of her possessions.

"Good morning, Isabel," said Elizabeth in a chipper voice.

"It is a good morning, indeed," replied Isabel as she accepted James's hand to step into the boat with them.

"Are we ready, ladies?" asked James.

"We're ready," replied Elizabeth. "And you'll both be happy to know I've packed us a nice lunch to eat along the way and I brought blankets in case we get cold. There's a bit of a chill in the air."

"You think of everything," said James. "I'll take care of the navigation while you take care of us," he chuckled. "Let's hope it doesn't rain."

James smiled as he listened to Elizabeth and Isabel chat the entire trip. A good portion of the conversation centered on Robert. Isabel couldn't seem to stop talking about him and her aspiration of securing a future with him.

"Here we are," said James as he slid the boat next to the Bennett wharf. He tied off the lines and helped Elizabeth and Isabel disembark. They all walked up the crushed oyster shell pathway toward the Hood Canal Bakery, passing by the Bennett brothers' company building. Isabel glanced over in that direction, wondering if Robert would see her. She wasn't ready for him to see her yet, especially when she didn't look her best after several hours of traveling in an open boat. *I wonder how and when I'm going to let him know I'm here? I need to come up with a plan.*

The bakery was the next building along the pathway. It was late afternoon, but Maggie and Rachel were still working on an order to go out the next day, which happened to be Wednesday, the Seabeck delivery day.

Elizabeth said, "Isabel, I see Maggie and Rachel are still working. Are you fine going in alone? I'm anxious to surprise my parents with our visit."

"Of course, Elizabeth. Please continue on your way. I'll be fine," said Isabel as she took her bags from James who had kindly carried them for her.

"We wish you well," said Elizabeth, already walking toward her parents' house. *Another step forward for this love story. Time to update my 'Robert and Isabel' entries in my journal tonight.*

Maggie was adding another apple pie to the pie safe when she heard the bells jingling on the entrance door. *Who could it be at this hour?* Rachel was taking a cake out of the oven and turned to see who had come in.

Isabel crossed the threshold and set her bags down. "I'm here!"

"Isabel!" said Maggie, "I had no idea you were coming. Welcome!"

"You two look like you could use some help. Feel free to put me to work. What would you like me to do?"

"We would welcome your help, Isabel. Your former employer increased the size of his order for delivery tomorrow. We don't ask Yu Yan to work late, so I'm afraid it's just Maggie and me," replied Rachel. "What good timing."

Maggie added, "As soon as we finish, Rachel and I will take you to the bunkhouse where you'll be staying. Jonathan and Jeremy built a nice addition to the building solely for women. All the Chinese ladies share a room together, but you'll be able to have your own room."

"I'm excited to work with both of you. It'll be interesting to see how you create the Seabeck orders. I've always been on the receiving end."

With Isabel's help, the bakery order was finally completed.

Maggie was pleased with Isabel's work performance. "Isabel, you were a great help to us. Thank you. Now, let's get you settled so you can rest. We'll need you here at six tomorrow morning."

"I'm sure you must be hungry," said Rachel. "I've put together something for tonight and tomorrow morning, which you can eat in your room. Shall we go?"

"I appreciate that, Rachel. I did work up an appetite. I'll grab my bags and follow you and Maggie."

* * *

The next morning Isabel awoke to the first day of a new chapter in her life. She sat up and gazed about her new living space. It was small but seemed comfortable enough. Besides, she didn't plan on being there long. If all went well, soon she would be Mrs. Robert Bennett. She realized she had been daydreaming too long and checked her pendant watch for the time. *I must stop, or I'll be late.* She got up, slipped out of her muslin nightdress and laid it neatly at the foot of her bed. *Someday I shall be wearing lace when I retire to bed.* She quickly dressed, pulled her hair back into a bun, then sat at the table and chair by the window to eat the breakfast of applesauce and rolls with jam, which Rachel had thoughtfully provided.

Isabel scurried to the bakery arriving on time, ready to work. When she walked in, Maggie and Rachel were buzzing about the kitchen placing the bakery items into wooden crates to be ready for the pick-up. Then the door bells jingled.

"He's right on time," said Maggie. "Good morning, Robert. Everything is ready to go."

Isabel whipped around with a pie still in hand, and gasped, her eyes wide. *Robert? I'm not ready to see him yet.* She set the pie down and smoothed her dress and hair. *I must look a mess.*

Robert was dumbfounded. Words failed him. *Isabel! What is she doing here? Am I to take her back to Seabeck? No one informed me of such.*

Maggie and Rachel looked at each other, both realizing what had just happened. They had been so consumed with the order, they didn't think to tell Isabel that Robert was the one picking it up. And, poor Robert, no one had clued him in about Isabel moving there.

Robert finally spoke, "Miss Warner. This is a surprise. I expected to find you at Seabeck today. How did—"

Isabel opened her mouth to answer, but Maggie interrupted,

coming to her rescue. "Isabel is our newest addition to the bakery. We discussed the idea the night of the Christmas party."

Robert wasn't sure how to respond. On the one hand, he was happy to see her. In fact, he felt his heart beating faster. But on the other hand, he was perfectly fine with her living further away, which meant he was in control. Finally, he said, "I'm quite sure Elizabeth's loss is your gain." Then he looked at Isabel, "Welcome to our community, Miss Warner."

"Thank you, Mr. Bennett. I believe I will be happy here."

Maggie and Rachel chuckled to themselves as they watched the pretense of formality between Isabel and Robert.

* * *

After returning from his Seabeck delivery trip, Robert wasn't any closer to reaching clarity about his relationship with Isabel. The entire way to Seabeck and back to the settlement, he wrestled with his feelings. While he sat in the boat, he gazed at Eleanor's portrait still secured inside his watch cover. She was the only woman he had ever wanted, but any chance of calling her his was snatched away years ago. He might as well face it and try to move on. *Move on with Isabel?* She was suddenly on his doorstep, and there was nothing to stop him.

Nearly two weeks had passed, and Robert had not yet interacted with Isabel. Then one late afternoon while he worked on a fur order, he heard the sound of the front door creaking open. He was alone, everyone else had left for the day, including Thomas. He looked up and saw Isabel. His senses were suddenly awakened by the aroma of a plate of cookies, which she was carrying.

"Miss Warner! This is a pleasant surprise. It looks like you've come bearing gifts."

"Indeed, I have. I baked these just for you."

"Since I'm the only one here, I guess I won't have to share. Thank you."

She answered flirtatiously. "You're most welcome." It was no accident that Isabel had arrived when Robert was alone. She was able to see the Bennett Bros. building from the bakery and observed that everyone except Robert left at the end of each workday. She recognized the pattern and made use of it.

Robert took the plate from her and placed the cookies on a table near the wood stove. He glanced at his teakettle, "May I offer you a cup of tea, Miss Warner? I have Darjeeling."

"I would happily accept a cup of tea, especially if its Darjeeling. It's my favorite."

"It's my favorite as well."

Robert filled the teakettle with water from a nearby pitcher and set the kettle on the stove. While he waited, he cleared off a work table and pulled over two chairs. Then he brought out two mugs and the tea. Soon the kettle whistled, prompting Robert to finish the tea preparation.

"I hope you don't mind drinking from a mug, Miss Warner. I apologize for not having any milk, but I do have sugar." Then he placed the plate of cookies on the table next to the sugar bowl.

"Everything is perfect," said Isabel as she approached one of the chairs.

Robert quickly pulled the chair out for her as she sat down, then sat across from her.

Isabel was in such a state of euphoria to be there with Robert attending to her every need, she could barely contain her emotions. She sipped her tea slowly, not wanting this special moment with Robert to end. As she lifted her eyes above the brim of the mug, they met his in such a way, he could not help but know she loved him.

The look on her face was impossible to ignore. He finally made the first move. "Miss Warner, would you like to walk with me tomorrow along the beach after you finish your work day?"

Isabel could feel her neck and face flush. *This is a dream come true. The cookie idea worked!* "Oh yes, Mr. Bennett. That would be wonderful. Perhaps we could finish with a cup of Darjeeling?"

"Are you willing to bring more cookies?" laughed Robert.

* * *

Early May 1857
Bennett Settlement

In the days and weeks that followed, Robert and Isabel continued to walk together along the beach, with Robert holding her hand. Isabel occupied his every thought, until finally, he began to surrender to her hold on him, and seriously considered marriage. His beloved Eleanor would always hold a place in his heart, but he knew a future with her was hopeless.

During one of their strolls, Isabel commented, "Elizabeth's babe is due soon. I'm so excited for her and James. They said it doesn't matter if it's a boy or a girl, as long as their babe is healthy."

"I hope to have children one day." Her eyes locked on him as she spoke. "With the right man."

She means me, Robert told himself. He had silently envied Thomas as he watched his brother enjoy fatherhood through the years, and wondered, *Is there still time for me to have what Thomas has?*

But at that moment, Robert chose to avert the subject and turned the conversation. "I meant to tell you, I'll be taking Jane and Thomas to Seabeck soon, so they can be with my niece when the happy event occurs. According to Thomas, it won't be long now."

* * *

Late May 1857

Seabeck

"You have a son, Elizabeth," declared the midwife.

Jane looked down at the sweet little bundle in her daughter's arms. "Lizzy, our grandson is beautiful," exclaimed Jane, as she brushed her hand across his soft, downy auburn-colored hair. "I'll tell James and your father they can come in now."

"Yes, I'm sure James has been pressed against the door. He was *so* nervous!"

Just as Thomas did during Mary's delivery, he brought in two handmade gifts for Elizabeth and James's baby. One from Jane and one from him. Once again, Jane had made a beautiful quilt and attached the special note. Jane also told them about the tradition of the quilts. Thomas had made the little leather shoes accompanied by his note. Elizabeth and James were overjoyed to receive such special gifts.

After spending two additional days enjoying their grandson, it was time for Jane and Thomas to return home. As planned, Randolph took them back.

The new parents named their son Alexander Franklin, after James's father. James gazed down at his son with a solemn expression. "I wish Father and Mother were still alive. They would have been excited to be little Alexander's grandparents."

"As are my parents," said Elizabeth. "I'm sorry I never had the opportunity to meet your parents, James."

"They would have loved you, just like my uncle does. Before you, he was the only family I had left. Being an only child, I have no siblings. You're very fortunate Elizabeth."

"I realize that." She giggled, "We'll have to make sure little Alex has siblings."

"I'm ready to work on that the moment you are," he chuckled.

Chapter 39

June 1857

Teekalet/Bennett Settlement

*A*fter returning from his latest venture trip in San Francisco, Philip sauntered into the bakery to greet Maggie. When she saw him, he was grinning. She noticed he was carrying a large package. *Oh, a gift for me. I love gifts from him,* she thought, gleefully.

Philip scanned the room looking for a surface not coated with flour dust. He spotted a large table and laid the box down. "Open it, my love," he said, still wearing his mysterious grin.

Maggie rushed to remove the ribbon wrapped around the large rectangular box. She smiled at Philip as she lifted the lid, then drawing a breath, parted the tissue, revealing the gift. Her eyes widened as she lifted up an emerald green silk satin dress. "Such beautiful detailing," she said. The bodice and hem were embroidered in a spiraling leaf design. Encircling the waist was a gold belt. Maggie was nearly speechless.

"Philip, I've never seen such a beautiful gown. I love it! But where will I wear it?"

"Darling, you're going to wear your dress to the Governor's Ball in Olympia next month." Then he brought out a hand written invitation from Governor Stevens and handed it to her.

"How exciting. I can't wait until next month. I see it's dated two months ago?"

"Yes, that's true. It was delivered to Teekalet to be given to me directly when I returned from one of my trips. Before I left on the upcoming trip to San Francisco, I borrowed one of your dresses for size and left it at the dress shop to have this gown made for you. I was pleased to find it ready for me when I arrived on this latest trip." Then he reached into his pocket and brought out a small velvet box and handed it to her. "This should go well with your dress, my love."

Maggie drew another breath and opened the box, which contained an emerald pendant and ear bobs. She gasped. "You're spoiling me, my Philip."

"I've been feeling guilty that we haven't taken a honeymoon yet. So much has happened and we've both been so busy. When I received this invitation, it seemed like the perfect substitute until I could give you a proper honeymoon." He winked, "I have a plan for that."

"I'm so anxious to try this dress on tonight."

"I expect you to model it for me. I'm planning to hire Thomas to make a pair of shoes for you to go with it. That reminds me, I'm free to invite my brothers."

"Jane will be excited. I'm sure she's ready to have some special time with Thomas. I wonder if Robert will ask Isabel?"

"Speaking of them, two weeks ago, Robert took Jane and Thomas to Seabeck to be with Elizabeth when she delivered her baby. They now have a grandson!"

"I'm glad you told me so I can congratulate Thomas. I planned to see my brothers next to invite them to the ball.

"Maggie, so you know, we'll need to plan for two days of being gone. I'll be using my ship to take us there, which will also give us a place to stay overnight."

"I'll tell Rachel. I never imagined I'd be going to a Governor's Ball."

"Don't forget. I want to see you try on that dress tonight."

"Until tonight then, my Philip," said Maggie, smiling, as Philip went out the door.

* * *

Philip found his brothers in their business building.

"You're back," exclaimed Thomas. "How was your trip?"

"It went well. More importantly, how was your trip? I understand Robert took you and Jane to Seabeck to be with Elizabeth during her delivery. Congratulations. I understand you have a grandson."

"Yes, Jane and I are excited to have another grandchild. Thankfully, Elizabeth didn't have any complications. We had a nice visit for a couple of days afterward."

"That's good news indeed." Then Philip brought out an envelope from inside his vest pocket. "I have something to show you two." He showed them the Governor's invitation. "This is the Governor's way of thanking me for retrieving the weaponry from San Francisco during the Indian uprising. He's extended an invitation to the Governor's Ball in Olympia, and has allowed me to invite both of you. I know Jane isn't going to let you pass this up, Thomas. And Robert, do you think you'll invite Isabel?"

"I think I might do that, Philip. We've been getting closer," replied Robert.

Thomas chuckled. "Jane will be in a flurry of what to wear. I'm sure she'll be going through her trunk. I best be ready to make her a pair of dancing shoes."

"Speaking of shoes, Maggie's going to need a pair of shoes to match her gown. Can you squeeze my order in? The ball is July 10th."

"I'll make it happen, and you don't have to pay me, Philip. Taking Jane to the Governor's Ball is payment enough. Are we going there on the *California II*?"

"That's the plan," answered Philip.

Just when Robert was summoning up the courage to invite Isabel to the ball, he happened to look out the window and saw her walking past their building heading toward her quarters. *She must be finished for the day. Now's the time.* He removed his apron and put his tools aside. "If you'll excuse me, brothers, I'm about to ask Miss Warner to the ball, while I still have the nerve."

"Brilliant," exclaimed Philip, with a grin.

Thomas patted Robert on the back, "Good luck, Robert. Maybe I'll be making a third pair of dancing shoes."

Robert rushed out of the building to catch up with Isabel.

Isabel was deep in thought about Robert when she heard the sound of oyster shells crunching underfoot behind her. She turned and saw him rushing toward her. "Mr. Bennett, are we taking a stroll together?"

"Yes, let's walk. I have something to ask you."

Isabel's heart pounded so hard she wondered if Robert might hear it. She felt herself blush from her neck up. *Could he be asking me to marry him this soon?*

Robert and Isabel walked on their usual path along the canal holding hands. It was a beautiful summer day. Fleecy white clouds drifted across a blue sky and shallow waves lapped gently against the shoreline, exuding a feeling of calm. They strolled together in silence, absorbed in themselves, both experiencing a sense of anxiety.

Finally, Robert broke the silence. He slowed down their pace, took a deep breath, and asked the question, "Miss Warner, would you go to the Governor's Ball with me?"

"The Governor's Ball? Yes, yes, I'll go with you. This is so exciting." Feeling slightly panicked, she thought, *What am I going to wear? Oh dear, perhaps Maggie and Rachel will help me. Nothing will stop me from going.* "When? And how? Do you know Governor Stevens?" She thought, *I really am rising above my station.*

"The ball is next month, and we'll be traveling there on my brother's ship. This will be my first time to meet the Governor. Have you ever been to Olympia?"

"No, I haven't. Oh, I can barely wait until next month! Thank you, Mr. Bennett."

Then Isabel moved closer to Robert. She put her arms around his neck and stood on her toes to reach his lips. Her lips parted, her eyes locked into his. Robert reflected back to their kiss during Christmas. This kiss promised to be all of that or more, and it was impossible for him to stop himself from declining her *invitation.*

He briskly pulled her closer and met her lips with vigor, then her tongue. As they passionately kissed, he felt as though he had gone into a trance. His entire body responded and he knew she felt it. Thankfully, they weren't in a secluded location. He may not have been able to stop. Suddenly, he pulled away.

"What's wrong?" asked Isabel, concerned she had moved too fast.

"Please forgive me, Miss Warner, someone could have seen us. I've taken advantage of you. You're so beautiful and inviting, I lost control for a moment. I'll be more careful in the future."

Isabel frowned, "I didn't feel that way at all."

"I think it's time I walk you back to your quarters. I need to cool off. I think for the time being, we should curtail our walks. I don't trust myself being alone with you."

Isabel gulped and held back the tears she felt welling in her eyes. "Whatever you say. I'll miss you. I look forward to our time together at the ball." *He must care for me, otherwise he wouldn't have invited me to the ball. Maybe he'll miss me so much, he'll realize he can't live without me.*

* * *

The next day at the bakery Isabel shared her news about the Governor's Ball with Maggie and Rachel.

"That's wonderful news, Isabel," said Maggie.

Rachel noticed Isabel's pensive expression. "Aren't you excited, Isabel? After all, you'll be with Robert."

Isabel answered with tears in her eyes. "I am excited, but I'm in a quandary of what to wear. I have one nice dress to my name, which looks like a flowery cotton sack. I want to be beautiful for Robert. I don't even know where I could buy fabric to make a frock, if I could afford it. I couldn't even sleep last night."

Maggie and Rachel looked at each other and nodded. They had become almost like sisters and always knew what the other was thinking.

Maggie spoke first, "Isabel, leave it to Rachel and me. I'm sure between the two of us, we can come up with a dress and all the trimmings. By the time we finish, you'll be the belle of the ball. I'm sure I have something in my trunk from my days in Frisco." She chuckled, "Before I met Philip, there *were* a few suitors who took me places, such as the opera house."

"I'll go through my trunk as well," said Rachel. "If we need to use needle and thread for some minor alterations, we should have enough time. We all seem to be about the same size."

Maggie smirked, "I have promised myself not to eat any more of our baked goods before the ball. Philip had a gown made for me in San Francisco just for this event. He used one of my dresses for sizing, which I haven't worn in a while. The gown fits, but it's a little snug."

Rachel laughed, "How are we going to know how everything tastes, if we don't test it? I guess we could round up a few *very willing* volunteers to be our official taste testers," she said in jest.

Isabel giggled. "You two are so sweet to me and so much fun. I feel like you're saving my life."

Maggie smiled at Isabel. "You're like a younger sister to us. There's one more thing. As soon as we decide what your gown will be, Philip and I will hire Thomas to make you a pair of shoes to match. You'll need to go for a fitting of course. At least you won't have far to go."

"I just can't thank you enough," said Isabel. "Now I won't be able to sleep from being too excited." *I'm going to be beautiful for Robert!*

Chapter 40

*P*roject *Isabel* was in full production. Maggie had resurrected a topaz gold silk satin gown. It had looked splendid on her against her fiery red hair. Maggie thought it looked even better on Isabel with her chestnut brown hair and dark brown eyes. Rachel contributed a gold and ivory paisley shawl, wrist length gloves, a reticule, and a cameo pendant necklace with matching ear bobs.

The week before the ball, Maggie said, "Time for a dress rehearsal, Isabel." The ladies gathered in Maggie's bedroom and dressed Isabel from head to toe. Thomas had made her a pair of ivory leather flat shoes at Maggie's suggestion.

"This is so much fun, Isabel," said Rachel. "Now let's style your hair. I brought my tortoise shell combs. Notice the carved cameos across the top. They go well with my pendant necklace and ear bobs. I always wear them together. My necklace and ear bobs are very dear to me as they were a gift from my sweet departed husband, so please be extra careful with them."

Isabel replied, "They *are* very special. I'm almost afraid to wear them. I promise to be careful, Rachel."

Maggie and Rachel styled Isabel's hair into a center part with long curls draping the sides of her face, and the remaining hair pulled back into a bun. When they finished, they removed the protective caplet from her shoulders and led her to the mirror hanging on the wall above the dresser. "Now, my dear, look in the mirror. You are stunning," said Maggie, feeling very smug.

"Robert won't be able to resist you," added Rachel.

Isabel saw an extraordinarily beautiful woman reflected in the mirror. She could hardly believe it was her. She gasped and a tear slid down her cheek. "Is this really me?" she asked.

"It is you, my dear," said Maggie. "And I'll be there with you on the night of the ball to help you dress. I'm sure Jane will join in. We'll all help each other dress. In fact, it will be necessary, and when we've finished and we make our entrance on the arm of our handsome men, we *will* turn heads."

* * *

"All aboard for Olympia," shouted Samuel, the first mate. The Bennett party boarded the *California II* while the crew loaded their bags. As the ship steamed out of the harbor, Philip showed the excited passengers to their cabins.

Thomas and Jane were staying in the cabin across from Maggie and Philip's cabin. Isabelle's cabin was next door to Maggie and Philip, and Robert's was next to Thomas and Jane.

After everyone had settled into their cabin, Philip invited them to his and Maggie's cabin to apprise them of the itinerary. "We have about an eight-hour trip before we arrive to Olympia. Ladies, you haven't traveled this route before. You'll enjoy it, it's beautiful country. We'll get a bite to eat in the dining saloon right away. Once we arrive in Olympia, it will be close to dusk so we'll have supper on board and retire to our cabins. Tomorrow, we'll have a few hours to explore Olympia if we so desire. The ball begins early evening at six o'clock."

During the voyage, Robert asked Isabel if she would like to take a stroll on the deck. "You'll be able to see so much more of the scenery from the deck," he said.

"I would be delighted, kind sir." *I'll be on my best behavior,* she promised herself. She grasped his extended arm as he guided her to the deck. After several hours of chatting and laughing, they crossed over the threshold of tension and were finally at ease with each other again. As they leaned on the railing side by side, Robert proudly pointed out special points of interest. He put his arm around her whenever she lost her balance from the movement of the ship. Isabel basked in the warmth of his touch, and thought, *I don't want this to end.*

* * *

It was long past dawn when the Bennett party woke up the next morning. They had slept later than usual. The gentle rocking motion of the anchored vessel had lulled them into a deep slumber.

As Philip splashed water on his face from the basin on the small dresser, he said, "Maggie, that's not like me to sleep so late. Was it the wine we shared last night or the tranquility of this peaceful little harbor?"

"I think it's because you're at peace with yourself, Philip. The Governor has honored you with his invitation to the Governor's Ball and you're sharing it with us. That makes you feel good," said Maggie as she wrapped her arms around him, giving him a morning kiss.

"Now that we're so rested, shall we prepare for the day and join the others. I'm sure they're up and around by now."

After a hearty breakfast in the dining saloon, the merry group disembarked, ready to explore Olympia.

"Well ladies, the Bennett brothers are at your service," said Philip in a jovial voice. "Are you ready to tour Olympia, the capitol of the Territory?"

Each brother extended his arm to his lady and the tour began.

In the two years since the Bennett brothers had come to Olympia, the city showed residual signs of growth. In many ways, Olympia had remained the same. Main Street was still comprised of dirt, muddy in the rainy season and dusty in the dry season. The surrounding area was still punctuated with tree stumps but was now lined with several wooden structures including a two-story Masonic Hall. There were a couple of hotels and a restaurant. The hub of activity remained near the waterfront since the dense forest, the steadfast denizen on the southern end of town, made over-land travel difficult. They were surprised to see the forests of fir, which once lined both sides of the bay, were now replaced by farms.

Also new to the brothers, was the wood causeway built to connect the main peninsula of Olympia to the eastern side of Swantown, later known as Budd Inlet.

Philip needed directions to the Governor's residence, so he led everyone to the general store. "Enjoy browsing ladies, while my brothers and I find out how to get to the ball tonight. The clerk should be able to tell us everything we need to know."

"I'm interested to see how this store compares to the one in Teekalet," said Maggie, her eyes already roaming around the space.

Thomas informed Jane, "This is also a post office. You could pen a letter to your family before we depart tomorrow morning and post it here."

"That's a wonderful suggestion. I shall do so."

After Philip received the information he needed, he said, "I learned we'll need to rent a carriage. The Governor's home is much too far to walk, especially in our finery." He pointed south toward the clusters of trees covering the incline in the distance. "That's where we're going. The state capitol is there now as well."

"A new adventure yet to come," said Maggie. "I've enjoyed visiting this town. Even though it's rustic, it's charming."

Jane exclaimed, "Mr. Sylvester's town square is my favorite."

Isabel added, "The people here are so hospitable. We would have missed seeing his beautiful home if the lady we met hadn't pointed it out. It's two stories high with a tower on top!" *Maybe Robert could add a tower onto our house to view the canal.* "She said Edmund Sylvester is one of the founders of this town."

"That house wasn't here when we arrived in '54," said Robert. "He lived in a log cabin near the bay close to the Indians."

Philip interjected, pointing toward the northwest as he spoke, "Do you see those mountains in the distance? They're called the Olympic Mountains, the inspiration for the founders naming this town Olympia."

Jane looked at Thomas, "It is truly a beautiful country. I'm glad we came in spite of all the adversity."

Philip looked at his time piece. "I'm sorry to cut this short, but we need to reserve the carriage and return to the ship. I'm sure you ladies will want as much time as possible to prepare for the ball."

* * *

Philip was correct. The three women used every minute available to freshen up and dress. Maggie and Jane helped Isabel first.

Once they had finished, Maggie said, "Isabel, Robert will be speechless. You are indeed a vision."

Jane added, "Yes, Isabel, you look truly beautiful. Robert will be overwhelmed with your loveliness."

Isabel stared at herself in the mirror. "I hope you're right. When I look in the mirror, I feel like I'm someone else."

Then Maggie said, "Make sure to keep your cloak closed until we're inside the Governor's home. It's all about presentation and the element of surprise. And it doesn't hurt to throw Robert off balance."

"Now it's time for Maggie and me to get dressed," said Jane. "I think it's best you stay here, Isabel. Relax and enjoy the moment. We shouldn't need your help".

"We'll tap on the door when we're ready to disembark. Be sure you have that cloak on when you step outside the door," Maggie said with a grin.

Maggie and Jane scurried off to their cabins to dress while Isabel continued to stare at herself in the mirror and fantasize about Robert becoming her husband.

Before long there was a tap on Isabel's door signaling it was time to leave. She put the cloak on and joined the Bennetts already gathered in the hall. Isabel was in awe of how beautiful Jane and Maggie looked.

Maggie was wearing her new emerald green silk satin gown complemented with the emerald jewelry Philip had given to her. Her red hair was styled with a part in the center and side coils with a feather headpiece as the final touch. A paisley shawl draped her shoulders.

Jane was wearing the only gown she possessed, but it was stunning. The silk satin gown was sapphire blue trimmed with white lace. She wore a pearl necklace with matching ear bobs and pearl studded combs. Her hair was also parted in the center but rolled back into a bun.

"You're both so beautiful," said Isabel.

She gazed at the men, especially Robert. "How handsome you all look," she said.

The men were wearing black tail coats and trousers with a white cravat and black top hats.

Philip looked approvingly at the women and said, "How fortunate we are, brothers, to be escorting these beautiful belles to the ball. I think you'll agree, we'll be the envy of every man there."

Robert and Thomas smiled, nodding with vigor.

* * *

The carriage ride was brief. Within a half hour, the driver was maneuvering his carriage into line with the other carriages on the tree-lined private drive to the Governor's mansion. There were throngs of people from Olympia society who had accepted the Governor's invitation. Included were members of the Legislature along with officers of the *USS Massachusetts*, which lay anchored in the harbor.

When the Bennett party exited their carriage, they gazed at their surroundings. Large evergreen trees dominated the property and bordered the beautiful grounds of the mansion. Upon approaching the mansion, they stepped up to a wide porch supported by four slender turned posts where the guests had formed a line to enter.

Maggie exclaimed to Jane as they all stepped into the foyer, "I've never seen so many beautifully dressed people at one time."

"And listen to the beautiful music. I do believe it's coming from string and wind instruments. This will be a memorable evening for us," replied Jane.

Isabel squeezed Robert's arm and looked up at him. "I'm looking forward to our first dance."

"As am I," replied Robert.

Philip spotted the Governor and Mrs. Stevens in the reception line greeting their guests. He turned to his little group and said, "Come, let me introduce you."

The Governor warmly greeted them as they were introduced. "I'm pleased to have all of you as my guests. May I present my wife, Mrs. Stevens?"

Mrs. Stevens extended her gloved hand. "Welcome to our home. Please, enjoy the reception. Afterwards, dancing will begin. And after that, we shall dine. Our chef has prepared a superb supper."

Maggie, Jane, and Isabel each curtsied as they thanked the mistress of the mansion.

The reception was a festive event. Lighted candles and chandeliers illuminated the room infusing it with a soft golden glow, and bouquets of flowers gave off a mixture of sweet fragrances. There were tables draped in white linen with plates of seafood accompanied with savory appetizers, and other tables held silver bowls of champagne punch, and for those who did not imbibe in alcohol, bowls of fruit punch stood ready.

The three couples separated, unintentionally. Philip and Maggie were engaged in several conversations. Philip had been introduced as Captain Bennett, making him a person of interest to many of the guests. Maggie chuckled to herself as she listened to her husband bring up the subject of her Lady Kay apple pie. *Oh my dear Philip, you never stop selling.*

Thomas felt a pang of hunger and decided to sample some of the seafood, and said, "Jane, shall we partake of some of these delicacies?" He picked up one of the china plates, neatly stacked near the trays of food. "Would you like me to prepare a plate for you?"

Jane took one look at the raw oysters on the shell, and said, "I'll have some of the shrimp, but no oysters, please."

Robert and Isabel meandered to the punch bowls. May I serve you a cup of punch, Miss Warner?"

"Yes please, Mr. Bennett, I would enjoy some."

Robert automatically served her the fruit punch and served himself the champagne punch. He was pleased with how the punch relaxed him. He was still a bundle of nerves when he was with Isabel. He just didn't know what to do about her. She was his salvation, but also his torment. He poured himself another cup, and then another, finding a new sense of courage.

"Isabel, er, I mean Miss Warner," he said, "I must confess I was stunned with your beauty when you removed your cloak. I found you breathtaking."

Isabel was enjoying this new relaxed Robert and felt a bit braver to reveal her inner thoughts. She held both his hands and looked up at him with her doe-like eyes, "I find you to be the most handsome and exciting man I've ever known. You're always on my mind. I have missed you in the past weeks. Our brief separation made me realize how much you mean to me. I can't imagine not having you in my life."

At that moment, the music began, signaling it was time for the first dance.

Robert extended his arm, "I believe that is our cue. Shall we dance, Miss Warner?"

They entered the ballroom with Philip and Maggie and Thomas and Jane following close behind. As the two couples watched Robert and Isabel, they grinned, each thinking the same thing. Robert was letting down his wall.

They all danced for the duration, taking short breaks off and on.

Philip whispered to Maggie, "Does this make up for not taking you on a honeymoon yet? Are you happy, Maggie?"

"Yes, my Philip, I'm having a wonderful time, and I'm very happy. You are the love of my life. You've treated me like a queen. I *feel* like a queen in this beautiful gown and jewelry."

Philip stepped back for a moment and gazed at her. "You are a queen. My beautiful queen." He glanced around, and discreetly kissed her.

Thomas and Jane were also having a meaningful conversation.

"Jane, you said you're glad we came. Did you mean it?"

"Thomas, I wouldn't have said it, if I didn't. To be honest, I feel like I have the man I married back, and then some. If you'd really like to know, I find you very exciting and as handsome as ever. All those years in Delhi, you always seemed preoccupied. I knew why, and that's the reason I said yes to come here."

"I love you Jane Bennett and you are still as beautiful as the day I married you."

Then Thomas invited his wife back onto the dance floor and twirled her around the room.

Isabel didn't want the dance to end. Every time Robert touched her, she felt a surge of energy ignite between them. *Does he feel it too?*

Finally, the late-night supper was served. The Governor had spared no expense for his guests. The side tables were laden with an extravaganza of food and there were bottles of champagne on every diner's table. The event was more than a ball, but a housewarming celebration for the Governor and his wife's new home.

Governor Stevens clanged his glass and stood. The West Point graduate was of small stature, but he had a commanding presence. When he spoke, people listened.

"Mrs. Stevens and I welcome you to our new home. I'll be forever grateful to President Franklin Pierce of these United States for appointing me to be your Governor of this new Territory. I am honored.

"I'll never forget my first night here. I had also been assigned the task of surveying a northern railway route from the Mississippi River to Puget Sound. I left immediately. It took me six months to reach Olympia.

"Word had reached the fine people of this community that the new governor was arriving soon. Preparations for a lavish reception to greet me were made at the Washington Hotel. I, of course, didn't know about it.

"I arrived alone on a cold winter day in November of '53. I was looking for a place to eat and warm up. I rode up to the Washington Hotel and dismounted my horse. I was cold and weary. I imagine I looked rather disheveled in my well-worn buckskins. When I asked about getting a meal, I was told they were expecting someone important, but I could go to the kitchen and ask the cook.

"Before long they realized the mistake they had made and apologized profusely. Then the celebration went forward. I was honored with a hundred-shot salute fired from a small cannon, along with flag waving, speeches, and a dinner, for which I was most anxious to consume."

The guests laughed. The Governor added, "Some of you were there that day, and I thank you. I raise my glass to you all. To you, our guests, may our home be ever at your service."

Everyone raised their glasses, and shouted, "Here, here!"

For the next hour, the guests took turns raising and clinking their glasses to salute the Governor and Mrs. Stevens. Each with their own special toast.

The Bennett brothers were very fond of champagne and filled their glasses full for every toast. As soon as a champagne bottle was emptied, it was replaced with a full one. Robert filled his glass in between the toasts. He was feeling too good to stop.

Finally, the evening was coming to a close. The guests were reminded of such when the mahogany wall clock in the hall struck the midnight hour.

Everyone gathered, thanking their hosts, and saying their

farewells. The women draped their capes over their shoulders and the men donned their top hats.

As the Bennett party stepped out the door, Maggie exclaimed, "Oh look at the beautiful lanterns glowing in the trees." They followed the light of the lanterns, which were hung every few feet in the branches to illuminate and guide the Governor's guests through the darkness of night back to the drive where their carriages awaited.

Isabel grabbed Robert's arm. He was tipsy and his walk unsteady. He was quite jovial. "Let me assist you, Mr. Bennett. You're a little wobbly. The carriage isn't far."

Philip and Thomas were grinning ear to ear. "I haven't seen Robert drunk like that since we were in England. Looks like Isabel has the situation under control," said Philip.

Thomas replied, "Well, I don't know about you, but I'm certainly feeling no pain. At least I'm walking straight."

The carriage driver delivered the happy couples back to the wharf where they boarded the *California II*. The crew had returned to the ship as well. Philip had granted them shore leave and opened a tab for them at the Gold Bar Restaurant.

The jovial couples walked down the hall toward their cabins, chatting and laughing. Robert's speech was noticeably slurred, so Isabel insisted on helping him to his cabin.

"Don't take long, Isabel. I'll come to your cabin right away to help you out of your dress," said Maggie.

"Thank you, Maggie. I'll be in my cabin waiting for you," replied Isabel as she led Robert to his cabin. "Let me have your key, Mr. Bennett, so I can unlock the door for you."

Isabel left immediately but held onto the key in case the door locked when it was shut. Robert staggered around in his cabin as he disrobed, carelessly tossing his clothes on the floor. Then he crawled into his bed and passed out.

When Isabel returned to her cabin, she immediately removed the cameo ear bobs and safely tucked them into their velvet pouch. They had been pinching her ear lobes the entire night. She rubbed them, *Ah, that feels so much better.* Isabel took one last look in the mirror of herself dressed in the beautiful gown. She sighed. *Maybe someday Robert will have a gown made for me, like Philip did for*

Maggie. Her thoughts were interrupted by Maggie's tap on the door. "Come in, Maggie."

After Maggie helped Isabel out of her dress, she wished her a good night. She chuckled, smiling broadly, "Philip will be helping *me* out of my gown. I best not keep him waiting."

Now alone, Isabel pulled the combs from her hair and shook it loose, letting it tumble over her shoulders. She carefully placed the combs in the velvet pouch. Then she slipped into a semi-sheer nightdress. She was ready.

Isabel slowly opened the door and paused, peering out into the dark hall, looking left, then right. No one was in sight. Quietly, she tiptoed across the hall to Robert's cabin and entered, closing the door tightly and locking it. She removed her nightdress and crept to Robert's bed. When she pulled the covers away, the moonlight spilling into the room through the porthole illuminated his naked chiseled body. She gasped, and her heart palpitated, rapidly. *Oh, how beautiful he is. And now, he is finally mine.*

She began her seduction. She thought about the man from her past who taught her how to please a man. She lost her virginity to him and believed at the time he was the love of her life, but when she asked for a commitment, she learned he was married. She vowed she would never make that mistake again.

Isabel stealthily positioned herself on top of Robert and straddled his thighs. Her long wavy hair fell over her face and draped onto him. Half-conscious as he was, blurred images of the woman he loved flashed in and out of his mind. He could feel the hot heat from Isabel's body, and with half-open eyes, looked up at the beautiful siren hovering over him. He put his hands into Isabel's hair, and grasping it, brusquely pulled her down to him, and kissed her hard and passionately.

Then she slithered down his body, touching him with her lips inch by inch, further and further. In his dazed state of mind, Robert was confused—was this real or was he dreaming? Once Isabel reached her destination with her lips, Robert lost control and succumbed to her seduction. He surrendered, and it was pure ecstasy for both of them. As Isabel blossomed, she moaned, "I love you, Robert."

Robert's inner voice replied, *I love you too, Eleanor.*

Afterward, Isabel put her nightdress back on and quietly slipped across the hall to her room.

* * *

At daybreak the following morning, the first mate sounded the horn of the *California II*, signaling the hour of departure for the voyage back to Teekalet. Thomas quickly hopped off the ship to post Jane's letter she had written that morning to her family in Delhi. As soon as he reboarded, Samuel called out to release the lines and weigh anchor.

As the ship left the Olympia harbor, Philip and Maggie and Thomas and Jane stood at the railing for a final glimpse of Olympia. Their magical evening at the Governor's Ball would always hold a special place in their heart.

After the two couples strolled the deck for a few minutes, Philip looked at his timepiece. "Breakfast should be prepared by now. Shall we partake?"

"Surprisingly, despite the amount of food and champagne I consumed last night, I actually have an appetite," said Thomas rubbing his stomach.

Philip chuckled, "Speaking of champagne, Robert's pretty quiet this morning. I wonder if he's up yet."

Maggie replied, "I haven't seen Isabel stirring yet either. I'll check on her, and tap on Robert's door as well. If he doesn't respond, I guess we'll let him sleep."

"He's bound to have a hangover," said Jane. "He probably won't mind missing breakfast. I noticed Isabel drinking champagne, but not as much as Robert. I'll go with you, Maggie." *A few moments alone with Isabel could be most enlightening.*

"Very good. Thomas and I will get seated in the saloon and wait for you," said Philip.

Maggie and Jane scurried down to the cabins.

Isabel had been awake for awhile, but she was too busy basking in the afterglow of her intimate evening with Robert to leave her bed. She sighed, and finally got up. She didn't want to miss a minute with Robert. As she dressed, she looked in the mirror, *I do believe I'm glowing. It's no wonder, my whole being was on fire—a fire impossible to extinguish. I love him so. I wonder if after last night he loves me? We were so good together. He'll probably feel obliged to marry me now.*

Suddenly, her reverie was interrupted by a tap on the door.

Maggie spoke loud enough to be heard through the door. "Isabel, it's Maggie. Are you up? Jane and I have come to let you know breakfast is ready."

Isabel opened the door and invited them in. "Good morning. I've been moving slowly this morning, but I'm ready to join you."

Jane couldn't wait to hear about Isabel's night with Robert. "How was your evening with Robert? I saw how he looked at you. You must have taken his breath away."

Isabel answered with a love-sick expression. "It was more than I could ever have dreamed." Her mind flashed to Robert's nude body. "Whenever I looked at that handsome man, I melted."

"I think it's pretty obvious, Isabel. You're in love with him," said Maggie.

"It's true. I've lost all reason when it comes to Robert. Is he up yet?"

"We're going to knock on his door next," said Jane. "It didn't sound like he was stirring when we walked past his cabin. I guess we're about to find out."

Maggie knocked on Robert's door and spoke through its thickness. "Robert, are you up? Breakfast is served."

There was total silence. "I guess we'll let him sleep. He probably won't want breakfast anyway. He was pretty wobbly last night," said Maggie. "Shall we go to breakfast ladies?"

A few hours later, Robert finally left his cabin and found everyone on the deck. He felt rough and looked rough.

"Well, it's about time you made an appearance, Robert," said Philip.

Thomas interjected, "You're not looking so good, Robert."

Robert replied in a quiet voice. "Well, I'm not feeling so good either. It's been a long time since I drank so much." He looked over at Jane, Maggie, and Isabel standing at the railing. "The ladies look well. I'll go pay my respects."

After Robert greeted the ladies, Isabel immediately grabbed his arm and said, "Would you like to take a stroll around the deck? It'll be like the walks we *used* to take."

"Of course, as long as we don't walk too fast," Robert replied extending his arm to her.

A few minutes into their stroll, Isabel had a question she was dying to ask. "Did you enjoy last night as much as I did?" Her eyes locked on him while waiting for his answer.

Robert managed to smile at her, despite the pounding in his head. "I don't remember the entire night, Miss Warner, but what I do remember I enjoyed very much. You looked beautiful in your gown, and I'm sure I was the envy of every man in the room."

Robert's answer wasn't quite what Isabel expected or wanted to hear. *He was so responsive last night. How could he not mention our act of love? Perhaps he'll remember once he feels better and thinks more about our night together. I'll just have to be patient until next time.*

* * *

Philip looked at his time piece. "Well, Maggie, in about an hour we'll be entering Teekalet Bay. We made good time. As I had hoped, we'll be going back home in the daylight."

"Philip, I had so much fun at the Governor's Ball last night. It was like being in a fairy tale, and you made me feel so special," said Maggie as she leaned on the ship's railing while enjoying the warmth of the summer sun on her skin.

"You are special, my darling. It made me smile to watch all of you having so much fun on the dance floor. I hadn't realized my brothers knew how to dance so well."

Maggie reflected for a moment. "You know, this trip was good for all of us in different ways. For us, it was like a honeymoon. For Jane and Thomas, it was a time for them to make up for the many months they were apart, and for Isabel and Robert, an opportunity for a budding romance to blossom."

* * *

The next day at the bakery, Maggie and Isabel were back to work.

"Welcome back, you two ladies of *high society*. I want to hear everything about the Governor's Ball and don't leave out a single detail," said Rachel giving each of them a hug.

"We'll chat while we work. I'm sure there must be a backlog due to our absence," said Maggie. "Thank you for taking on the extra load, Rachel, so we could go play."

"You're most welcome. I was pleased to do it." Rachel smiled at Isabel, "I'm guessing you have some favorable news about Robert to share?"

"It was so wonderful, Rachel, and thank you again for loaning me your jewelry and accessories. I put everything safely into Maggie's trunk."

Maggie added, "Rachel, would you like to come over tonight to pick up your belongings?"

"Do you mind if I come another night instead, Maggie? I'm making a dress for Annie for her birthday and I'm running out of time. It's a surprise for her."

"Please feel free to take your time, Rachel. Isabel did such a nice job of placing my gown and underpinnings into the trunk, I didn't have to do a thing. She placed your gloves, shawl, reticule, and jewelry pouch right on top."

Isabel smiled, happy with the compliment.

* * *

Philip answered the door. "Why, Samuel, what brings you here?" *He must have had the mill ferry him here. I wonder what could be so urgent?*

"I'm sorry to disturb you at home, Captain Bennett, but I thought you should know about this right away." Samuel brought out a small item wrapped in a muslin cloth. He unwrapped it, revealing a cameo pendant necklace.

"Our cleaning lady, Gertie, brought this to me. She found it in the bed in cabin two while she was changing the bedding. I figured someone must be very upset knowing this is missing. It looks valuable."

Philip's mind flashed back to the night of the Governor's Ball. *Isabel was wearing this necklace, but cabin two? That was Robert's cabin! That sly devil!*

"Thank you, Samuel, I do know who this belongs to. You did the right thing. Please let me know how much the pilot charges you and I'll reimburse you immediately. And tell Gertie her honesty is commendable. I won't forget it."

As soon as Samuel left, Maggie was by Philip's side, "Philip, I couldn't help but overhear. That's the necklace Rachel loaned to Isabel. Thank goodness I still have Rachel's jewelry pouch in my trunk. I'll put her necklace in it without her ever having to know it had been lost. No need upsetting her. *I'm most displeased with Isabel. That was extremely careless of her. I won't ever be lending her any of my jewelry in the future.* Did I hear Samuel say cabin two?"

"Yes," replied Philip.

"But wasn't cabin two Robert's cabin?"

Philip nodded. "Now, you're catching on."

Maggie's mouth dropped open. "Oh my."

"For now, let's just keep this between the two of us. Robert was so drunk, I wonder if he even realizes she was with him in his cabin. We'll watch and see how this plays out."

"Yes, for both of their sakes, we will be discreet."

Chapter 41

A month had passed since the Governor's Ball. Philip had just returned from a business trip in San Francisco, where upon checking with Hank at the post office, learned there was mail waiting for him. It was a letter from his home town of Weymouth, England. As he read it, he thought, *This is a matter to discuss with Robert and Thomas.*

After letting Maggie know he had returned, he kissed her and told her he needed to discuss some family business with his brothers. "I'll tell you all about it when I come back."

Philip found his brothers, as usual, at their business building.

"Welcome back," said Thomas and Robert in unison.

Philip's eyes scanned the room. "It looks as though you two have been busy. I hope you're caught up. We have another piece of business to discuss."

Robert raised an eyebrow. "No risky ventures, I hope."

"No, nothing risky, but it's going to require one of us to go to England, and soon."

"Now, you have me curious," said Thomas. "What's going on?"

Philip held out the letter. "This letter from our solicitor in Weymouth was waiting for me at the post office in Frisco. It seems we need to make new arrangements about our parents' estate. The people who have been living there for the past several years have aged to the point of not being able to maintain it any longer. First, it sounds like the place needs some work to get it back to the way it once was. Then, we need to decide whether we continue to rent or lease it, or, shall we sell it? Mr. Reynolds indicates the people plan to move out by the end of the year, so one of us will need to be there once they've vacated."

"If you have time, Philip, this is as good a time as any to discuss it. Let's sit at the table. We have a bottle of whiskey in the cupboard. Can I pour you a drink?"asked Robert.

"I'll bring out three glasses," said Thomas.

As they sipped their drinks, Robert was reminded of his hangover after the Governor's Ball. He looked down at the amber liquid he sloshed around in his glass, and said, "Next time we're together at a social event where free alcohol is being served, *please* don't let me over drink. I don't remember boarding the ship or even getting to my cabin that night. And the next day, I paid dearly with a terrible hangover. I could barely hold my head up."

"I can vouch for that," chuckled Thomas, "You were worthless for the next couple of days."

Philip grinned at Robert, "While we're on the subject of the ball, you and Isabel looked pretty cozy. It's been a long time since I've seen you so relaxed with a woman. Have you seen her much since the ball?"

"We've had a couple of walks, but I'm continuing to take it slow and easy. I'm still confused about what I should do. You know, maybe I should be the one to go to England. Some distance between us might be good, and it will give me a chance to clear my head. I need to make a decision one way or the other. Besides, you two have wives who might not like you being gone so long. Thomas, do you think you'll be able to pick up the slack here?"

"With our extra help, I should be fine. Matthew and Christopher have learned quickly and they're doing a fine job overseeing our Chinese workers. It's worth it for me to stay here and carry the load. Jane and I have been apart too much."

"Then it's decided. Robert you're elected to go," said Philip. "And if we're all in agreement, we'll leave it up to you to evaluate the situation and decide what's best for all of us—to keep it or sell it. I'm figuring if you go the Panama route, it'll take you about two months to get to England."

"Hmm, that means I best leave soon," replied Robert. "I guess you fellas won't be seeing my face around here for four or five months." *Isabel isn't going to like this.*

Philip already had a plan in mind. "We'll time your departure with my next business trip to San Francisco. I'll take you to

Panama where you'll cross the Isthmus on the Panama Railway to the Atlantic side. From there, you'll catch the next steamer to New York and then one to England. On my return trip, I'll stop off at Mazatlán and combine some business with Alberto and visit Emily."

"I'll look forward to hearing how our daughter is doing. Jane and I will send a letter with you to give to Emily," said Thomas. "Now that I think about it, I'm sure Jane will want to go with you. I once told myself I'd be going on the next trip to Mazatlán, but not this time. I'm needed here. At least, Philip, you brought our children and our new grand baby to us last December. That was a wonderful gesture on your part."

"It was my pleasure to bring everyone together."

"Jane is going to be so excited when I tell her this. She'll enjoy seeing Jonathan working by your side, Philip."

"I'm sure he'll make his mother proud. When we stop in Frisco, I'll plan an extra day there so we can all pay a visit to Jeremy and see how he's doing."

"Brilliant!" exclaimed Thomas.

The brothers clinked glasses. "With our situation in hand now, I shall take my leave, brothers. I have an impatient wife waiting for me," laughed Philip.

* * *

Early September 1857

Bennett Settlement

It was Wednesday, the Seabeck delivery day. The bells on the door jingled as Robert entered the building.

Maggie smiled, "Good morning, Robert. You're right on time as usual."

"Good morning, ladies." Robert's eyes landed on Isabel for a brief moment. He knew she would be disappointed with what he was about to say. "Before I load up, I have some news to share with you ladies."

Maggie knew about his news. Philip had told her, but asked her not to say anything until Robert had a chance to announce his plan.

"You have our attention, Robert," said Rachel.

"Yes, please tell us," added Isabel, who didn't know whether to be nervous or excited.

Robert continued. "This will be my last Seabeck delivery for a while. Some family business back home in England has come up, which needs immediate attention. I've been elected to be the one to go, so Thomas will take over the deliveries until I get back."

Isabel was crestfallen. "How—how long will you be gone?"

"Due to the distance from this side of the continent and how much time I'll spend in Weymouth, I'll be gone about four to five months."

"When are you leaving?" asked Isabel, obviously distraught with Robert's spur of the moment announcement.

Maggie and Rachel observed some tension between the couple and decided to give them some space. They made themselves busy and finished filling the crates with the bakery order for Robert.

Robert took a step closer to Isabel. "I'll miss you. I'm glad we had an opportunity to spend time together at the ball. It was a memorable night. This might be a good thing. I'll have a chance to think things through." *She drives me crazy. I have to make a decision. I don't want to give her false hope until I know for sure if I'm ready to make a commitment to her. This trip is perfect for me to get some distance and clear my head.*

"A good thing?" asked Isabel. She kept her voice low, barely able to disguise the bitterness she was beginning to feel.

Robert bent down and kissed her on the cheek. "I'll try to say goodbye before I leave. Now, I best load these goods into the boat, or I'll run out of daylight hours."

"I certainly hope I see you before you go," said Isabel. *And I want a proper kiss, not a peck on the cheek.* She watched him go out the door, still holding back tears. *I needed more time to tell him. I've missed my monthly flow, but I won't know for sure until I miss another one. One more month was all I needed. I couldn't say anything until I knew for certain, and now he'll be gone. He's ruined everything. At least when he returns and sees me carrying his child, he'll do the honorable thing and marry me. Maybe while he's doing his thinking, he'll recall our night together in his cabin. He'll realize he can't live without me.*

Chapter 42

Mid-September 1857

Bennett Settlement/Teekalet

*J*onathan glanced at his pocket watch, "Mother, you need to hurry," he said as he picked up one of her bags.

"I just hope I haven't forgotten anything," said Jane as she scanned the room. Then she remembered the two baskets of preserves she had prepared for Jeremy and Emily. She dashed to the kitchen and returned with the baskets. "I knew I was forgetting something."

Thomas shook his head and chuckled. "It's a good thing there are three of us to carry everything you're taking."

Jonathan put one of Jane's bags under his arm and took the baskets from his mother. "Are we ready now? Uncle Philip and Uncle Robert are already on the wharf waiting for us. I've learned not to keep Uncle Philip waiting. He's very stringent about time."

Thomas offered the crook of his arm to Jane which was all that was available to offer. One of her bags was under his other arm and both his hands were needed to carry the remainder. Feeling the weight of the bags, he asked, "What all are you taking? You're not going to be gone that long."

"Gifts for our grandbaby and our children. I raided our pantry, and I've been sewing like crazy for little Georgiana."

Thomas smiled back at his wife, "You're a thoughtful mother and grandmother."

When the Bennetts reached the wharf, Peter was ready with the workboat to transport them to Teekalet where the *California II* awaited them.

Thomas kissed Jane goodbye. "I'm going to miss you, my lady. Tell our children how much I love them."

"I will, my darling. I'm so excited to see them, in spite of it being a short visit."

While Jonathan helped his mother board, Robert pulled Thomas aside. He handed Thomas a folded letter. "Would you give this to Miss Warner for me? I had told her I would say goodbye before I left, but I think it's better this way. She looked like she was holding back tears when I told her the news of my trip. I wouldn't even know what to do if she broke down in front of me. It's not something I handle well."

"I'll wait until you're at Teekalet and boarding the ship before I hand it to her." Thomas gave his brother a hug. "You take care of business in Weymouth, and I'll take care of business here." Then he looked over at Jonathan waiting to say goodbye. "Jonathan, come and give me a hug, and watch over your mother for me."

"I will Father." He looked over at the boat. "It appears I'm the last one to board. See you later."

Thomas watched the boat disappear and walked back to the business building. He walked over to one of the work tables where Matthew and Christopher were working.

"Well, lads, Robert is on his way to England. I'm counting on your support for the next four or five months. I know Robert did a good job apprising you of his tasks." He looked out the window in the direction of the bakery. "I'll be gone for a few minutes."

Holding Robert's letter in his hand, Thomas walked toward the bakery. It seemed so quiet with part of his family gone. The only sound he heard was the familiar crunch of the oyster shell path and the distant caws of seagulls.

As Thomas entered the building, the bells on the door jingled announcing his visit.

Maggie was the closest to the door and greeted Thomas. "Hello, Thomas. Is Jane gone now? I guess you're going to be a bachelor for a little while. Can we help you with anything? A sweet pastry to take home with you?"

Isabel's ears perked up when Maggie asked if Jane was gone. *Gone? Surely not yet.*

"Yes, they left early this morning." Thomas looked over at Isabel and held out the letter. "Isabel, Robert left this for you. He said he was sorry he didn't get a chance to say goodbye." *Brother, you're turning me into a liar. I admit he didn't ask me to lie, but what else am I supposed to say? Tell her he doesn't want to watch her cry? I don't want to watch either, I'm getting out of here before she reads whatever he wrote.*

"Good day to you, ladies. I mustn't tarry. My work awaits." Thomas quickly exited the building and didn't look back.

Isabel looked down at the somewhat crumpled letter in her hands. She was shocked that Robert hadn't kept his promise to say goodbye to her.

Rachel could see that Isabel was emotional. She offered a suggestion, "Why don't you take a break to read your letter?"

Isabel looked up, still numb from the shock and answered in a solemn tone. "Yes, Rachel, that's a good idea. Thank you." She went outside to sit on the bench under the apple tree for some privacy.

Isabel couldn't help thinking it was a beautiful fall day. Perfect for a short romantic walk to say farewell. The air was crisp, but not too cool, and the leafy trees were turning into beautiful colors of gold, red, orange, and bronze. The ground was a mosaic of color carpeted by leaves. If not a walk, they could have been sitting on this bench with him holding her hand as he said goodbye. Then ending the goodbye in a kiss so passionate, he would be unable to forget her.

She took a deep breath and unfolded the letter. Tears now set free, dropped onto the letter, as she read the disappointing words. The letter was a polite goodbye without a clue of what he felt for her. He mentioned again he had a lot of *thinking* to do. The final blow was how he signed it, *In deepest friendship, Robert Bennett.*

She vehemently crumpled up the letter, threw it on the ground, and stomped on it, crushing the leaves it fell upon.

You buffoon! Do you have to be drunk to show any emotion? Then she thought of their child she might be carrying. She bent down and picked the letter up. She smoothed it, folded it, and put it in her apron pocket. She looked down and put her hand lovingly on her belly. *Little one, you will be my miracle. He is an honorable man and will not turn his back on you. I will become Mrs. Robert Bennett and we will all be together in his beautiful house. And I will ask him to build a tower on top so that we may view the canal together. Yes, little one, we need to be patient for his return.*

Isabel composed herself and went back into the building to resume her tasks. Maggie and Rachel exchanged glances. They had no idea what was in that letter, but they doubted it was what Isabel had hoped for.

Chapter 43

Late September 1857

San Francisco

*T*en days later after leaving Teekalet, the *California II* steamed into the Golden Gate harbor. Philip planned to stay in the harbor only long enough to replenish fuel and water.

Jane stood at the railing and gazed out at the city where her son now lived. Philip had told her she and Jonathan would have just enough time to say hello to Jeremy while the ship was being refueled.

With the gift basket in one hand, Jonathan helped his mother disembark with the other, then hailed a cab. "Let's go surprise Jeremy, Mother. We only have an hour."

The driver stopped in front of the brick building of the private investigator, Oliver Scott. Jonathan asked the driver to wait for them, as they wouldn't be staying long. When they entered the reception room, they learned that Jeremy and Oliver were out on a case.

The receptionist remembered Jane and Jonathan. "It's so nice to see you both."

"And you as well, Dorthea," replied Jane. "Would you give this basket to Jeremy and tell him to expect to see us on our way back from Mazatlán in about three weeks?"

"It will be a short visit. We'll just be passing through so we can only stay a day," added Jonathan.

"I'll let them know as soon as they come in. I'm sure they'll be most pleased to find your gift basket waiting for them."

They thanked Dorthea and headed for the cab.

The driver took them back to the ship with a few minutes to spare. When they returned, the crew was finishing up loading water barrels onto the ship.

Philip was surprised to see Jane and Jonathan back so soon.

Jonathan explained, then said, "I'll let Samuel know we're back, Uncle Philip, so we can be on our way."

"Very good, Jonathan."

Robert helped Jane board the ship and stood with her along the railing and watched the city disappear as the ship went back out to sea.

As they left San Francisco behind, Jane felt a sense of melancholy to have missed an opportunity to see her son.

Robert was still next to her and noticed she looked sad. "Jane, are you all right?"

"Oh Robert, don't mind me. I guess I'm just an overemotional mother. I'm so disappointed I didn't get to see my Jemmie. I was so excited to hand him my gift basket and watch him peek inside to discover what I had brought him. He loves surprises. At least he will have the pleasure of the gift when he returns and finds it waiting for him. He'll know I was there. I'll have to be patient and see him on our return trip."

"Jane, you're a wonderful mother, and you're not overemotional. I'm sure he'll be excited about your gift. He'll know you're coming back. And remember, Philip will make sure that you will continue to see the children whenever he can make it possible. He's very thoughtful that way."

"You're right, Robert. And here I am talking about myself when you're about to be gone for several months with decisions to make. I hope all goes well for you, Robert. It's obvious you've been struggling for some clarity in your life. Maybe this trip is exactly what you need."

Robert hesitated answering for a moment as he stared out to sea. "Perhaps so, Jane."

* * *

Two weeks later, the *California II* entered the Bay of Panama. Although it was considered a port, it wasn't a typical port. There were no deepwater wharfs, so ships had to anchor several miles from shore, which meant passengers and baggage or freight had to be transferred to shore by small boats.

"Well, here we are, Robert," said Philip.

Robert embraced Jane and Jonathan. "I guess this is goodbye."

Philip shaded his eyes and looked out toward the shore. "I see a small boat heading this way."

"Good thing I traveled light, there's not much room in that boat," chuckled Robert. "I'm looking forward to the train ride. Evidently it will only take a day to cross the isthmus. The train hasn't been running for very long. They finished it in '55. I understand it took five years to lay forty-seven miles of rail. Quite a few people died laying track."

"How did you learn so much about the train?" asked Philip.

"When I made my last Seabeck delivery, I told Randolph and James about my upcoming trip to England and that I would be taking the Panama route. There happened to be a customer who overheard our conversation. He had traveled that route and told me all about it."

Philip nodded at the boatman who had just arrived before giving Robert a bear hug. "I'll miss you brother. Send a letter off as soon as you get there, so I know you arrived safely."

"I will, Philip." He grabbed his bag and climbed down the rope ladder hanging down the side of the ship and jumped into the transfer boat. He looked back up at his brother, smiled, and waved.

Philip watched over Robert until he saw him reach the shoreline and step onto land. Then he yelled out to Samuel, "Weigh anchor. Next stop, Mazatlán."

Chapter 44

November 1857

Weymouth, England

It was a grey day when Robert arrived, fitting he thought, for visiting his parents' gravesite. It had been thirteen years since his last visit to his hometown—the last time he saw his parents alive.

With fresh flowers in hand, Robert walked through the entrance of Weymouth Cemetery. The cemetery had grown. He figured if he could remember where his grandparents had been laid to rest, he would find his parents' headstones. He recalled they had been buried near an English oak tree and a stone fountain. His eyes roamed across the landscape until they stopped at the two landmarks. The tree was much taller now. He carefully walked through the maize of headstones until he found his grandparents' markers, then his parents. There he saw for the first time, his parents' names with dates of birth and death engraved into a block of granite. Sadness and guilt swept over him as though a dark cloud had cast a shadow upon his solitary figure for neglecting his parents in their later years. Then he realized someone had placed fresh flowers on his parents' graves. *Who would have done that?* He kneeled down and added his flowers, wishing he could thank the person who must have cared about his parents in his absence. He remained kneeling to converse with them, then ended his visit with a prayer.

Being back in England brought back many memories about Eleanor. He had thought he pushed her out of his mind until he saw her one day in the town center when he and his brothers last visited their aging parents. She appeared to still be married and prosperous. He realized she was a mother when he saw two children walking beside her. It was at that moment, he gave up all hope of ever getting Eleanor back.

During the entire trip to England, Robert continued to wrestle with his feelings for Isabel and he had still not come to a decision to make a commitment to her. He knew she loved him, but could he love her as long as Eleanor still owned his heart? Robert opened his watch cover and gazed at Eleanor's portrait inside. *Oh, Eleanor, you are lost to me. Somehow, I need to move on.* He decided after his meeting with the family solicitor, he would write a letter to Isabel.

The meeting with the solicitor was productive. The question of what to do with the estate was made easy for Robert since the solicitor already had a vetted lessee ready to sign if the Bennett brothers agreed. The only contingency was a guarantee the house and grounds would be restored to a satisfactory condition.

"You've made it easy for me to make a decision, Mr. Reynolds. I'll agree to those conditions. I have my brothers' approval to go along with whatever decision I make. If you would be so kind as to give me a key, I will look the place over. As soon as I ascertain what needs to be done, I'll get things started. Your service has been excellent, Mr. Reynolds, thank you."

"It's a pleasure to be of service, Mr. Bennett. I've known your family for many years. Your parents were fine people." The solicitor handed Robert the key and shook hands with him.

"One more thing, Mr. Reynolds. Is the post office still in the same building in the town center? I'd like to send a letter to my brothers and update them."

"Yes, it's in the same building. Not much has changed around here."

* * *

After leaving the solicitor's office, Robert went straight to the family estate. He was saddened to see how much it had gone downhill. It reminded him of the visit he and his brothers made in '44. Like the people who had lived here, their parents' age had prevented them from maintaining the house and grounds. He remembered how he and his brothers went to work and put everything in order.

He spent several hours looking the place over and made a detailed list of what needed to be done and who should be hired. He planned to ask for referrals from Mr. Reynolds along with a manager to oversee any improvements that weren't completed by the time he left.

It had been a long day, so he went back to his hotel. Once he settled in, he sat down to write two letters. The one to his brothers was easy; the second letter, to Isabel, was not.

Robert had finally decided to rid himself of his indecisiveness and make a commitment to Isabel. *I know she loves me. She's beautiful and the fact that I'm twenty years her senior, doesn't seem to bother her. She's young enough to give me children. I might still have time to have what Thomas has. I care for her, but if I keep Eleanor locked inside my heart, I'll be unable to fall in love with her or anyone. I believe I'm ready to free myself to find love again. I'm going to ask Isabel to marry me.*

Robert felt like a great weight had been lifted. He left his room and descended the stairs with a contented look on his face. First, he went to the bar and ordered a whiskey and water. He smiled at himself, *one drink and that's it*. After keeping his promise to himself, he sat down at a table in the dining room for a quiet meal. As he ate, he mulled over everything he had written in his letter to Isabel. *I haven't mailed it yet, there's still time to change my mind. No, I'm tired of being alone. I'm going forward.*

Robert slept well that night. His mind was at peace.

The next morning Robert woke to the sounds of a waking town. After living at the peaceful canal, such sounds seemed foreign to him. It was time to get up anyway. It was chilly out, so he put on his leather jacket. The jacket was special to Robert since Thomas had made it for him for his birthday. It was also special because it was unique. Thomas had cleverly designed it with an inside pocket which looked nearly invisible.

Robert often kept his money there. Today, he inserted the letters into the pocket. He decided he would have breakfast downstairs and then head to the post office. He hadn't been to the town center yet. He wondered if he'd notice any changes.

After breakfast, he walked to the post office. The town center was buzzing with people. *The population has grown*, he thought. He worked his way through the throngs and finally saw the post office building.

He brought the letters out from his pocket and held them in his hand. He handed the letter to his brothers to the mail clerk first. He looked at the second letter and hesitated. There were impatient people in line behind him, making it obvious he was holding up the line. He stepped away. "Wait on these people," he said. He stared at the letter. He stepped back in line, still holding the letter.

Suddenly, he heard a woman's voice call out his name. He turned to see who it belonged to. *Who knows me here?*

"Robert!" the woman shouted again.

He followed the sound of the voice. His eyes widened, his jaw dropped, and his heart pounded so fast he thought it might explode. "Eleanor?" He quickly tucked the letter back inside his jacket pocket and stepped out of the mail line.

Eleanor rushed toward him. "It's really you! What are you doing here?" Eleanor's eyes zoomed in on his ring finger. *No ring?*

Robert's voice softened as he answered her. "I'm here to handle my parents' estate. There's been a change of status so one of us had to come and I was elected since I—." He stopped short, not wanting to admit that he was the one who wasn't married. *She'd think I'm pathetic,* he thought. "The reason doesn't matter."

"It's been so long, Robert." Eleanor glanced down at his hand again. "Do you have time to have a cup of tea with me?"

"It would be my pleasure, Eleanor."

Eleanor grabbed his arm. Her touch felt as natural as it did so many years ago. "Do you remember the little tea house we used to go to? Would you like to go there?"

"Your wish is my command."

Eleanor laughed lightly. "Robert, that's what you always used to say to me."

"It just slipped out!"

When they walked in, the owner recognized them. He saw Eleanor frequently and knew quite a lot about her life. It was a small town.

"Oh my Lord," the man said. "Are my eyes deceiving me? Is it so? You two are back together after all these years? I always liked you two together. I didn't know you were back Robert."

With a perplexed look on his face, Robert answered, "Hello, Mr. Taylor. I'm only here for a little while. It's very nice to see you're still here."

Robert pulled out the chair for Eleanor and seated her. Then he sat across from her.

Mr. Taylor came over to wait on them. "I know exactly what you two want to order. Darjeeling tea and crumpets with berry jam." He puffed up with pride. "Am I correct? How's that for a memory?"

"I'm impressed," said Robert. "Eleanor, shall we order our usual for old times sake?"

"Brilliant, Robert." She glanced at his hand again.

"You heard the lady, Mr. Taylor."

"Robert, you did it again. You always used to say that. I feel like I've gone back in time."

"I wish we could, Eleanor. You know you're just as beautiful as ever?"

Eleanor counted back the years in her head. "Robert, can you believe it's been over twenty years? A lot can happen in such a span of time." Then she extended her hand to his side of the table.

Robert looked down and noticed she wasn't wearing a wedding ring. "I see you're not wearing a ring, Eleanor."

"It's true, and I see you're not wearing a ring. I'm a widow. Are you a widower?"

"I've never married, Eleanor." Robert paused a moment, then locked his eyes to hers and whispered, "I suppose it's because I've never found another you. I've never stopped loving you, Eleanor."

"And I've always loved you, Robert."

"How can you say that when you told me to leave and you were marrying someone else?"

"Robert, will you come with me to my cottage? There is so much to tell you and I don't want to say it here. It's walking distance."

"As you wish."

Robert paid the bill and said goodbye to Mr. Taylor.

* * *

"Please, make yourself comfortable, Robert. Would you care for some sherry?"

Robert sat down on the settee but declined the sherry. He wanted to be alert for this conversation.

Eleanor sat next to him, grasped one of his hands, and proceeded to pour her heart out. "Robert, I was in a loveless marriage. All my husband cared about was that I gave him a male heir. He owned me. You didn't know, but my father arranged my marriage to a man with title and wealth. I loved you so, I would have married you even if my father would have disowned me, but I married Anthony to save you."

"What do you mean, save me?"

"My father threatened to destroy you, and if I left England to go with you and he couldn't reach his long arm out to hurt you, he threatened to destroy your father instead. Anthony knew about you as well and unless I submitted to him, he also threatened to harm you. So you see, I had to give you up to save you."

"I had no idea. Your father was a scoundrel. I'm assuming he's passed on?"

Eleanor nodded. "Both my parents are gone now. I visit their graves regularly."

"I visited Weymouth Cemetery yesterday soon after I arrived and was surprised to find fresh flowers on my parents' grave. I wondered who had placed them there. Do you know who had cared about them?"

"Oh Robert, I must confess. I visited your parents regularly while they were alive. I was desperate to maintain a connection with you. And now, I frequently visit their gravesite and bring flowers."

"I didn't know. They never mentioned it in their letters."

"I asked them not to tell you. I thought there was no hope of us ever being together again, but I just couldn't let go of you completely."

"Do you have children, Eleanor?" He didn't want to admit he had seen her with her children thirteen years prior. Not at that moment at least.

"Yes, I have a son and a daughter. They're adults now. My son lives nearby on our estate. I should say *his* estate. When my husband died, he left almost everything to him. My son and I are *not* close. He's so much like my husband. You'll be surprised to know that my daughter moved to America. She lives in Kentucky. We were close. It was hard on me to see her move away. How fortunate it was that I saw you at the post office. I had just mailed a letter to my daughter, Josephine."

She looked deep into Robert's eyes with tears welling, and said,

"Oh Robert, I confess, I still love you so much. I hope you still feel the same. I'm free now. Can't you see? I believe we're meant to be together. I want to be with you in every way, and I don't care about any rules. I've been following everybody else's rules all my life."

Robert leaned toward her and kissed her gently. He knew now why he hesitated to mail the letter. His instinct wouldn't allow him. "Eleanor, marry me." He longed to kiss her passionately but was afraid he wouldn't stop at only a kiss. "I yearn to make love to you at this moment, but I want you to be my wife first."

"I don't care if we're married before we make love. We've been apart too many years, Robert."

"Eleanor, before you answer, there is something you should know. I don't want any secrets between us. Recently, I've become involved with a young woman. For years I rebuffed every woman who offered herself to me. You are the only woman I ever wanted, but finally, I accepted that I had lost you forever. I didn't want to continue my life alone. I have kissed her and desired her, but nothing else has happened. I haven't made a commitment to her, but was very close to doing so. I knew I could never love her the way I have loved you, but I was willing to accept it and move on with my life."

"Thank you for telling me, Robert. How could I blame you? You couldn't have been expected to live a life alone. I can only be grateful that I found you in time. Yes, Robert, of course, I will marry you."

"I should have asked you first, are you positive you're willing to come to America with me? I have a home there and my family lives near me. I must warn you, life there is more primitive than what you experience here."

"There's nothing to stop me now, Robert. As long as we're together, that's all that matters. Yes, I will come.

"At least I'll be in the same country as my daughter. She's made me a grandmother now.

"My son and his wife are childless thus far. It's ironic, isn't it? Like my husband, Richard is obsessed about producing a male heir. He has such an ego, I'm sure he blames his wife for the *deficiency.*

"Robert, are you sure about this? You must realize that it's too late for me to have any more children. Are you willing to give up having your own children?"

"Eleanor, you are my heart. I won't allow anything to separate us now that we've found each other. Besides, I have wonderful nieces and nephews. We're very close."

"If you're sure."

"Yes, Eleanor, I want you to come back with me as Mrs. Robert Bennett." He kissed her gently again, and said, "Once we're married, we're not wasting a second to be together as man and wife."

She glanced toward her bedroom, "I thought about inviting you to my bed tonight, but if you insist on waiting, you could sleep on the sofa. I can't bear being separated from you ever again."

Robert chuckled, "My darling Eleanor, you're testing my self-control. No, I must return to my hotel, for if I don't, I fear I will awake in your bed to the morning light."

"You're so poetic, Robert. A woman can always hope," she laughed.

Robert took her in his arms and kissed her. "Now, my darling, I'll say goodnight. My time here will be even busier than expected. I want to finish business here as soon as possible and afterwards, book passage for the two of us on the next ship departing for America. An idea has come to me. I want us to be married on the ship. I'll be checking to see if there will be a chaplain on board."

"That sounds so romantic, Robert. I'll start tomorrow to take care of my affairs. I'll ask my solicitor, Mr. Reynolds, to assist."

"Now I know we were meant to be together, we have the same solicitor," he laughed. "Expect to see me on your doorstep early in the morning. We can go to *our* solicitor's office together. Then, we will go to the jeweler and pick out our wedding rings."

"That's sounds marvelous, Robert. I'll be ready."

Chapter 45

November 1857

Bennett Settlement

$\mathcal{I}$t was Wednesday, Seabeck delivery day. Maggie, Rachel, and Isabel were finishing up the orders when they heard the familiar sound of the bells jingling on the front door.

"Good morning, Thomas," said Maggie in a cheerful voice.

"And to you too, ladies." Thomas inhaled the aroma of the bakery goods. "It always smells so good in here."

Maggie asked, "How are you faring during Robert's absence? He must be in England by now."

"Philip and I are waiting for a letter from him. He said he would post one right after his arrival."

"Would you let us know how he is doing when you hear from him? When do you think he will be returning?" asked Isabel.

"Of course, I'll be happy to let you know. I expect him back sometime in March or April." Thomas was uneasy talking about Robert with Isabel. He felt a sense of flight. He looked out the window. "I best be going, it looks like we may get some snow." He quickly loaded the goods into his cart to take to the workboat awaiting him at the wharf.

Isabel gazed out the window as she watched Thomas leave. At the moment, Thomas was her best source of information to learn anything about Robert. There was no doubt now she was carrying Robert's child. She calculated she was four months along, since it had been four months since the crimson wave had visited her. She wouldn't be able to hide the pregnancy much longer. She had altered her clothes to hang looser, but soon it would be obvious that she had a baby growing inside her. *Will I be greeting him with a mountainous belly or our babe in my arms? Will I receive a letter from him confessing he wants me to be his wife?* At that moment, a wave of nausea came over her. She had thought the morning sickness stage was finally over, but once in a while it crept in. The aroma of the pies and cakes lingering in the room always triggered the feeling. *So far Maggie and Rachel haven't caught on. They don't realize the real reason I'm using the privy.*

Isabel needed to leave, and announced to Maggie and Rachel, "I'm not feeling well. Since we have finished the order, would you mind if I leave for a while to lie down? I can come back in a couple of hours if you need me?"

"You do look a little pale, Isabel. Take your time, we have everything under control here. Yu Yan will be coming in soon for her shift, so we should be fine," replied Maggie as she studied Isabel.

After Isabel left, Maggie said to Rachel, "Something seems different about Isabel. Have you noticed, Rachel?"

"Yes, I have. Especially her mysterious trips to the privy, the fact that she's been arriving late, and I believe she has gained weight."

The two women looked at each other, aghast, realizing the reality of what was staring at them in the face.

"It can't be true, can it, Rachel?"

"After having two children, I recognize all the signs. I fear it is true."

"But the father? Robert? I can't imagine him taking advantage of her."

"All I know, is it takes two," replied Rachel.

* * *

Two hours later, Isabel returned to the bakery. She had relieved herself of the nausea and rested.

"I'm feeling much better now," she said to Maggie and Rachel. "Put me to work."

Maggie and Rachel exchanged knowing looks and nodded to each other. Isabel noticed the undercurrent between them. "Is something wrong?" asked Isabel.

"Perhaps we should talk while there's only the three of us here." said Maggie. She motioned to the table and chairs. "Come, sit with us."

Isabelle flushed from the neck up. *They know.*

Wanting to make Isabel feel more comfortable, Rachel said, "I'll make us some tea." Because of Isabel's condition, she chose peppermint.

Maggie waited for Rachel to return with the tea before bringing up the serious subject, so she started with a polite question. "Did you rest well? You look more refreshed."

"Yes, the nap was most helpful," replied Isabel.

Rachel arrived with the tea tray. "Here we are with our tea," said Rachel, pouring three cups.

Isabel sniffed the fragrance of her tea through the steam rising from her cup. "This smells heavenly. Is it peppermint?" Suddenly it struck her what their little *talk* was to be about. She flushed even more, although she didn't think it possible. "You both know, don't you?"

Rachel smiled compassionately. "Yes, Isabel, we know. You must have been feeling so alone."

Maggie interjected, "You do realize we're your friends, don't you? We are here for you, Isabel."

Isabel began to cry, then sob. "You probably guessed that Robert is the father. He left before I could tell him. I wasn't certain yet."

With a bewildered expression, Maggie asked, "When did this happen? I've always thought of Robert as nothing but a gentleman."

Isabel dabbed her eyes with the kerchief that Rachel handed her. "It was the night of the Governor's Ball. As you know, Maggie, when we returned to the ship, I assisted Robert to his cabin. If you remember, he was quite wobbly from the overabundance of champagne he consumed."

"Yes, I remember. We were all having a laugh about it. Robert has always been so serious and *inward.*"

"Shortly after you helped me out of Rachel's dress and you left, there was a knock on my door. I was about to climb into my bed and had blown out the candle, so the room was dark. I asked who was at the door and Robert announced himself. I was surprised but pleased for the opportunity to enjoy more of his company and opened the door. I adore him so. Without asking me if he could enter, he stepped into my cabin and closed and locked the door behind him. I wasn't at all worried about him locking the door. I thought he was just trying to protect my reputation because of him being in my room alone with me.

"I drank champagne too, but not as much as Robert. I felt very relaxed, however. The next thing I knew he was pressing his nude body against me and laying me down on my bed. As he kissed me, he said he loved me, and I told him I loved him. He said he could no longer resist me, and he must have me. Oh, Maggie and Rachel, I knew it was wrong, but I'm so in love with him. I was afraid I would lose him if I resisted."

Maggie and Rachel were stunned.

That doesn't sound like Robert, even he if he was drunk. He looked like he was ready to pass out and sleep through the night, thought Maggie. Then her mind flashed back to last July when Samuel brought Rachel's necklace to Philip. *The cleaning lady said she had found the necklace in the bed of cabin two. Why was Rachel's necklace found in Robert's bed if he was in Isabel's bed in her cabin? Was the cleaning lady mistaken? Something is truly amiss.*

Rachel put her arm around Isabel. "My dear, I'm sure Robert will do the right thing when he returns. He's an honorable man. I can't imagine him not being thrilled to have a child with you."

Isabel caressed her belly. "I already love this child, it's a part of Robert."

"We're going to take good care of you Isabel. You're not alone anymore. Robert will have quite a surprise when he returns," said Maggie. All the while she offered support to Isabel, Maggie just couldn't shake the feeling that Isabel's description of Robert seducing her didn't sound like him. *Philip has told me stories about women throwing themselves at Robert. Not once did he succumb to their wiles. He was always alone, with his heart still in England. And what about the necklace?*

Rachel agreed, "Yes, he certainly will be surprised."

Isabel hugged both Maggie and Rachel. "Thank you so much. I have felt desperately alone. You are both so good to me."

Their conversation was interrupted by the sound of the bells on the door. Yu Yan had just arrived for her shift.

"It looks like our conversation is over for the moment," said Maggie. She turned to the Chinese woman, greeted her, and showed her the tasks for the day.

Rachel said, "Isabel, I'm sure you are emotionally exhausted, why don't you take the rest of the day off?"

"Yes, I concur with Rachel," said Maggie. "We'll see you tomorrow."

"I would appreciate that, thank you." While leaving, she patted her belly, *We're no longer alone little one. I can't wait for you to meet your father.*

As Isabelle left, Maggie's eyes followed her, *This is indeed a puzzle. The one thing the Bennett brothers all have in common is integrity, rooted deep within them. I wonder what Philip will say when I tell him tonight, and then he'll tell Thomas.* She sighed. *We'll see what Robert has to say when he returns. He won't have the reception he's expecting.*

Chapter 46

Mid-January 1858

Liverpool, England, The Atlantic Ocean

*T*hey heard the blast of the ship's horn, warning passengers it was time to board.

"This is it," said Robert as he helped Eleanor board the *Arabella*. "Our future together begins today."

"I'm so happy, Robert. How soon will we be married?"

Robert brought out his watch and flipped open the cover to check the time. "I would say in about an hour."

Suddenly, Eleanor caught a glimpse of her portrait inside the case. "Robert, you still have my portrait after all these years?"

They stopped walking for a moment. "Yes, my darling. I couldn't count the times I have gazed at it hoping against hope we would be together, somehow, someday. And then, when I nearly gave up hope, you happened back into my life."

"And it's because we each had a letter to mail. Yours to your brothers and mine to my daughter. How ironic it is that both letters were being sent to America. Fate must have been giving us a helping hand. If one of us had come at a different hour, we wouldn't have found each other, despite being in the same town. Do you believe in fate, Robert?"

Robert thought about the *other* letter that he nearly mailed. "Yes, Eleanor, I do believe in fate. I also understand that we can't change the past, but we can move forward into the future. Now, let's find a porter to take us to our cabin."

The porter opened the door for them and gave Robert a key. "Thank you," said Robert while handing the man a tip.

With a slight bow, Robert gestured toward the doorway and said, "After you, my lady."

"Oh, Robert, this is beautiful. How much did you spend?" Then she saw the roses. "White roses. My favorite! You remembered! How did you get roses in January?"

"First, this is our honeymoon suite, so the cost doesn't matter. You're worth every pound. As for the roses, I ordered them from a florist who grows out-of-season flowers in his greenhouse, the same florist where I bought flowers to take to my parents' gravesite. It was then that I learned about his greenhouse."

"This is so romantic, Robert."

"Take some time to freshen up, my darling. I'm going to check with the captain about our ceremony. I'll be back in a few minutes. Soon we will be Mr. and Mrs. Robert Bennett."

"Hurry back!"

* * *

"I now pronounce you husband and wife," proclaimed the minister. "You may kiss the bride!" Robert and Eleanor looked into each other's eyes, then embraced, kissing gently.

Robert whispered, "It's taken over twenty years for us to be together. Now, we are united, forever. I love you, Eleanor."

"I love you too, Robert."

After the couple's brief romantic interlude, the captain stepped forward. "Congratulations, Mr. and Mrs. Bennett. I'm pleased to tell you that I took the liberty to have a bottle of champagne delivered to your cabin, with my compliments."

Robert extended his hand, "Thank you, Captain Eaton. You've been most generous. We appreciate you allowing us the use of your cabin for our ceremony assuring us the privacy we desired."

Robert turned to the minister and paid him. "A fine ceremony," he said as he put his arm around Eleanor. "Mrs. Bennett and I thank you."

Robert extended his arm to Eleanor. "Shall we stroll around the deck for some fresh air?" He grinned, "Once we're in the honeymoon suite, we won't emerge for awhile."

Eleanor chuckled, "I take it we'll be dining in tonight?"

After supper, they spent the evening talking, making love, then talking. They had twenty years to catch up on. As they laid entwined in each other's arms, Robert reflected back to the Governor's Ball. "I dreamed about you one night last summer, Eleanor. We were together like this. You told me you loved me, and I replied back that I loved you. It seemed so real at the time."

"I wonder if I'm dreaming right now. I can hardly believe we are here, at this moment, in each other's arms. Please, God, don't let me wake, if I am dreaming. I beg you Robert, give me proof I am not dreaming."

Robert smoothed Eleanor's hair and kissed her cheeks, her lips, her neck, and the length of her body. Then he returned to her lips and kissed her gently, then passionately. He whispered, "Does this feel real, my darling?"

"Yes, oh yes, Robert, but I need even more proof."

"I'll be happy to oblige," he whispered.

* * *

Mid-March 1858

Teekalet Bay

The ship *Sophronia* blasted its horn as it entered Teekalet Bay.

"Robert, this is the most beautiful country. I'm looking forward to living here and meeting your family."

"You'll be meeting them soon."

Robert helped Eleanor disembark while their baggage was unloaded. A small steamboat was tied next to the wharf in readiness to ferry passengers to their destination. The steamboat was the mill's latest acquisition. Robert started loading their baggage and helped Eleanor board. Soon the pilot arrived.

"Welcome back, Mr. Bennett." He tipped his hat to Eleanor. "My name's Andy." He looked back at Robert. "Your brother Thomas told me to keep a lookout for you. He asked me to blast my horn when we come within close proximity of your landing. I ferried your brother Philip to your settlement the other day. He had returned from a business trip in Frisco. Looks like everyone is going to be there waiting to welcome you back."

Andy released the lines and jumped onto the steamer. "Make yourselves comfortable. Ma'am, if you care to have a better look at the scenery, you two can sit on the bench next to the railing."

"Thank you, Andy. I would like that," Eleanor replied, smiling sweetly.

The steamer chugged down the canal. The wind from the speed of the boat whipped through Eleanor's hair. *What a beautiful vision*, thought Robert. As they traveled toward the Bennett wharf, Robert described the points of interest along the way. Eleanor snuggled close to him, taking it all in.

Robert put his arm around her. "I'm so anxious for you to meet my family, my darling. I wonder if you'll recognize Philip and Thomas. It's been so many years since you saw them last. They're in for a shock. They don't know about us."

"I hope they're happy for us, Robert."

"I'm sure they will be."

Robert could see the wharf in the distance. There was one person who wouldn't be happy about him and Eleanor. While he had not yet made any promises to Isabel, he knew she wouldn't be happy. He wasn't looking forward to hurting her. Andy had given him the impression the family planned to be on the wharf to greet him when they heard the blasts. He hoped Isabel wouldn't be there.

"There's the Bennett wharf," shouted Andy. He sounded the horn three times.

"I'd like to stand, Robert, so I can see your family better," said Eleanor.

"I'll wrap my arms around so you don't lose your balance." Robert positioned Eleanor in front of him giving her a front row view with both his arms around her.

"We're close, I can hear Philip's dog, Britta, barking."

"I'm so excited, Robert."

* * *

"There's the signal," yelled Thomas. Everyone knew about the signal and scampered down to the wharf to greet Robert. Britta followed Philip and Maggie and barked, adding to the excitement. Maggie wondered what was about to happen with the surprise waiting for Robert.

The whole family was nervous about the *situation*. No one wanted to miss Robert's reaction. Jane caught up with Thomas and Jonathan.

Rachel had told Peter to go ahead of her. She was lagging behind to help Isabel down the path to the wharf. Isabel was over eight months along and needed assistance walking down the incline to the wharf. She was both nervous and excited to see Robert. *How will he react when he sees me? I'm as big as a house!*

As the steamer approached, the group waved at Robert. Isabel had moved to the front so she could see Robert more easily. She stood with her hands clasped under her far-extended belly.

When the boat was just a few feet away from the wharf, Eleanor turned to face Robert and embraced him, giving him a lingering kiss. "I love you, Robert," she said.

After the kiss, while still locked in their embrace, Robert peered over Eleanor's shoulder and could easily see each and every person waiting on the wharf, particularly, Isabel. He was dumbfounded. *Why, she's with child, and quite far along, it appears. I guess I wasn't the only man in her life. That certainly makes things easier for me. I never wanted to hurt her.*

As the boat inched toward the wharf, everyone, especially Isabel, was stunned to see a beautiful woman in Robert's arms, and this beautiful woman had just kissed him, passionately.

A Note From Lilly

Thank you for reading Book Two, *Perils in Paradise* of the *Intrepid Journey* series. I hope you enjoyed the continuing saga of the Bennett family. If so, I would be most grateful if you could take a moment and leave a review on the book's Amazon page.

The Bennett Family Saga continues in Book Three of the series, to be published in the near future. If you would like to learn when it is available, feel free to visit my website at www.lillyrobbinsbrock.com, where you may subscribe to be notified. While you are there, check out my blog.

Make sure to visit me on my Facebook page at www.facebook.com/lillyrobbinsbrock, where you are welcome to interact and find tidbits of interest surrounding the book project. I look forward to sharing my next novel with you.

Lilly

Acknowledgements

Each time I begin a book project, my family faithfully supports me and tolerates my obsessive personality while I am in writing mode. They deserve a heartfelt thank you. My husband, Phil, read and edited at least three drafts. His male perspective and creativity was invaluable. My daughter, Alecia, was extremely helpful on my original draft as the story evolved. It was always an exciting moment when she came up with an idea for a particular character. My sister, June, has always been supportive and a great proofreader. She's been a cheerleader on every project.

I also want to thank my editor, Tracy Cartwright of Editing by Cartwright. I appreciate her editing skills. It was a pleasure working with her.

And finally, a huge thank you goes to my other daughter, Vivi Anne. She continues to work by my side utilizing her skills and education to format the book as well as to design and create the book cover.

I feel very fortunate to have such a wonderful group of people surrounding me.

About The Author

Lilly Robbins Brock was born in Olympia, Washington where her pioneer family homesteaded in the late 1800s. She loves history and one of her passions has been researching her family tree. Learning about the past lives of her hometown inspired Lilly to write Book One of her historical fiction novel series, *Intrepid Journey: An Untamed Frontier*, and now, Book Two, *Intrepid Journey: Perils in Paradise*. She is presently working on Book Three to continue the story of the Bennett family saga.

Lilly has also written three nonfiction memoir/biographies to honor three members of the Greatest Generation who served our country during World War II. The first book, *Wooden Boats & Iron Men,* is about a PT sailor and his love for PT boats. The second book, *Ever A Soldier,* tells the story of a soldier who saw action on the European front. The third book, *Victory On The Home Front*, is about a Rosie the Riveter and her husband who was a fighting Seabee.

In her professional career, Lilly has been a legal secretary, teacher, and for the past thirty-five years, an interior designer. She and her husband are now retired. They live in a quiet country setting on the shores of the Columbia River in Cathlamet, Washington, which has become the perfect place to pursue her lifelong desire to write stories, and where she wrote her first book, *Food Gift Recipes from Nature's Bounty.*

Made in the USA
Coppell, TX
25 August 2021